ANGELS

and

BANDITS

by

Brodie Curtis

Westy Vistas Books

Westy Vistas Books, Colorado, USA

brodiecurtis.com

First Edition: April 2022

ISBN 978-1-7337835-2-1 (paperback)

ISBN 978-1-7337835-3-8 (e-book)

The publisher is not responsible for websites (or their content) that are not owned by the publisher.

Cover Design and Divider pages by Momir Borocki; Editing and Interior Design by Sue Millard, UK, www.jackdawebooks.co.uk

Printed in the United States of America

ANGELS

and

BANDITS

by

Brodie Curtis

PART I
1936 to 1939

"When once you have tasted flight, you will forever walk the earth with your eyes turned skyward, for there you have been, and there you will always long to return."

—*Leonardo DaVinci*

Chapter 1

The morning summer sun beamed through Weldy & Beane's backroom window and the heat was becoming oppressive. Eddy Beane wiped at his brow and manoeuvred around the sewing table, the presser, and racks of suits, trousers, slacks, shirts, jackets and dresses, until he reached the door to the alley and cracked it to generate a cross breeze. It let in sounds of the world outside his own, truck engines, automobile horns, and voices of women chatting as they walked along the pavement. However, the day to day traffic on Savile Row wasn't his concern. Commitments to customers had to be met.

He picked up the first of the day's orders and went to the rack to select the roll of cloth the customer had chosen. Then he turned up his sleeves, spread the cloth on the cutting bench, and began to lay out his patterns.

The doorbell rang, and Eddy hurried from the back room to the front counter. The customer waiting there was a tall, trim, dark-haired man dressed in a sporty brown blazer.

"Good afternoon, sir."

"Hello, young man. Are you new here? I expected to see Mr. Weldy."

"My uncle is away at the moment, sir," Eddy said, "back this afternoon."

The man said with a hint of curiosity, "Do I detect a French accent? I didn't know Weldy had any foreign relatives."

"No sir, it is my Aunt Maddy. Beane was her, err, *nom de jeune fille*. I don't know the English word. She was called Beane before she married Uncle Al."

"Ah! Her 'maiden name.' I see—Weldy and Beane. Is your father Mr. Weldy's partner?"

"No. He died in Flanders. During the War."

"I see," the man said, extending his hand. "My name's Park."

Surprised, Eddy shook his hand. "Edouard Beane. People call me Eddy."

"You were brought up in France, eh?"

"Yes. I was born in Hazebrouck. *Maman* and I came to London only four years ago."

Mr. Park seemed to be appraising him. "Then we've both left the land of our birth," he said, and Eddy thought his smile was sympathetic. "I'm a Kiwi, from New Zealand. Moving to London is a big change in one's life. I wish the best for you here in England."

"Thank you, sir."

"Anyway, I'm here to pick up some alterations that Mr. Weldy was to make for me if you'd be so kind. Two items."

"Yes sir." Eddy went to the back room, located the hangers sheeted in brown paper with the label 'Commander Keith Park,' and hung them on the rack at the end of the counter.

Commander Park tore open the brown paper to inspect a black suitcoat and a blue military jacket, decorated over the left breast pocket with a pair of wings and a colorful chevron bar. He felt inside the jacket sleeve where it had been mended and said, approvingly, "Like new."

Eddy was fascinated by Commander Park's jacket. The full-dress embodiment of the Royal Air Force. "You're RAF, sir?"

"That's right. Now, what's the damage?"

Eddy was puzzled. "It is mended, sir."

"No. I meant, how much do I owe you?"

"Oh, I must look that up in Uncle Al's book. One moment please."

Park said cheerfully, "Never mind, tell your uncle to put it on my account and we'll square up at the end of the month."

Park took the hangers and turned to leave.

Impulsively, Eddy said, "Sir!"

Commander Park stopped and looked back. "Yes?"

"If I may. What is it like?"

"What's what like?"

"To fly. To fly *un avion!*"

Commander Park paused. "That's hard to explain. It is something you must experience for yourself." He grinned. "I tell you what: I have a monoplane trainer at my disposal. A two-seater. If you're keen, I'll show you what it's like. Be at Hanworth at ten o'clock on Saturday morning."

Eddie could barely speak. "*Merci!* Where is Hanworth, sir?"

"It's in Feltham. You'll find it."

~ ~ ~

Wednesday crawled into Thursday and Thursday trudged into Friday before Eddy dared to tell his aunt and uncle about his invitation. Aunt Maddy was excited for him, but as he feared, Uncle Al was more reserved. Eddy wondered if he thought he had overstepped his bounds with Commander Park.

The continuing heat-wave gave the workroom a steamy, slightly sweet smell that made Eddy crave fresh air. Aunt Maddy had left a pair of men's trousers on the bench beside the Singer sewing machine for Eddy to press. He held them up by the hems, admiring the neatness of her work as he matched the inseams, then laid one leg of the pants flat on the presser and pulled the handle. Steam hissed from the sides. He opened it, shook the cloth to dissipate the steam, and repeated the process on the other leg before he folded the pants and placed them on a hanger. He wrapped them in a paper bag, attached a name tag, and hung them on a rack with other completed alterations.

The telephone on the front counter rang and Uncle Al answered. "Commander Park! Good afternoon, sir."

Eddy's stomach did flip-flops, and he froze, unable to stop listening. On the other side of the workroom, Aunt Maddy also paused in her work.

"The alterations," Uncle Al said, "we'll just put those on your account, sir. I'm glad you're pleased with them." There was a lengthy pause on Uncle Al's side of the conversation, and he glanced at Eddy with a sad smile. "I'm afraid I can't give you a telephone number for Eddy's mother, sir. She died almost four years ago. Eddy lives with Mrs. Weldy and me."

He listened again.

"Yes, Mrs. Weldy and I went over to Hazebrouck in 1932 to find Eddy and his mother. Unfortunately, Thérèse was already quite ill.

She and Eddy came with us to England and she saw doctors at Guy's Hospital, but she couldn't be cured. Eddy stayed on with us."

There was another pause. "Yes, sir. He's becoming an excellent tailor. Thank you, sir. I'll mention that to Mrs. Weldy. I know Eddy is delighted that you asked him to join you at Hanworth tomorrow. Mrs. Weldy and I are grateful to you for giving him the opportunity. If I may ask, sir, what should he wear?"

After another short pause, Uncle Al concluded the call and turned to Eddy with a grin. "You're to meet Commander Park at Hangar C in the morning at a quarter to ten. Wear a light jacket, and you're to take sunglasses with you." Al reached inside his breast pocket. "Take my Windsors."

Startled, Eddy stammered his thanks. Aunt Maddy came over and hugged him.

"Flying with Commander Park! It'll be the thrill of a lifetime!"

Eddy grinned shyly.

When he returned to his work he heard Aunt Maddy ask Uncle Al, in an undertone, "What did Commander Park ask you to mention to me?"

"He said that you taking in Thérèse and Eddy was the most decent thing he's heard of in a long time."

A lump formed in Eddy's throat.

But he could no longer ignore his work—the alteration orders, garments, and packages stacked around the work room. So he took up the needle and thimble and tried to will the hands of the clock to move faster. It wasn't that he didn't appreciate his job at Weldy & Beane, but an unexpected chance to fly was impossible to lay aside. He tried to concentrate on his stitching, thinking of the great pride that he took in having helped his aunt and uncle build a thriving business. Together the three of them had devised an efficient system for tailoring and adjusting a vast array of styles, all of which required long hours of labor to meet customer deadlines.

The business was good—good enough for Uncle Al and Aunt Maddy to have purchased a four-bedroom house in Peckham. They paid him generously. Working alongside them was pleasant and he loved living with them and his little cousins, Georgie and Anna Thérèse. The children were well-provided for, and a true joy to be with. He couldn't complain in the least about his life—but a chance to fly in an aeroplane with Commander Park was the most exciting thing that had ever happened to him.

Chapter 2

At seven o'clock Saturday morning, Eddy was up and dressed in slacks, comfortable lace-up boots, and his light zip-up jacket. He got in Aunt Maddy's way so much while she made breakfast that Uncle Al sent him to fill the kindling bucket and coal scuttle for the parlour. As soon as he had eaten, he kissed Aunt Maddy, shook Uncle Al's hand, and headed for the door.

Uncle Al asked Eddy, "You're sure you know the way?"

Aunt Maddy chuckled. "Now, Al, I've seen Eddy studying our map for the last three days!"

"Okay. I just thought I could help. I've been there you know," Uncle Al said and didn't even draw a breath before he continued. "Hanworth is huge. I saw the Graf Zeppelin land at Hanworth in 1931. Fifty thousand people came to watch, and there was still plenty of room. They'd drawn a circle on the turf—probably sixty feet in diameter—and set out the words 'London Air Park' with white stones. And the Zeppelin was enormous—hundreds of feet long—like a giant gray rocket. I felt like an ant standing beside it."

Eddy fidgeted.

Aunt Maddy said, "You certainly got around before you married me, didn't you now, Al Weldy."

A three-year-old boy blasted through the kitchen doorway, with rumpled pyjamas and a raging case of bed head. He tackled Eddy's pant leg and hung on for dear life.

"Take me! Take me Eddy!"

"*Quelle énergie!*"

Eddy picked the lad up and gave him a hug. "Not this time Georgie. Maybe when you get older, we can fly together; we'll see."

Aunt Maddy took Georgie from Eddy. "Come on son. Let's go upstairs and wake Anna Thérèse."

She kissed him on the cheek, letting Eddy slip out the back door. He rocked his old Unibus scooter off its stand, started it up, and set out for Feltham.

~ ~ ~

Eddy made the grounds of London Air Park by 9:30, and was directed to Hangar C. He sat on his scooter for ten minutes, checking his pocket watch until he couldn't bear to wait any longer, and then braced himself to walk through the hangar's open front entrance.

"Young Beane! Over here," Commander Park said. He set an oil funnel down on the workbench and wiped his hands clean with a rag. "Just making sure my Hawk is ship-shape."

The man who had been helping Park closed a panel on the Hawk's fuselage and extended a dirty hand to Eddy. He had a grease-mark on his left cheek. "Tiger Lewis."

"Edouard Beane."

"What's that?"

"Edou..."

"Blimey. I'll call you Frenchy if it's all the same to you."

Park said, "Tiger here keeps the Hawk's engine running smoothly."

"Pleased to meet you, sir," Eddy said to Tiger.

Tiger nodded and went back to the work bench.

Eddy turned back to Commander Park. "Why do you call him Tiger? I see he is a stout man. *Fort.* Perhaps he is fierce?"

Commander Park laughed. "That well may be. But the reason we call him Tiger is that he is the very best flight trainer on a Tiger Moth. If a person's going to learn to fly, there's no better instructor than Tiger."

Eddy flushed with embarrassment. Had his ignorance of aeroplanes blown the good will that he had established with Commander Park?

"Come over here, lad, and have a look at the Hawk."

Park stood in front of the aeroplane's nose, facing its cockpit.

"What is the first thing you notice about her?"

Eddy took a moment. "Her wings, sir. They look like one long wing that goes through the cockpit."

"It's called a monoplane. One, sleek, level wing. Tiger's plane has two wings, above and below the cockpit. A biplane." He raised his voice, "I say, Tiger. Top her up with fuel, will you? We'll help push her to the station for you."

Tiger returned, removed the chocks, and took hold of the tail fin with both hands.

Commander Park directed Eddy to the left wing. "Give a push, would you? I'll take the starboard wing."

Eddy took his place, and the three men pushed the Hawk out of the hangar to the fuel tank where Tiger took up the hose and pumped. Commander Park watched a bi-plane taxiing towards the runway and said to Eddy, "I spoke to your Uncle and Aunt yesterday. They're a fine couple."

"Yes, sir, thank you. Aunt Maddy and Uncle Al have been wonderful to me. They came to Hazebrouck to find *Maman* and me. When she died, I don't know what I would have done without them."

Commander Park's interest had been piqued. "How did that come about?"

"They came into *Maman*'s shop. It had a red awning and black lettering on the front window: TAILLEUR BEANE. They were looking for *Maman* and of course they saw the name and came in."

"When was that?"

"August 1932. Almost four years ago."

Commander Park's expression encouraged Eddy to continue. "I was in the back room when they came in. I heard *Maman* gasp. I thought something was wrong. I hurried through the door and she was at the counter, facing Aunt Maddy and Uncle Al. '*Est-ce que tout va bien?*' I asked her and I'll never forget her answer: '*Tout va bien, nous avons eu une grosse surprise.*'"

"A big surprise indeed," Park said. "But I am a bit confused. Had your mother ever met your aunt or uncle before?"

"She knew my Uncle Al during the War. He was my father's... *meilleur ami*. Best friend?"

"That is correct."

"They were lost to each other when my father was killed." Eddy's throat tightened and he looked away.

"I'm sorry, lad."

"It is all right," Eddy said. "My father was a very brave soldier. My uncle told me how he was wounded the day my father died. My father held his position so my uncle and many others could escape. Even so, my uncle nearly died that day. He was taken back to England, to the hospital. He didn't know what happened to *Maman*. And *Maman* thought Uncle Al had died when my father died. It was many years after that when he and my Aunt Maddy came to look for her—on their wedding trip. It was a wonderful blessing that they came."

"I see. Quite a story, young Beane," Park said.

Tiger came over, wiping his hands. "Finished, sir," he said to Commander Park. The three men took up their positions again to push the Hawk onto the grass infield.

"Thanks, Tiger," Commander Park said. "Just see us into the air, and you can be off to your teaching."

"Now then, Beane, climb in. I'll help you up the back of the wing. Strap yourself into the rear seat and put on the headphones." Park cupped his hands together for Eddy to step up, and Eddy scrambled over the side of the cockpit and strapped himself into his seat. Park did the same. Then his disembodied voice burbled seemingly from the bodywork. "If you can hear me, speak into the voice tube."

"I can hear you, sir."

"This is how we'll communicate in the air. Straps tight?"

"Yes sir."

"Very good." Commander Park signaled to Tiger by twirling his index finger and Tiger made a mighty pull on the Hawk's propeller. Its engine sputtered, then roared to life, and gray smoke gusted past Eddy from under both sides of the fuselage. Park gave a thumbs-up, and Tiger nodded, pulled the chocks from the wheels, and turned away towards the buildings and his next pupil.

The Hawk slowly moved forward and began a wide turn towards the runway.

"It takes big, strong movements to turn an aeroplane on the ground. The Hawk moves deliberately, like a big, boxy lorry. You have to be firm. If you steered your scooter like this, you'd end up in the ditch."

The Hawk's nose was now pointing straight down the runway, with its engine roaring. Eddy could not believe how noisy it was. He gripped the back of Commander Park's seat in excitement.

"I'll bring her to fifty knots for lift-off," Park shouted over the engine.

The Hawk sped shuddering down the runway, and when its front wheels rose from the grass Eddy felt the vibrations smooth into nothing and he watched, fascinated, as the ground fell away beneath them. The engine sound beat on his ears. The Hawk was two hundred feet off the ground and climbing, and the runway light stanchions shrank until they were no bigger than a pin head.

Park said, "Now I'll toggle the stick a little to level the wings. And trim the nose up." The Hawk's wings rocked back and forth, and Eddy held his breath.

The brilliant sunshine was a strain on his eyes, even through his Uncle's Windsors. He turned away from it and looked down at the earth the Hawk had left. A long black cylinder seemed to have been burnt into the grass. What in blazes was it? It was moving at the same pace as the Hawk, and he realized he was looking at the Hawk's shadow.

"We're on a westerly course," Park said. "We navigate our way by landmarks. Look starboard."

"Starboard, sir?"

"To your right. *A droit.* That's Bedfont Lakes. Just past the Wood. Do you see it?"

"Yes sir."

The cockpit of the Hawk rocked more than Eddy had imagined it would. He saw Commander Park pull back a lever, and then his knee move as though he pumped a pedal with his feet. The plane shook, and Eddy bit his lip.

"A light plane like this bounces around a good deal," Park said cheerfully. "Watch over my shoulder, and you'll see me constantly making adjustments to the controls to keep us stable. Not long ago, I co-piloted a fully loaded Blenheim bomber. Smooth as an ocean liner compared to the way this crate rides. Of course, it weighed fourteen tons; that is more than eight times our weight today.

"Now we'll make a turn, lad. To larboard. That's left."

"*A gauche.*"

"Yes. Just twenty degrees to start. Hold on."

"Yes sir."

10

The left wing dipped, and Eddy's body slid into the left edge of the cockpit. He grabbed onto a strap that dangled overhead to his right and hung onto it with a death grip. Slowly, the Hawk began to level.

"How was that, lad?"

"For a moment, I thought I might fall out, sir."

"Were you holding on tight?"

"Oh, yes, sir."

Commander Park's chuckle echoed through the voice tube. "Takes some getting used to." He pointed to larboard towards a round body of water bisected by a spit of land. "Know what that is, down there?"

"No, sir."

"Queen Mary Reservoir. Another good landmark near Hanworth. What do you think of flying, now?"

"It's the most exciting thing I've ever done, sir. I feel different—I'm not sure how to explain. I... I wish I could stay up here forever."

"I feel that way, too, lad. Even after thousands of flights."

They passed through a wisp of low cloud. It was suddenly much colder than in the open sunlight. It occurred to Eddy that he had just passed a cloud, when on the ground all the clouds passed over him.

"I'm going to make another turn to larboard. Then, we'll fly straight over Feltham, turn to starboard, and land from the north. Hold on."

"Yes sir."

As the plane tilted, Eddy found himself looking down at workmen's cottages, laid out in straight narrow streets. Rows of houses that were so close together they reminded him of marks on a ruler's edge. The streets ran together in triangles and quadrangles seamed with the tiny movements of automobiles. A spire towered over a road lined with commercial buildings. It was a whole new way of looking at the city. From above.

The Hawk began its final turn to starboard and Eddy realized his experience above the earth would soon end. He had been in the sky with Commander Park for only a short time, but what he'd observed in the air and on the ground had pushed everything else from his mind and given him an experience he would remember for a lifetime. That didn't change the fact that later that afternoon he would be back at his trade. And again Monday morning, and everyday thereafter except Sundays. He tried to tell himself that someday he

11

would fly again, but his spirits sunk at the reality that flying with Commander Park would become just a memory.

Suddenly, the noise of the engine dropped to nothing. Eddy's heart leapt into his throat. Had the engine failed? Were they going to crash?

"You back there, lad?"

Eddy could not speak a word.

"Beane!" Park shouted.

Eddy managed to croak, "Yes sir?"

"I thought I'd lost you. Feels like we're falling out of the sky, doesn't it?" He didn't wait for an answer. "It doesn't take much power to land. Gravity does the work. I'm lining her up and letting her level."

Eddy watched, every nerve on the stretch, as Park pulled back on the stick. The runway grass surrounded the Hawk as it descended, and he realized again how vast the aerodrome was. To their right were rows of parked biplanes. Beyond them, he saw an aeroplane lining up to land, another taxiing, and pilots walking about the hangars. Then the wheels hit the ground with only the slightest bounce. Park gently slowed the Hawk's pace, and they rolled to a stop near the hangar.

He let the engine die. Tiger Lewis and another ground man pushed the Hawk away from the runway, and Park climbed down. Eddy took a deep breath and followed him. It was all over.

"Thought you'd be in the air with a student," Park said to Tiger.

"My lesson cancelled," Tiger said. "How'd she run?" He looked tired. The grease on his face was still there, and now his jacket was black with it.

"Simply lovely. You have her purring." Park chuckled. "Tough day, Tiger?"

"You don't know the half of it, sir. I need seven of me! More and more people want flying lessons. Always on Saturday and Sunday! And I've got planes to fuel up, planes to clean, and all these grounds to keep tidy. How can I keep up?"

"You need more help," Park said. "Perhaps another ground man?"

"I'd give my firstborn for a good weekend man."

Park said, thoughtfully, "How about Beane here? He seems quite keen on aeroplanes and the field."

Tiger turned to Eddy. "What about it, Frenchy? If the Commander likes you, I'll try you out. You want to start today? If you can pull your weight, it'll be three pounds for you for a full day Saturday and Sunday."

Time stood still for Eddy as he mulled his answer. Obligations to Aunt Maddy and Uncle Al weighed heavy, but an irresistible urge had gripped him. "I ought to speak to my Aunt and Uncle, I think. If they agree, I come here *demain matin.*"

Tiger turned to Commander Park, a question on his lips, but Park replied before he could ask. "He means he'll be here tomorrow morning."

"Good lad. Eight o'clock."

Eddy said, tentatively, "Tiger?"

"What is it, Frenchy?"

"Can we put my pay towards flying lessons?"

Commander Park smiled.

Chapter 3

E ddy, with his sleeves rolled up, climbed onto the fuselage of the Tiger Moth and Tiger handed him the aviation fuel hose so he could fill the Moth's top tank. He inserted the nozzle and turned the toggle to Open. The chilly fall breeze brushed his bare forearms.

A hundred yards away from the fuel station, seven biplanes were parked in a row but, unusually for a Sunday morning, there was no flying taking place.

'Not as busy as I expected,' Tiger had said to him earlier that morning. Few of the pilots who kept aeroplanes at Hanworth had turned up for pleasure flights, so Eddy hadn't had much work preparing planes or pushing them to the runway. All he could hear over the pulsing of the gasoline was intermittent hammering from the next hangar over. 'Dammit anyway,' Tiger had said, 'I would've booked some more lessons if I'd-a-known our day fliers were going to stay home. Tell you what, Frenchy: just pay for the fuel and you can take 'er up.'

Tiger was generous like that. Yes, he squeezed every bit of work out of Eddy each Saturday and Sunday, but Tiger had made good on his promise to teach him to fly. Eddy had flown most weekends and was confident and comfortable behind the windscreen of the Moth even though Tiger constantly reminded him he had much left to learn. Working with Tiger in the hangar, Eddy had begun to learn how to maintain aeroplanes, from engine gaskets to control dials. The past three months had been the happiest of his life.

Eddy waited impatiently for the eighteen gallon tank to fill. The pungent whiff of gas signaled power and freedom and he was eager to take the Tiger Moth in the air.

While he waited, he heard the drone of an engine. A sleek yellow monoplane with black trim was approaching from the east.

14

"Wonder who that is?" Tiger said. "Looks like a Swallow, but I don't know whose. It must be stopping to refuel, so hurry it up, Frenchy!"

"*Presque fini!*"

"In English!"

"Sorry," Eddy said. "Almost finished. Here," Eddy said. He handed the nozzle down to Tiger.

"Okay. Let's get 'er pushed out of the way. Fuel that Swallow and then you can take 'er up." Tiger secured the fuel hose on a hook next to the tank.

"This will be your third solo," Tiger said, taking his place behind the right lower wing and preparing to push the Moth away from the fuel pump.

"*Oui*—sorry! Yes."

"Fly smoothly, lad. I'll be watching. Remember what I've told ya."

Tiger's assessment of the trainer plane had been burned into Eddy's brain by frequent repetition: 'She's easy to fly, but difficult to fly well.' Eddy had seen Tiger give dozens of lessons and heard his scorching remarks when the pupils had gone home. During a good number of lessons the Moth had stalled. Tiger didn't have any trouble restarting the engine with his instructor controls, but a student who stalled more than twice usually saw his flying dreams end at basic instruction. Eddy hoped to impress Tiger with a smooth climb and level cruise, then a "wheeler" landing where his front wheels touched first as the Moth slowed down and the little trailing rear wheel merely feathered to the grass. If he did well, Tiger might be convinced to let him move on to aerobatics like rolls and loops. Most students never made it that far because the controls of the Moth responded slowly, requiring a sure and competent hand that they didn't yet have.

While he and Tiger waited for the Swallow to make its approach, Eddy checked the clouds. Altocumulus, in patches of whitish-gray at about ten thousand feet. According to the flying instruction book Tiger had loaned him, they were a sign that rain was coming late that evening or in the morning. That didn't bother him, because the bad weather wouldn't be setting in till long after he was back on the ground, and once again working in Weldy & Beane's backroom.

Tiger fished a sheet of paper out of his breast pocket, read it, and folded it away again with a sigh. "Jackson, Dinkins, Woodward. What an afternoon."

Eddy realized it must be a list of students scheduled for lessons. Tiger had more inquiries for flying lessons than he had time to give them. Eddy dreamed of one day earning his instructor license, and Tiger trusting him to take on the lessons he didn't have time for. Until then, he had to keep practising, keep learning, and hope his improving skill would be recognized.

The Swallow was approaching, at first in a sober downward glide.

"I know where I've seen it before. That's Howey's plane from Cambridge," Tiger said.

Its engine roared suddenly, and the nose of the plane lifted again. It banked hard and buzzed over Hangar C and the updraft sucked a tin sheet off the roof that flew fifty feet in the air before pitching back into the turf where it stuck, upright and swaying.

"Bloody hell!" said Tiger.

The Swallow banked away to the right, then rolled to line up into the wind once more. Eddy had to admire the smoothness of the manoeuvre, but Tiger was furious.

"Christ Almighty, if that's one of Howey's students—what's he playing at?"

The Swallow landed, this time without incident, and taxied to where Tiger and Eddy were waiting. The middle-aged instructor had risen from the rear seat of the open cockpit and was shouting angrily in the much-younger pilot's ear. Tiger hailed him as he climbed down.

"What the hell are you teaching him, Howey?"

"Damned if I know, Tiger," Howey said. "Ask him! Bloody fool!" The younger man was still in his seat. He had taken off his flying helmet and was brushing his thick blond hair into place. He held his chin high over the collar of his heavy wool sweater in a pose that was *bourgeois* through and through, and made Eddy think of some of the customers at the tailor shop, the ones that treated him like dirt under their shoes. The young man seemed not to care about the damage he'd caused.

"What the hell was he playing at?"

"He said he wanted to look around. He's got far too high an opinion of himself."

The student had by now climbed onto the wing and hopped down, and he strolled over towards them.

16

Tiger didn't wait for him. He stepped forward and shook his fist in the young man's face. "What the hell did you think you were doing? That tin sheet could have killed somebody, you bloody dimwit!"

The young man slowly pushed Tiger's fist away. "Let's start again, shall we? I am Dudley Thane. And you are?"

"Tiger."

"Tiger who?"

"Just Tiger."

"I see," Thane said. "Well, Mister Tiger, perhaps I was rather exuberant. It's shocking, though, the slipshod way buildings are put up these days. Send the bill to Howey, there's a good fellow." He nodded at Eddy and said, "Be a good lad and bring me a cup of tea," and strode away towards the hangar like a gust of wind blowing a stack of papers off a table.

"Your prize student?" Tiger asked Howey.

"A prize twit. I've about had it with that one," Howey said. "He's quick on the controls and he has a light touch, but his skull's stuffed with shite. A Trinity man. Oh well, he pays, I suppose." He extended his hand to Eddy. "I'm Tom Howard. You may not believe it, but I give flying instruction from the airfield at Fen Ditton."

Eddy introduced himself and they shook hands.

Tiger said, "Refuel the Swallow as quick as you can, Frenchy. The sooner Howey gets this Thane character off my airfield the happier I'll be."

Howey laughed. He said to Eddy, "Don't judge me by my student, son. Thane's an oddity. He's a spoiled baby spending Daddy's money. In this business, you have to learn to deal with all sorts."

"You don't expect me to make tea for that arrogant bastard, do you?" Eddy asked Tiger.

"If you do, you're sacked. Fuel up, and then go flying."

Chapter 4

In the summer of 1938, nearly two years after beginning his weekend work at Hanworth, Eddy was at home in Peckham with Uncle Al and Aunt Maddy. Georgie and Anna Thérèse had been tucked into bed and he and Uncle Al were sitting at the newly-purchased dining room table. He rubbed a finger along the table's beveled edge and then stopped in case his fidgeting would draw his uncle into another lengthy anecdote about its purchase. Al's story would prevent him from even starting on the proposal he was poised to make, and his mouth had already gone dry with nervousness.

Eddy had worked grueling seven day weeks since he had started under Tiger. Most evenings he would have been too dog-tired for a meeting with aunt and uncle, but not tonight. His future was at stake.

Aunt Maddy placed a tea service with three cups in front of them and took the chair beside Eddy. He sat up straight to meet his aunt's and uncle's curious glances.

"Well now!" Maddy said. "What is this about, Eddy? We haven't sat down to talk, just the three of us, for some time now."

"I am sorry, but it is very important. It has to do with flying."

Aunt Maddy sighed. "Flying, always flying."

Eddy sat in awkward silence and Uncle Al prompted. "Do you want to leave Weldy & Beane?"

Eddy took a deep breath and began. "I want to thank both of you for letting me learn to fly. Now I have an opportunity—to start my own flying business."

"A flying business!" Uncle Al said. "At Hanworth?"

"Yes. Tiger Lewis has been telling me that he turns away requests every week to transport business parcels, and even businessmen. I can do that."

"We're both very proud of you," Aunt Maddy said, "but I dread the thought of you in the skies every day."

"You don't need to worry about me, Aunt Maddy. I've flown going on five hundred hours, already. I have my "A" license now, and my flight instructor's license, so I am qualified to give flying lessons—there is a great demand for them. I can earn my living—a good living—doing what I really want to do."

There was a pause. Uncle Al glanced at Aunt Maddy, who was sitting now with her fingers pressed to her lips.

"I see," Uncle Al said. "But wouldn't one need an aeroplane to take on a business like that?"

"Oh, of course! Tiger knows of an Aeronca C-3 100 monoplane I can purchase. It has an extra seat, so I could give flying lessons from it. It would be perfect for trips to the Midlands, and even northern France."

Uncle Al took a sip of tea. "Commander Park says you are a good pilot. But buying an aeroplane is a big step. How much does this Aeronca cost?"

"Eight hundred pounds," he said.

Uncle Al and Aunt Maddy looked at each other, grimacing.

"That's only one-half of its price, new," Eddy said.

"I don't know anything about aeroplanes, but is it in good order?"

"Yes, and it's only two years old."

"Then why would the owners sell it to you for half its value?" Uncle Al asked.

Eddy hesitated. "Well, the owner overshot the runway, so it's had some damage." He saw his uncle's expression change and hurried on. "But it's as good as new, now. Tiger says the best mechanic at Hanworth has fixed it up."

"You want to buy a crashed aeroplane and fly it every day?" Aunt Maddy asked.

"Tiger has flown it, and he says it is operating perfectly."

Uncle Al still looked troubled. "You haven't got eight hundred pounds," he said.

"If I can come up with two hundred pounds, the seller will arrange financing for the rest. I have one hundred set aside from my earnings at Weldy & Beane and at Hanworth. I would like you and Aunt Maddy

19

to lend me the other hundred. I'll pay you back as soon as I can, with interest."

"Do you believe you can earn enough to repay the loan as well as earn enough money to live on?"

"I think so." Eddy paused while he marshalled his financial arguments. "Each hundred hours of flight operation will cost me thirty pounds. Flying lessons are a shilling a minute, so ten hours will bring in thirty pounds—my hundred hours of flight will bring three hundred pounds—that's a profit of two hundred and seventy."

"That's assuming your hundred hours are all flying lessons," said Uncle Al.

"I've thought of that. When I'm not teaching, there'll be the money for carrying passengers. Just last week a businessman offered Tiger thirty pounds to fly him to Manchester and back on the 30th. That job will fall to me, so I'll have that to start. The Aeronca has room for quite a number of parcels, and papers, and small sized cargo. I'll charge a fee for everything I can carry. I've worked out that my flying business will bring in at least one hundred pounds over expenses each month, right from the start!"

Uncle Al leaned back and put his thumbs in the armholes of his waistcoat. He and Aunt Maddy looked at each other, as if Eddy weren't there. Then Al said to Eddy, "Why don't you go out for a smoke, while we two have a chat about it?"

Eddy felt he had the battle half won. He finished his tea quickly and went into the garden, pulled a cigarette from his jacket pocket and lit up. He understood the concerns his aunt and uncle would have. They weighed on him, too. They would be afraid for his safety, question his business savvy, and worry about the impact of his departure from Weldy & Beane. A hundred pounds was no small sum for them to find, and he expected to wait for some time before they could answer him. He wouldn't hold it against them if they declined. But he would definitely find another way to purchase the Aeronca. Flying was what he wanted to do for the rest of his life.

The evening sunshine was still sparkling through the young growth on the sycamore trees behind the house, but the air was beginning to turn chilly. He lit a second cigarette. Would Tiger loan him a hundred pounds? He thought it unlikely. But what about the bank? He could ask Uncle Al to guarantee the debt, or perhaps Commander Park.

He was halfway through his cigarette when Uncle Al appeared at the door and motioned him in. He and his Uncle took their seats again, and for a few moments none of them spoke. Eddy wondered if they were working up their nerve.

"We love you very much, Eddy," Aunt Maddy said.

His shoulders drooped. She was going to let him down lightly, but the answer was going to be No. "And I love you both," Eddy said, trying to hide his disappointment.

She went on, thoughtfully. "Do you remember the day we met you? It's nearly six years ago, isn't it? You and your mother sat with Uncle Al and me in the garden behind the lovely house in Hazebrouck."

"I remember." Eddy had loved the elegant manor house. It had arched windows and the outside was covered in climbing ivy vines. He remembered walking with *Maman* along its long, graded gravel drive, towards the flagpole on which the tricolor of France danced with the breeze. The path to their own small house ran off to one side, through *Maman*'s garden which in summer was filled with tomatoes and pepper plants, cucumbers and tall, climbing beans. "Yes. Madame du Claire's house."

"She helped your mother open her tailoring shop."

"Yes, she did."

"Your mother gave us tea. Do you remember that she sent you off on an errand?"

"Yes. She sent me to the market, for bread."

"That was when she told us she was sick and didn't have long to live. I made her a promise then that I would take you in as my own. And that I would give you a good life in England. So your uncle and I have been discussing whether loaning you this money would honor our promise to your mother."

"I understand. You are concerned about my safety. And I know it's a large sum for you to find."

Aunt Maddy said, "Your mother was immensely proud of you. She felt you had many abilities that wouldn't fully develop in a little town like Hazebrouck. She believed there would be great opportunities for you if you came to live in London. We see your abilities, too, my dear. That is why we will give you the hundred pounds." She kissed him on his cheek.

"We admire your spirit," Uncle Al said. "If flying is in your blood, you'll do it whether we approve or not—and I can see you've looked carefully at the money side of things. So we trust you."

Eddy shot up from his chair and bounded around the table to shake Uncle Al by the hand. "*Merci, merci mille fois, c'est épatant! Vous verrez—* you will see. *Je vous promets.* I promise. I will make you proud!"

He took a deep breath and closed his eyes in sheer happiness. *Merci beaucoup, Maman.*

Chapter 5

Dudley Thane touched down smoothly in Tom Howard's plane, setting the Swallow's wheels onto the grass at Fen Ditton with only the tiniest bounce. He knew he was returning the plane thirty minutes late and Howey wouldn't be happy. But how could he possibly keep track of time when he was practicing rolls and dives high above Cambridgeshire?

Nevertheless, he'd have to stomach appeasing the man. The financial reality was that this occasional hiring of Howey's trainer was all Thane could afford. His paltry trust allowance would never cover the costs of purchasing his own machine. Even worse, his Pater, his Father, had reached his boiling point with Thane's excuses for not securing suitable employment since graduating from Trinity. There was no extra funding to be found there.

None of that mattered to Thane when he was flying Howey's plane. Soaring in the sky, his mind was free, and his troubles vanished. Each week as the days plodded along he grew progressively more antsy and agitated until his appointment to fly the Swallow finally came.

Taxiing to the hangar, he was less than pleased to find Howey standing hands on hips with a flying student at his side, waiting for Thane to climb down.

"You're late and you've burned up my fuel," Howey said. "What about my four o'clock lesson? Did you think about that?"

"I'll fuel her up," Thane said.

"I've had it, lad," Howey said.

"Now, Howey, it was just—"

"No more warnings! Any more humbug and you won't fly again from Fen Ditton!"

"Ah, Howey."

"Do you understand?" Howey jutted his chin out in a stony pose.

The older man's stare bored through Thane and he lowered his gaze. "Yes."

A female voice called gaily, "Dudley! Yoo-hoo!"

Thane's fiancée, June Stephenson, was walking over from the hangar, a vision of glamour in a cocoa-colored skirt and tightly-fitting white sweater. Her flowing brown hair was tied off with an orange band. She waved at him.

Thane brightened. The sight of June's smile washed away the menace in Howey's warning. "Point taken, Howey. If you gentlemen will excuse me, I'm off to—more agreeable matters."

He jogged away to June, lifted her into a playful bear hug and kissed her.

"Isn't it a lovely day!" June exclaimed. "Perfect for flying!"

"Second only to you in perfection, my love."

"Tell me where you went," she said.

"Oh, nowhere in particular. I worked a bit on my aerobatics," he said, keeping to himself the unpleasantness with Howey.

"I'm so jealous Dudley—wouldn't it be wonderful if we could both fly?"

"Yes, dear. You know I'll take you up the very minute your Pater permits me to."

"I'll look forward to that more than you know." She paused. "But I don't want to be a passenger. I want to learn to fly, just like you. I'm thinking of taking flying lessons. I'm going to speak to Daddy about it."

Thane laughed. "I expect he'll insist that you do two hundred hours of practice, not just the hundred he wants from me."

She asked teasingly, "Don't you think I'm capable?"

"Oh, kitten, it isn't that." He kissed her hand. "Think of how busy you are with our wedding preparations! And after that you'll be learning to run our household and our staff and arranging to entertain our guests. You won't have the time. Let me look after the flying. I'm quite certain your Pater will see it the same way." He took her hand and began to lead them towards the car park.

June stopped them. "Dudley, you aren't listening."

He kissed her cheek. "Now, kitten, I want you safe and beautiful at home—you and the family we're going to have." He saw her beginning to frown, and added, "Let's talk about this later."

"Yes," she said, "we need to talk if you think I'll be staying home and tending to our household. I fear we may have very different ideas about our future, Dudley."

"Kitten..." Thane said, mulling how to extract himself from a delicate topic with her that he should have had the good sense to avoid. Hmm, flowers, a nice, colorful bouquet. That would be the ticket to smoothing things over.

"Well," she said, "I suppose now is not the time. As far as me taking flying lessons, we can talk it over during dinner with Daddy tonight. We'll see what he thinks."

Thane realized he had completely forgotten about Mr. Stephenson's dinner invitation. "Oh, kitten, I've done it again." He drew her near and kissed her on her cheek.

"Dudley! What do you mean?"

"It's the whist tournament this evening. All of our housemates at Neville's Court have entered. I've signed on as Griff's partner." He had been looking forward all week to single malt scotches and laughter with his best friend Griff and their Trinity mates. "We've paid our entry fee so I can't really back out." Even better, he could avoid old man Stephenson sitting stiff as a board throughout dinner, with that menacing gaze that seemed to bore through him, followed by the usual relentless questions about Thane's plans to pursue a livelihood. How much longer could he put off replying to the proposal that he should join Stephenson Enterprises? There was no way he could ever lower himself to start work as a clerk—especially not in June's father's firm.

She pulled away from him. "Do you really want me to tell Daddy you're turning down his invitation in favour of a silly card game?"

"Of course I don't, dear girl, but it can't be helped." He was looking forward to the spectacle of Griff pursuing the Newnham beauties, and maybe even some harmless flirtations with his own old flames. "At least your Pater will have his princess all to himself. He might just thank me."

"You're impossible—and I truly don't think you understand!"

"I'll make it up to you; I promise. Griff and I will sweep up the prize money and tomorrow I'll take you to Market Street."

25

"I don't need any more gloves or perfume," June said. "I need you! You don't seem to give me much of your time any more. Are you engaged to Griff, or me?" Her lips flattened into an angry straight line. After staring at him for ten uncomfortable seconds she said, "Truthfully, I don't know what exactly I am to you. Am I your showpiece, to be displayed when convenient? It's tedious, Dudley."

Chapter 6

Eddy was concluding a flying lesson on a warm August afternoon. The student, Tarrington, was sweating slightly at the controls, but he had brought the Aeronca down safely at Hanworth without needing Eddy's intervention.

"You're doing very well, Mr. Tarrington," Eddy said, as they climbed down from the cockpit. "A couple more hours and you can fly solo."

"I hope so, Mr. Beane. Thank you."

They shook hands, and Tarrington walked away towards his car.

During the summer of 1938, Eddy had arrived at Hanworth just after sunrise and stayed to sunset, seven days a week. He was either in the hangar caring for every square inch of his Aeronca, or he was in the air. He'd given dozens of hours of flying lessons and had a waiting list for prospective students. He'd delivered parcels throughout Britain, to Liverpool, Birmingham, Bristol, Southampton, and even Edinburgh. He'd been paid forty pounds to fly to Paris and pick up five cases of 1928 Clos de Mesnil Grand Cru champagne for Lord Goldbaum's end of season ball. He had already paid his aunt and uncle back their hundred pounds and his bank account was growing steadily.

Eddy stretched his arms over his head to unwind from the confinement of the cockpit. He fetched a rag, a screwdriver, and a pair of pliers from the hangar and opened the Aeronca's engine cover to check the oil and fuel levels and inspect the gaskets and hoses. Everything was in order, but the rubber seal around the passenger side door had been making an annoying hiss during flight, so he began to inspect it to find the cause. A deep voice behind him said, "Good afternoon, Beane."

He looked round and was surprised to see Commander Park. "Commander! Good afternoon. Nice to see you, sir."

"That's a fine machine," said Park. "I'm glad you are taking such good care of it. Tiger tells me you are in the air more than any pilot here. He speaks highly of your flying ability."

"Thank you, sir. I heard you had gone to South America."

"Argentina, actually. But I'm at Fighter Command now. Air Commodore commanding Eleven Group under Air Chief Marshal Dowding."

"A promotion? Congratulations, sir."

"Thank you. Do you follow matters on the Continent, Beane?"

"When I can, sir. I don't like what I've read about that man Hitler and his Nazis."

"Indeed. That is precisely what I've come to see you about. Come for a walk so no-one can overhear us, and I'll tell you about it."

Hanworth was quiet in the late afternoon and they strolled together to the end of the grass infield. Only one aeroplane was in sight, a Tiger Moth banking before it made its landing approach. Park offered him a cigarette and lit them both, and they watched the Moth land. Eddy could see himself reflected in the Commodore's sunglasses, but not the expression behind them. He was startled when Park said, "Would you like to serve your country, Edouard?"

"In Fighter Command, sir?" Eddy's heart leapt. "Flying fighter planes?"

"Not yet. Perhaps in time." Park put a hand on Eddy's shoulder. "At the moment, I have an even more important task for you. Here is the situation. We've begun to produce excellent fighter planes with Rolls Royce engines. They're called Spitfires."

"Yes, sir. I've heard of them."

"I tested one in '36," Park said, "just about the time I met you. Our Spitfires are fast, manoeuvrable, and they climb like the devil's behind them."

"They sound impressive. I haven't seen one yet."

"Hitler is producing fast light bombers at an alarming rate, and Spitfires are precisely what we need to repel them. But we don't have enough of them. They cost four and a half thousand pounds each, plus another thousand for the guns and radio. Dowding and I must convince the ministers to open the Royal Exchequer because Hitler is arming for war, and we've got to be ready. We need many hundreds of Spitfires. The trouble is that we are up against other Arms'

28

requests for battleships, tanks and machine guns, not to mention the usual civilian needs for hospitals, schools, orphanages and the like."

Park paused. "That is where you come in."

"Sir?"

"We believe Hitler has far more Heinkels and Junkers than show up in our official counts. We're sure that they are hidden away under netting outside a new Luftwaffe base. Wunstorf. We need evidence if we are to convince the Treasury that our need for Spitfires really is urgent. We need photographs." Park paused to take a long drag on his cigarette. Eddy felt he was being sized up, same as the day they met at Weldy & Beane.

"Are you asking me to take those photographs? Sir, my Aeronca doesn't have the range to fly to Germany. Why don't you use an RAF reconnaissance plane? Or a Spitfire?"

Park raised his sunglasses. "We can't risk the political fall-out if an RAF plane is caught in German air space. You, on the other hand, are a private individual who flies to the Continent in the course of commerce. Like your recent flight to Paris." He looked straight at Eddy and waited.

"But also—if I'm caught, I'm on my own?"

"This mission is vitally important to your country. And to France, the country of your birth."

"Give me a minute, sir."

"Of course."

Eddy walked away, his mind in a whirl. The Aeronca, which earned him his living, was no fighter. With a cruising speed of not much more than eighty miles per hour, it would be a sitting duck if he met any German fighters, because they could dive four or five times as fast. But if what Park said was true, and Hitler was tooling-up for war, then there would be no civilian business for the Aeronca to do.

Commodore Park had turned to look over the Aeronca. Eddy judged him to be more than just a uniformed military man; he was a warrior, ramrod straight, who would have the guts to do himself what he had just asked Eddy to do.

Another military man came to Eddy's mind, his Papa.

He remembered *Maman*'s funeral, six years earlier, when the mourners had gathered for the funeral tea at The Four Bells pub in Lassingwood. One of Papa's messmates from the War, Bill Jenkins, had pulled Eddy aside and recounted stories about his father. Eddy had choked up listening to Jenkins recount how his father died while standing his ground on the trench wall against a German assault so many British soldiers could escape. Clearly, his father had been well-liked in the Army and a courageous soldier. Eddy had the look of his father, Jenkins had told him, and "if you have your father's qualities, you'll be a helluva man just like him." Like Park, Papa would have had the guts to accept this mission.

For the first time, today, Eddy felt he had a chance to do something to measure up. He ground his cigarette butt into the turf with the heel of his boot, and rejoined Park.

"Well?" the Commodore asked.

"What are the distances going to be like?"

Park nodded slightly, acknowledging the question as a provisional acceptance of the task. "Probably four hundred air miles. What's your usual range between refueling?"

"Two hundred miles."

"We can fit a second fuel tank for you. We'll arrange for you to refuel at a friendly airfield in Groningen, in the Netherlands." He extended his hand to Eddy. "I have faith in you, lad. You'll do it."

Eddy swallowed hard and shook his hand. "I'd be honored to."

"That's the spirit. Come on. I want to see this crate of yours in the sky. How much fuel has she got in her, right now?"

"She's nearly full," Eddy said.

"Good. Let's take her up! After that, I'll talk you through the operation. I'm convinced there is a way to shoot the photographs we need and get you back home safely."

Chapter 7

In Groningen, in the dark before dawn, Eddy walked from his overnight lodgings to the airfield. The Inn where he and Corporal Tinker had stayed was comfortable enough, but he was to fly to Wunstorf at first light, so he had slept maybe four hours, tossing and turning as he anticipated what he expected to be the most eventful day of his life. A distant security light guided him into the hangar. Inside, he lit a lantern and a cigarette, and played the light over the Aeronca's propeller, intake, and flaps. Everything looked in order.

The hangar's layered scents, pungent of oil, grease and solvent, sharpened his senses to his task.

He heard the rattle of tools and saw a light, and turning his lantern towards it, there was Tinker and the glowing tip of his cigarette, already preparing to supervise their mission.

"Morning," Tinker said.

"Good morning."

Given his dutiful nature, Eddy wasn't surprised that Tinker had been first to arrive at the hangar. They had flown together a dozen hours to prepare for the mission over Wunstorf, and Eddy had come to appreciate Tinker's quiet confidence and to respect his skills. Tinker had sharpened Eddy's ability to set a course by altimeter and compass, and to match ground features with a map.

Eddy had learned to use a little hand-held Fairchild K-14 camera that Air Commodore Park had given him. As practice, they had taken photographs of Biggin Hill and Duxford from varying altitudes, of the structures and aeroplanes on the ground. The work had continued for a week until Park was satisfied that Eddy could capture the required quality of images. Park had sent a sample of exposed film from the Fairchild to Photo-Interpretation at the War Office, and they had agreed that the images it produced were perfectly adequate. Details of the aircraft he had photographed on the ground could be clearly identified: elliptical wings of Spitfires; long, straight wings of Hurricanes; turret guns on Defiants; the top bubble on a Bristol Blenheim.

Eddy placed the camera on the tandem seat. It was no bigger than the Kodak that Uncle Al used to take pictures of Georgie and Anna Thérèse, and Eddy had been dismayed when he first saw it. Park had read the doubt on his face. "It's made for 'spotting'—general aerial reconnaissance. We can't very well mount a camera with a bigger lens on the underside of the Aeronca and let you go wandering over German airspace, now can we?"

Yesterday afternoon, Tinker had dozed during most of their flight from Hanworth to the Netherlands and Air Commodore Park's advice had rolled over and over in Eddy's mind. "Fly over Wunstorf early in the morning when everything's a bit confused. The Germans aren't at war at the moment, so they can't be sure you are a threat. You might be a private pilot from Hanover who lost his way. When you've taken the photos I need, stay on course. Don't deviate or turn back—that would look suspicious. Just keep going, and head for the clouds if you can. Stay calm. They will leave you alone in there. Why would they risk a collision in a cloud when they don't know who you are or what you are up to? Turn back only when you're sure they are not still watching."

Now, as Eddy pumped fuel into the Aeronca, he understood he was about to risk his life; despite his preparations, the Aeronca might have a mechanical problem, and although he had had plenty of technical training he couldn't do anything about the Germans if they decided to force him to land or shoot him down. He had lied to Aunt Maddy about this trip. His cover story was that he was flying to the Continent to deliver a businessman to meetings in Lille, and that he would be away while he waited to bring his customer back.

He felt guilty about the lie. What if he didn't come back? There wouldn't even be a funeral. Life would move on without him, and he couldn't say that he would leave much of a permanent mark. He had lived with Aunt Maddy and Uncle Al for only a few years; just a short chapter in the book of their lives. He loved them, of course, and his little cousins, and they loved him back, and he thought the fact that he was young and unmarried should make it easier for them. If he did die, Georgie and Anna Thérèse might miss him at first, but they were young, and over the years their memories of him would fade. The children would demand all Maddy's and Al's attention and that would take their minds off his death, surely?

He replaced the nozzle on the gas pump and took a walk out into the darkness to clear his head. He ought to trust that his training and practice would enable him to take the photographs that the Air Commodore required, and that the Aeronca would come home without incident.

"Frenchy," Tinker called. "I reckon we should test the RND before you take off."

Eddy came at once. He pushed away his morbid thoughts, and climbed up to his seat, taking care to avoid the Radio Navigational Device, which had been mounted on the inside of the cockpit, near his knee.

Tinker called up to him, "Turn it on."

Eddy switched on the knob, and the RND's high, intermittent beeps pierced the cockpit.

"It works all right."

"Good," Tinker said. "We'll mount the beacon on an antenna here as soon as we've got the light to see what we're doing. Then you can home into it on your way back, Frenchy, just like we practised. Home in on the beeps. Remember you won't be able to hear them until you are within fifty miles. After that, they'll get louder as you get closer. When they're this loud you'll be on top of us!"

"Got it," Eddy said.

"Good. Now, off with you. I'll radio Commodore Park to let him know you are in the air." Tinker made a mighty pull on the Aeronca's propeller, and the engine thrummed into action.

The Aeronca's wheels lifted off the grass runway into the first light of morning. Eddy climbed to five thousand feet, leveled, and set his compass bearing. Dawn came gray and hazy behind thick clouds. He couldn't yet make out much beyond his windscreen, as if he were flying in a vacuum where nothing else existed, forced to rely on compass and altimeter.

On Air Commodore Park's advice, he and Tinker had waited several days for these conditions: An eight-eighths layer of stable stratocumulus clouds over northern Germany with a ceiling of a mile, at most. He leveled off just below the ceiling, as Park had advised.

Minute after minute, he flew east into visibility, and danger. Now he could make out landmarks: the Ems River, the moorland at

Aschendorfer Obermoor, and then the town of Cloppenburg, recognizable by the Amtsgericht, a rectangular, red-roofed district courthouse, with vast grounds and tall, steepled belfry. Forty more minutes passed, and he was over the water of Steinhuder Meer, and knew he would be approaching Wunstorf.

Soon he could see military buildings in the distance ahead, grouped around runways, hangars and barracks, with the tiny shapes of soldiers patrolling outside.

But he couldn't see any planes. Were they in the hangars, or was Air Commodore Park wrong about Wunstorf as a potential enemy air base? He remembered Park's instruction: "You must fly as low as you can. Get me detailed pictures of those bombers."

He let the airspeed drop and brought the Aeronca down to a thousand feet. Even so, it was some time before he spotted the evidence Park wanted. Brownish-green netting had been suspended across much of the perimeter of the airfield by thick ropes tied to trees several hundred yards from the runways, but he could make out the distinctive shapes of fuselages and wings beneath it. Several giant propellers protruded from the netting and here and there he could make out a glazed nose that matched those of Heinkel bombers in the photographs that Park had shown him.

Click. Click. Click. He aimed the Fairchild at the netting and snapped as many photographs as he could until he had passed completely over the airfield. Then he banked to take a second pass.

As he turned he saw that three planes, much smaller than the bombers beneath him, were being pushed out of a hangar and onto the runway. Fighter planes. Messerschmitts!

His heart began to thump. He set down his camera, pointed the Aeronca's nose towards the cloud ceiling, and started to climb away from them.

The Germans got their fighters lined up frighteningly fast. The leader roared down the runway and by the time Eddy had flown over the field the other two were in the air behind him. Why had he gone for a second pass! Still, the ceiling was less than fifteen hundred feet above him and if he could get into it he should be safe.

The fighters were making sweeping turns towards him. The leader had a large number 34 painted in white behind its cockpit.

Just a few hundred feet more!

"*Allez, allez, allez!*"

The Aeronca's engine sputtered and he realized his main tank was nearly out of fuel. As he hastily switched to the auxiliary he saw the lead fighter flying straight at him, so close that he could see the pilot's thick white scarf. The Aeronca's engine roared back to life and the Messerschmitt passed over her nose like a comet. But the fighter hadn't fired. Eddy realized Air Commodore Park had been right. The Germans were harassing him away, but so long as he looked inoffensive, they would hesitate to attack.

He had reached the cloud ceiling. The cold whitish-gray vapor flicked around him and surrounded the Aeronca with blessed invisibility. He was completely within the cloud layer, floating in a chilly other-world, as if he had entered the heavens, cut off from earth, hidden from enemies. He took a deep breath, knowing his feeling of safety might be an illusion.

He marked his altitude, spun the dial on his compass and set a westerly bearing for Groningen.

A roaring engine startled him, zipping through the clouds to starboard. It was probably a Messerschmitt, but he couldn't see it, and the roar diminished and faded to nothing. He flew on, listening, for several uncomfortable minutes but heard no more.

There was no use turning on the Radio Navigational Device yet; he was far out of range. When he dared to drop below the ceiling to find a landmark, he was passing the bend in the Weser river at Windheim. He re-entered the clouds.

He was still nervous. Even in this swirling, white domain it was possible the clouds might part, and a Messerschmitt might swoop down onto him. If he was squarely in its gunsights, bullets would stream into his engine like hammer blows, making him the pilot of a ball of flames. The Aeronca had no defense. He could only monitor his instruments, stay on course and will his Aeronca to come through. It had been his constant companion, his workhorse and, quite apart from his motivation to save his own neck, he didn't want it to end up as a pile of twisted metal in a foreign land.

Time passed slowly in his white world. In thirty minutes, the clouds began to thin and break up. Eddy checked the skies around him: No Messerschmitts. Below him were the fertile squares and rectangles of Lower Saxony farmland. He made for the next patch of clouds and turned the knob on the RND. He should be in range of the beacon soon.

Nothing. Minutes passed.

He had retraced the course as far as the Ems River before the first faint beep came through the RND's speaker. He took a deep breath, and for the first time, dared to think that he was going to complete his mission to hand the camera and its film to Air Commodore Park, and see his satisfaction when he knew he had the evidence he wanted. He checked his compass reading and made a tiny correction to port. The beeps grew louder and his confidence in a safe return grew.

He checked his map. The small town below him might be Magnuskerk. Yes, that must be right: a body of water shaped like a seahorse. Soon he saw another Dutch town, which must be Sappemeer. The web of roads that came into view led him to Groningen, and then he recognized the ground plan and the clustered buildings of the airfield.

The beeps of the RND were sounding loudly now, as if they were cheering his arrival.

His wheels touched down safely, and he taxied to where Tinker stood waiting.

"You made it, then," Tinker said.

Eddy looked down at him from the cockpit. "Did you dare to doubt me?"

Tinker chuckled.

"Things got a little hairy over Wunstorf," Eddy said. "They scrambled three fighters to have a look at me."

"You always knew they might. Did you get the photographs?"

Eddy lifted his camera into view. "I did."

"Good lad. We'll refuel, then, and make for Hanworth. The Commodore will be waiting. I telephoned him when I saw you coming in, and he says, 'Good work' and he'll meet us at Hanworth to receive the camera. He wants to get the film to the P-I officer immediately."

Eddy climbed down and stretched. He felt as though he had been flying non-stop for a week. He walked away for a smoke while Tinker tended to the refueling.

Air Commodore Park had asked him to do something extraordinary, and he had done it. As he relished the sense of achievement, his thoughts turned to his parents, and the promise he had made to *Maman* the day she had been put to rest nearly six years before.

That day, in late October 1932, light had been fading in the late afternoon sky. He had walked to St. Martin's parish church in Lassingwood, the small town in Oxfordshire where Papa had been born and raised, with Aunt Maddy holding onto his arm. A brisk breeze had been rustling the tan-colored leaves of a chestnut tree, and some had fallen across the weathered headstones below St. Martin's sooty walls. While the Vicar spoke *Maman*'s funeral liturgy he had prayed for her soul; then he had promised *Maman* that he would grow up to be a good man and that he would make her proud. *Maman*'s headstone was at St. Martin's among the rest now, and he would return there as soon as he could to pray for her, and to tell her what he had just done.

Perhaps Papa and *Maman* were looking down and keeping him safe, because his *Maman*'s last wish had been to be reunited with his father in heaven. She had asked Aunt Maddy to seek permission for her to be buried at St. Martin's, a parish in the Church of England, even though she was a devout Catholic. Because it had been at St. Martin's, as a boy, where his father had come to his spirituality. Eddy smiled to himself, hoping that her choice had somehow brought his parents together again.

"Frenchy," Tinker said, drawing him back from his musings.

"Yes?"

"I'm glad you're back safe. By the way, the Commodore said he hopes we're both hungry. He is treating us to cocktails and dinner at his club. He wants to hear all about the mission."

"I'll bet he does." Eddy moved away from the Aeronca so he could light a cigarette.

"I can't wait," said Tinker, following him. "Have you ever been to a London club?"

"No, I can't say I move in those circles."

"Come on, let's finish fueling up and get home. This is a date I don't wait to miss."

Chapter 8

Three weeks after the Wunstorf mission, Eddy was sitting with Air Commodore Park and Corporal Tinker at Park's club, glass of scotch in hand. He was comfortable now with the room's dark, inlaid wooden panels, its extraordinarily tall windows, and its portraits from centuries past. On the night he had returned from photographing over Wunstorf, nervous reaction to the day's mission had vexed him throughout dinner. Although it had been a celebratory occasion, the club's pervasive aura of self-assured, masculine power had taken him entirely out of his own element.

This evening, Park, Eddy and Tinker were smoking in comfortable silence. Between Eddy's first visit and this one a camaraderie had grown from them working together as a team. They had conducted four missions over German airspace and now they were waiting to meet Air Chief Marshal Dowding.

Dowding arrived, wearing his blue RAF jacket with chevrons that stretched from his lapel button to his shoulder. They all stood to greet him.

"Edouard, meet Air Chief Marshal Dowding," said Park.

"I am Edouard Beane, sir. I'm pleased to meet you." They shook hands.

"And you know Corporal Tinker," Park said to Dowding.

"Yes," Dowding said. He stared at Eddy; his lips turned down slightly under a wispy, graying mustache. "You are the pilot who has been observing for us over Germany?"

"Yes, sir," Eddy said.

"You have photographed Bombers at Wunstorf and Warnemunde. Junkers at Dessau. The ball-bearing plants at Schweinfurt. You have given us precisely the evidence we needed, Mr. Beane," Dowding said.

Eddy dared to smile. Those four missions had just made September 1938 the busiest month of his life, and the most rewarding.

A waiter approached, clearly intent on service, but Dowding waved him off. "I won't be staying," he said to Park. He asked Eddy, "I take it you know why we need the photographs?"

"Yes, sir," Eddy said. "You need evidence of Germany building up its air force so our Ministers will release funding for more fighters."

"That is correct," Dowding said. His crisp, efficient speech pattern reminded Eddy of Park when he gave instructions for a photography mission.

"It is critical, now more than ever, that Fighter Command gets more fighters. Just last week an agreement was made at Munich to give Hitler a part of Czechoslovakia for Germany. Many at the Air Ministry believe that all that has done is to whet the man's appetite for more conquest."

"In fact," Park added, "we have been asked by the Air Ministry to submit Fighter Command's report on the actions we have taken to prepare for the defence of Great Britain."

"To that end," Dowding said, "we have devised a unified system of radar, ground observers, raid plotting, and radio control of our aircraft. But our system simply cannot work without an adequate number of Spitfires." He paused, his long face set with lines of determination. "Park tells me you are French-born?"

"Yes, sir," Eddy said, cautiously. He didn't immediately see what Dowding was driving at.

"France will be attacked by Hitler within a matter of months; I'm sure of it. Your work is as vital for France as it is for us."

"Ah. Of course."

"Fighter Command's report, with your photographs, makes our case for more Spitfires in the strongest possible terms," Dowding said. "We need one more set of evidence to submit along with it. Are you willing to obtain it?"

"Yes, sir. I am," Eddy said.

"Good. Air Commodore Park will explain your mission." Dowding prepared to leave, but as an afterthought he leaned towards Eddy. "Young man, Air Commodore Park tells me you have proved your mettle. Continue to show the same spirit and we will find a place for you in Fighter Command."

"Thank you, sir."

At that, Dowding rose and took his leave. Eddy watched him stride stiffly away through the open club room. His own mind was full of Spitfires. He saw himself climbing into the cockpit of England's sleekest war machine, sliding the hood into place, pulling back the throttle, feeling its wheels leave the earth, and soaring towards high mountains of clouds. Nothing could stand in his way.

"Well," Park said, breaking his daydream, "You made a good impression on him."

"Did I?"

"He sized you up the moment you were introduced. If you hadn't impressed him, he would have left without telling you about Fighter Command's report."

Tinker chuckled. "I've seen him dismiss junior officers in less time than it takes to crank a propeller. The men call him 'Stuffy.'"

Park raised an eyebrow at Tinker. "All right. Let's get to business. We have information that Germany's production of Dornier light bombers has stepped up. The factory—Dornier Flugzeugwerke—is expected to produce two thousand more of them in the next couple of years."

"Is this my next mission, sir?"

"Yes. The facility is already immense, and they are extending it further. We have information that the new Dorniers are parked under camouflage outside the buildings. We need photographs of the whole complex. You see, Beane, the Germans are spending a billion Reichsmarks a year on military aircraft and—we spend a pittance compared to that. It has to change. Tinker, hand me the map."

Tinker reached into his satchel, retrieved a map and gave it to Park, who unfolded it and laid it in front of Eddy. He put his finger on its southern border, where Germany met Austria and Switzerland. "Here, in Friedrichshafen," Park said. "That is where the factory is."

Eddy had a look. "It's a long way, sir. I will probably need two fuel stops."

"Yes, this is the farthest we've sent you so far, Frenchy," said Tinker. "But the good news is that this mission should be less dangerous than the four you have completed with me. Friedrichshafen is on the east shore of Lake Constance and only a few minutes airtime from Switzerland. There is a fair bit of industry in the area. The weather's usually good in early October, so I expect there will still be a considerable amount of air traffic, which will make you less conspicuous. Best of all, you can fly in and out in the middle of the day, snap your photos, and leave German air space very quickly. I won't need to come along and man the beacons."

"Excellent! When do I go?" Eddy asked.

"I took a look at the weather charts," Tinker said. "Three or four days of showers are settling over most of France. Let's make it next week."

Air Commodore Park lit a cigarette and said, "Listen, Edouard. I am sure you're flattered that Air Chief Dowding acknowledged your contribution and you're bound to be excited by his suggestion that someday you might join us at Fighter Command. But I need you to put that out of your mind. Your mission to Friedrichshafen is to bring us the last vital pieces of evidence to make our case for more Spitfires. Keep a cool, clear head and concentrate on your mission. Do you understand?"

"I do, sir."

"Good lad." Park signaled the waiter over. "Shall we order?"

Chapter 9

Eddy left the airfield hastily the next day to join the Weldy family dinner. He hoped to put the pressures of his mission to Friedrichshafen out of his mind, at least for the evening. Uncle Al took his usual seat in the carver chair at the head of the table. Little Georgie was seated next to him, and Anna Thérèse was perched in her highchair on the side next to Aunt Maddy. Eddy hurried to the table, washed and hastily brushed into a semblance of tidiness.

Eddy sat down next to Georgie, who looked up to him and smiled with a five year-old's unbridled delight. Uncle Al nodded, warmly. Anna Thérèse was busy with a rubber rattle toy that mercifully made only a quiet noise when she shook it. Eddy almost always had to forego the cozy familiarity of dining with the family in light of his workload at Hanworth and his missions for Air Commodore Park. Nevertheless, even with his frequent absences, when he sat down he was once again one of them, as though he had never been away. It comforted him beyond words.

"Daddy! What's for dinner?" Georgie asked.

"Lamb and peas," Uncle Al said. "And Mummy said if you eat it all, there's rhubarb fool."

Aunt Maddy came in carrying a stack of hot plates, her hands protected by a folded tea-towel.

"Eddy, dear, would you push that trivet a bit nearer for me?"

"Aunt Maddy, I warn you I'm going to be home for dinner much more often."

"Promises, promises," she said, putting down the plates.

Eddy hoped his face didn't show the guilt he felt. "Thank you for waiting for me this evening."

"We are just happy to have you back with us," Uncle Al said. "This past month we have seen hardly anything of you. What have you been carrying to the continent? Passengers? Cargo?"

"Plenty of both," Eddy said. Air Commodore Park hadn't specifically prohibited him from speaking of his missions, but good sense dictated that he didn't disclose, even to family, that he had flown to Germany each of the past three weeks. "With luck, though, I'm going to fly mostly within England from now on. Business has been good, and it looks as though yours has too. Your new furniture is impressive," he said to Al, to try to keep him from talking about flying. He ran his palms over the white linen tablecloth. "It reminds me of Madame du Claire's manor house."

Uncle Al smiled. "Thank you, Eddy. It's all second hand, from the auction rooms. The table and chairs came with the sideboard in one lot. I had to bid a fine price, I must say! Your Aunt Maddy upholstered the seats."

"Another line of work, Aunt Maddy?" Eddy asked.

"Don't you think I have enough to do?" she said, with a smile. "Georgie!" She broke off with a sharp admonition to little Georgie, who had slipped away to the sideboard while Eddy and Al were talking and was about to poke his finger into the bowl of rhubarb fool. "Al, please take him on your knee, dear, till we're ready."

Eddy captured Georgie and lifted him onto his knee, which surprised the little boy into sitting still. "*C'est ça,*" Eddy said. "Your *Maman* will be pleased with you, little *Chanticleer.*"

Georgie looked up at him. "What is Shantyclear, Eddy?"

"*Chanticleer* is a cockerel, and the cockerel is a special bird for people from France."

"Is that because they can eat him?"

Eddy chuckled. "No. It's because he is proud and very noisy, just like you."

Aunt Maddy brought in steaming dishes of peas and potato, and sliced lamb. Eddy waited while she said grace and then patted Georgie and said, "Sit in your proper place, now."

Aunt Maddy gave Eddy a plate bearing the largest slice of lamb and smiled at him. "It means so much to have you with us at family dinner."

"It means just as much to me," Eddy said, helping himself to peas. "I'll be here every night I can."

"That would be wonderful. You've been so busy since you bought the aeroplane."

"I've been lucky. I've got away to a good start," Eddy said.

Georgie stared at his plate and stuck out his lower lip. "Can I have woobarb, Mummy?"

"Yes, dear. But not until you've eaten your lamb and peas."

Uncle Al was noticeably quiet during dinner. Eddy had a sinking feeling that his departure from Weldy & Beane to pursue a flying career had left his Uncle in difficulties. Trained tailors who put in fifty hours in a week didn't grow on trees. Had he left his Aunt and Uncle in the lurch after all they had done to give him a new, comfortable life in England?

Aunt Maddy ate slowly, feeding Anna Thérèse a couple of mouthfuls for every one she took herself. When the main course had been polished off, she said to Georgie, "Well done! You've eaten all your lamb and all but a smidgen of your peas. Now you can have your blessed woobarb."

Georgie bounced in his chair with glee, and when Aunt Maddy set a bowl in front of him he attacked the fool with the zeal of a puppy, his spoon diving in again and again. Eddy damped his handkerchief to wipe the streaks from Georgie's chin.

"Al, would you take Anna Thérèse, and set Georgie up with his blocks, while I clear away? Eddy and I are going to wash the dishes, aren't we dear? Then I'll take the children upstairs for their bath."

"Yes dear. Come along, my little lamb. And you too, little mister!" Al picked up Anna Thérèse and disappeared down the hallway with Georgie bounding ahead of him.

Eddy helped Aunt Maddy clear the table. "Has Uncle Al run out of anecdotes? He seemed unusually quiet," he said. "Is there any trouble with the business?"

"No, dear. It's not that." Maddy filled the sink with hot water. Eddy waited for her to explain. He thought it must be something difficult because she had said no more until she had whisked up a foam with the soap-holder and begun to wash the plates. "Weldy & Beane has more business than ever. We've taken on a new tailor. We are both so proud of you! We know your flying business makes you happy, and that makes us happy, so you mustn't feel guilty about leaving our shop."

"Thank you for saying so. It's just...Uncle Al seems distracted tonight."

Aunt Maddy sighed and handed him a plate to dry. "He had some news today. It's to do with the War, and that always unsettles him."

"The War? Is it about my father?"

"Yes, I think it is. Years ago, before we were married, when I ran the Four Bells pub, Al told me about something that happened when he and your father served together in Flanders. It seems to have come back around—I expect he'll tell you about it once the children are in bed."

Eddy went on mechanically drying dishes. The Great War had ended twenty years ago. How could it possibly re-enter their lives now? What was this secret story? Was Al in trouble? *Maman* had sometimes said there were secrets that should stay buried.

When the dishes were all dried and put away, Aunt Maddy sent him off to the sitting room where he found Uncle Al in his over-stuffed chair by the fire, with his feet stretched towards the tiled hearth. A bottle of brandy and two glasses stood on the occasional table beside him and next to it were several unfolded pages of a letter.

"I don't often see you drinking brandy, Uncle Al."

"I don't suppose you do."

"Is everything all right?"

"Yes. But come and sit down. Would you like one?"

"Yes, please," Eddy said.

Uncle Al poured brandy into the other glass and handed it to him. After a few moments he said, "An officer from the Ox & Bucks called on me today, at the shop."

"Ox & Bucks? Isn't that the regiment you and my father were in during the War?"

"That's right. The officer brought me a letter that they received last month. It had been addressed to your father and me at regimental headquarters, from someone in Germany."

Germany had been the enemy then, as she seemed likely to become again very soon. What business could someone in Germany have with his father and his Uncle—two former British soldiers—twenty years after the Great War?

"I don't understand."

"Seems odd, doesn't it?" Uncle Al had a sip of brandy. "The letter's in French. Aunt Maddy and I have looked at it, and I think we have the gist of it. But of course, our French isn't as good as yours. Would you mind reading it through and giving us a translation into English?"

Eddy nodded, and Uncle Al handed him the letter. It had been receipted with a bold black stamp and a date written in: 'RECEIVED 27 SEPTEMBER 1938 REGIMENTAL HEADQUARTERS. OXFORDSHIRE & BUCKINGHAMSHIRE LIGHT INFANTRY'. It was addressed to his father and his Uncle at Cowley Barracks.

He read aloud, pausing between phrases as he translated from the French:

I believe that you will remember me. I am called Jens Kluber. You took me prisoner in Flanders just before Christmas in 1914. I remember you well, and I know that one of you, at least, understands the French language. Then, in the most surprising of circumstances, you also met my cousin Axel and his man Uwe on Christmas Day, 1914. Axel sent a letter home to our family in Germany that told them about you. He told them how the English and German soldiers met in a truce and you all shared Christmas dinner. He told our family about your long conversations with him and Uwe, and how you saved me the night you captured me. He said you had treated me well, which is true. That is why I must write to you now.

You gentlemen have become a legend to us—the benevolent Englishmen we could not hate. I have found your names in Cousin Axel's letter, and the name of the regiment in which you served. I don't know if you survived the war, but hope that if you did, your regiment will send this message on to you.

I am writing to you because I have nowhere else to turn. Now is a time of great tragedy in Germany. Hooligans have taken over our country—

"Hooligans?" said Al. "Your aunt wasn't sure if she had understood that properly."

"Yes," Eddy said. "*Voyoux*—it means louts, thugs,"

"She was correct, then. Thugs."

Thugs have taken over our country, under the guise of politics. They won't tolerate anyone who doesn't agree with them. I have seen Nazis commit atrocities on our streets. I am a simple grape-grower, and I can't stop them. I hate what we are becoming. I fear for our younger people.

But I write not for myself, but for Axel's daughter, Lotte Schroder. She is a teacher of languages, well-educated and kind-hearted. Axel's son, Otto, despite the same upbringing, has thrown in his lot with the thugs—he is a Nazi. He and his brutish friends beat people and steal in the name of

46

patriotism. Otto is enraged with his sister Lotte because she criticizes the Nazis. He hates her sympathies for our workers here in the Mosel region, and for those less fortunate. Their father Axel didn't come home from the war so he's not here to help her. Their mother, Elke, died five years ago. So, Otto holds much power over Lotte. It is difficult to explain how much danger she is in. I fear Otto will harm her if she stays here, because she will never support his beliefs.

I can see only one solution. She must leave her home, and go somewhere far away, where Otto cannot find her. Can you help me?

Jens Kluber.

Eddy finished reading aloud and sat thinking. The letter astounded him.

Uncle Al prompted him. "Well? What do you make of it?"

"I don't know enough to judge. You've told me before about the Great War, and the British and German soldiers meeting at Christmas in a truce, but I don't remember you mentioning this fellow Jens."

As usual, when a wartime anecdote was on its way, Uncle Al turned to cigarettes. He still smoked Chesterfields. He offered one to Eddy now and lit them both before he continued. "Your father and I took Jens prisoner one night when we were on patrol in no-man's land. We took him to our reserve trench to turn him over to the military police. Jens was scared to death."

"Anyone would be scared."

"He looked so young, and to tell you the truth, he had wet his trousers!"

Eddy chuckled.

"Well, we gave the boy a drink, and some food, and that cheered him up a bit. Your father talked with him for quite a while, in French. He told him our prison camp would be much more comfortable than the German trenches." Uncle Al smoked, smiling. "I know the letter says we saved him, but that's too strong. We took him alive. We didn't shoot him or cut his throat and drop him in the mud which is what happened to many other Englishmen and Germans. That is the best I can say about what we did for Jens. We met his cousin Axel three weeks later, on Christmas Day, 1914."

"Yes. You told me the soldiers from both armies laid down their weapons and met in no-man's land for a greeting. And that you think about it every Christmas."

47

Uncle Al took a drag on his cigarette and sat back. "It was astonishing, Eddy. Unbelievable. We shared food with men we had shot at, and who had shot at us. We smoked and drank with them— Axel had some wine from his family's vineyard, and he shared it with us. He was speaking French, and your father spoke good French, so they struck up a conversation. Soon, we were talking like old friends." He paused. "The truth is your father and I saw Axel as a decent sort. Just a lad who lived in the cold hell of a muddy trench far from his home and followed orders, same as us."

He smoked for a few moments in silence.

"Axel asked if we knew anything about a young cousin of his who had been taken prisoner, and we realized it was that lad Jens. I never saw Axel or Jens again, so it's quite a surprise that he has felt the need to contact me after all these years. I can only think that he is desperate to help Axel's daughter. She is dear to him. I understood that when your Aunt Maddy first read the letter. Even so, I can't imagine things getting so difficult that a man would go outside the family for help. To a relative stranger, in another country—"

Eddy sensed the doubt in his Uncle's voice. Uncle Al had a family to protect. A business to run. Eddy thought Jens was probably honest— at least, if he was a trickster, what was he trying to achieve? To pry himself into Uncle Al's life and make money out of him if he could? What if Axel's daughter was really not the paragon of virtue Jens made her out to be?

Uncle Al spoke again. "This young lady might well be in grave trouble. I have read these Nazis are a terrible bunch. Maybe I should offer to take her in."

"But you are not sure?" Eddy asked. He thought his uncle was torn, between his obligations as a husband and a father to protect his family, and a good-hearted humanitarian desire to help Axel's daughter. After all, Uncle Al and Aunt Maddy had taken him into their home when *Maman* was gravely ill and had not given it a second thought. But he was family—and Jens and Axel and Lotte were not. No, they were Germans. It was the Germans who had killed Papa and left him to lie forever under the mud, without a marker. What was more, the Nazis rule Germany now and they would have shot down his Aeronca if they knew he had been taking photographs above their airfields. Eddy would have been very relieved if Uncle Al had wadded up Axel's letter, tossed it in the bin and forgot it had ever existed.

His uncle, though, was still thinking. Finally, he said, "I'm remembering Axel and The Christmas Truce. And I'm thinking about your father. The day before we met you and your mother in Hazebrouck, I took your Aunt Maddy to visit the battlefields in Flanders. I found the place your father died. Past Zillebeke, near Sanctuary Wood and Hill 60. It's not far from where we captured Jens and met Axel during the Truce. I took your Aunt's hand and we walked to the trenches. They were still there, but the wooden frames were rotting, and mud had slid down into the bottom. I felt oppressed in there—I damned-near couldn't breathe. Your aunt held me tight until I came out of it. I scraped up a handful of dirt because I realized something, Eddy. That miserable patch of earth will always be part of me. And everything that happened there. I'll never get away from it."

Uncle Al closed his eyes. "Eddy, your father will always be alive inside my soul, and he would take this girl in; I know he would."

Eddy accepted that his Uncle had made his decision even though important questions were unanswered. "You know that the facts in the early part of the letter are correct," he said. "But you have no way of knowing whether Jens's story about Lotte is true."

Uncle Al looked at him, intently.

"Where do they live?" Eddy looked at the heading on the letter. "This is from a vineyard with a Saarburg address. I'll find a map. Back in a moment." When he returned he said, "Saarburg is just down the river from Trier. There's an airfield south of Trier, so I could fly over and see what I can find out."

Uncle Al held up his hand, like a stop sign. "Hold on, lad! I only wanted you to translate the letter, to make sure your Aunt and I hadn't misunderstood anything. This isn't your problem. I don't want you involved."

Eddy grinned at him. "But you're thinking about transplanting a strange young woman into our family, so I am involved! Look, they're French speakers, so I'm in a better position than you to find out what's really going on. I'm making a trip to the Continent next week. I can arrange to stop in Trier and look in on Jens and Lotte—if I can find them. I will ask what her situation is with her brother, and judge whether she is as good a person as Jens says she is." He took a sip of brandy. "I'll ask her if she really needs to escape Otto—and if she really wants to leave her home. Would you trust me to gather the evidence for you? I'm not so likely to be swayed by wartime sentiment as you are."

Uncle Al stubbed out his cigarette with an abruptness that told Eddy he had trodden on dangerous ground.

"Sentiment? It seems like common decency to me. I can't ignore an appeal like this."

"I'm sorry. Of course it's your decision."

"And your Aunt Maddy's!"

"Yes. Obviously. But that doesn't change what I said. I'm in the best position to find out what's really going on. I'll tell you the truth about the girl—you know I will. After that, you can decide if you want to take her in." His own cigarette was down to the stub, and he put it out in the ashtray between them.

After a moment Uncle Al said gruffly, "These Nazis are a dangerous lot."

"Yes." It sounded as though he was forgiven. "Shall I let you know when I've arranged my trip? Then you can send a telegram to the vineyard to let them know I'm coming. Perhaps Jens could pick me up at the airfield."

"What if you come face to face with Otto? Jens says he's a thug, after all."

"And I have wit on my side," Eddy said, with a grin. "I'll steer clear of him."

Chapter 10

E ddy had to contend with uneasy feelings about his flight to Friedrichshafen as he and Tiger were standing outside Hangar C, watching for the landing approach of one of Tiger's students who was completing his first solo flight. His qualms weren't about the flight to Friedrichshafen, which he would be making the next day; they arose from his detour to the Moselle region of Germany. It had seemed easy enough to volunteer for a quick stop to help out his uncle, but after a think the potential complications gnawed at him. Adding a take-off and a landing at an unfamiliar airfield. Dealing with Jens and Lotte whom he knew nearly nothing about. Possibly coming face to face with Nazis.

"He's coming down nice and smooth," Tiger said.

"What—who?"

"That's Purifoy," Tiger said, irritated at Eddy's inattentiveness. The Moth had begun a gentle glide to the ground. "Pay attention, Frenchy. Let's hope he brings my plane home in one piece."

"Watching a solo is nerve-wracking," Eddy said. "Just waiting and hoping it all goes okay."

The older man nodded. "To be honest, these days I'm more worried about the Tiger Moth than I am about the students." Eddy raised an eyebrow, uncertain if Tiger had been serious. "You've got a new one starting this morning, haven't you?" Tiger asked Eddy, and without waiting for a reply, added, "A woman. I hope she won't wreck anything."

The student brought the biplane down safely and taxied towards them. Tiger strolled to meet him, no doubt to give him his congratulations on becoming a pilot.

Eddy hung back, idly watching. His own thoughts went back to his upcoming mission for Air Commodore Park. He had grasped that Friedrichshafen must be particularly important since he'd been given his instructions not only by Park, but also by Park's superior,

51

Air Chief Marshal Dowding. That wasn't what troubled Eddy because he had no doubts he could get what they needed. He was more concerned about the letter that Uncle Al had received from Jens. It required a stop in German territory that Park and Dowding didn't know about, and certainly would expect Eddy to avoid. He regretted having volunteered so rashly to assess Jens and Lotte, without fully considering his duty to Park and Dowding. He had prioritized his family over his country but, in his heart, that was a choice he had to make.

The roar of a sports car engine broke into his thoughts, and he turned to see a shiny red MG convertible come sweeping in through the airfield gates. The driver was a young woman of about Eddy's age, wearing sunglasses and a headscarf over her long brown hair. She drove up to him, lifted her sunglasses and said confidently, "I'm looking for the flying instructor—Mr. Beane."

Her hazel eyes seemed to sparkle and her cheekbones were high and perfectly-shaped under her scarf, like a movie star's. Her rosy red lips were slightly parted although she had finished speaking. For a moment he was speechless. She looked at him coolly, waiting.

He gathered his wits and said, "I'm Eddy Beane. How can I help you?"

"I have an appointment with you to discuss the possibility of taking flying lessons. The man said eleven o'clock, so here I am. My name is Stephenson."

"Oh! Yes, of course." Privately Eddy cursed Tiger for having written only the surname in the diary. Was she Miss, or Mrs? It would be just his luck if this one was already married or engaged. "Pleased to meet you, Miss Stephenson."

She smiled back at him. Good: she wasn't married.

"Would you mind parking the car round the corner? We're waiting for a student to taxi in from his first solo flight, so the hangar apron needs to be kept clear."

She revved the engine a little, put her sunglasses back on her nose, and drove decorously to the end of the building. She parked in the shade, next to Eddy's elderly Unibus scooter, and he tried not to feel envious about the contrast between his tired-looking transport and the sporty MG. Not for the first time it occurred to him that his scooter would suggest to affluent students that he was poverty-stricken and beneath notice. Miss Stephenson's arrival convinced him that even if it cost hundreds of pounds he would purchase an automobile that reflected his standing as a successful aviator.

She got out of the car and waited for him to join her. A very self-possessed lady, indeed.

"I would like to look at your aeroplane."

"Of course." Eddy walked her to the grass infield where his two-seater monoplane stood.

"What make is it?" she asked.

"It's an American model, an Aeronca," Eddy said. "There are not many like it in England." They stood by the two-bladed propeller, looking at the cockpit. "I don't suppose you know much about aeroplanes yet, Miss Stephenson?"

"I have never seen one of these," she said. "Those side by side seats are unusual for a trainer, aren't they?"

"You are *cor-recte*," Eddy said and he flushed slightly, recognizing that his French accent had become more marked as it often did when he was nervous or over-awed. Recovering, he said, "Most training planes are a tandem design, with the instructor sitting behind the student. I like this side by side layout. I find it permits me to watch my students operating the controls."

Miss Stephenson unfastened her scarf, and her hair lifted on the breeze as she walked around the plane. She paid attention to its fuselage, the fixed landing gear, tail fin and small rear landing wheels. The questions she asked were short and to the point. He suspected that she had allowed him to misjudge her—he had certainly been distracted by her sports car, her white-toothed smile, and undoubtedly voluptuous, *attrayante* figure. He felt vaguely guilty that he had doubted that she was a serious prospect for flying lessons.

"Tell me, Miss Stephenson, who referred you to me? I'd like to thank him."

"Mr. Lawrence. He's one my father's friends," she said. "He spoke highly of your abilities. And please, if we're going to work together, drop 'Miss Stephenson' and call me June."

"Of course—June. And I'd like you to call me Eddy. I must thank Mr. Lawrence for his referral. I'm glad he stirred your interest in flying."

"Actually, it wasn't Mr. Lawrence who did that. I was already interested."

53

"Oh?"

"My fiancé used to come back so very happy after he'd flown. He told me he had landed here at Hanworth on occasion. His name is Dudley Thane. Do you know him?"

Dashed by the mention of a fiancé, and with his mind half running in French, Eddy missed the subtle implication in the words "used to." "No, I can't put a face to the name." He pulled himself together and tried to remain professional. "Now, what are you hoping to accomplish if you take flying lessons with me?"

"I want to become a pilot."

"To fly for pleasure—or to earn your living?"

"I want to be skillful, and safe," she said and looked him in the eye. "I want to be able to fly a plane the way I drive the MG. Without having to think about it."

He was impressed by her directness.

"Okay. You will need fifteen hours of flying instruction to achieve your "A" license. That permits you to fly all types of aircraft. Of course, you will also have to do many hours of study on your own. Would you like to climb up, now, and sit in the cockpit?"

"Yes, I would, very much."

Eddy opened the door and gave her a hand to climb in. Her grip was warm and firm, and the orchid smell of her perfume wafted over him in a sweet cloud. She favoured him with the hint of a smile, as though she knew exactly the effect she was having on him, and he steadied himself and climbed up after her.

"I see what you mean about dual seats," she said. "Very friendly."

Damn the fiancé. He took a calming breath and explained the power, rudder and aileron controls, and the meaning of the various instruments on the panel.

"It's a more complicated job than driving a car. You've got to think in three dimensions when you're in the air. You have to keep an eye on altitude, pitch and roll, as well as making your turns. You're not following a road surface."

"But I shan't have to worry about policemen warning me I'm going too fast," she said, with a grin that showed how much she was enjoying herself. "Or about other silly drivers getting in my way."

"That's true, but there will be other traffic flying in and out of the airfield. And if you were to fly my plane into a tree or a mountain—"

54

"I'd probably end up dead," she agreed, cheerfully.

"I was going to say," he countered, "that I'd be out of a job, because I'd have nothing to teach with."

She laughed. "Now you're teasing me. I have no intention of causing anything so messy as a crash. I'm relieved you have good reason to teach me how to avoid it."

Twenty minutes later, Eddy walked June to her MG. He handed her some papers and said, "These explain our take-off and landing procedures, so please study them carefully. We'll go over all of this during your first lesson." He decided he had better acknowledge the lucky man who was engaged to marry Miss Stephenson. "If there is anything you don't understand, perhaps your fiancé can help out."

"I'm going to study very carefully, mister instructor," June said. "But Dudley will not be helping me. He's very much an ex-fiancé. Shall we go back to your office now? I think we should talk about money and set some dates for my lessons."

Afterwards, as Eddy watched June drive away in her MG, he could scarcely recall what they had discussed. The most important fact was that she wasn't engaged any more. Her hazel-green eyes, her lovely complexion, and her smile were burned into his mind. He thought—hoped—that there was more than a student's eagerness in the way she had shaken hands after signing on for a series of lessons. She would come for the first of them the following Tuesday.

He couldn't wait.

Chapter 11

The following afternoon Eddy was at his worktable in Hangar C, unpacking a new set of gaskets that had arrived in the post. Tiger came out from underneath the fuselage of his plane and straightened his back.

"Well, Frenchy, we've got company at last," he said. Air Commodore Keith Park and Corporal Tinker came into the hangar. "Hallo Commodore, we've been expecting you!"

They all shook hands, then Park laid a large map on the worktable and began to outline Eddy's fifth photography mission. His demeanor was pleasant, as usual, with the same aura of confidence, and he spoke with the same efficient pacing as for the previous four trips, but Eddy thought it was significant that Tinker stood to attention throughout. It confirmed his feeling that this mission was particularly serious.

Tiger, less easily awed, said, "When did they promote you to Commodore, sir?"

"Oh, it's quite recent. Now, we are marked on your schedule for the next two days, are we not?"

"Yes sir," said Tiger and Eddy, together.

"Good. Air Marshal Dowding has an enormous opportunity to use the photographs I am sending you to get at Dornier Flugzeugwerke. But I must—must—get them to him by Friday."

Eddy noted the Air Commodore's change of tone. "I see, sir. You'll have them."

"I'm going to share something with you in the strictest of confidence," Park said. "Do you understand?"

"You can count on me, sir," Tiger said.

"Yes sir," Eddy said.

"Okay. You know the *Daily Express*—Lord Beaverbrook's newspaper?"

Eddy and Tiger each nodded.

"Beaverbrook has been supportive of the current government's policies towards Hitler and his Nazis. He is in favour of appeasement. Like the agreement at Munich that Air Marshal Dowding told you about when we met him at my club."

Eddy remembered Dowding's stern expression as he had explained Fighter Command's quandary. If Britain was to oppose Hitler, then more fighters were going to be needed, but the current government seemed more interested in appeasing the man.

"Well, Dowding has a chance to meet with Lord Beaverbrook in secret this weekend, in Kent, at the house of an MP named Winston Churchill."

"Churchill?" Tiger said. "He's a Tory."

Park made a tight smile. "Many believe Churchill is above party politics. Over the years, he has held a vast array of positions within our government. Most importantly, he believes that war with Germany is inevitable. He's arranged this meeting to give Dowding a chance to convince Lord Beaverbrook of the gravity of the Nazi threat. If Beaverbrook can be convinced that Germany is amassing bombers and hiding them from the rest of Europe, he will have to drop his support of appeasement and perhaps he will even champion Fighter Command's case with the Treasury for more Spitfires."

Eddy realized that his role in obtaining the photographs might well influence national policy at the highest levels.

"We have a good deal of evidence from your previous missions which Dowding will present to Lord Beaverbrook," Park said, "but we need photographs of the Dorniers to complete our case."

Eddy was studying the map, his gaze tracking the route he was likely to fly from the Channel to the Somme, Nancy, France, and the Rhine Valley. Remembering his promise to Uncle Al, and considering the gravity of the mission, guilt gnawed at him. How dare he propose a detour on his way home when he would have in his possession photographs of Dornier Flugzeugwerke that were the key to Dowding's argument? But it was just as vital to his own family to learn about this German girl, Lotte. His Aunt and Uncle had to know more before they invited her into their home.

"Sir, I will need to make a stop on the way back." He put his finger on a small town near Germany's border with Luxembourg. "In Trier. It's on the route home, if I refuel at Liège, rather than Nancy."

Tinker looked at the map, and grimaced. "Trier is in the Mosel, you know."

Park said, "I don't fancy you landing in Germany with my photographs."

"It will be a quick stop, sir. Just a few hours. It's a job I need to do for my Uncle."

"Your uncle Alan Weldy?"

"Yes, sir. I need to make a pick-up for him." He kept his face impassive and hoped the Air Commodore wouldn't question him too closely.

Park thought for a moment, and asked, "Business?"

Eddy nodded, hoping Park hadn't seen his momentary hesitation.

"I see. Well, your commerce is our cover, of course. Be as quick as you can."

"Thank you, sir."

"Corporal Tinker will go over the details," Air Commodore Park said. He shook Eddy's hand, laid an envelope of five pound notes on top of the map, and left the hangar.

Three hours later, Eddy was fully briefed. He completed his engine checks and loaded his Aeronca with a change of clothes, maps, and Park's camera. He telephoned Uncle Al and asked him to send a telegram to the vineyard in Saarburg to request Jens to meet him at the airfield at Trier the following afternoon.

In an hour's time he was flying over the Channel's grey waters with their white wave-crests and heading for his first fuel stop at Nancy. He looked forward to arriving in time for dinner and a good night's rest.

The thought of dinner reminded him how much he'd like to spend an evening with his newest flying student. June Stephenson was a total delight. After their meeting, she had balanced springily on her MG's running board and smiled at him before sliding into the seat and driving away. He regretted that any plans in that direction would have to wait until he had completed the Air Commodore's mission.

~ ~ ~

When dawn broke next morning, Eddy was already seated in the Aeronca. The ground man at the airfield wound the plane's propeller and soon Eddy was aloft, putting his sunglasses on to continue his eastward flight over the French countryside. The sky was clear, and he had no difficulty in following the Moselle River towards its headwaters in the wooded hills of the Vosges. After that, his next landmark was the majestic Rhine Valley and the city of Basel where he made his second fuel stop. Over Switzerland, he adjusted his course towards Zurich, heeding Air Commodore Park's advice to stay south of the German border.

To his right the Swiss Alps rose dramatically in powerful rocky faces and sharp peaks, with attendant white clouds. He was glad his mission didn't require him to fly over them. In the thick green forests below, lakes reflected the sun back at him in flashes of light. A train puffed along past a cabin that stood as a lonely outpost in a mountain valley. The forest gave way briefly to reveal a small village with bright red roofs and a white church spire, tiny and toy-like, and the roads ran away from the houses through meadows and into the trees again. He checked the map and marked his position on the line Corporal Tinker had drawn as the route to Friedrichshafen. When he saw the tall buildings of Zurich, he adjusted his course and headed northeast for Lake Constance.

Eddy passed the time remembering Air Chief Marshall Dowding's suggestion that one day he might join Fighter Command. How much more quickly would he reach the lake if he were soaring above the cloud tops in a sleek Spitfire? Manning the cockpit controls in a RAF flight suit and wearing a high-altitude oxygen mask. He could almost taste the thrill of executing loops and dives in Britain's newest war machine.

The lakeshore that represented the eastern border of Switzerland brought his mind back to the mission. The waters were peaceful, the sun-flecked surface dotted with sailboats and a solitary little steamer. There were two commercial planes in the sky, one to the east, one to the north, but both were in the distance, at least a thousand feet higher than his Aeronca. Far beyond the northern plane, the gothic spire of Konstanz, Germany's cathedral, pierced the sky. Eddy prepared his camera, and quietly lost height until he could clearly see mallard ducks paddling in little fleets along the lake shore.

Then he made for Dornier Flugzeugwerke.

The aircraft factory was larger than any he had flown over in London, Manchester or Birmingham with massive buildings spreading across several acres. There were three building cranes, with white puff balls of steam floating up from the engines as the huge arms swung slowly back and forth. A dull gray maze of scaffolding covered an immense half-built wall.

He photographed the complex as a whole from steep oblique, at six thousand feet, before he descended to capture detail of the buildings. As Park had said, there were rows and rows of Dorniers under camouflage netting, and he circled them for photos from all angles.

He was so absorbed by his work that he barely heard the noise of the approaching aircraft until he glanced to his port side and saw it flying towards him. Long, flat wings with black crosses outlined in white. A swastika on its tailfin. German. Military. Less than a hundred yards away and heading straight for him.

Everything stopped, like a fixed image—the spinning ring of his propeller, clouds in the distance, and his hand rigid about Park's camera.

The Nazi aircraft banked away and came back at his tail.

Eddy's heart was in his throat. At any moment bullets might shred the Aeronca. The Nazi plane slipped sideways to fly alongside him. It didn't look like the fighters that had pursued him at Wunstorf. It had fixed landing wheels braced under its nose and tail wings, like the training planes at Hanworth. Eddy realized with immense relief it had no guns.

The Nazi plane flew next to him, almost touching his left wing, for ninety seconds. The pilot's head, in its black leather flying helmet and goggles, was turned towards him, and his right hand held a camera pointed at the Aeronca. They passed side by side over Friedrichshafen, over the hotels at the shore, and out over Lake Constance. Then his pursuer made a sweeping turn to the east, and back to Germany.

Eddy flew west with Park's precious camera lying on the seat next to him. He didn't trust his hands to be steady enough to pack it away into its case. Never in his life had he experienced a moment of terror such as he'd felt when the black crosses appeared. He felt as if he'd cheated death. His refueling stop could not come soon enough—he was desperate to put his feet on the ground and smoke a cigarette.

As his head cleared, he wondered why the Germans had chosen to take pictures of the Aeronca, rather than force him to land or even shoot him down. Perhaps the fact that there was no war yet had restrained them, as Park thought it might. But the knowledge that they now had images of his aeroplane chilled him. A heart-stopping reminder of the reach of the Nazis.

Approaching Basel, Eddy spotted the twin spires of The Minster, and descended over the Rhine, reaching the airfield at noon. He smoked while his plane was refueled, savoring the calm of the green foothills to the Swiss Alps. He weighed whether he should abandon his plan to visit Jens and Lotte. On the one hand, the Nazis now had pictures of his aeroplane, but on the other, what could they do with them? He could still fly on to Trier, and he would be in and out of German airspace in a matter of hours. Once he reported the incident to Air Commodore Park, chances were that he wouldn't even return to Germany, at least not in the Aeronca. He decided to press on.

From Basel he flew north, following the Rhine towards Strasbourg, and turned north-west when he saw the city's cathedral spire in the distance. Thirty minutes later, he was flying over Saarbrucken with its industrial buildings and its many bridges over the Saar river.

Re-entering German airspace gave him a sinking feeling. On the ground he would meet Nazis wherever he went, and they wouldn't all be marked by white crosses and swastikas. But he had to go on to Trier. Uncle Al needed to learn more about Jens's strange request, and the uncertainty would eat away at them both if he ignored it.

He followed the Saar River, which looped through the forest like a navy-blue string thrown onto a dark green carpet. Every few miles there was a small town. Where the Saar joined the Moselle, he looked out for Trier and its airfield. He made his approach into the wind, landed gently, and taxied towards the terminal building.

Chapter 12

That morning, as Eddy had flown east, to the north of the Swiss Alps, Lotte Schroder had cleared away her brother Otto's breakfast plate and cutlery, and carefully picked up egg scraps from his *Bauernomolett* that had fallen off his fork and he hadn't bothered to eat.

"Otto, there is egg stuck to your face," she said.

He looked up and closed the binder that he was studying. "Eggs? Where?"

"On your mustache," she said. While he was busy wiping his face she noticed the binder was marked with a black swastika within a white circle bordered in red. White lightning marks signifying his SS unit were within a diamond pattern in the top right corner. It was the same binder he often studied in the evenings and he had made it very clear that she was never to touch.

"So my dear sister, now am I clean? Have you pressed my uniform?"

She set the plate and cutlery in the basin and brought his clothes from the table near the kitchen door where she'd set them after ironing. He accepted his uniform with a grunt and carried it upstairs.

Lotte took a handful each of sand and soap from their respective canisters and began to scrub the skillet. As she worked, she mentally reviewed the day's lessons that she had planned for her students. Her English class would study verbs and their opposites, such as "Like" and "Dislike." She frowned a little as she thought of example sentences: "I like cake." "I dislike my brother." Her 'secondes' were studying French, and with them she planned to ask if they knew there was a difference between common nouns, like *la ville* and *la ferme* and *le marché*, and proper nouns, like *La France* and *Montigny-les-Metz*.

With the dishes draining in the rack, she emptied and put the coffee grinder away. She hung the skillet on a hook near the cast-iron stove. The evening meal would have to be something simple, because she had an appointment to meet her father's cousin Jens. She understood that Jens had arranged to meet the son of an Englishman that her father had somehow become acquainted with during the last war. She wasn't sure why Jens wanted her to be there. Even more curious was Jens's insistence that Lotte should not tell her brother Otto about the meeting, even saying that if Otto demanded to know where she was going, she should lie to him. It was all very odd. Jens was normally a stolid businessman who inspired trust by being predictably ordinary.

Otto came tramping down the stairs into the living room.

"Lotte! Come in here, please," he said.

She sighed but went to him. He was standing at the mirror fixing his tie. His military black shirt had two embossed lightning flashes on its collar which identified him as an SS man. His black wool breeches were held up by a belt adorned with a four inch silver buckle shaped like an eagle, and his black knee-high boots glimmered.

The black swastika on his armband chilled her. She had seen armbands like it a week ago, their wearers throwing merchandise through a broken store window into the street—hats, coats, and dresses dragged out and pitched onto the shattered glass. Her friend, Lilli Mandel, whose family owned the store, was standing outside, her face blotched with tears. Outraged, Lotte had hurried forward, but Lilli's puffy eyes had shown such fear that Lotte stopped in her tracks. She had no choice but to watch in silence as the store's entire stock was doused with fuel and burned. Every day since then, she had chastised herself for lacking the courage to stand up to the Nazis. But how could she be brave when nobody would help her?

Otto said, "Lieutenant Helmuth will be joining us for dinner tonight."

Otto's friend was large, loud and to Lotte's dismay, seemed smitten with her. He would speak directly into her face with foul tobacco-laced breath, and every time he visited he asked her for a social date.

"That's not possible," Lotte said.

"Of course, it is." Otto turned to look at her, coldly. "What is the problem?"

"I have an appointment with Cousin Jens when school is out. He needs me to translate for him at a business meeting."

"If it's straight after school, then you'll be finished by dinner time," Otto said.

"I don't know when we'll be finished."

"Oh, I expect we could wait until as late as 7:30," Otto said. Lotte thought he was making an effort to humor her, and her suspicions were aroused. He adjusted his tie. "It will give us time to drink a few mugs of pilsner before we eat. Oh, and Helmuth is fond of schnitzel. See that there's plenty of it. This is imperative."

Lotte was appalled. Now Otto was asking her to deal with Helmuth when he was full of lager. "I'm sorry Otto, but I can't do it."

"You must!"

Lotte was running out of excuses. She shook her head. "I won't."

Otto turned on her with eyes of fury and gripped her jaw with his right hand. He drove her backwards, until her spine pressed against the wall. "You will have dinner for Helmuth and me at 7:30! Do you understand?"

Lotte couldn't open her mouth until Otto loosened his grip. She gasped for air and said, "Yes."

Otto relaxed, then suddenly let her go and embraced her with every appearance of fondness. "Lotte, I'm sorry—I was upset, but this is an especially important dinner. For both of us."

She sat down and rubbed her jaw. "How could your dinner possibly be important for me?"

"Surely you've noticed how Helmuth looks at you. If you play your cards right, I think he will marry you."

Lotte suppressed a gag. "I would never, ever marry that man."

Otto's eyes narrowed. "Of course you will. He is rising fast in the party. He has met Himmler, personally. One day he will have an important appointment. Why—with all the languages you speak, someday you might find yourself the wife of the man in charge of Paris or London. You'd like that, wouldn't you?"

"Helmuth is fat and rude," Lotte said. "I will not have anything to do with him."

"First, he's stout, not fat. There's a difference. He has the broadest shoulders of any man I know." He chuckled. "And I've seen how powerful he is. With your blond hair and school cleverness and his size and strength, the two of you will make perfect German children."

Lotte nearly gagged at the thought of massive Helmuth on top of her. She recoiled, slowly moving away from Otto, but he put his hand over hers, firmly.

"My dear girl; I know what's best for you," Otto said. "You are, what, twenty three years old? It's unnatural for a woman to still be single at your age. So I will help you find a husband. If you satisfy his needs and give him children, Helmuth will be a fine husband. You'll never do better than him. Besides, if you marry him, he'll favor me in the party. So if he'll have you, you must marry him. And one more thing: keep your silly ideas about fairness for Jews and workers to yourself. Tonight, you'll support the Nazis every bit as strongly as I do." He squeezed her fingers tightly, making her wince. "No more discussion."

She opened her mouth to object, but Otto glared at her and slashed his flat hand across his throat. She knew exactly what he meant.

Otto took a last look in the mirror and placed his cap on his head. Apparently satisfied, he left the house without a further word.

Lotte put her head in her hands. Their house had become her cage. She walked to the mantle and stared at the photograph of her family taken when she was a baby. Her father, Axel, was holding her on his knee. Elke, her mother, and Otto, who was then just three or four years old, stood on either side of him. They were all impeccably dressed, the picture of a perfect family. Even though the photograph was rigidly posed, kindness and goodness shone in her father's eyes. She had no memories of him, but she felt deep down that if he had come home from the war he would have made Otto into a better man, and then her problems with Nazi Helmuth would never have arisen. Father, father, I need you!

Otto was no longer the brother she had adored. He used to play with her kindly when she was small—pretending to chase her, counting, *Ein, Zwei, Drei,* while she ran away, laughing with glee. Being older, he would always catch her, but he would swing her high and then give her a playful tickle to make her squeal with delight before they'd start all over again. Later, he would give her a piece of chocolate, telling her he had climbed a mountain or dived to the bottom of the river just to find it for her. Back then, she had believed he would do anything for her. But the boy Otto had vanished forever.

Chapter 13

At Trier Eddy parked the Aeronca near the terminal building in front of a dozen other planes. Most were biplane trainers and one looked like a cargo plane, and he was relieved that none of them had military markings. There were no pilots about, but a man was standing at a window in the terminal building. He wore circular glasses, and it was his stillness that worried Eddy: he seemed much too interested in the Aeronca. When he saw that Eddy was looking at him he withdrew from the window into the gloom of the building.

Feeling a little uncomfortable, Eddy put away Commodore Park's camera at the back of the dashboard box and, as a further precaution, stacked his maps in front of it before he climbed down from the cockpit. While he was setting the wheel-chocks a thin, balding, middle-aged man approached him, asking tentatively, in French, "Mister Beane?"

"Yes. Are you Jens?" Eddy asked, also in French. "Jens Kluber?"

"That's right," Jens answered. They shook hands. "I am happy to meet you. I thank you with all my heart for coming."

"Delighted, sir. My Uncle Al sends you his good wishes."

"Oh yes. And please send him my salutations in return. Now, come. I will take you in my delivery truck to meet our dear Lotte. We can't go to her house—her brother Otto might be there—we are going to meet her at a beer hall near Saarburg. Nobody will take much notice of us because it's still Oktoberfest here. There will be music as well as beer, and if we sit at the back we will avoid the ears listening at doors."

Eddy had expected a brief, private gathering with Jens and Lotte. He was disconcerted that they would meet in a public place where his chances of encountering Nazis would undoubtedly increase. His fact-finding for Uncle Al was becoming more than he had bargained for. He hesitated for a moment, weighing the risks to his mission for the Air Commodore. He could make up an excuse and return to the Aeronca. But he had come all this way to find information for his Uncle Al and he couldn't give up now. Getting to the heart of the letter, by meeting this young lady Lotte, was a short ride away. And, after all, it would be an adventure. He followed Jens to the truck and climbed into the passenger seat.

"I have made all my deliveries on the way here," Jens said. He indicated the empty cargo bed with a jerk of his thumb. "We go directly to Saarburg now—into the forest and back to the Saar River."

Within minutes they were driving through the deep shade of evergreen trees which smelled of pine and freshly cut wood. Here and there they passed bungalows with dormer windows cut into their thatch roofs. When Jens drove out of the forest again, they were close to the river in Saarburg. Ancient stone walls climbed up from the bank like stairs and an old castle looked down from the summit of the rocks. Tidy houses in various shades of white lined the riverbank. Where the road entered town, the lamp-posts on Saarburg's streets were hung with red banners, each carrying stark black swastikas in a white circle.

Jens drove on through town and out into the countryside again. There were no trees or field crops here but rows and rows of vines, heavy with pale green grapes, gleaming in the afternoon sunshine, and trained up wooden posts made from tree branches. The rows of vines filled all the land from the riverbank right up into the hills.

"What kind of grapes are those?" Eddy asked.

"Riesling. Everybody grows the Riesling grape round here."

"You seem to have a good harvest in prospect."

"Oh, these are not our grapes," Jens said with some amusement. "We must drive eight kilometers yet. Our vineyards are on a good south-facing slope. We have the stony soil that grows a perfect grape for the Moselle wine. It is, I think, the finest white wine in the world."

"But of course," said Eddy, politely.

Jens glanced at him. "You are fond of wine?"

"My mother was knowledgeable, but alas, she died when I was sixteen. I have lived since then with my aunt and uncle in England." He considered explaining about Aunt Maddy and her ownership of The Four Bells, but nothing in her association with the pub suggested she was at all interested in wines.

Jens chuckled. "The English, they are not known to be connoisseurs of wine."

"Perhaps not, but my aunt and uncle enjoy a glass with their dinners from time to time."

"Good," said Jens.

The beer hall turned out to be a white, two story building with windows flanked by green wooden shutters. An unpainted deck extended from the second floor, and under the eaves above the second floor entrance there was a statuesque bierkeller sign, a carved wooden lion's head. Jens parked in the gravel lot next to the hall, among rows of other automobiles and trucks.

Eddy followed Jens in. A raucous sing-along was in progress, smiling revelers sitting at long rows of tables and drinking large mugs of beer. The band was playing on a small stage at the far end, and the singer was waving his feathered Tyrolean hat in the air, leading the choruses. Those who were standing swayed with the music, raising their pilsners in time with the beat. Some stood arm in arm, linked at the elbows. Those who were sitting at the benches put down their drinks and clapped in time with the zither and the drums.

Jens led Eddy through the cheerful crowd until he found Lotte standing towards the back of the crowd. Her long, blond hair was styled off her forehead, and she wore a black vest over a dress with a paisley pattern. She greeted Jens with a hug.

Jens shouted, over the music, "This is Eddy Beane. He is the son of the British soldier your father met in the war."

She gave Eddy a kind smile, took his hands and leaned forward to make herself heard over the music. "Hello Eddy. I'm Lotte Schroder."

"I am pleased to meet you."

Jens ordered pilsners for all of them.

Eddy felt far more comfortable than he had expected to be in a room full of Germans. The people were joyful with welcoming expressions. Eddy thought they were probably decent, working people, enjoying a break with family and friends. He couldn't see a single Nazi uniform. The scene reminded him of the good people of Hazebrouck enjoying their Bastille Day parade, and of picnickers on the Common at Peckham on Summer Bank Holiday.

When the sing-along ended, the room was less noisy, and Jens quietly told Lotte and Eddy the story of the night he was taken prisoner by Uncle Al and Eddy's father. Eddy was relieved that Jens's version closely matched his Uncle's, though he kept to himself his knowledge that Jens had pissed himself that night.

"You are here now because I remembered how kind your Uncle was to me," Jens said. "That is what gave me the courage to write to him. It is a terrible time now in Germany. Did you see those swastika banners in Saarburg?"

Eddy nodded.

"The Nazis rule Saarburg, the same as they rule all of Germany. Lotte's older brother, Otto, is a Nazi. He is as bad as any of them."

Eddy looked at Lotte. "I'm sorry."

She made a tight smile, with no humor in it.

"Over the past few years, the Nazis have worsened," Jens said. "At first, they just used to wear their brown shirts and sing their silly songs, but they didn't cause much trouble. Now they do what they want." He turned to Lotte. "Tell him," he said.

"Me?"

"You speak better French than I do."

~ ~ ~

Lotte said, "Cousin Jens is right. Last week they broke the windows of Mandel's clothing shop. The Mandel family is Jewish, and Lilli Mandel is my friend. The Nazi thugs threw everything out into the street—coats, dresses, trousers, and hats—they stole anything they fancied and burned everything else."

"What does Otto have to say about this?" Eddy asked her.

Remembering the viciousness of Otto's assault that morning, she took a deep breath before continuing. "He thinks it is all right for them to do this. He says Germany is for Germans, not Jews. He demands that I agree with him. But I won't." She left out that disobeying Otto was a different matter and altogether more personal.

"Let me tell you a story," she said. "Last summer the Nazis paraded through Saarburg. Some were in their brownshirts, and the soldiers were in gray uniforms. Otto and his thugs wore their SS blackshirts. They carried red Nazi banners and they sang a song; it was something about the blood of Jews spurting from their knives. It chilled me. Then one of the Nazis pointed at a man on the sidewalk and screamed 'Communist!' They set on him all together, like a pack of rabid dogs. They beat this poor man with their fists, and he fell to the ground. There was blood streaming from his face. I saw it. Otto kicked him. The look in his eyes was evil."

Lotte sat back, unable to say more, feeling a mixture of horror and sadness.

Jens said, "I have tried to talk with Otto, to tell him that Nazis are not the real Germany. He should forget them, and work with us at the vineyard. But he won't listen. I believe he is lost to us."

"So, neither of you are Nazis," Eddy said. "Then what are your politics? Are you communists? I hope that doesn't put you in danger."

Lotte was startled. Eddy had used the word 'communist' so lightly. Clearly, he didn't know that in Germany merely uttering the word within earshot of the Nazis could result in a beating. She scanned the sunny faces around them that were all turned to the stage and was relieved that no one seemed to have overheard him. "Politics. How much time do you have?"

Eddy smiled briefly. "Actually, not long. I can stay for perhaps another hour. I must land in the Netherlands before dark."

"Ah!" Jens said, clapping his hands. "I intended to give you a case of our Riesling to take to your Uncle—but I forgot it! I must go and fetch it. Lotte, will you stay and talk to Eddy? I'll be back in thirty minutes."

"Of course, Uncle."

Jens hurried out. Lotte smiled at his forgetfulness, even though part of her suspected a ruse in order for her and Eddy to talk privately.

She said to Eddy, "You asked if I'm communist. I don't think of myself as political at all. I don't go to meetings or read party literature. I just teach the English and French languages to the children of Saarburg."

"Something about you suggests much deeper convictions."

"It is true," Lotte said, "that I want the best for our workers. Especially people who work at our family's vineyard. They should get fair pay, enough to raise a family. They should be taken care of if they get hurt or sick. Their children should be educated. Does that make me a communist? I don't think so. I think my views align with social democrats."

She took a drink of pilsner. Eddy's expression betrayed nothing and she wondered where he stood. "What about you?"

"Oh—there is nothing wrong with wanting everyone to make enough money to have a good life," Eddy said. "I own a flying business, you see, and I have to think about my costs, including what workers are paid. If they are too high, I won't have any customers and my business will fail. So these are difficult questions." He smiled. "But at least you and I have something in common."

"Oh?"

"We're not Nazis or communists."

"Here, in Germany if you are poor, you don't ask for more pay. You join the Nazis. If you become a thug like the rest of them, they'll take care of you. Perhaps."

"Jens wrote my uncle that you need to get away from Otto for that reason," Eddy said.

Lotte sighed. "Yes. He thinks I must leave here. But this is my home. Otto is my brother. I have my students. How can I even think such a thing?" She paused. "I lie in my bed and wish that Otto and I were a family again."

"What will happen if you stay?"

"Otto will not stop until I am a Nazi, just like him, because when I don't support him, other Nazis notice. And Otto loses face."

"But surely he can't tell you how to think."

She lifted her chin to show the bruises under her jaw. "This morning he shoved me against the wall. He held me by the throat. He told me that tonight I must serve dinner for him and another Nazi, and back the Nazi party while I do it, or else—" She made the same throat-slashing movement Otto had used.

Eddy reacted with the same astonishment she had seen in good German people when they witnessed Nazi brutality. Seeing physical evidence of aggression exposed the Nazis' evil nature like no newspaper report could. He asked, "Did you go to the police?"

Lotte laughed shortly. "No one stops the SS. They are the worst kind of Nazi. Otto is an SS man. He can do anything he wants." She took a drink of beer. "His Lieutenant wants me—he lusts after me. He is large, brutish and mean. That's the man Otto's bringing to dinner

71

tonight. Otto believes if he delivers me to this ogre he will advance in the Nazis. I'd rather die."

The music stopped abruptly. Two men wearing black trench coats and fedoras had appeared in front of the stage, flanked by two men in black SS uniforms who carried Luger pistols and long knives at their belts. Silence fell over the beer hall.

"What's going on?" Eddy asked.

She gestured to him to be quiet, and muttered, "That's my brother Otto. The one on the left. The large SS man is his Lieutenant I told you about. Helmuth. The other two are Gestapo men! If they come to us, tell them you are a wine merchant from France, here on business with Uncle Jens. But don't speak to them unless they ask you directly." She gripped his hand. "Promise me!"

Eddy nodded.

The Gestapo men were strolling through the beer hall, looking intently at the faces of the people sitting at the tables. One of them carried a photograph, which they referred to as they examined each group. The big room was still, as if everyone were holding their breath. Each time they moved to the next group of people, Otto's and Helmuth's jackboots thumped loudly on the wooden floor.

"They are looking for someone," Lotte whispered.

"Who?"

"A Communist perhaps. Or a Jew. Even another Nazi if he has stepped out of line."

"What will they do if they find him?"

Lotte flashed a look that must have made him feel ignorant for asking.

Helmuth grabbed a man by the collar and slapped him across his cheek several times, while the other three stood by and watched. Helmuth abused him loudly in German. Nobody else said anything.

"That's not the man they're after," Lotte whispered. "Helmuth has a grudge against him. He is saying something about their years in school."

The Gestapo and SS men were still walking from one table to another. Now they were only one away from Lotte and Eddy. She could see Eddy had shifted in his seat, as if he were considering making a run for it. But even if he made it outside, Eddy couldn't return to the aerodrome without her or Jens. If he ran, Otto would

72

catch him and beat him, and if the Nazis suspected him of spying they might even kill him. She put her hand over his to calm him.

"Sit still. Do not attract attention."

Helmuth must have heard her voice. His gaze fixed on Lotte and he laughed in an unpleasant way. He said loudly in German to Otto, "Look who is here."

One of the Gestapo men tousled Eddy's hair, not to injure, but to humiliate. He said *"Jude"* in a shrill, scornful voice. The other Gestapo man laughed.

Helmuth said "Otto," then spoke harshly to him about Lotte. Otto's face turned red, and he glared at her with a startling rage in his eyes. He seized Eddy by the shoulder. *"Nein,"* he shouted.

Lotte stood up and pushed Otto away. "Leave him alone! He is Jens's business customer, and you are insulting him."

"Then where is Jens?" Otto asked.

"He has gone to fetch some samples of our wines."

Helmuth lit a cigarette. He picked up Lotte's beer mug and drank from it, insolently, and spoke some more to Otto. The Gestapo men spoke amongst themselves, then one of them asked Helmuth a question. Helmuth spit into the tankard and put it down on the table as though it was fouled. The Gestapo men seemed to relax but Otto remained tense.

"What is this?" Eddy asked Lotte, in French.

"The Gestapo man asked if you are my Jewish lover—to insult me. Helmuth asked Otto why I'm not at home cooking their dinner. Then he told Otto he has lost control of me. He said that he isn't sure any more if I am—" She flushed and said crisply, "He says I'm not suitable any more to be a bride."

She saw Eddy's face flush, although she couldn't tell if it was in embarrassment or anger. Either way, she had to deflect the emotion. "It was a joke, I think, but Otto's furious at me, for being seen with a stranger in this beer hall. I have told all of them that you are here from France, for business with Cousin Jens."

She was about to say more when the other Gestapo man spoke angrily to her. He put his fingers to her lips, made a gesture like pulling a zipper closed, and spoke to Otto. Otto grabbed her arm and jerked her off the bench. She yelped but Otto dragged her down the aisle between the tables and out through the back door.

~ ~ ~

The Gestapo men and Helmuth laughed. Eddy sat aghast, but they ignored him, moved on to the next table and resumed their search. The moment they turned away, Eddy jumped up and ran after Otto and Lotte. The back door opened into a side alley with automobiles parked along it. He saw Otto holding Lotte by her throat, pinned against the passenger door of a black sedan. She was struggling, her hands on Otto's wrists. Eddy ran up and grabbed Otto's collar with both hands and jerked him backwards. He lost his grip on Lotte's throat and turned on Eddy, growling with rage. Eddy punched him in the face, and he fell to the ground with blood gushing from his nose.

Lotte straightened up, gasping and unable to speak, leaning against the car door. There was a loud crack as a bullet struck the auto. Eddy spun around and saw one of the Gestapo men was running towards them with a gun in his hand.

"Get in!" Eddy pushed Lotte into the automobile. He jumped in and hit the starter button and the tires spun as he accelerated away. There was another shot and the shatter of glass. "That's our taillight," he said under his breath. "Lotte! Which way to Trier?"

Lotte struggled upright in the passenger seat. She coughed several times.

"Can you point, Lotte? Help me! We must get to the airfield in Trier."

She pointed out the window, to a road on the right.

"Good girl."

Eddy pushed the accelerator to the floor. "How are you feeling now? Your own brother. It's unbelievable. It looks like I must take you with me, Lotte. You can't stay here."

She nodded without speaking.

Now with a moment to think, he was astonished at what he had just done. He hadn't been in a fist fight since he was nine or ten years old growing up in Hazebrouck, when he had stood up to the class bully in the schoolyard. Otto's cruelty had set a furor off inside of Eddy that he hadn't been able to control. The truth was the blows he struck felt good, and just, but there was surely hell to pay if Otto and his thug friends caught him before he left Germany. Even with the danger he was facing, most surreal was the young woman sitting next to him, on the run from her own brother and about to fly away from her homeland.

"I hope you don't feel you are being kidnapped?"

"No," she said. "Cousin Jens had told me that I should be prepared to go to England. He saw that there would be a breaking point with Otto before I could see it." She sighed and massaged her neck where Otto's cruel fingers had dug in. "It is very sudden, but if I stay I don't believe I'll live through the night. Now," Lotte said, pointing towards the Saar River, "cross the bridge, there. We must avoid Saarburg."

He appreciated her caution. It wouldn't be wise to drive a stolen sedan through a town that flew red swastika banners. Silver ripples shimmered on the river in the late afternoon sun. He overtook a farm wagon laden with hay, the horses plodding steadily.

He was getting used to the unfamiliar controls of the car; the left hand driving position was not too different from the cockpit of the Aeronca. Everything about it, from its leather upholstery to its chrome-rimmed dials and walnut dashboard, spoke of expensive luxury. "This is quite a car I seem to have stolen. What is it, a Mercedes-Benz? Who in their right mind would leave such a beautiful car unlocked?"

Lotte smoothed her blond hair back from her face. "I don't know. It's not Otto's. It must belong to the men he was with." She twisted in her seat to look into the rear of the car. "There's something on the back seat." She reached back and picked up a binder, which she showed to Eddy. "This has the same swastika and SS lightning flashes as the one Otto likes to read." She flipped through pages of rules and procedures, then stopped. "These are lists of people's names," she said, horrified. "And their addresses. People I know, who hate the Nazis."

"Then I don't think we need worry about giving the car back to its owner," Eddy said grimly.

"There's a pistol on the seat, too," she said.

"Can you reach it?"

"Yes."

"Hand it to me." He checked its magazine. "A Luger. Fully loaded. Good." He set its safety catch and slipped it into his waistband.

Lotte said, "Cross the Moselle there, to your left, and the airfield is just a few kilometers north." Minutes later, they were speeding through the airfield's gateway. Eddy parked the Mercedes next to the Aeronca.

A man came towards them. Eddy recognized the man with circular glasses whom he had seen in the terminal window. He stood, arms extended, between them and the plane.

"Halt!"

Eddy drew his Luger and pointed the barrel at the man's forehead. He said in French, "Lie down, right there, on your belly."

The man stopped but he didn't seem to understand. He repeated "Halt!"

"Lotte! Tell him to get on the ground. On his belly."

Lotte translated into German. The man hesitated but he lowered himself and lay flat on the concrete.

"Ask him why he stopped me," Eddy said.

The man didn't answer, so Eddy put one foot on his hand. He screamed and spoke rapidly to Lotte.

She translated. "He just received a telegram that was sent to all German airfields instructing them to detain an Aeronca with your tail number."

"We'd better tie him up. See if there's anything in the car."

Lotte dived into the back seat of the Mercedes and came out with a pair of handcuffs.

"Perfect."

Eddy cuffed the man's hands behind his back, then he helped Lotte into the cockpit of the Aeronca and belted her into the student seat.

"This is where you need to help me," he said. He set the throttle to idle and put her fingers round the brake. "Take a firm hold and keep it absolutely steady till I come back." He jumped down and hand spun the prop, and with puffs of smoke the Aeronca's engine started. He pulled the chocks from the wheels and ran back to the cockpit.

"I'll have to climb over you, sorry," he said. "Sit tight!" He settled into his seat, pulled back on the throttle and with a roar the plane began to move.

Lotte looked back. "Eddy," she said, "They've followed us!"

One glance was enough. A black sedan had pulled up beside the prostrate man in glasses. A Gestapo man and Helmuth were firing their pistols at the plane, their bullets pinging off metal. Eddy pulled the Luger from his waistband and handed it to Lotte.

"I've got to fly," he shouted, over the engine. "Shoot anybody who tries to stop us."

He gave the Aeronca full power and the aeroplane bumped forward, faster and faster, until its wheels lifted off the runway and they were airborne. Once he was sure they were safely away, he looked across at Lotte. She was still looking back, with the Luger grasped in both hands. He chuckled to himself when he realized her straps had restrained her from turning far enough to fire. He touched her arm to get her attention.

"Put on your headphones," Eddy said, miming. He waited a moment for her to comply. "Talk to me through the voice tube. Can you hear me?"

"Yes."

"Put the safety catch back on the gun."

She did so.

"We're safe now. Have you ever flown before?"

"No."

"Just relax. Your stomach may flutter. Your ears may clog. That is normal. You will be all right."

"They tried to kill us."

"Yes, they did. But you were brave."

"I would have shot them if I could," she said.

Eddy flew due west, heading for Luxembourg. Lotte sat in silence, staring forward. His heart was still racing. He kept checking the sky behind them, but no plane seemed to be following them. He doubted that the Nazis would respect the Luxembourg border—so maybe it had just been good luck that a plane hadn't been available to chase the Aeronca.

"Lotte, please hand me the map from the box in front of you."

She dug through the box and did as he asked.

Reassured now that he was not being followed, Eddy set a course for Liege. The sun was half below the horizon, and he estimated he had just enough time to reach the airfield before dusk fell. As he began to relax, he realized how foolish he'd been. Commodore Park had been right; he should never have stopped in Germany. He had mixed his personal agenda with his mission, misleading the

Commodore and Tinker, thereby jeopardizing a cause far greater than any single person.

He might have just destroyed his future. Air Marshal Dowding himself had as good as invited him to join Fighter Command, so the chance he wanted more than anything, to fly Britain's amazing new Spitfire, had been at his fingertips. He'd thought of Dowding's offer every hour of every day since. Had he just thrown it away? He would have to face the consequences with all the honor he could muster.

But he allowed himself a sly grin, knowing he'd just beaten the Nazis on their own turf and a big part of him wouldn't change a thing. His pride from doing that was immense; the same kind of feeling he'd had when he knew his mission over Wunstorf had been accomplished. Maybe the warrior that had been his father was in him after all. More than anything, he was certain that he had saved Lotte's life and hers was very much a life worth saving.

Chapter 14

Lotte was lying face down on her bed in the inn. She hadn't said a word since she and Eddy had landed in Liège in near total darkness. She had been listless in his arms as he had helped her out of the cockpit, with the sadness in her heart from abandoning her home hurting worse than Otto's cruelty. What grieved her most was the loss of her family, though she now knew that had happened long ago. Otto had given her no choice; he and his thugs would have killed her if she stayed. They would have disposed of her body and blamed a Communist, a Jewish person, or any Nazi enemy, so she would not only have left the earth without justice for herself, but her disappearance would have been the excuse for injustice to others.

After a while she sat up and wiped the tears from her face. Eddy was sitting in the armchair at the other side of the room and his friendly smile made her feel a little better.

"I'm sorry."

"Don't be," he said. "Have a wash, it'll make you feel better. The lavatory is down the hall. I'll go and order you some food."

"I can't eat."

"Then you can drink some brandy."

Eddy returned fifteen minutes later with a bottle and two glasses. He poured two tots and sat beside her on the edge of the bed. "Tell me what you are thinking."

Lotte sighed. "My life—everything I am—has been erased. I have no country. No home. No family."

He took her hand. "I came to find you because my Uncle Al had a special connection with your father. He and my Aunt Maddy will help you. They will take you in and look after you."

"But they don't even know me."

"I know they will do it because they did it for me. You and I are much the same. I grew up in France. When *Maman* got sick, Aunt Maddy and Uncle Al came to find us and took us to live in England. *Maman* died six years ago, and I've lived with them ever since. Before that, they had never even met me! But they have taken me into their home and have cared for me like one of their own children. They are good people. I miss *Maman*, of course I do. But my life in England is better than my life before. Yours will be, too."

Lotte squeezed his hand. "I'm sorry you lost your mother. I lost mine about the same time." He'd once faced complete upheaval and being alone in the world. The distress she was feeling had once been his, too, and his assurance that his Aunt Maddy and Uncle Al would help her make a new life comforted her. She vowed that she would bring a positive contribution to their family.

"You are a good person," Eddy said. "You're brave. You resist those barbarians. You reject their evil ways."

"I only try to do what is right," she said, gathering strength. "The Nazis have taken our country, but what they stand for is wrong! It is not Germany! People must oppose them." She paused. "But for the moment they are very strong."

"Starting tomorrow you will make a new life, far away from the Nazis. Let me tell you about my Aunt and Uncle, and their little children." Eddy went on talking softly, and she hungrily took in details of life with his family. He described London, the tailoring shop, and some of the places he had flown to in the Aeronca. When the brandy glass was empty, Lotte realized how tired she was, and lay back on the bed and closed her eyes.

"I will sleep now," she said. "Thank you for everything you've done."

"Goodnight. Sleep well." Eddy pulled a blanket over her and turned off the lamp.

~ ~ ~

Eddy had tried to sleep in the armchair, but he was flagging the next day. He phoned Corporal Tinker before taking off from Liege, to warn him the Aeronca had been damaged by gunfire, and between tiredness and his need to watch for potential failures, the flight seemed unbearably long. When the Aeronca touched down at Hanworth, Eddy was not surprised to see Tinker waiting on the infield. He was dismayed, however, to see that Air Commodore Park was with him. He would have liked twenty-four hours grace in which to wash, change his clothes, and eat, and most of all to catch up on sleep, before facing the Air Commodore.

"Tinker called me earlier," Park said. "He said your crate had been damaged, and that if you were not here by noon, he would send a spotter over the Channel, Folkestone to Calais." So Tinker had told him everything. "Wanted to see the evidence for myself. Those holes weren't made by a Messerschmitt cannon. Small arms fire?"

"Yes, sir." Eddy turned back into the cockpit and helped Lotte down.

Air Commodore Park said to Eddy, "You omitted to mention that you were bringing in a passenger." Lotte was holding the Nazi binder they had found in the car, and before Eddy could respond, Park asked her, "Are you connected with Weldy & Beane?"

Eddy couldn't blame Park for the assumption. She certainly looked very efficient.

"The reason for my journey to England is a long story," Lotte said, in English. So far she had spoken to Eddy only in French, and he was surprised that in English her German accent was hardly noticeable.

"I'll hear it later, then," Park said. "Beane, did you bring back what you were in fact sent for?"

Eddy climbed up into the cockpit. It seemed a long time since he had hidden the camera, and in their rush to leave Trier he hadn't thought to check whether it was still there. He reached into the map box. Nothing. He pulled the maps out and searched every inch of the compartment. Still nothing. His heart sank. He looked down and the Air Commodore's eyebrows signaled impatience. Corporal Tinker's expression was stony.

Lotte stepped towards the plane. "Eddy, are you looking for the camera?"

He tried to say 'yes,' but could only nod.

"It must be on the floor. I took it out of the box when you asked for the map."

Eddy searched underneath her seat. She was right. He picked up the camera, climbed down, and handed it to Air Commodore Park, trying not to show how relieved he was. "Mission accomplished, sir."

Lotte offered Park the binder. "You may find this interesting, sir," she said. Park's gaze narrowed as he turned it over and saw the swastika on its cover. He nodded his thanks, then turned to Eddy with a grim face. "This is—unexpected. I suspect there's more to this trip than meets the eye."

"Yes sir, I'm afraid so."

"And you, young lady—where exactly are you going?" Park asked.

"She's come to stay with my Aunt Maddy and Uncle Al," Eddy said.

"I see." Park seemed to consider further questions, but after a moment he said, "I'm going to assume all your paperwork is in order. If it isn't, you need to make sure it will be, PDQ. Well, young man, take her home. But you will be at my club at five o'clock prompt this evening. I want a very full report on this trip."

"Yes sir."

~ ~ ~

That evening, Eddy presented himself at Air Commodore Park's club in St. James's. Park and Corporal Tinker were already seated in leather armchairs in the parlour. Park greeted him affably, offered him a whisky, and invited him to begin.

Eddy told his story economically, but even so, it took longer than he would have liked. The waiter noiselessly attended them and had topped their glasses three times with Glenlivet before Eddy reached the end of his report.

Park sat for a moment in silence, and then said, "That is quite a story you have laid out, Beane. Let me summarize to be sure I have understood it. Over the Dornier factory, you came face to face with a German reconnaissance plane, likely a Fieseler Storch. The pilot took photographs of your plane. I hazard a guess that the Germans had recognized your ID number. They realized you've been a regular visitor to their military sites and decided to neutralize you. You got away by the skin of your teeth and I think you've been damned lucky."

"That's about the size of it, sir," Eddy said.

"Your Aeronca is known to them now. We can't risk sending you to carry out any more investigative missions."

"I'm disappointed, sir, but not surprised."

"What bothers me, now, is the girl you brought over from Trier. What's her name?"

"Lotte Schroder."

"Yes. Why is she here?"

"I've brought her to stay with my Uncle Al and Aunt Maddy, sir."

"I see. At their invitation?"

"Yes sir."

"I have to ask. She is a foreign national and she has a German name. It seemed strange to me this morning that she had no luggage. I'm guessing that she has no papers, either. In these times, this is serious—more serious than you seem to realize. So tell me about her, and don't leave anything out."

Eddy knew that the Air Commodore wouldn't forgive him if he lied. He settled down to tell Park and Tinker about his father's and Uncle Al's service together in Flanders, and how they captured Jens and had an unlikely Christmas dinner on the front line with Lotte's father, Axel. He recounted the contents of Jens's letter, and his Uncle Al's big-hearted concern for Lotte.

Air Commodore Park sat back for several minutes, puffing on his pipe.

"Did you say Fraulein Schroder teaches French and English? How many languages does she speak?" Park asked.

"At least those two, and of course German, sir."

"She is against the Nazis, you say?"

"She hates everything they stand for," Eddy said.

"If she is really what she appears to be, she may be useful to us. On that score, I need to speak with my colleagues at SIS. They will check out who she is really is. They will be very thorough. If she can be of use, we'll handle the paperwork so she can stay. Either way, we will let you know."

"Yes sir."

Air Commodore Park paused. Eddy could feel an admonition in his stare.

"You misled me about your stop in Trier, young man. Your purpose was noble, but it nearly compromised the mission." He sipped his scotch. "In view of your service up to now, I am prepared to let this pass. Never let that happen again. And don't make me regret this."

"Yes sir. Thank you, sir."

"Nevertheless, now that the Germans are on to you, your intelligence work is finished." Park sat back in his chair. "I want you to enlist in the RAF."

"Sir! *Fantastique!* Thank you!"

He ignored a little voice in his head that was telling him to ask questions about Park's plans for him and to consider the pros and cons of such a big decision—and change—in his life. He already saw himself in the cockpit of a Spitfire. It could fly at three hundred and sixty miles per hour and was supremely manoeuvrable. He itched to get the feel of it and throw it about the sky, to climb, turn, spin and roll.

He rose and shook hands with the Air Commodore and Tinker. "How soon can I fly a Spitfire?"

Tinker chuckled and waited for Park to break Eddy's euphoria. "First, you'll have to learn to march. Master that, and perhaps you'll fly a training plane." Park allowed himself a thin smile, with just a hint of teasing. "Listen, Edouard, we want to build Fighter Command with the best sort of young men and from the missions you have completed for us, I believe you have what it takes to be one of them. I must warn you; it will take a tremendous amount of work."

Tinker said, "Frenchy, there's something else you need to understand about RAF fighter pilots. Most of them are university-educated young men, from upper-class families. They enter the RAF as officer candidates. You, on the other hand, will have to follow the route we have established for natural flyers who went to the wrong school. When you come out, you'll start at a lower rank. You'll be a Sergeant Pilot. If you are to succeed, you'll have to learn to get on with the wealthy lads—who will be your superiors in rank—and some of them will act as though they are your superior in everything else."

"All right Tinker," Park said. "Edouard. You're going to Duxford. Tinker will prepare the paperwork. Report to the airfield first thing on Monday morning. Now go home and pack your suitcase."

Neither Park's circumspection nor Tinker's warning dampened Eddy's enthusiasm, but another voice spoke in his mind, the voice of June Stephenson. He hesitated. "Sir?"

"Yes?"

"Can I delay my enlistment for one month? I have some commitments with my business I must honor."

Park raised an eyebrow. "Can't Tiger handle these things? He will wind up your affairs. He'll do right by you."

"There are some private flying lessons sir—that I've assured a student I would provide. Skipping out would be in very poor form."

Air Commodore Park agreed, irritably. "One month, then. No more."

Chapter 15

The runways were empty at Hanworth, and the skies were clear, perfect for a flying lesson. Tiger was working contentedly in Hangar C, but Eddy was waiting for June Stephenson, and trying not to spend all his time looking towards the airfield gates or checking his wristwatch. The seconds ticked wearily by. He went out into the sunshine and walked round his new car, a four-door Morris Eight in burgundy and black—one hundred and fifty pounds' worth, bought in conscious competition with June's shiny red MG. Then he came back to the Aeronca and examined it yet again from nose to tail, prop, wings, trailing edges, wheels. Everything was in order, but he was still listening for the roar of the MG's engine.

He glanced at his watch for the tenth time and stopped himself. He was determined not to go out again and look for her. To his relief she drove up punctually at three o'clock and he strolled out as casually as he could to meet her. She parked the convertible next to his Morris without appearing to notice his new car. She pulled off her headscarf, smoothed her brown hair and re-tied the scarf before she stood up from the low driving seat, stepped over the door onto the running board, and hopped down.

"Good afternoon Eddy! Am I late?" She reached into the car for a jacket and put it on.

"Hello June, *ne t'inquiète pas*," Eddy said as calmly as he could. "You are on time."

She joined him beside the Aeronca.

"I've so looked forward to my lesson."

"Good. Have you done your homework?"

June unfolded the checklist he had given her at the end of their initial meeting and handed it to him. "I've got them by heart now: Flaps, throttle, prop speed, cylinder head temperature..."

Eddy laughed. "*Bien.* I give you full marks."

A brilliant white Aero two-seater came scorching up to the hangar and parked beside them. Its top was booted, and the driver flashed a smile at June Stephenson, cut the engine and hopped out.

"June!"

"Dudley?" June said. "What on earth? How did you know I was here?"

"I inquired at the manor." The young man pushed his thick, blond hair off his brow and smiled knowingly. "The sight of a five pound note works wonders with Longmarsh's household staff."

Eddy was certain that he'd seen him before.

June said shortly, "Dudley, I'm busy. We have nothing more to say to each other."

"Ah, now, don't be like that, kitten. Is there somewhere we can talk? I'm sure we can straighten things out." Dudley reached for June's hand, but she pulled away from him.

Eddy was about to intervene when Tiger came running out of the hangar. He shook his grease-stained fist at Dudley. "You! You're the damn fool who nearly took the roof off my hangar! Get your bloody car off my infield!"

"Nice to see you, too, sir," Dudley said. "How about I move my car round the side, eh. I want to talk to Miss Stephenson."

"Well, I don't want to talk to you," June said. "I am going to have a flying lesson."

Dudley looked at Tiger, who was still stiff with rage. "I trust you'll calm yourself down before you take off with her."

"I'm not her instructor," Tiger said. He nodded at Eddy. "He is."

Dudley laughed scornfully. "He's just a grease monkey. I remember he fueled my plane. This dear girl is not going to share a cockpit with the likes of him."

Eddy kept his temper and said, "Sir, you are out of turn. I am a fully-qualified pilot and licensed flight instructor."

"Oh, are you indeed? And who exactly are you?"

"My name is Edouard Beane."

"*Oui*," Thane said, appearing amused, "Charmed, I'm sure." He turned back to June. "Now, June darling—I can see this isn't going to be safe for you. Come with me to Fen Ditton. You can fly with me."

"That's enough!" Tiger said. "Miss Stephenson. Are you going with this fellow or flying with Frenchy?"

"I'm not leaving."

"Then, sir," Eddy said to Thane, "I must ask you to leave."

Thane looked mulish, but Tiger stepped forward and said, "Go on! Get that bloody car out of here!"

Thane said to Eddy, "Take good care of her old son—and in case you don't understand plain English, *Prenez soin*. Well, *au revoir*. I'm pretty sure we shall meet again." He returned to his Aero, revved the engine, and sped away.

The three of them watched the sportster screech out of the gates in an uncomfortable silence. Finally, Tiger said, "I don't think much of your boyfriend, Miss Stephenson."

"He isn't my boyfriend. He was my fiancé," June said. "I broke it off."

"Then ya have a bit of sense," Tiger said, under his breath.

Eddy was both encouraged and troubled by the scene he had just witnessed: encouraged because this beautiful young woman had chosen him over her ex-fiancé, at least for today, but troubled because if she were capable of dismissing Thane, with his good looks and his moneyed background, she would have no time at all for him. He and June Stephenson lived in completely different worlds and he simply wasn't her kind.

"Well June," he said. "Let's get on with your lesson, shall we?" He opened the Aeronca's door on the passenger side and helped her to climb up into her seat, then walked around the plane and climbed into the pilot's seat. "Let's see you buckle up. I'll help if you need it."

She fastened her lap harness, and he secured her shoulder harness.

Tiger looked in at his door. He had put on sunglasses and his smile was unusually mischievous, as if he could read Eddy's mind. "Okay, Squire. What's your pleasure?"

Eddy was glad that June couldn't see him from the student's seat. He said stiffly, "Full procedure, if you please."

Tiger made a mock salute. "Gas on. Switch off. Throttle closed. Brakes set."

For June's benefit, Eddy pointed to the important aspects of the controls. "Fuel is on, and the mixture is rich. The magneto ignition switch is in the off position, the throttle is closed, and I'm holding down the brakes."

"Just like the checklist," she said.

Eddy repeated to Tiger: "Gas on. Switch off. Throttle closed. Brakes set."

Tiger gripped the propeller blade at its highest point and pulled it firmly downwards through its arc, so it made a full circle. "Brakes and contact," he said to Eddy.

"That is to prime the engine," Eddy explained to June. He double checked the brakes, said, "Brakes and contact" to Tiger, and turned the ignition switch on.

Tiger gripped the propeller blade and swung it again, harder and faster this time, and the Aeronca powered into action. The deep throb of the engine filled the cockpit. The propeller became a spinning circle in front of them. The seats vibrated and thin streams of exhaust rose over the sides of the cockpit, accompanied by a faint smell of gasoline. Eddy signaled to Tiger to pull the chocks away from the wheels. Ahead of them, the runway was open.

June seemed to be mesmerized by the whirring of the propeller. Eddy touched her hand to make her look at him. "Put your headphones on."

She smoothed her headscarf and did as he asked.

"Can you hear me?"

Her voice came back to him through his headphones. "Yes."

"Keep them on all the time we are in the air, otherwise you won't hear a thing over the engine."

"I could hear you perfectly well without them," she said. "I was just, well— absorbed."

"You wouldn't hear me when the engine cranks up. Bien. At the moment, I'm holding the brakes, because we do not want to move until the oil in the engine heats up."

"Got it," June said.

He pointed out the dials she should be observing. "There. Now we can taxi out to the start of the runway for a final check." He let off the brake, and they began to move slowly across the infield. Just before the runway itself, Eddy turned the Aeronca into the wind.

"You can see the windsock is swaying a bit, towards us. That's good. It means we'll have the wind blowing over our wings." Eddy pointed to other control dials. "Mag check. Good. Carb heat check. Good. Now, this is where you can join in. Hold the brakes, with me—here."

June put her hand over his on the brake lever. Her fingers were warm and firm and unafraid.

Eddy opened the throttle. "This is the run-up," he said, as the engine roared. "We need to generate plenty of power before we try to lift off."

He aligned the Aeronca's nose with the white line painted down the center of the runway. This time he put June's hand on the throttle and covered it with his own, and with their hands pulling back together as one, the plane accelerated smoothly and sweetly into the air. Eddy savored both feelings and regretted having to take his hand from hers to work the trim.

"How high will we climb?" she asked.

"Three thousand feet," he said. "It will take us several minutes."

June's sigh of pleasure came through his headphones. "Do you ever get tired of this?" she asked. "It's amazing. The whole of London is at our feet. That's Richmond Park. I never knew it had so many ponds. And the Thames—I can see all the way out to Gravesend."

Nearly all new students had to be jerked away from the wonder of aerial sights to their business of flying. When the altimeter read three thousand feet Eddy leveled the plane and June said with sudden concern, "Oh, are we falling?"

Eddy chuckled. "No. It only feels that way. Your inner ear is playing tricks on you. I'm going to teach you how to fly level. The horizon is your friend. When we keep the dashboard and the horizon a constant distance apart, we are flying level. Go ahead, try it."

June worked the yoke and the throttle, following Eddy's instructions.

"You are aiming above the horizon," Eddy said. "Check your altimeter. We're climbing again."

"But I set us on that gray line out there."

Eddy chuckled. "That gray line is the cloud deck—the false horizon."

"Oh." She sounded disappointed, so he glanced over, and a hint of a pout had washed over her lovely face.

"Don't worry, I made the same mistake when I started. I think all of us pilots do."

She seemed to cheer at his use of the word "us." He moved her hand on the yoke.

"Let's try turning now. We'll turn to starboard, that's to the right. One wing is going to go down, and the other up. It's called banking. Don't be alarmed—you won't fall out! Now, I want you to move the yoke to the right."

The Aeronca tilted and changed direction steadily to starboard.

"How does that feel?"

"The yoke is heavy," she said. "But its smooth, kind of like pulling a weight on a rope with a pulley."

Eddy smiled, making a mental note to remember her simile. "Flying is constant checking and balancing. We check our position visually, against landmarks and the horizon. We look at the control dials. We adjust."

"Pressure good. Altitude good," she said, rather self-consciously.

"That's it! Now, we're heading back the way we came. Let's talk about landmarks. You must learn to recognize them to know where you're going. There's one easy landmark that every pilot in London pays attention to. What do you think it is?"

"The river, of course. So we will be heading west?"

"Yes, Perfect," Eddy said. "Enjoy the sights while you can. There are only a few patchy clouds to look through and it's rare to see London so clear of smoke." June gazed down at the Thames, segmented by its bridges. The Tower, St. Paul's Cathedral, the Houses of Parliament, and Westminster Abbey all stood in bright sunshine. She nearly had her nose on the window. Her rapt attention was as cute as a puppy watching for its master, and Eddy remembered how Commander Park had smiled at his own wonderment on his first flight.

"People say they see shapes in the clouds," she said. "But now that I'm up here with them, they're not like that at all. There." She pointed at a lonesome, small cloud half lit by sunshine. "It's more like cotton wool being pulled apart and then pushed together again."

"But that's not all. Look up now and straight ahead, above us a bit."

"Oh! Another aeroplane. My word it's coming at us fast!"

"In five seconds, it will be behind us."

"But when you see them from the ground, they seem to move so slowly."

"Everything changes up here."

"Indeed it does."

"We are traveling much faster than you realize. We're not far from Hanworth now, so you must prepare to land."

"Oh," she said, disappointed again.

"Pay attention. Landing is much more important than taking off." He directed her so that the Aeronca was correctly lined up on the airfield. "I want you to pitch the nose a little lower. Point it at the runway. Can you feel it? You're making a gentle descent. That's it. Well done."

"I feel I'm really flying!"

"You are."

"But are you going to help me land?"

Eddy laughed. "Indeed, yes. A good pilot must have as many successful landings as take-offs."

"Funny," she said, sardonically.

"Keep your hand there, so you can feel what is happening, but let me do the work. I'm going to idle down the engine." Eddy pulled back on the throttle slightly. "We'll come in just above the runway and let our wheels float to the grass."

"Like we're gliding."

"That's it."

They taxied to the infield just off Hangar C.

The moment the plane stopped, June unfastened her harness and turned excitedly to Eddy.

"Thank you so much! You let me fly your plane! I love it, Eddy, truly I do. I can't tell you how much I am looking forward to our next lesson. I must keep flying with you."

Eddy was nearly speechless. "Y-Yes. *Bien entendu.* You did very well. Come on now, time to get down."

He assisted her to climb out of the cockpit. Everything about her took his breath away. Her bubbly, infectious nature. Her smile, her luxurious wavy, brown hair, the floral scent of her, the touch of her fingers on his ...

Impulsively, she turned to him again. "I'm far too excited to go home yet! There is a tearoom just along the road—the Rose Hill Tea Room—do you know it? Will you join me?"

He couldn't possibly say no.

She asked Eddy teasingly, "Your car or mine?"

So she had noticed the Morris, after all. He found it hard to give an answer that wouldn't sound censorious. She was still high as a kite after her flight, and he didn't quite trust her judgement. However, he didn't feel all that calm himself. He knew very well that she was a girl used to being in charge, and on such a sunny afternoon her open car was definitely more attractive than his closed-top sedan.

He smiled at her. "Yours, of course."

~ ~ ~

At the Rose Hill Tea Room, she suggested, "Let's sit outside. It's too lovely to hide indoors."

There was a flagged patio on the sunny side of the building, decorated with pots of crimson dahlias, and bordered with sweet peas and cosmos in shades of pink. June chose a table, and they sat down.

"Isn't this heavenly? I love the scent out here."

He agreed and when the waitress came he let June order what she fancied, which turned out to be a pot of tea and a plate of buttered scones.

"Delightful," June said, and set to pouring tea. Her hand was unsteady, and the tea sloshed out of his cup, into the saucer and onto the tablecloth. "I'm sorry. But every time I think about flying, I get goosepimples. Oh, Eddy. That was the most exciting hour of my life."

Eddy said, truthfully, "Today was a gift from heaven."

"Wait until I tell the girls!"

He thought he would rather not know what she might tell them about himself. "What do they say about you taking flying lessons?"

"They think I'm looney." June dabbed with her napkin at the spilt tea. "Most of them are scared by heights and that makes them afraid to fly." She giggled and looked up at him. "I tell them: If you saw my handsome flight instructor, and heard his French accent, you would know why I do it."

Eddy blushed.

"I didn't mean to embarrass you," she said.

"You are the first woman I've taught. Men who buy lessons have ambitions. They want to fly to impress people with their money, or to make a business more efficient. But I don't know whether a woman thinks the same way. Tell me, honestly, why you want to fly."

"Oh," June said. "I told you that. Don't you remember; my fiancé learned to fly when we were up at Cambridge together. Dudley used to come in from flying with such an enthusiastic glow that I was quite jealous."

Eddy hadn't thought about Dudley Thane since they'd taken off and he tried to conceal his disappointment that he had to deal with the thought of him again.

June said, "He's my ex-fiancé, remember. I'm so very sorry that he turned up. After I broke our engagement off I didn't hear from him for some time. But he's started to bother me again. It's so annoying." She had a sip of tea, and her hands were still not quite steady.

Eddy tried not to be discouraged, but Thane turning up had been like a bucket of cold water on his prospects with June. The man's car, his clothing, his education, his attitude—all of it was from a world he didn't enter. Oh, he'd seen it before, from the men who came into Weldy & Beane and demanded their goods this very second, who made a fuss about a button, a seam, or a lining, usually without foundation. *Maman* had always seethed at the behavior of men like Thane, and so did he. He was disappointed that June had once taken up with Thane and even agreed to marry him. She was probably no different from the sort of people he despised.

"Anyway, that's quite enough about Dudley," June said. "I became set on learning to fly. The hardest part has been convincing Daddy to let me take lessons. We argued and argued."

"It's not so strange that your father was reluctant to let you fly. Perhaps he is concerned about your safety? Or perhaps he does not trust you?"

"He didn't want me to have a car either, but he came round!" She laughed. "I have to prove I am good enough to fly solo because my next challenge will be to convince him that I need an aeroplane!"

So June expected her father to buy an aeroplane for her amusement. That seemed like something Dudley Thane would say. It was clear that Mr. Stephenson could afford to give her the best of everything: she had plenty of food and clothes, a fine automobile, and an excellent education. Eddy supposed she also had access to social engagements in the highest circles and was expected to marry into the aristocracy. Eddy, brought up with his *Maman*'s disdain for royalty and her insistence that all people should be of equal standing, suppressed an inward sneer at the thought of June marrying a prince. She might of course prefer a rich young man from her father's circle of industrialist acquaintances. She could have her pick. Her ex-fiancé Dudley Thane was one of those sorts or the other —very much unlike Eddy.

He took a sip of tea, watching June sit back with a pleased but distant expression, probably lost in her thoughts on today's flying experience. Just as he had been after his first flight with Commander Park. Was he being too hard on her? Maybe so. She lived the same upper class life as Dudley Thane did, but he couldn't paint her behavior with the same brush. Thane had judged Eddy to be working class and an incompetent flight instructor based on seeing Eddy pump aviation fuel into Howey's Swallow the only other time they had met. June, by contrast, had recognized from the start that Eddy's knowledge of aviation was vastly superior to hers. She had never questioned his ability to teach her even though Eddy was just a working pilot with fewer years of education. The thing to do, he supposed, was to judge June only on her own actions.

She broke into his thoughts. "When will you let me sit in the pilot's seat?"

"Oh, very soon." He found her enthusiasm hard to resist, but he had to be cautious, for safety's sake. "Let's get a couple more lessons behind us. We need to be rock-solid on take-off and landing. And one of the things I insist on with all my pupils is that you learn how to get out of difficult situations, while I'm right there to help you. You still have to experience a stall."

"What's a stall? Is it like when you miss a gear when you're driving a car?" She giggled again. "I did that when I was learning to drive. I made Daddy so wild."

"Stalling is a bit like that, yes. The plane loses speed—effectively it stops flying."

She gasped. "In mid-air?"

"That's right. In technical terms, it happens when we exceed our critical angle of attack. We'll talk about what that means. I'll put you into that situation with me at the controls, so you can learn how it feels, and how we handle it."

"All right if you say so. I can't wait to go up again with you, whatever we do. If we have another day like today, I just might not want to land. I might want to stay up in the skies with you forever." She smiled. "But when we do land, let's come here again. Agreed?"

She offered her hand on the bargain. There was a happy smile in her hazel eyes, and when Eddy shook hands with her, Dudley Thane and social class were the last things on his mind.

"*Bien sur!* I mean, yes, I would like that very much."

Chapter 16

F ive days later, Eddy left Hanworth earlier than usual and strolled along to the Common, hoping to meet Aunt Maddy and little Georgie, who liked the playground there. The late afternoon breeze felt good, and Eddy couldn't remember the last time he'd strolled for pure enjoyment. It was a pleasure, too, to have time to think about June Stephenson. She had returned for her second lesson, this time without any complications from Dudley Thane. She was making good progress—eager and unafraid, paying attention to detail, applying what she had learned at home to the business of keeping the Aeronca in the air. She'd invited him along to the tea room again, too. Just thinking about her was intoxicating, and he was still mildly tipsy with his memories of her when he arrived at the Common.

As he had expected, Aunt Maddy was supervising Georgie on the swings, gently pushing his rump to make the swing go.

"Higher Mummy! Higher!"

"Hold on tight then." Maddy saw Eddy and smiled. "Oh, look, here's your Uncle Eddy. He'll push you much harder than I do."

Eddy chuckled at being called "uncle" even though he and Georgie were actually first cousins, notwithstanding their eighteen year age difference. "Hold on, Georgie," Eddy said, as he took Maddy's place. "Ready? Go."

The swing flew up and Georgie squealed in excitement.

Eddy kept pushing until Georgie had his fill and scrambled off and ran over to the monkey bars where other children were climbing up and down.

"I'm glad you've joined us," Aunt Maddy said. "Come and sit on the bench. We can see Georgie from there, and I can give my old ankles a rest."

They sat in the sunshine watching the little boy considering how to climb the bars.

"We don't often have time to just sit and chat, do we? You're always so busy. I can't remember when you last took a day off from Hanworth."

"I know," Eddy said. "Business has been good. It seems a shame to wind it down but I'm counting the days till I go to Duxford. I'll miss all of you, of course, but I can't wait to fly a Spitfire."

"That will be soon enough. At least we get to enjoy you today."

Eddy didn't reply, and instead lit a cigarette. Georgie was testing his strength by gripping the first ladder bar and swinging his legs out, then returning his feet to safety.

"What's on your mind, Eddy?" Aunt Maddy asked. "I know there's something. Is it the RAF training?"

"Yes, it is partly the RAF." He took a long drag. "There's something else though. I met a girl."

"Oh Eddy! That's lovely. Is it Lotte?"

Eddy paused, wondering if he should have opened this door. "No Aunt Maddy, it isn't. I mean, Lotte is an attractive girl and a very nice person. We went through a lot together, and I'm fond of her. But she is not the girl I'm talking about." He puffed on his cigarette. "How is Lotte? I haven't seen her since the weekend."

Aunt Maddy gave him an old-fashioned look. "You're avoiding the question. Who's your lady friend?"

"And I'm asking about Lotte," Eddy countered. "If you tell me how she's doing, I'll tell you about my—lady friend. Perhaps!"

She chuckled. "Stubborn is your middle name, Edouard. All right. We're happy to have Lotte with us. She's good with the children and helps out, and she's more cheerful than I would have expected after what she went through. But the poor thing—all she had was the clothes on her back! Luckily, we're about the same size, so I lent her a few things, and we went shopping."

"You're very kind," Eddy said. "I hope you haven't had to spend too much on her."

"Don't worry. She'll pay me back. She needed some smart outfits because she's been attending interviews."

"Oh?"

"There was a telephone call for her on Monday morning from a government man who said Air Commodore Park had asked him to contact her."

"That sounds promising."

"Yes. They wanted to interview her immediately so I told her to take the District Line to St. James's Park. She left the house before eight again yesterday and didn't come home until the evening."

"Do you think she got the job?"

"I don't know yet," Aunt Maddy said. "I really can't say. Lotte told your Uncle and me that someone in the Government has asked her to come in every day this week, but they have asked her not to talk about it for the time being."

"I see," Eddy said, not all that surprised, and made a mental note to ask Lotte about her dealings with the government. When Maddy said no more, his thoughts returned to June, as they did nearly every minute of every day.

Aunt Maddy broke the silence with a friendly nudge of her shoulder against his. "Well?"

"Well what?"

"Tit for tat, Monsieur Beane. I've told you about Lotte. Now tell me about your lady-love."

Eddy puffed on his cigarette. "Her name is June. I am giving her flying lessons. And she is wonderful."

"Dear me. This sounds serious," Aunt Maddy said, with a glint in her eye.

He felt deep relief from being able to talk about June at last. "Yes, but it isn't easy. To be honest, it's possible my interest might be unrequited. What makes it worse is that, even if June likes me, I don't think she would be allowed to marry me."

"Why?"

"Her father is rich and she's his darling. I don't think he would stand for me. On top of that, her ex-fiancé turned up at Hanworth and we had a bit of a tiff about her flying lessons. He's a wealthy society boy and made sure to throw it in my face. June chose not to go off with him, and I've cherished the time we've spent together, but he made me realize she is above my touch." He sighed. "But I can't get her out of my mind."

Aunt Maddy sighed a little too. "I think I need a cigarette." They smoked in silence watching Georgie work up the courage to swing himself hand over hand across the monkey bars.

"Your Uncle Al and I don't care for people who flaunt their wealth and privilege any more than you do," Maddy said. "It can be uncomfortable, but sometimes we must put up with it in order to get what we want."

She exhaled cigarette smoke and smiled. "There's only one occasion when Al really splashed out. When we got married, we didn't waste money on a honeymoon. We bought the house and got the business going first. What he didn't tell me was that all that time, he was putting money aside for a holiday in France—a proper wedding trip—on the Golden Arrow!" She sighed at the happy memory. "Oh those Pullman coaches! The luxury! Inlaid wood, gilt fittings, thick carpets. I thought I'd died and gone to heaven."

She glanced across the playground at Georgie. Satisfied that he was still at the monkey bars, she went on with her tale. "It was so gorgeous, but the cost bothered me. And I was worried about the business we would be missing at Weldy & Beane. I remember when we settled into our compartment the couple who took the opposite seats. The man held his bowler in his lap and nodded, but the way they looked at us said we were in the wrong place. I was wearing my best day dress. It had an embroidered pattern and bone buttons and all, but it was nowhere near as expensive as that woman's dress. Hers was bespoke, town-tailored, silk. The man laughed and whispered into her ear. She was wearing a big cartwheel summer hat but I know what they were saying behind it. They got up and left. I think they spent the rest of the journey in the dining car."

"They sound like nasty people," Eddy said. He wondered why Aunt Maddy had decided to launch into a lengthy anecdote just now. Usually she sat quiet while Uncle Al did the reminiscing.

"I suppose. I wanted to go home, but Al wouldn't let us. I was afraid we'd meet a customer and she'd say, 'Why, Maddy Weldy, what a surprise to see you here! Will my mending be ready for pick-up on Tuesday?' I told Al I wanted to go back. But Al hugged me, and insisted we stay. He was my rock. The thing is, Eddy, if I'd run away from those society people that day, we would never have come to France. We wouldn't have met you and your *Maman*."

Eddy smiled at her as he took in her meaning. "I'm glad you told me, Aunt Maddy. Well! I'm not ready to give up on June, not just yet."

Maddy said, "Times have begun to change, Eddy. I have heard of marriages across class lines. You are about to become a pilot in the

Royal Air Force, so that will be a point in your favour. Listen, dear, I lost seventeen years I should have had with your Uncle Al. You know the story. When he went off to the War with your father, we knew we loved each other." She exhaled a stream of smoke. "But Al was wounded in Flanders and we lost touch because we didn't fight for what we had." She paused. "Maybe things turned out for us the way God wanted; I don't know. But your Uncle and I lost all those years we ought to have spent together. We let a love slip through our fingers that should have been taken first time around and it's only pure, gorgeous luck that we ever got together again. So I am the last person to tell you a match is impossible."

She took his hand. "What I'm saying is, if your heart is set on this young lady, go and get her."

Chapter 17

Eight days after arriving at Hanworth, Lotte emerged from St. James's Park Underground Station in London to a chilly breeze and gray skies. She walked round the block to 54 Broadway, an imposing building whose brass plaque identified it as the "Minimax Fire Extinguisher Company." This was her fifth visit, however, and now she knew that "Minimax" had nothing to do with fire extinguishers.

A glance over her shoulder confirmed that she was once again being followed by the man in a dark raincoat and a black trilby hat. He looked aside when she caught his gaze. She hadn't noticed him on the underground this morning, but the carriage had been crowded as always and she knew he must have been there, watching her, reporting on her, just as he had been throughout the week.

"You must expect to be watched," Mr. Bunting had told her on Monday morning. She hadn't quite worked out what authority Bunting had within the British Government. He was always plainly dressed in a dark suit. He had interviewed her each day in a small, windowless room that gave no clues as to his rank or position. "Relations between England and Germany are strained at the moment and the circumstances under which you arrived were, as you are aware, most unusual. We take every precaution."

So Lotte understood that surveillance was a necessary government procedure. Nevertheless, she felt a measure of pity for this man whose duty was to shadow her uneventful travels between the Weldys' house in Peckham and these offices on the outskirts of Westminster.

She entered the building, trotted up the dingy stairs to Mr. Bunting's floor and checked in with the woman at the desk, who told her, as she had all week, to wait. Five minutes later, Mr. Bunting himself came to greet her. She thought that was a hopeful sign, as each of the past three mornings he had sent his assistant, a younger man who had managed to be polite yet totally distant. She followed

102

Bunting through a maze of corridors to an unfamiliar part of the building. The entered a large room laid out with dozens of wooden partitions in no discernable pattern and then filled with desks in a way that brought to mind a Saarburg neighbor's warren of rabbit burrows.

This time Bunting showed her into what she assumed was his own office; it was larger and better lit than the room in which she had sat for long hours on the previous day, which had been furnished with only a small table and three hard upright chairs. This room had a heavy desk, a swivel chair behind it, and two chairs in front of it upholstered in brown leather, but still there were no family pictures, souvenirs, or mementos. Bunting closed the door and motioned for Lotte to sit in front of the desk, facing the window. "It's been a long week for you, Miss Schroder," said Bunting, as he took the swivel chair. "How are you coping?"

If Lotte had answered completely truthfully, she would have said that the past four days at 54 Broadway had been the most mentally-grueling of her life. Bunting's staff had probed the details of her home, friends and acquaintances in Saarburg, her brother and her family, Jens and the vineyard, her education and teaching position, her love-life and her political leanings, and of course her escape with Eddy from Otto and the Gestapo. English, French and German native speakers had come and gone, changing language with a frequency that sometimes required her to catch herself before she spoke in the wrong tongue. A woman named Mrs. Rose had taken a great deal of time asking her questions about the Nazis in Saarburg and in particular the Nazi parade during which the Mandels' clothing shop had been destroyed. Between interviews, she had sat for oral and written language examinations in English, French and German, and an intensive test in Germanic history.

"I don't mind, sir," she said.

"Our investigations appear to confirm the details of your upbringing," said Bunting, "and that you are proficient in English and French."

"Yes, sir."

"I have just reviewed a report from sources in Germany, which confirms you were living a relatively quiet life in Saarburg—teacher and a member of the Lutheran church. You read Bible stories to children every third Sunday. You lived with your brother, Otto, who is a Nazi in the SS, at your parents' house. They are both deceased. You are rarely seen with Otto in Saarburg. Within the past month, one of your teacher colleagues has observed bruises on your jaw, neck and forearm. How did you get those?"

Lotte was stunned that this Englishman sitting behind a desk in London could gather such private information in a matter of days. "My brother Otto did that to me."

"Why would your brother do such a thing?"

"Because I refused to support the Nazis as he demanded." She looked away from Bunting. "I am sure your report says that I told Mrs. Rose that Otto would have killed me if I stayed in Saarburg. I believe that to be true with all my heart."

"I see," Bunting said quietly.

"You have been observed at *kaffee und kuchen* with Lili Mandel, who is the daughter of a Jewish merchant family, and with Greta Lund, who is well-known in Saarburg as a communist sympathizer. Tell me how you know them."

Lotte was taken aback. "Of course I am friends with Lili. We went to school together. As for Greta Lund, a teacher-friend introduced us earlier this year. I enjoy speaking with her."

"What did you talk to her about?"

"Greta is a very knowledgeable woman, so we spoke of many things."

"Such as?"

"Music. She liked many kinds."

"Which kinds?"

"Hans Albers, Lilian Harvey and Willy Fritsch, and even The Comedian Harmonists. And of course Schumann and Strauss."

"Did you discuss political matters with Greta Lund?"

"Yes. She is on the side of the workers. She believes that their employers and the government should do more for them."

"Do you agree with her views?"

"Mostly."

"Are you a communist?"

"No."

"But you say you are not a Nazi, even though your brother is SS?"

"Absolutely not!" She felt blood rising in her temples. "I am German and I love my country. But it is in the hands of the Nazis and I will never agree with their ways."

Bunting leaned back in his chair and took a pipe from his jacket, packed it and lit up, watching Lotte all the while. He smoked in silence, then pulled a large brown envelope from a desk drawer. He opened it, then with a slight softening of his expression drew out a folded card and placed it in front of Lotte. "Please review the information. It is your Alien Registration Card."

The words "Registration Card" were printed at the top, emboldened and underlined, and a head and shoulders photograph of her was fixed at the bottom. Her name, date of birth and date of arrival into England were printed correctly. Her status was listed as single with no children, and Al's and Maddy's house in Peckham was listed as her address. The next line listed "SIS" as her employer. She looked up at Bunting.

"What is SIS?" she asked.

"We are SIS. You are going to work for us."

"Oh!" She was so relieved, she very nearly accepted at once. A calmer voice, however, prompted her to ask what he wanted her to do. "What is my job?"

"You will be working as a translator for us, mostly translating documents, written in German, into English. Now and then you may be asked to transcribe recordings of German conversations to English, or to listen in on conversations between German-speakers and then provide a transcript." He puffed on his pipe. "I must emphasize that you will treat your work for SIS as strictly confidential. Your acceptance of this must be unconditional."

"What will happen," Lotte asked, "if I do not agree to work for you? Please understand that I am not refusing. But I would like to know what the alternative would be."

Bunting took his pipe out of his mouth and leaned slightly towards her. "I very much hope you will want to work for us. We see the growing Nazi movement in Germany as a huge threat to national security. We will need all the information we can gather, to be ready to counter it. As someone who has already made plain your position —by fleeing Germany—I believe you will want to assist us."

"I see," Lotte said. "Yes, I do. And it's important that I earn money, too, so the work is very welcome. But I have not yet looked at any other work I might be suitable for."

Bunting said, without hesitation, "I'll be honest with you Miss Schroder, you cannot look for other work. If you refuse the position I have offered, you will be extradited—returned to Germany. And you need to make your decision before you leave this office."

Lotte's pulse rate doubled, and she clasped her hands on her knee to keep them from trembling. She said as steadily as she could, "That is very clear."

"However, I hope that you will accept willingly, and that extradition will not be necessary."

"So, if I take the carrot, I don't get the stick?"

Bunting permitted himself to smile, and it made him seem more human. "I take it you accept the position?"

"I do."

"Then please sign this form now. You should also sign your card."

She did so and returned the form to him and put away the precious card in her handbag.

Bunting continued, "If you are asked about your employer, you will answer that you are employed by the Home Office. You cannot speak of your work to anyone, not even to the Weldy family or your friends. If you do, we will know. Your employment will be terminated, and you will be returned to Germany immediately. Is this understood?"

"Yes, sir," Lotte said, wondering if she had entered the dangerous shadowy world of a spy novel.

"Very well," Bunting said. "Now I'm going to give you a taste of what you'll be doing. Consider this your first assignment." He opened his desk drawer again and pulled out a letter, which he gave to her.

She looked it over. It was written in German and addressed to a residence in Liverpool, via Thomas Cook's Lisbon office. She said, "This is a letter from an old woman in Frankfurt writing to her granddaughter, Mary Anderson, who is a hairdresser. The old lady is complaining that her doctor forbids her to eat beef—or asparagus!—because of her gout. Do you really need me to transcribe this?"

Bunting grinned and pointed to the letter with the stem of his pipe. "Is there anything odd to that, do you think? Does anything strike you?"

"The handwriting is uneven. But she is an old woman with painful joints, so perhaps that is to be expected. However, the word asparagus appears to be written in a more deliberate style. Also why is the letter addressed to the office of Thomas Cook, if the granddaughter is employed and living in Liverpool? Doesn't she have a regular address where the postman might deliver her mail?"

"Excellent observations," said Bunting. "Political operatives—spies —are adept at concealing important data in otherwise innocuous communications," he said. "It may be a word that seems out of place, or written in another hand, or a sequence of numbers, a date, or some other sort of code. We're going to train you how to spot their tricks. In fact, there is nothing of import in that letter. I keep it merely as an example for our new recruits. Let me have it back." Bunting returned it to the drawer and rose. "Now, Miss Schroder, let's get you settled at a desk."

Chapter 18

That night, after the Weldy children had been put to bed, Lotte sat with Maddy, Al and Eddy in the parlour, gathered round the hearth.

Lotte said, "I have some good news. I have a job with the Home Office."

"The Home Office," Al repeated. "Really?"

"Yes. I start Monday. To begin with, I will be working at 54 Broadway. But when I complete my training I may be moved to a different location. It might not be in London."

"That sounds—curious," Eddy said. "What will you be doing?"

"I have been hired as a translator. The important thing is, because I have accepted the job, I have also received my papers. I am authorized to live in England."

"Splendid," Al said.

Maddy agreed. "We're so happy for you."

Eddy smiled but he said nothing.

"I think I am well-suited for the position," Lotte said. "I will be paid a decent wage, so I should be able to rent a flat before very long. I hope you won't mind me staying here till then."

Maddy's smile faded. "Dear, we are very happy for you. But I'm sad to hear you're thinking of moving out."

"Oh," Lotte said. She hadn't presumed that the Weldys wanted her to prolong her stay. Surely they wanted things to return to normal for their family as soon as she was able to muster the resources to live on her own. "You have the children, Maddy, I wouldn't want to be a bother."

"Remember," Eddy said to Lotte, "I'm about to leave for Duxford. My bedroom will be empty."

Maddy and Al looked at each other, consulting without words in a manner that Lotte envied—a happy, settled couple.

Al turned to Lotte. "Stay with us," he said, "at least for a while. Save your wages. Find your way around London. I understand that if you're posted in another city, it won't be convenient to live here any more, and you'll have to strike out on your own. But until then, if you are comfortable with us, we would very much like you to stay."

Lotte had a lump in her throat. These generous people, whom she had just met, were giving her the warmth and security that had been missing for so long in her own home in Saarburg. "Thank you."

"Then its settled," Maddy said, beaming. "You'll live with us."

"Wonderful!" Al said. "Let's ask Tess Walden's daughter to sit with the children tomorrow evening and we'll all go to dinner. My treat!"

"I would love to Uncle Al," Eddy said. "But I have an engagement with June Stephenson."

"Oh?" Maddy said. "An engagement?"

Eddy reddened with embarrassment. "It's not that kind of engagement, Aunt Maddy. I'm giving June a flying lesson tomorrow afternoon and we've made plans for tea after."

"Well, now, taking tea won't stop you having dinner with us. Why don't you bring June with you?" Maddy said.

Eddy fidgeted. "It won't work, not tomorrow. But I've told June all about you and Lotte. She wants to come and meet you, and we'll set that up soon, I promise. Just not tomorrow."

Chapter 19

June leaned back in her wrought iron chair and raised her face to sunshine peeking through a cloud-filled sky. Sitting with Eddy on the patio of Rose Hill Tea Room after another flying lesson, she stretched her arms wide, uncoiling her body from the cramped confines of the Aeronca. Eddy seemed content to wait for her to settle.

"Look at this weather," she said. "It's hard to believe how awful it was when we were in the air."

An hour earlier the sky had turned dark, and rain had streamed over the windscreen so that visibility had been down to nothing. While Eddy kept checking the altimeter and compass in order to fly straight and level, she had bombarded him with questions that had betrayed her apprehension. He had remained calm and given answers that calmed her as well. Eventually the aeroplane broke out of the squall and the danger had passed.

Gazing at his impassive, almost sculpted profile and his wavy black hair, she realized he was the most attractive man she had ever met. He emitted a mysterious aura that her heart told her was one of goodness, and she would relish spending the time with him to learn his secrets. She hadn't felt so happy in a long time. She had to concentrate to pour their tea without spilling it.

"It's good you have seen how disorienting bad weather can be," Eddy said.

"I was very relieved when we got out of it."

"We just had a tiny taste of what flying is like in rainy conditions. The Aeronca shouldn't be up during a storm. Now you know why we study the weather before we take off."

"I'm glad my first flight in rain was with you."

He smiled wryly. "I told you I'd put you in difficult situations. I admit I didn't plan this one."

"And I was thinking you have a wireless connection to the weather gods," she said with a little grin. "Oh Eddy! I can't tell you how happy I am that I'm really going to get my license—and be a pilot. Because I am, aren't I?"

Eddy's smile broadened. "Ah, but there's a lot more for you to learn before you fly on your own. First things first: Next time we fly I think you should take the pilot's seat. But for your own safety, I won't let you go solo until you're ready."

"So much instruction! Am I a slow learner?" she asked, teasing.

"No, you're one of the quickest," he said. "But I wish you weren't, so you'd need more lessons with me."

June shook her head at his compliment and had a sip of tea. "I simply refuse to believe you'll be gone from Hanworth this time next month."

"Well, I shall. If you're going to be ready for the license exam before I go, you'll have to put your back into it."

"I'll fly by myself if I have to. Steal a plane and fly away to find you."

"I think Tiger would have something to say about that," Eddy said, smiling.

She didn't take offense because she was the one who had pushed the point. She knew she was coming across as over-confident. But it was cute that he was willing to pay her compliments.

"You know," she said, thoughtfully, "there must be tremendous opportunity in aviation. Look at you—all the business you can handle, and there's even more for the taking. Isn't that right?"

"Yes. I'm doing quite well, thank you," he said.

"Of course, you are," she said. "I know I'm not your only pupil. You couldn't have bought your Morris if you weren't making a good living."

Eddy nodded, hiding a smile.

"Besides, I overheard you and Tiger talking about a cargo load that needed to go to Paris. You told him to find someone else to take it."

"I only turned it down because I'm going into the RAF."

"I dare say, but you're limited by the size of your aeroplane too. Limited cargo space, limited seating, and limited range. Here's the thing, Eddy—flying as an industry is just getting started! You will see

111

businesses built and fortunes made carrying cargo and passengers by air. It won't be many years before ocean travel will be finished. Maybe rail, too."

He said, slowly, "Yes, I can see that coming—but there may well be a war first."

"Oh, war! What a nuisance all that stuff is! I must convince Daddy to let me keep flying, so I can start a flying business. Now, if I had an experienced pilot as my partner...." She looked at Eddy. "I just might persuade him to invest. But, no, you have to go off and join the RAF."

"I do love to fly, and I do love working with people," he admitted. "There is a lot of sense in what you say. But the thing is, if we do go to war, men of my age are likely to be conscripted into military service whether we like it or not. Even if we started a new business, it would die before it got going. On the other hand, war will speed up the development of flying technology and I'll learn far more about aeroplanes and flying in the RAF than I ever could here at Hanworth."

June mulled over his views. "In that case, you should definitely go. Learn as much as you can, and then come back and we'll build our flying business when the war is over. That won't be long, will it?"

She grinned at him. Her imagination had already worked out their future; a tidy office, herself and Eddy discussing business side by side, with a fleet of cargo planes in the big hangar. Something about him suggested a modern perspective that made him capable of an equal partnership with a woman. Besides, when she outlined her plans to him, she could wear the blue one-piece flight suit that she was wearing now, knowing how its tight belt accented her curves.

He grinned back, in a lop-sided fashion, and she wondered if he thought her enthusiastic, naïve or both.

"The first step," she continued, "will be to introduce you to Daddy."

"I don't know about that."

"Why not?"

"I'm just a working pilot, June. Not the sort of man your father deals with."

"You are about to fly aeroplanes for the Royal Air Force. Personally invited to join-up by Air Commodore Park. Remember? I heard you and Tiger talking about him. And you are misjudging Daddy. He isn't a snob. He built his business 'by pulling himself up by his bootstraps' as he likes to say." She chuckled. "Sometimes I call him our John Thornton."

"Who?"

"Oh. A wonderful character from a book called *North and South*. Anyway, Daddy will be interested in your story."

"Will he mind that I am not English?"

June laughed. "He may. But I will convince him you are hard-working and respectable, all the same! You shall be my Eliza Doolittle, and I will be Professor Higgins presenting you to society. Which means of course, Mummy."

He picked up the bill that lay on the table between them and frowned at it.

She realized that he didn't have the foggiest idea what she was talking about, and to go on about literature with a man who clearly hadn't studied it would be cruel. She put her hand over his. "I'll pay," she said, and when he held onto the bill, she added. "At least my own share."

"You will not," he said, indignantly. "I can certainly afford five bob."

"Well, then," she said, "perhaps I should tell Mummy you have been paying me some flattering attention." He drew back, but June kept her hand on his, savoring their stalemate. Finally, she relented. "All right. Let's go back to the airfield. I expect you have other students waiting to fly."

Walking together to her MG, she was excited that he had made clear he was reluctant to part from her. Even so, he had been convincingly clear-headed about the reasons he must. She chuckled to herself that his clear-headedness had stopped with his stubborn chivalry in demanding to pay the bill. He would be her tiger to tame.

As June's MG zipped through the empty mid-day streets of Hounslow, Eddy stayed quiet. Whatever his reason for silence, it gave her time to think. She was attracted to him, but when their instructor-student relationship came to a close he would probably vanish from her life. She didn't want that to happen. What she really wanted was to pass her exam and for him to celebrate by sweeping her up in his arms. She glanced at him, sitting in the cramped passenger seat, looking steadily at the road ahead. He seemed perfectly content to do nothing more. She rested her left hand on the shift, longing to reach across those few inches to touch him as they sped along.

At Hanworth she parked outside Hangar C, turned off the engine and looked at him. "You haven't said a word since you got in the car. Are you all right? I hope it wasn't my driving."

"Sorry. No, of course not." He began to get out of his seat. "I'm afraid I haven't been very good company."

"No, you haven't." She stepped over the door in her usual lithe fashion and came round the car to meet him. "Maybe I should give you something to cheer you up." She took his face in her hands. His immediate stillness told her she had startled him, so she put her lips to his and kissed him. Their kiss lingered, and he slid his arms around her and pulled her tight. When he let her go, she couldn't stop gazing at him. And it seemed to be the same for him.

"Better?" she whispered.

"*Bien sur*," he whispered back.

As impetuous as her kiss had been, she was certain then that she done the right thing. She gave him a radiant smile. "You'll have to meet Daddy very soon, I think." Then she got back into the MG but Eddy hadn't moved. He was standing beside the car, locked in place with his gaze fixed on her and his expression appearing very much bemused. She found it cute that he was reluctant to part, for she was as well, but they both had obligations and besides, their first kiss had been quite perfect—short and very sweet. She blew him one more kiss and drove away.

~ ~ ~

Three days later, the Aeronca was climbing steadily; today June sat in the pilot's seat and Eddy was observing her from the other. The altimeter now showed five thousand feet, the skies were clear, and wind was less than ten knots. A perfect flying day and a perfect day altogether since June had greeted him with a kiss when she had arrived at Hanworth thirty minutes earlier. His gaze was fixed on the RPM and engine temperature dials, but he had no idea what he was doing. When he licked his lips he tasted her lipstick. His own skin smelt of hers. His temples pounded as he remembered looking into her hazel eyes, smoothing back her wavy brown hair, and kissing her. Every minute until they kissed again would be torture.

"Well," June said. "I'm disappointed."

"What?" Eddy asked, jolted back from his musings. June had lit a flame in him like nothing he had felt before but that had to be put aside. This was her first time in charge of the cockpit's controls and his duty to supervise her was paramount.

"There's really nothing special about the pilot's seat."

"What do you mean?" Eddy asked.

"It is just as cramped as the one I usually sit in."

It was at times like this, when Eddy first allowed a student to take control, that he most appreciated the Aeronca's side by side seat plan. It let him watch how a student checked the dials and made adjustments to the ailerons, rudder or power. He got a keen sense of their confidence, or nervousness. June had made all the proper pre-flight checks and accelerated smoothly along the runway to takeoff. So far, her performance had been perfect, and self-assured, and he was proud of her.

He chuckled. "What is special is that you are in control of all the instruments to keep us flying safely."

"I am. You told me to climb, and we are still climbing. What altitude do you want me to level out at?"

"At least nine thousand feet. The Aeronca's not designed to go much higher. This lesson is going to be about stalls and what to do about them, and we need plenty of height, so we will be safe to practice."

"Does that mean plenty of time to recover if I get it wrong?"

"Exactly." Eddy glanced at her profile, the subtle upturn of her nose, and the rosy blush on her beautiful cheek. Don't! he admonished himself. The cockpit was only safe if it was all business. "You told me that when you were learning to drive you stalled your car."

"Lots of times, in the first couple of days. The MG likes to trip me up even now, if I don't balance my pedals properly after a stop."

"That is a mechanical stall. It's not what is going to happen today." He had told her to read up on aerodynamic stalls in preparation for their lesson, and her nod of understanding told him she had done it. He continued. "You've studied aerodynamics. You know it's the differences between airflow and pressure, above and below the wings, that enable us to fly. But to experience a stall we're going to pitch the plane's nose upwards, to the point where those differences no longer generate lift."

June leveled the Aeronca when the altimeter showed nine thousand feet. They were skimming through a layer of small white and fluffy clouds.

"Pay attention. I want you to feel what happens. The engine will not stop, but if we don't make adjustments smartly, the nose will drop, and we'll spin towards the ground." Eddy pulled the yoke and angled the nose up but without adding any throttle. "Now, tell me what you can feel. What's the plane doing?"

"It feels wobbly. And the controls are mushy."

"Good. What else?"

"The sound of the wind is different. Less powerful."

"That's right. Now."

The Aeronca's nose dropped.

"Oh! I don't like that."

"Push the yoke forward, smoothly. Pull back on the throttle to give us more power."

June did so, and the plane leveled out safely.

"Perfect. June, I must say, you are becoming a pilot."

Her smile lit up the cockpit. "Can we land this plane now so I can kiss you?"

Desire for her washed over Eddy; he simply couldn't deny it. He thought of landing as she suggested for a second but compromised by reaching for her hand. "Later, Miss Stephenson. Climb back to nine thousand. We'll practice the stall again. We're going to do it two or three more times; after that, we'll see."

"Yes, mister flight trainer."

Under his instruction June performed the stall recovery procedure again. This time he got her to turn the plane downwind, so the nose dropped much more than it had on the first stall. June handled it well. He put her into a stall a third time and again she corrected it without help. Eddy was pleased with her increasing skill, though he knew his judgment was clouded by his own anticipation of landing the plane and embracing her to celebrate a job well done. He took deep breaths to stay on task.

"Lose height now, to get better visibility and find your landmarks," he said. "But maintain our angle of attack, or we'll go into another stall and we won't have the altitude to deal with it."

June dropped the plane's nose slightly, and they picked up speed over the sprawling grounds of Kew Gardens.

"Turn to larboard," Eddy said. "What is your landmark?"

"The big house there." She pointed to a vast, green lawn surrounding a manor house with six imposing white columns. "That's Osterley, isn't it?"

"Yes," Eddy said. "Is it anything like your own family's house—Longmarsh, isn't it?"

"You'll see for yourself on Friday, now won't you?"

"You tease." Eddy pointed forward. "Turn southwest and keep to the eastern edge of Cranford Wood. That way we'll stay clear of the air traffic lanes into Great West Aerodrome. They test aircraft there, so it's a dangerous place to linger."

The plane banked gently. As they came around, June said, "What's that ahead of us? It's odd."

A dark mass, like vapour, was rapidly approaching out of the sun. Eddy realized with shock that it was a mass of birds. He could see the wavering of their wings. "It's a flock of geese!" He pulled the yoke to climb. "Hold on!"

The mass became an array of heavy grayish-brown bodies and beating wings. A bird struck the propeller and thudded into the windscreen. June ducked as the safety glass crinkled across her helmet like a spider's web. The engine roar changed to an unfamiliar note. Eddy punched a hole in the crazed windscreen so he could see out and leveled the plane as best he could, but the prop was spinning unevenly, one blade sheared away. The geese were gone.

The yoke felt slippery. He raised his palm and saw it was running with blood. He wrapped it with his handkerchief and took back the controls.

June sat up, cautiously, pushing glass off her flying suit.

"June! Are you all right?"

"I don't know." There was a hint of panic in her voice. "I can't see where I'm going."

He tried to sound reassuring. "It's all right, darling. I've got the controls. I've pushed the glass away so I can see fine. We're still high enough to glide down safely. It's not far to the Aerodrome, thank God."

He tried the ailerons and the rudder, and was relieved when the Aeronca responded, sluggishly but obediently, like a trusted mount. He scanned the horizon for other air traffic. Nothing, thank goodness. He powered down, heading for the Aerodrome. He would only get one shot at this landing, because there was a sea of tree-tops between them and the runway and the broken propeller wouldn't lift them enough to make another pass. He kept the Aeronca's nose a little higher than usual as he judged their rate of descent and brought her down in a long glide just above the treetops. Then her wheels brushed the runway, the tires took hold, and they rolled to a stop.

He cut the engine, unbuckled his safety straps and reached across to brush the rest of the ruined windscreen off June. He took her head in his hands.

"You're bleeding!" she said.

"It's all right, darling. Just a cut. But you, my darling. Are you all right?"

"I am fine, Eddy." She took off her flying helmet and ran a shaky hand through her hair. "That's more than I can say for the goose."

He laughed. "I'm glad to hear it."

A lorry truck drove up and stopped in front of the damaged Aeronca.

"You all right in there? You've made a mess of your crate, ain't you?" its driver asked.

"Emergency landing. We hit a flock of geese," Eddy said.

"You were bloody lucky to bring her down in one piece."

Privately, Eddy agreed, but he didn't want to say so in front of June. He helped her down from her seat, and said to the driver, "If you'll allow me to use your telephone, I'll arrange to have the plane taken back to Hanworth. Then I'll need to call a taxi."

~ ~ ~

Eddy and June waited under sycamore trees outside the Aerodrome. The unusually warm October weather and peaceful sounds of wind rustling the leaves belied the frenzy of their afternoon and June's still-racing heartbeat. He offered her a cigarette, but she declined.

118

"You seem very calm, considering what you've just been through."

She smiled. "Because I'm with you. I knew you would keep us safe." It was true. When the goose struck, the safety glass had crumpled and fallen over her like a fish net, forcing her back into her seat. Eddy must have taken the controls from her. She had no idea at the time that he had cut his hand, but she guessed it must have been painful, judging from the amount of blood on his white handkerchief. And he had still kept them both safe. The same feeling of safety as when she had been a little girl, climbing into Daddy's lap upon awakening from a bad dream.

He put an arm around her shoulders. "That's very trusting. I hope your father will see it in the same light."

"He doesn't need to know."

Eddy relaxed his hold a little and turned to look at her. "You need to be honest with your parents, June. Flying is a risky activity. You'll run into other problems and I may not always be there to sort them out."

"I hope you will be."

He took her hand. "I do too. Still, you don't want your father to hear about this from someone else."

She kissed him. "I'll have a talk with Daddy before you meet him."

Chapter 20

On Friday afternoon, Eddy was driving his Morris Eight southwest out of Putney. This trip to visit June and her parents was his first long journey in the saloon, and he was well pleased with its smartness and comfort. He grinned to himself, having realized that purchasing the saloon spared him the embarrassment of arriving at the Stephensons' country estate on his worn Unibus scooter.

The A3 wound gently out of the dreary streets of Wandsworth, through the leafy suburbs of Wimbledon and Surbiton and past the turning for Chessington Zoo. Perhaps June would find it amusing to spend a day there with him before he left for RAF Duxford—although, as the zoo was quite close to the Stephensons' place, he realized she was probably very familiar with it and she would end up taking charge, as usual, to be his guide.

Approaching Oxshott, Eddy took out the sketch map June had drawn for him. He must take the next turning, the one towards the heath. She had marked the final turn off that road with a drawing of a giant cedar tree, which was easy to find from a half mile away with its stately branches spread wide like fans. He turned beneath its shade and headed down the graveled drive between laurel and rhododendron bushes. A hundred yards on, at the crest of a little hill, the bushes ended and revealed Longmarsh, the Stephenson family's mansion. Its elegance took his breath away. It was built of light-colored brick in the Georgian style, wide and handsomely symmetrical with a wing each side of the main front door. Ivy vines clad the walls and were neatly clipped at each window. The lane led down to a driveway in front of the house, which circled a lawn with a spouting fountain and a classical figure as its centerpiece.

A beige Rolls Royce with burgundy-red fenders was pulling away from the front door, following the sweeping curve of the driveway round the neatly mown lawn and central fountain, heading up the drive towards him. Eddy moved the Morris well over to the left to let it pass and the chauffeur in the open driving seat acknowledged him with a slight nod, but the person in the body of the limousine had his head down, evidently reading. Feeling suddenly shy, Eddy waited till the Rolls was out of sight before he dared to drive down to the house, and he parked the Morris a long way from the grand portico.

He screwed up his courage and approached the front door. It opened silently before he reached the top step.

"Good afternoon, sir." The manservant in the doorway was dressed in a suit of black with a dazzling white shirt and a bow tie. Eddy, unfamiliar with country house staff, wasn't sure whether he was a butler or footman. At any rate, his manner was cool, not to say stiff. "May I help you, sir?" His tone suggested rather the opposite.

"I have an appointment at four-thirty with Miss Stephenson and her parents."

"Indeed, sir. May I ask your name?"

"Edouard Beane."

"Please wait here, sir. If you would care to sit down?" He indicated a massive wooden chair at the other side of the entrance. "I'll enquire and be back shortly."

Eddy sat down and waited. When the manservant returned his manner seemed to have softened a little. He said, "Follow me, sir."

Eddy followed him into a spacious hall with a patterned marble floor. At its center, a table displayed the largest flower vase of dahlias he had ever seen, an explosion of orange, white, and yellow.

June came skipping down the staircase into the hall, wearing a white blouse with an orange loop pattern tucked into her sleek tan skirt. Eddy thought she looked a perfect picture.

"Eddy!" She hugged him and then turned to the manservant, who was waiting for instructions. "Thank you Rankin—that will be all. Oh, will you ask Mrs. Wilson to bring us tea in the parlour? Now, Eddy, come with me and let's walk in the gardens. Daddy's just finished a business meeting, so he'll need a few minutes."

Rankin retrieved a cream colored cardigan without being asked and handed it to June.

She thanked Rankin, put her cardigan on, took Eddy's hand and led him through the corridor to a door at the rear of the house.

He followed her outside and into a stunning landscape of flowers and greenery. Purple monkshood stood tall above clumps of golden heleniums that burned brightly against the dark, clipped-yew hedges, and there were dahlias everywhere in shades from crimson and orange and yellow to pinks and whites. It made the vase in the hall almost seem shabby and he was astonished to the point of disorientation; she had to pull him along to the path.

"Is something the matter?"

"I've never seen anything like this before. Even in France."

"It is late in the season, but Foster makes sure we still have good color. He's been the gardener here since Daddy bought the place. This is a last fling before the frosts."

"*Que c'est beau!*"

They wandered along the stone pathways.

"It's very, very beautiful," Eddy said. He sniffed the air. "Is there mint growing here? I can smell it but I can't see it."

"Yes. There is lots of it in the vegetable garden on the other side of the hedge."

Where the path met the edge of the terrace, a stone fountain had been planted-up with white begonias, which had filled the bowl instead of water. June led Eddy to the stone balustrade and looked across the lower garden.

"This is my favorite place," June said, "because of the rose beds. In the summer the scent of them, with the lavender and carnations is just gorgeous."

"The view is magnificent. What are those bushes on the other side, the ones with big purple and blue flower-heads?"

"Those are hydrangeas. They last so long, and they always make me happy." She turned to face him. "I came out here this morning, specially. To think."

"What about?"

"About you."

"Good thoughts," he said, lightly.

"I'm serious!"

"So am I," he said.

She paused, and leaned over the balustrade, framed against the autumnal foliage and flowers like an idyllic portrait, one that perfectly displayed her beauty. Her expression was confident yet thoughtful and the breeze blew a lock of hair across her face in just the right hint of whimsy. It was an image he wanted to keep forever, like a snapshot close to his heart.

"It occurred to me," she said, "that I have known you for less than four weeks. But they have been the best weeks of my life."

"Mine, too, my darling."

"You have taught me how to fly, in every sense."

He smiled. "You have no idea how hard it's been for your instructor to stick to his lessons. You are the best student I've ever had. And I also must say—the best in every way."

She took his hands. "Thank you. My handsome flying instructor is a man of many qualities. No wonder I have fallen in love with you."

He drew her close and kissed her. "And I have fallen in love with you. *Tu es belle, mon amour.* I am the most fortunate man in England. But—"

"What? No buts allowed, today of all days."

He drew a deep breath, his gaze scanning the property. "All this— your father's wealth, this house, these gardens, all the luxury you're used to—it frightens me, *mon amour.* By comparison, I have little to offer."

"My heart means more to me than this house and all Daddy's money ever could. And my heart wants you. Even when you go away to the RAF. I'll miss you terribly, but I'll wait. We can be together whenever you have leave."

"You're sure?"

"More than I can ever say." She embraced him.

He nuzzled his nose into her neck, then reluctantly drew back. "That will have to do for now. We must be calm and self-possessed when I meet your parents."

~ ~ ~

Rankin led June and Eddy into the parlour, where June's father and mother were seated on matching velvet-upholstered chairs. Mr. Stephenson rose to greet him.

"How do you do, Mr. Beane?" He shook hands with Eddy. "My wife."

Eddy turned to June's mother and took her hand. "*Enchanté,* Mrs. Stephenson."

"Mr. Beane." Her hand lay limply in his, and after a moment, she withdrew it.

June sat down on the settee and indicated Eddy should join her.

Mr. Stephenson returned to his chair and said, "I gather you are June's flying instructor, Mr. Beane. Tell us; how is she progressing?"

"Very well, indeed, sir. She mastered the basics very quickly and she has earned the opportunity for a solo flight. She will be well-prepared for her licensing examination and I fully expect her to pass."

"That is good to hear," Mr. Stephenson said, but Mrs. Stephenson's pale stare seemed to bore into Eddy. Mr. Stephenson went on. "There is something I want to ask you about. June told us that she was involved in a flying accident."

"It was hardly serious enough to call it an accident," Eddy said. "But, yes, sir, we encountered an unexpected situation."

Mr. Stephenson's eyes narrowed, giving him the look of a seasoned barrister. "In the air, I imagine all unexpected events are dangerous."

"We flew into a flock of geese. One of them hit our propeller and damaged our windscreen."

"June said you landed without power?"

"Oh Daddy! I've told you—everything was quite all right. I wasn't frightened, not a bit."

He addressed Eddy again. "I believe you know Mr. Lawrence?"

"Yes, sir," Eddy said, not quite seeing the connection, but trying to be polite. "He flies a Miles Sparrowhawk out of Hanworth. A most impressive machine."

"Indeed. A racer. He says it achieved a hundred and sixty miles an hour in some competition recently—the King's Cup?" Mr. Stephenson sipped his tea. "Anyway, Lawrence has given me rather more information about your goose incident than June has so far cared to admit."

"I see."

"Such an incident is quite dangerous, grave in fact, is it not?"

June stiffened beside Eddy, and Mrs. Stephenson's limp fingers tightened on her lap. He took warning.

124

"We lost some engine power," Eddy said. "Yes, it could well have been a dangerous situation."

"You were forced to land a damaged aeroplane at an unfamiliar aerodrome. Mr. Lawrence gave his opinion that June's life was in danger as well as your own. I think you ought to explain yourself."

Eddy controlled the tension he felt. "Willingly, sir. First of all, a bird strike is highly unusual."

"How unusual?"

"As unusual as a train running into a tree on the track. I have flown nearly a thousand hours and I have not experienced such a thing before. We lost some power, but we had no trouble gliding to the Great West Aerodrome, and we landed safely."

"About your aeroplane; Lawrence tells me it is American. Was that part of the problem?"

Eddy took a moment to compose himself before answering. June was fidgeting, and he flattened his palm, as if to ask for her patience.

"No, sir. Neither its make nor its design had anything to do with the problem we encountered."

"Wouldn't a machine made here in England have been far more robust? For instance, a Hawk Trainer made by Fred Miles's company?"

"No, sir, I'm sure any light aeroplane would have been equally affected in that situation." Sensing Stephenson's bias against imported machines, he added, "In fact, although Aeronca is an American manufacturer, my plane was built here in England, at Peterborough."

The fact seemed to give Mr. Stephenson pause, so Eddy continued.

"Mr. Lawrence may have mentioned Tiger Lewis, the flight instructor from Hanworth? He was an RAF pilot during the Great War."

"Yes. But I don't think Pamela knows about him, so please go on."

"Well, Tiger—Mr. Lewis—has given flying lessons for many years and is very well respected at Hanworth. I'm sure Mr. Lawrence would confirm that. It was Tiger who recommended I purchase the Aeronca. For one thing, it has side by side seats and that means I can easily observe my students checking the instruments and working controls such as the yoke and the rudder bar. On the other hand, the Hawk that you have heard about is a tandem arrangement, where the instructor sits behind the student and in my opinion is much less able to supervise. What's more, the Aeronca's gliding stability is well known. Your daughter is safer in my plane than in any other of its class." He leaned forward, with an air of determination. "The goose strike we experienced required quick action, of course, but at no time did I believe either of our lives was in danger."

Mr. Stephenson seemed satisfied. It was his wife who shook her head in an unmistakable signal to Eddy that the views of June's parents might not be in concert.

"I hate this flying," she said. "And to think my daughter has taken up with another bloody aviator after the engagement travesty with the first one!"

June stood up. "Enough!" Her fists were clenched, and she was shaking. "Eddy is the best pilot at Hanworth." She turned to her father. "Did your chap Lawrence tell you that? There is no pilot I would rather fly with. Things happen in the sky—and the goose strike was dreadfully unlucky. But I am glad it happened during my training. Eddy showed me how a dangerous situation can be managed calmly and safely. I will be a better pilot for having gone through it!

"And you," June said to her mother, "how dare you throw my broken engagement in my face—in Eddy's presence—when I was the one who broke it off!"

"Calm yourself, dear," Mr. Stephenson said to June. He stood up, and Eddy got to his feet, convinced he was about to be thrown out. However, Mr. Stephenson's voice was quiet as he said, "Mr. Beane. Shall we take a walk in the garden? June—Pamela—by your leave Mr. Beane and I need to have a few words alone."

Mr. Stephenson went out into the garden and Eddy followed him along the path he had trodden with June only half an hour before. The sun had dropped below the level of the yew hedges, and the garden felt chilly.

"I do my research, young man," Mr. Stephenson said, "and June is right about you. The people you work with say you have considerable merit as a pilot. And Lawrence told me that you seemed to have proved your mettle to Commodore Park."

"Thank you, sir."

"June is our only child, Mr. Beane, and we love her dearly." He stopped at the begonia fountain, reached inside his jacket pocket and pulled out a silver cigarette case.

"Would you care for a cigarillo?" The case was engraved with a reclining lion and the initials 'WAS.'

"Thank you," Eddy said. Mr. Stephenson took one himself, then popped open a gold lighter and lit them both.

"You see Beane, we want to protect her. To a fault? I hope not."

"Understandable, sir."

Eddy drew on the cigarillo and coughed convulsively. Mr. Stephenson smiled, with an unexpected twinkle in his eye, and waited for him to recover. "It's not usual to inhale fully, Mr. Beane. As with cigars, you breathe in through the mouth and out through the nose without taking the smoke any deeper. I'm relieved to see that you are not made in the same worldly mould as June's previous young man."

"Thank you, sir," Eddy managed to say, between gasps. Mr. Stephenson puffed and looked away, giving Eddy a moment to become accustomed to his smoke. Eddy took a tiny puff, tasting the fine tobacco before exhaling. These few private minutes with June's father were unexpectedly reassuring. He was far from familiar with the man but something told him they might one day be able to find common ground, despite their vast social class difference. June's mother, however, had emitted only hostility towards him and, more importantly, his relationship with June. He would have to deal with that, and he didn't have the foggiest notion where to begin.

The older man became serious. "Tell me: Is June capable of becoming a pilot?"

"Very much so, sir. She has studied her lessons and applied them on every instructional flight. She is intelligent, as you know better than me, and she has a light touch on the controls. She has earned her opportunity to solo. I have no qualms about letting her take my Aeronca up on her own."

Mr. Stephenson reached into the flower border and picked at some seed heads. "Himalayan poppies. A brilliant blue. A prize indeed when they bloom in late spring, but very difficult to grow south of London." He gathered several of them. "Would you like some seed to try in your garden?"

"I would only waste them, sir, I'm afraid. I am not a gardener, and if I gave the seeds to my Aunt Maddy, she has small children and I suspect the poor plants would be trampled."

"Ah well. I'll give these to Foster and ask him to sow them as soon as he can." Stephenson pushed the seed heads into his jacket pocket. "I believe you are fond of my daughter?"

"She has been my favorite student, sir."

"I'm quite sure of that. But I think she is more than a student to you." Eddy squirmed as if the yew hedges were closing in on him, but Stephenson merely smiled and puffed on his cigarillo. "You probably didn't notice at the time of your—ahem—shared moment with June— but this fountain is in full view from the house windows."

Eddy reddened, and said, "I don't have any excuses to offer, sir."

"Don't be embarrassed. I know it's rather awkward for a father to stick his nose into his daughter's matters of the heart. I'm sure June will have been honest with you, and you knew she broke off her engagement to Dudley Thane more than two months ago. I am sorry that Mrs. Stephenson brought it up."

"Don't worry about that, sir. Actually, I've met Mr. Thane. He turned up at Hanworth a few weeks ago."

"I imagine that was a rather uncomfortable moment." He didn't wait for Eddy to respond. "Young Thane is a Cambridge-educated fellow and he will inherit a large estate. You can't compete with that but, quite frankly, I couldn't either at your age. I suspect that your character might far surpass his. At least, that is how I will judge you, and I'm happy to let things run as they will between you and June. Her mother, on the other hand ... " Mr. Stephenson puffed on his cigarillo and looked Eddy in the eye.

"Thank you, sir," Eddy said. "I appreciate your approval—and your warning."

"Which, you understand, you will pretend I didn't give."

"I understand, sir. I promise I'll do everything I can to be worthy of your daughter—in your eyes, and in Mrs. Stephenson's."

Chapter 21

Their relationship having survived tea at Longmarsh, June's next challenge had been to convince her mother that Eddy was a fit and proper person to escort her to the wedding of the daughter of Mr. Dennison, Mr. Stephenson's business partner. Since the meeting at Longmarsh, Daddy hadn't been a problem but her mother had obstinately refused to let Eddy attend. 'It wasn't suitable.' June argued that she herself didn't know Mr. Dennison or his daughter, the bride, but Mummy and Daddy would be expected to greet all of his business associates, leaving her to twiddle her thumbs. Her mother relented only when June pointed out that Eddy would be off to RAF training in a week.

Now she and Eddy were walking into the church behind her parents, her hand in the crook of his arm.

The four of them were ushered into their pew just behind the bride's family. They knelt and briefly prayed, and when they resumed their seats June took Eddy's hand. It felt a little clammy. Maybe he was overawed by the Cathedral's grandeur, the massive stone columns and marble carvings and the beams of light that poured through the huge stained glass windows, but she thought it was more likely he felt he was the Stephensons' newest display piece since the other wedding guests had certainly been appraising them as they walked from the narthex to the front pews. She didn't think Eddy needed to worry about that though; attention had been fixed on the enormous diamond brooch which her mother had chosen to wear on the bosom of her frock, and which twinkled aggressively from the vee of her fur stole.

A violinist and a pianist struck the sweet opening notes of Edgar's *Salut d'Amour*. "Such a lovely piece," she whispered to Eddy.

"Yes," he said, softly, without the faintest hint of recognition.

June tucked her hand under his arm once more. When he appeared into the Stephensons' entry hall just an hour before, in a dark blue suit cut perfectly to flatter his athletic build, he had looked so striking that even Mummy took a second glance at him. June had anticipated her making scornful remarks about his attire, but Eddy's suit had been a gift from his uncle and was just as apt for one of Daddy's business meetings as it was for the Dennison wedding. His shirt was brilliantly white and set off with a rich burgundy tie. The only thing her mother could find to say was, "Trust a Frenchman to wear a red tie. How flamboyant." June had looked at her mother's diamond brooch and smiled pityingly.

The organ struck up Wagner's processional from *Lohengrin* and June turned to watch Mr. Dennison escort his daughter down the aisle. Her own father stood at the end of the pew, his usual stoic expression softened, and she thought she saw a tear at the corner of his eye. He glanced at her and gave a little smile. She was sure then that having allowed Eddy to escort her today meant Daddy approved of him—even with Mummy standing stiff as a sentinel beside him. Mr. Dennison delivered his daughter to her waiting bridegroom and the bridesmaids and groomsmen arranged themselves with care behind them.

"Dearly beloved, we are gathered together here in the sight of God," began the Minister. Eddy squeezed her hand and for a moment she imagined the two of them at the pulpit, nervously poised to say their vows, with his adoring smile reassuring her that there was nowhere else in the world she would rather be.

She had never felt so sure during her engagement to Dudley Thane. That kind of love had been elusive from the start. "Not tonight, darling, I have an appointment," or "No, my dear, I'm spending the evening with Freeman," or White, or Bailey, or whoever was his current drinking companion. Her ex-fiancé's excuses were endless and they always seemed to have to do with his friends. It became painfully clear which he preferred. His main destination was the club, and his aim was to drink scotch. Her doubts about Dudley had grown, and the qualities that had drawn her to him had vanished.

Eddy was different. He hadn't been in her life for very long, but he craved time together exactly as she did. Even so, he not only understood, but sensed when she needed to be away from him in a way that made them one, yet each their own person. Their impending separation hung over them like the sword of Damocles.

Perhaps they could marry before he joined the RAF. Would Eddy be able to apply to live in married quarters while he was in training?

She had no idea. She sighed, realising that she mustn't let the wedding vows being taken at the altar today persuade her into a situation she couldn't control. And although Daddy had been gracious towards Eddy so far, he would never tolerate a hasty rush into marriage. She would have to let things develop naturally. In time, Eddy's many fine qualities would surely impress even Mummy.

"Wilt thou have this Woman to be thy wedded wife?" the Minister asked the bridegroom. She and Eddy glanced at each other. Only her mother's irritated cough turned their attention back to the ceremony.

Afterwards there was a long photographic session outside the porch at the Cathedral's west end. June and Eddy waited while her father spoke with a heavy-set man wearing a black-silk top hat and their wives stood dutifully at their sides. During the conversation, a young man cut through the crowd towards them. With a sinking heart, June recognized Dudley Thane.

"Hello, June, my dear," he said, extending his hand to her.

"Hello, Dudley," she said, not taking it. His blond hair was too long, and his smile lopsided. Even out here in the open air, she could smell whisky on his breath.

Thane sketched a laugh and shrugged. He looked at Eddy. "I see I have been replaced by the Frenchman."

"Good afternoon, Mr. Thane," Eddy said, coolly.

June recovered her wits and asked, equally coolly, "Well, how have you been, Dudley?"

"Top-notch, dear," Thane said. "I've carried on with my flying. I'm off to the RAF next week."

"That will be splendid for you. Eddy has joined up, too."

"Really?" Thane took a long look at Eddy. "I'm surprised that our Royal Air Force is reduced to taking Frenchmen."

Eddy said, "I've lived in London for six years, Mr. Thane. I am a naturalized British citizen. And my father was as English as you are."

"Oh," Thane said, grudgingly. "I suppose I'll see you in Scotland next week."

"No. I'll be reporting to Duxford," Eddy said.

"Ah. The Volunteer Reserve," Thane said with leisurely scorn. "Then I shan't be seeing you—my base is for officers—educated men. In a few months, I'll be flying Spitfires. Tell you what, old man, make

131

it through basic training and perhaps they'll give you a Stinson or a Rapide for cargo runs to Kenya." He made a sardonic grin at June.

She took Eddy's arm, and Thane said, with mock anguish, "Mercy me. I am supplanted by an uneducated Frenchman. How the mighty are fallen." He looked at June. "Both of us. Tsk, tsk."

"That's enough!" June said. Eddy's arm was tensed with an anger he couldn't express in these surroundings.

"I get the message," Thane said. "Cheery-bye, dear, if that's where your taste lies. Goodbye." He waved a theatrical farewell and disappeared into the crowd.

Chapter 22

The day for June's solo had finally arrived. Eddy had booked her in for early afternoon, so he could use the morning before her arrival to give the Aeronca a good cleaning. He parked the plane outside Hangar C and lined up the supplies: two buckets of water, one mixed with a strong-smelling detergent; a long-handled brush; a step ladder; and cleaning rags. He began in the cockpit, wiping down the dials and the inside of the windscreen.

Tiger shouted to him from inside the hangar. "Frenchy! Telephone call for you."

Eddy climbed down from the cockpit and jumped over the cleaning supplies on his way to the office.

"Hello?"

"Darling, it is me," June said. "Didn't we schedule my solo for half-past twelve?"

"That's right."

"I thought I'd better let you know I may be late. Mummy wants me to have lunch with her. I know it's only eleven o'clock now but I don't think I'll arrive at Hanworth until two, even if I hurry."

"That's okay; I'll wait."

"Will you? Don't you dare go up without me!"

"Don't worry about that!" He was as excited as she was for her solo. "I haven't scheduled anything afterwards. You'll want to celebrate. But your tardiness will cost an extra kiss."

June laughed. "That's no hardship!"

"Drive safely, *mon amour*. I'll see you soon."

"Bye bye."

Eddy hung up the phone, grinning from ear to ear. Just the sound of her voice intoxicated him. He thought back to their series of flying lessons and was proud of how she'd arrived at the airfield so thoroughly prepared, and professional, right from her first day. No student of his had been more ready to solo, and he looked forward to letting her speed down the runway like a falcon released. Very soon, she would pass her licensing exam, and then, when she was no longer his student, he would not have to maintain appropriate instructor decorum for a moment more.

He walked back to the Aeronca, set up the step ladder, and climbed up to swab the wings with detergent.

He whistled *Alouette* as he worked. You would approve of her, *Maman*, he thought happily. June's parents had invited him for dinner, and later in the week June would dine with him at Aunt Maddy's and Uncle Al's house in Peckham. He was sure she would get on fabulously well with his adoptive family, and with Lotte who was nicely settling in as one of them, but he realized, sadly, that those visits would be among their last together. He was due at Duxford in less than a week. So every second counted. He would take her to the theater one night, a concert on another. Definitely a day at the Zoo. Galleries, tea houses, and cafes; they would be together every day and night he could manage.

With the wings of the Aeronca cleaned and rinsed, he inspected the propeller blades. They were new, since the goose strike, and he rotated them to look along their length and confirm neither was bent. He ran his hands over their edges to check for nicks. They were in perfect condition.

Being with June made his life complete. Just sitting with her, holding her hand, as they gazed at each other across the table. Walking with her. Driving his Morris with her sitting next to him. He had never felt so alive.

He did not want to think about their coming separation, but leaving for the RAF weighed on him, especially since Dudley Thane's supercilious greeting at the Dennison wedding. Thane's contempt for Eddy had been evident from his raffish blond coiffure to his Oxford brogues. Was Thane typical of the educated and wealthy 'best sort' whom Air Commodore Park wanted to mold into Spitfire pilots? Park would only ensure Eddy was assigned to a Spitfire squadron if he proved his worth during training. He feared that success would mean he would be thrown in with men like Thane who would deride his primitive education and his Frenchness. That prospect, coupled with his impending separation from June, made him wonder if enlistment in the RAF would prove to be a prison sentence. He sighed, trying to convince himself that when one day he sat at the controls of a Spitfire, everything would work itself out.

He tried to find the positives. Duxford was only a couple of hours' drive from Oxshott, so between June's MG and his Morris he was sure they could manage to be together as often as he had leave. But it might be years before his duties in the RAF ended—especially if there really was a war coming.

His cleaning job was nearly done. Rinsing the Aeronca's tail section with the long brush, his thoughts returned to his girl. Maybe they should marry at once. He was sure the Stephensons could arrange whatever special license was required. Marrying wouldn't prevent him having to leave her when he went north for training, but it would save them having to—well—wait. He smiled to himself when he thought how eager June would be to agree.

He checked his watch. Five minutes to two. She would be here any minute—his astonishing, wonderful darling. He swabbed the last bit of the tail and began gathering up his cleaning supplies. *Alouette, gentille alouette, Alouette, je te plumerai...*

A Rolls Royce drove onto the airfield. With Indian red fenders and beige trim, it was nearly the twin of the one Eddy had seen pull away from Longmarsh, but this car's roof was fully covered, and when the driver opened the rear door, it was Mr. Stephenson who got out.

"Mr. Beane," he said. "Good afternoon."

"Hello, Mr. Stephenson. What a surprise." Eddy set down his bucket and mop and they shook hands.

"I respect a man who cares for his equipment," Stephenson said. "Good show."

"Have you come to watch June's solo flight?"

"I have indeed."

Stephenson retrieved his cigarette case from his jacket pocket.

"I'm sorry, sir, but one must not smoke this close to the plane."

"Oh! Of course. Tell me, Beane, when are you off to the RAF?"

"I report Monday morning, sir."

"It's a heady time to be joining up, young man."

"Yes sir, I know."

"I sometimes meet Anthony Eden down at my club. I assume you know who he is?"

"I've heard his name, sir."

"He was Foreign Secretary until quite recently. He opposed the agreement that Chamberlain made with Hitler in Munich. Wouldn't vote on it last month in the House of Commons."

Eddy remembered Air Marshal Dowding's misgivings about the Munich agreement. "There's a lot of talk about war coming sir."

"Yes. Eden thinks we will have to stand up to Hitler, and the Italians too. If it comes to that, we'll need young men like you to carry the load. So I find it quite admirable that you will be putting on the RAF uniform, young man."

The roar of June's MG engine broke into their conversation, and they both turned towards the sound. June parked by the hangar, stepped over the car door, and hurried towards them.

"Daddy! What a surprise!" She kissed her father on his cheek. "Thank you for coming. How did you ever get away from your business?"

"No trouble, darling. I'm the boss, after all."

She turned to Eddy. "Mister flight instructor." She gave him a rather reserved peck on the cheek in comparison to the kiss she had laid on her father.

"I'll put these things away," Eddy said, gathering back up his cleaning supplies. "June—get dressed and make your pre-flight checks."

"Yes, sir," June said.

Fifteen minutes later, Eddy and Stephenson stood side by side to watch the Aeronca glide down the runway. As its wheels left the turf it waggled for an instant and Eddy heard Stephenson catch his breath, but as the airflow evened out the plane rose steadily. June's climbing angle was perfect, giving Eddy immense pride. She banked gently to larboard, the Aeronca's fuselage gleaming yellow in the afternoon sunshine as she flew past them. Eddy glanced at her father, who was watching with a rapt expression.

"Mr. Beane," Stephenson said, "Tell me about her flight plan. What is she going to do?"

"She will climb to 8,000 feet and turn south as far as Lower Halliford. She'll follow the Thames to Richmond, then she'll turn west and head home."

"What is that, about thirty miles?"

"More or less."

The Aeronca droned away between wisps of clouds and disappeared.

"Am I allowed to smoke now?" Stephenson asked. "While she is—er —airborne."

"Yes sir," Eddy said. "Let's stand over by the hangar where we'll be able to see her coming back in."

Stephenson offered Eddy a cigarillo, which he accepted, and lit them both. They smoked in silence, with Eddy taking care to hold the smoke in his mouth, and exhale through his nose. Stephenson seemed entirely comfortable in his company and Eddy hoped they might be on the road to familiarity.

"Mr. Beane; Eddy. There is an important matter I'd like to discuss," Stephenson said.

Eddy had no idea what was coming. June's solo? Their courtship? He blew smoke and said uncomfortably, "Certainly, sir."

"This is business," Stephenson said. "Your flying business. June has asked me to purchase your aeroplane. Would you entertain an offer?"

Eddy hid his relief. "Oh, yes sir. June is very capable. And yes, I'd entertain an offer. In fact, there's no one I would rather have in charge of the Aeronca." He paused, hearing the familiar drone of the Aeronca's engine. The yellow fuselage was visible in the sky to the east and was rapidly approaching the airfield. Stephenson followed his gaze and turned to watch the plane. Eddy hoped Mr. Stephenson's appreciation included him—the direction of their business transaction—and June's progress under his instruction.

Was Stephenson beginning to consider him worthy of his daughter?

Eddy and Stephenson tamped out their cigarillos and walked back to the end of the runway. Landing was June's final test. Eddy's heart beat quicker as the Aeronca drew nearer. June had been well prepared but the moments of powering down and pointing the machine's nose towards the approaching earth were nervy even for an experienced pilot. June cut the throttle, and the roaring of the engine stopped. The plane's nose dropped a little more than Eddy had expected.

"My God!" said Stephenson. "She's falling from the sky!"

137

Eddy patted his arm. "No, she's fine, sir, look. She cut power correctly. The plane is gliding now and its forward airspeed will be enough. Just a few more seconds."

The Aeronca touched down with only the slightest bounce. At the end of the runway, June turned quietly and taxied towards them. Her megawatt smile could be seen even through the windscreen. Mr. Stephenson slapped Eddy on the back and said, "That's my girl!"

Eddy opened her door of the Aeronca and held June by the waist as she jumped down. Then he gave the love of his life a celebratory kiss.

Chapter 23

The weekend passed in a flurry of drives with stops for tea, dinner at Longmarsh followed by a lengthy walk in its gardens, and frequent exchanges of words of commitment.

On the Monday morning June drove with Eddy in her MG to RAF Duxford. Arriving at the crushed gravel parade ground, she parked boldly in front of the flagpole at the entrance to the main building, but that was as far as her courage would carry her. Once she had switched off the ignition, she and Eddy sat in silence. There was much to say, but words wouldn't console her for their imminent parting. He would become a denizen of one of the many accommodation buildings they had passed, eighty miles from her family's home; a world away.

Eddy drew his handkerchief and offered it to her. "I think you need this, *mon amour*."

She said, uncertainly, "Am I crying? Dear me."

"It's okay, darling," Eddy said. "I'll keep a stiff upper lip for both of us."

"I promised myself I wouldn't."

"Cry if you must, darling. It's just as sad for me."

She fought back a sniffle. "I've had you for a month and it's been the best time of my life—and now—"

She felt her heart would break with loss. During their short time together, the meaning of her life had changed. She craved time with him. It was her happiness. How could she adjust back to being alone? She was already missing him.

Eddy lifted her hand to his lips and kissed it. "I'll think of you constantly dear. Time moves so fast; we'll be together again when I have leave and that will come before you know it. It will be hard to be apart but I'll squeeze every bit of knowledge out of the RAF that I can. Think of it as my duty for our future."

She leaned towards him and he kissed her.

"It's time for me to go. *Souviens-tu—Je t'aime.*"

"I love you," she said, and slowly let him go.

Eddy got out of the MG and collected his small duffle bag from the boot. He walked back to her, kissed her through the open window and disappeared into the building.

She started the car but didn't dare yet put it in gear. Her stomach was churning and she needed to collect her thoughts. A fighter plane passed overhead with a roar, reminding her that Eddy would be flying RAF aircraft that were many times faster than their Aeronca. The fighter banked into a turn so sharply that she could see the top of its glass canopy. Her man would soon fly with the same dangerous verve. What would it cost him, to gain the aviation knowledge he was seeking? She would miss his company, his touch, his kiss, but she feared every bit as much for his safety.

~ ~ ~

Eddy completed his entry papers and handed them to the clerk. He was directed to a white-washed barracks, and when he stepped inside he saw a large room containing two rows of bunk beds, the ends facing each other in a tidy symmetry. Some were already taken by other young men. Halfway down the room he found an empty one, with a footlocker labeled "E Beane" next to one labeled "P Grace." Its meaning was clear so he stowed his few possessions. June had been gone only thirty minutes, but already he was living in a different world.

Another young man came in and approached and examined the top bunk. He wore a bespoke suit set off with a brilliant blue tie, his hat was in his hands and the way he held himself reminded Eddy of the men in the drawing room at Air Commodore Park's London club. Then he turned and appraised the room and the other men with a thoughtful and confident expression.

The man glanced at the names on the footlocker then looked at Eddy. "Mister Beane?"

"Yes. Eddy. And you are Mister Grace?" Eddy asked.

"Phillip Grace," the well-dressed man replied. "Mind if I take the top bunk?"

"Not at all, the bottom suits me fine."

Grace began to transfer items from his leather travel bag into his footlocker. "Do I detect—*un accent français?*"

Eddy sighed. "I was raised in France but have lived in England many years now."

The young man's manner and immediate inquiry into his nationality brought Dudley Thane strongly to mind. Grace looked every bit the aristocrat Thane was, but Eddy couldn't figure out what he would be doing at RAF Duxford. Wasn't Phillip Grace well-educated, like Thane? He should be training with the toffs. Why wasn't he with the officer candidates, in Scotland or wherever Thane was?

A stream of other men had entered the barracks room in the meantime and they too were unpacking. They were mostly dressed like Eddy was, in slacks with wool jackets that were tidy rather than expensive. Now there were maybe forty altogether. Several looked to Eddy like lads about to spend their first nights away from home, wide-eyed like deer caught in headlights. He realized that although he wasn't as self-assured as Phillip Grace, the two of them were streets ahead of the others in confidence.

A man in uniform came into the barracks and closed the door sharply. He stood in the middle of the room, straight as a ramrod. He had slits for eyes and lips pressed together like the sides of a vise.

"Ten-shun! Front of your bunks!"

The men moved quickly to stand at the end of their bunks, chins up and hands at their sides.

"Now listen carefully you shabby lot! You will see two "Xs" marked on the Parade Ground. You have sixty seconds to form a straight line between them. There's the door. Go!"

The young men rushed out the door and scrambled in a disorganized pack towards the marked "Xs." A short lad just in front of Eddy stumbled and fell into a puddle and Eddy was about to land on top of him when Grace caught his arm and kept him upright.

"Come on Beane!" Grace said. "Let's take our places."

Eddy stood next to Grace in a line of young men facing their humorless leader.

"You will call me Sergeant Shaw. I am responsible for you lot." Shaw approached the line and stopped in front of the short young man. He flicked a forefinger at the clot of mud on the man's cheek. "Shabby lot indeed. What's your name, son?"

"Declan Potter, sir."

"Where from?"

"London."

The sergeant flicked at the lank brown hair peeking over Potter's ear. "A street urchin. You are in the countryside now, Potter, one of the sheep, and you'll be sheared like one."

Shaw addressed the whole group again. "Welcome to the Royal Air Force's Duxford airfield. You've each enlisted as a pilot candidate. That's all well and good, but it's not my concern. To fly for the RAF, you must first learn the ways of the military. Fitness and discipline. You will have a full measure of both before you leave my care. And before you even touch an aeroplane. First of all," he looked at Potter, "you'll be cleaned and put into proper dress."

Shaw strolled to his right and stopped in front of Grace. He looked him up and down and Grace looked back with total composure. Shaw said, "The dungarees you are about to put on won't come from your fancy London tailor. You'll all be equal once you're in uniform. Isn't that right, lad?"

"Yes, sir," Grace said.

"Hmm. Squad! Follow me to the quartermaster. About turn. Quick march."

They did their best to obey. Eddy found himself marching behind Phillip Grace in his finely-woven wool jacket. Shaw had made it very clear that money and class were not going to be advantages here. Despite the discipline the RAF was clearly going to impose, the idea of equality was reassuring. There was also the fact that Grace had helped Eddy to avoid the embarrassment that the mud puddle had brought on Potter. Neither of them would have to face the trials of Sergeant Shaw alone.

Chapter 24

Nine months after leaving London for his RAF training, Eddy and Grace were going out of the small graystone boardinghouse where they were billeted in a little village on the east coast of Scotland. Grace, his roommate, called it "their bonny little quarters." The accommodation was spartan, with its iron bed frames and white ceramic wash-basin, but other than that they had little to complain of. Mrs. Gibson kept the sheets clean and fed them well.

It was just after breakfast and the morning was already charged with excitement, more so than any other since Eddy had joined the RAF at Duxford in Cambridgeshire. Today, he and Grace were to have their first solos in a Spitfire.

The wind was whipping off the firth, and Eddy drew his jacket collar tighter against the cold. "Summer? My eye! It's bloody cold."

"Ah, this is like the gulf stream, old man," Grace said. "It's colder at home in Northumberland this morning; bet on it." His usual good-natured smile was bright with anticipation.

Grace had occupied the top bunk over Eddy for the whole of the eight months they spent at Duxford. The group of young men had started each day by assembling on the parade ground in their polished boots and buckles at seven o'clock to endure forty-five minutes of Sergeant Shaw's ridiculous marching drills. "Tin soldiers," Grace had called them. After marching, it had been classes and flying instruction. In the afternoon there was sport, and evening study, with lights out at ten.

They had somehow survived Shaw's methods, but not his derision. He called Eddy "Froggie" and Grace "Yer Lardship." Eddy put up with it fairly well because Shaw derided all the other men equally. He also had tolerated Duxford's sixteen hour days because they were only a little more demanding than his time in tailoring and at Hanworth, but Grace was an Oxbridge man, like Dudley Thane, and for him the new routine was a shock. So on the days when Grace was too worn out to polish brass and leather, for inspection, Eddy had offered to do it for him. In return, Grace helped Eddy shore-up the gaps in his education when Duxford's training required mathematics and physics.

Their friendship had flourished in affable insults about Grace's laziness and Eddy's relative illiteracy, and mutual commiseration about Shaw and his routine bullying. Grace hadn't spoken about his family much, though Eddy had heard another pilot refer to the Grace family's Northumberland estate as "vast." The only clue Grace had given Eddy about his lifestyle was a proclamation he'd once made that life's greatest pleasures were "a good grouse-shoot and hooking a fat salmon," activities that Eddy had never experienced and presumed were pastimes of the wealthy. And Grace hadn't asked Eddy much about his family.

Eddy never did learn why an educated man, like Grace, would be at Duxford training with men who had come through the Volunteer Reserve, rather than being groomed for an officer role with other educated gentry who joined as regular flyers. Grace hadn't offered an explanation and Eddy hadn't pressed him for one. Most important to Eddy had been that Grace had shown him that not all young aristocrats behaved as badly as Dudley Thane.

After eight months at Duxford, Eddy's orders had come in and he was assigned to an airbase in Scotland north of Edinburgh, where both regular RAF pilots and pilots from the Volunteer Reserve would be trained on Spitfires. Eddy and Grace had been assigned to the same airbase, and they'd been together nearly all the time since arriving in Scotland.

"I don't know about Northumberland," Eddy said, "but it's warmer out here than in our room."

Grace laughed and said, with sudden energy, "I hear a Spitfire calling me. Let's be off."

His saloon car was parked beside the narrow street, and he and Eddy set off on their drive to the airbase. They passed rock-outcroppings, spiky coverts of gorse and thick tufts of fescue. Neither man spoke. Each was lost within himself, already feeling the adrenalin of take-off.

Eddy's years of flying gave him confidence in his abilities but, still, soloing in a Spitfire was a challenge that would give any pilot pause. His tandem training with instructor Sergeant MacLeod these past weeks had been his aviation awakening. He had climbed to heights where ground details vanished—and as a result, learned why he had to deal with a cumbersome oxygen mask. During his first dive in a Spitfire, G-forces had pinned him to the back of his seat. And Mac had laughed at his shock. By now Eddy had come to grips with the aeroplane's capabilities. The Spitfire's look, acceleration and handling were outstanding. And the boom of its engine made his Aeronca and even the Miles Magister he had trained on at Duxford seem mere whispers in comparison.

Throughout his training he had heard talk that recent events were forcing Fighter Command to put new pilots into the cockpits of Spitfires much sooner than had been done in the past. Air Marshals Dowding and Park had no choice. Hitler had taken Czechoslovakia for his own in March of 1939, just a few months before. War with Germany seemed more probable each new day, and the British had to have adequate numbers of fighter pilots trained up to deal with the Luftwaffe. Eddy wondered if all the men were as ready as he was.

He stared at the crags and gorse along the route and hoped he was up to it.

~ ~ ~

"Remember, laddy," said Sergeant MacLeod, in a strong Glaswegian accent, "she's a greyhound. Open 'er up gently."

"I'll remember," Eddy said.

"Be in fine pitch," Mac said. "O'erwise, the runway won't be long enough."

Just two days ago, a new man called Ross hadn't switched from coarse to fine pitch and had slammed into the beach, destroying himself and the aircraft.

"Now, man, yer no a nit-wit. I'll just remind you to bring 'er back in one piece."

Eddy took a deep breath and faced the bank of dials, gauges, levers and rods, all of which he had mastered through dozens of hours of classroom instruction. They were his responsibility now, and his only friends in the air—there was no one else to rely on. He reached up to pull the canopy forward, shutting it against the summer sky and other Spitfires overhead that flickered like diamonds in the sun. He

145

pressed the starter. Orange and yellow flames poured from the exhaust and ran alongside the fuselage.

He flipped off the parking brake, held the spade stick steady and pulled the throttle open, and began to taxi towards the runway. The Rolls Royce engine bellowed and he adjusted left aileron and left rudder as he had been taught, equalizing the monster torque of the propeller that forced the Spitfire's right wing downwards. Once she was in mechanical synch, he pointed her down the runway, gaining speed with the airframe vibrating slightly and the wheels rattling over the grass. Her wings lifted effortlessly and she was airborne.

He sought a light fingertip touch on the sensitive elevator while he muscled the ailerons into setting. A pilot's harmony with his plane's instruments could never be learned in the classroom. It was born of experience, tact, and physical balance. Up, up, climb—he could hear Mac's dry advice in his head. "Don't clip our hangar roof, now, 'cause I dun't have time for a mess."

Eddy had no intention of making "a mess."

The Spitfire carried him clear and rose elegantly into the sky to join the others, flying towards the coast. He found he had been holding his breath. Over his right shoulder, Grace's plane was five hundred yards back. He eased back the throttle, pumped the undercarriage into place, kept the plane's ailerons and roll axis level, and tried consciously to relax. He thought briefly that Mac would be pleased with how he had climbed.

The Spits were racing above the graystone houses of the village. Mossy green earth gave way to gray crags and chalky cliffs and the white, foaming line where the ocean's green-tinged fluorescence turned to solid blue.

Eddy checked his altimeter as he climbed. He pierced a gap in the altocumulus, its white puzzle pieces bordered in dark blue. The temperature dropped three degrees for every thousand feet of height, but he hardly noticed the chill as he tended the controls and searched the sky above for the Spitfires he was to join. They were flying three Angels higher. The pre-designated flight ceiling was Angels twenty, or twenty thousand feet.

Reaching their level, Eddy had to position his plane at the wing-tip of his Squadron Leader. If his airspeed was too high, he risked overtaking the formation and missing his mark. He aimed his Spit's nosecone at the roundel at the front of his leader's fuselage, smoothly let off the throttle to reduce his speed, and eased into his place aside the leader. Only a slight tipping of his wings betrayed his inexperience. 'Relax,' he told himself, and took a deep breath.

The formation leveled and flew straight for several minutes. The leader was ahead of him to the left, another plane behind him to his right. Nine more were behind that one, creating what would look to people on the ground like a slash in the sky. Grace, in plane T 202, was among them.

At a word from the squadron leader the formation banked to larboard, and Eddy had to mind his gap between the planes as they crossed over the beach and descended west towards the airfield. The Spitfires spread apart to approach for landing one by one.

They were powering down. A good first flight. Exhilarating, quickly over, but landing required the same attention to control and finesse that he'd needed for takeoff. Five thousand feet and dropping rapidly. He assessed the rush of wind along his canopy as he balanced the pull of gravity and the speed of his approach.

An unfamiliar high-pitched wail broke his concentration. To his right, a Spitfire was diving steeply. He saw it had Grace's tail number.

"For God's sake pull up," Eddy said aloud. The dive continued, the wail rising in pitch for ten horrific seconds. Then the plane hit the ground and exploded.

Eddy could hardly breathe.

The green infield seemed to him to grow larger, threatening to swallow his own plane. Only thousands of hours of flying experience enabled him to mechanically complete his procedures of dropping the undercarriage, putting the engine in fine pitch, and lowering the flaps.

He landed, parked, unstrapped and climbed down, and ran towards the outfield where the ruins of Grace's plane lay burning. He stood helplessly next to Sergeant MacLeod.

"Can't 'splain it. Was sure that one could fly," Mac said.

Eddy, reaching back to the childhood consolation of churchgoing, murmured the Rosary under his breath. Part of him was gone. Phillip Grace had been at his side during RAF training for going on a year. He hadn't been able to rely on June for that, nor his family in Peckham. With Grace he had toiled and sweated and laughed and enjoyed the pleasure of a smoke and a drink in their rare nights off base. Their training had formed a common ground and despite their class difference the two young men had become friends.

But Grace was gone—abruptly and permanently removed from Eddy's life—forcing him to face his RAF future alone.

His squadron had suffered three fatal crashes in a week. Chappie had landed with his undercarriage up and spun across the grass like a Catherine wheel until his Spitfire burst into flames. Ross had crashed on the beach. And now Grace.

God alone knew why.

He couldn't face going back to the house yet. Grace's crash was tragic and a shock, and there were too many questions. Everyone would ask them, and there were no answers. He needed to be alone, to try to come to terms with what had just happened. He had to stick out another month of flying training before his scheduled leave, so he would have to be ruthless with himself and get in the right mindset to survive. If he did, he could return to London to see June Stephenson. Then he could soak up the preciousness of life. And get ready to fly again.

Chapter 25

June and Eddy waited in the foyer at Claridge's to be escorted to her father's table. Eddy stood straight and serious. To June he seemed an imperial vision in his sleek, air-force blue dress uniform. It was the last day of August 1939, and ten months of training in the RAF had darkened his moods, adding a seriousness he hadn't had before. June knew it would be up to her to bring levity and affection back into her airman.

Perhaps afternoon tea with her parents wouldn't be too bad. She had resisted Daddy's invitation at first, worrying that Eddy might be outside his comfort zone, but Daddy had insisted, and it wasn't in either of their interests to refuse. She hoped her suggestion that Eddy wear his dress uniform would help him to face tearoom decorum under Mummy's critical gaze.

The host led them into Claridge's fashionable art deco reading room which had pale yellow walls, a brilliant white paneled ceiling, and an immense glass chandelier. The room was filled with guests, but quieter than June expected. Perhaps people were feeling oppressed by the recent alarming news that Germany was mobilizing for war on the continent.

Her parents were sitting at the center table and Mr. Stephenson rose to greet them. He kissed June on the cheek and said to Eddy, "Hello Sergeant Beane. I am glad you could join us."

"Hello, sir. Thank you for this very kind invitation." They shook hands. Eddy greeted Mrs. Stephenson, who responded with a faint smile. June had to concede Mummy had come a long way as far as Eddy was concerned. She acted civilly towards him now, especially when he was in RAF full-dress. Once, after Eddy's visit to their house in Oxshott, Mummy had even confided in June that it was 'a pleasure' to see her daughter so happy. It was taking far longer than June had hoped it would, but Mummy's resistance to Eddy seemed to be waning.

The tearoom was filled with finely-dressed patrons, with hardly a seat to spare around any of the tables. June noticed several men in uniform among them, but none were wearing RAF blue.

A tea set was placed on the table, and a waiter wearing an immaculate white jacket served up.

"Your uniform becomes you, Sergeant," said Daddy.

"Thank you sir," Eddy said, and added with a smile, "though it's not nearly as comfortable as the dungarees and work shirt I used to wear at Hanworth."

"June tells me you are flying Spitfires now."

"Yes, I am being trained to fly Spits." Recognizing Daddy's expectant look, Eddy added, "They are fast and manoeuvrable. Magnificent machines."

"You've done well since you joined up. Has it really been five months since we last saw you?"

"About that, sir."

"Very good," Daddy said. "The newspapers are warning that the Germans are brewing for trouble. How do you young men feel about that?"

"We've heard those reports, too. If war is declared because of the Germans, we will be ready to face them."

June tried to look as confident as Eddy, but the prospect of war chilled her. She knew nothing of war except that many men would die and losing Eddy would destroy her. She felt a duty to project strength and keep his spirits up but didn't know if she had it in her.

Another trolley arrived and a three-tiered rack was presented: on the bottom, finger sandwiches filled with poached salmon, or boiled eggs, or cucumber and ham; in the middle, olive bread and cheese spreads, apricots, figs and a variety of scones, and sweets on top, including tarts and delicious-looking Battenberg Cake. Eddy brightened at the sight of the elegant presentation, and after June and her Mummy served themselves, he filled a small plate with some of each delicacy.

"Edouard," said June's Mummy, after a server wheeled the cart away, "It does sound as though you have done well in the RAF but our friends the Wallaces and the Purifoys have sons in the RAF who fly Spitfires like you do and they hold the rank of Lieutenant. Why are you not a Lieutenant too?"

June sighed with exasperation at Mummy's never-ending fixation on matters of appearance. She probably knew the answer to her own question. How could Mummy ever endure a luncheon or an afternoon tea if the discrepancy between Eddy's rank and those of the university-educated sons of her matronly friends might be mentioned? June was about to come to Eddy's defense when a good-looking man with a thick, dark mustache approached the Stephenson's table.

"William! Good to see you, old man," he said.

"It is good to see you, too, Anthony," Daddy said. "Pamela dear, you know Anthony Eden, don't you?"

"Of course," Mummy said. Eden shook her hand. June noted that her Mummy hadn't asked about his wife. Mummy was an expert in reading people and situations, and June was certain there was a reason.

"Anthony, may I introduce my daughter June," Daddy said.

"I'm very pleased to meet you, June" Eden said, taking her hand briefly.

"And June's escort is Sergeant Edouard Beane."

"Beane, Beane," Eden said, as though searching his memory. "Aha! You're one of Park's men." They shook hands, with Eden prolonging the clasp a moment longer than June would have expected. "Excellent. I've read your reports, Beane. You had some interesting adventures over foreign territory, didn't you?"

Eddy nodded.

June was astonished and judging by her parent's wide-eyed expressions they were equally puzzled.

"Your photographs have been most helpful," Eden said. "I see Park has got you into uniform. Splendid. We need men of your quality flying for us. Things are about to boil over with that bloody little man Hitler. Speaking of which, I'm afraid I must be off."

Eden bowed to June's parents. "It was nice to see you again."

"Indeed it was," Daddy said.

As Eden left, he put a hand on Eddy's shoulder. "Good luck, Beane."

June's parents were both looking at Eddy. Mummy's expression in particular had brightened, as though acquaintance with Anthony Eden had doubled his social value. Finally, she said: "Edouard, this is a surprise. You didn't tell us you worked for Air Marshal Park. And you know our former Foreign Secretary? And whatever did you photograph? I wish you would tell us more."

Daddy sighed and touched her hand. "Pamela, my dear, I don't believe Edouard is at liberty to tell us what he has done for Air Marshal Park. I suspect Anthony may have mentioned something we should not know. Let's keep this bit of information to ourselves."

"Thank you, sir," Eddy said, with evident relief.

June, on the other hand, was delighted. Mummy was, for the first time, smiling at Eddy.

~ ~ ~

Eddy too had noticed the warmer attitude of Mrs. Stephenson. He and June exchanged parting phrases with her parents outside Claridge's, and as the Stephensons' Rolls Royce drove off he reflected that he and Mr. Stephenson were becoming quite comfortable with one another. If he was also making inroads with June's mother, all the better. Hopefully the afternoon with her parents had been one more step towards being together with June forever.

"It's a lovely afternoon, dear," June said. "Let's walk to Grosvenor Square."

"Yes," Eddy said, taking a deep breath. "Even though that went well, let's do anything rather than sit at a table and make small talk."

They strolled up Brook Street towards the square, holding hands. He was still savoring June's mother's adieu at Claridge's: "I trust we will see you again soon, Edouard. Take care of yourself." She had continued to smile at him. It seemed that Anthony Eden's recollection of him had finally convinced her to unbend.

June asked, "Will you have to keep secrets from me, too? Or will you tell me?"

"What about? Oh, you mean my work for the Air Vice Marshal?"

"Of course," June said. "I need to know whether I am in love with a spy, or a secret agent!"

Eddy hesitated. He had often wanted to tell June about his photography missions, rescuing Lotte, stealing the Mercedes and being shot at on the Trier airfield, but he knew Air Vice Marshal Park would not approve. Park had never strictly forbidden him from speaking about his photography over Germany, but clearly, he would expect that information about the missions should be kept close. More recently, when Eddy had joined the RAF, he had signed documents that bound him to secrecy over national security matters. On top of that, he was familiar with all the Government warnings about "careless talk costs lives."

"As your father said, I'm not at liberty to talk about it, my love. But someday, I'll tell you the full story. I promise."

"If that's the best you can do, be warned; I'll hang around just to hold you to it."

They entered Grosvenor Square between borders of neatly-trimmed shrubs that still carried a few late-season blooms. Pathways led through the manicured lawns and were populated with other late afternoon strollers. Bordered by commercial buildings, a school and an embassy, the square was a green oasis in the midst of stone and concrete.

June stopped and reached into her bag. "I have something for you."

"Oh?"

She handed him a long white scarf. "I'm told its dreadfully cold at the altitudes where your Spitfire flies. Will you wear this, and think of me?"

"Of course I will. Thank you." Eddy kissed her with an intensity that the passers-by nudged each other and smiled. He saw nothing of them, because June held him tightly and he sensed a wanting in her that matched his own. She put a hand on his cheek and said, "You have won her over."

Eddy drew back slightly. "Who? Your mother?"

"Yes, of course. Mr. Eden's behavior convinced her. It was quite perfect."

"If that means she won't stand in our way any longer, I'm over the moon."

"That is exactly what it means," June said. "She'll give you her blessing now."

Eddy kissed her again. Then he dropped to a knee and took her hand. "June, my darling, will you—"

She pressed her fingers to his lips. "You need to talk to Daddy."

PART II

1940

"Was there perhaps a new race of Englishmen arising out of this war, a race of men bred by the war, a harmonious synthesis of the governing class and the great rest of England; that synthesis of disparate backgrounds and upbringings to be seen at its most obvious best in R.A.F. Squadrons?"

—Flight Lieutenant Richard Hope Hillary (20 April 1919 - 8 January 1943)
    A Battle of Britain RAF Pilot

Chapter 26

The twelve Spitfires of 57 Squadron were approaching RAF Hawkinge in echelon. At the command of Squadron Leader Patrick "Dobbers" Dobson they broke formation, banked into the wind, and landed one by one on the grass of the airfield in front of a giant hangar painted in drab green and brown camouflage. Eddy Beane taxied across to join the rest of the Squadron.

It was his first trip to RAF Hawkinge, a vast meadow outlined by trees, situated only three miles from the English Channel. Seagulls circled above one of the buildings: that must be the mess. On the south perimeter, machine guns poked over stacked sandbags like stray twigs on a bird's nest.

Eddy unstrapped his harness and climbed down, breathing in the briny smell of the sea.

Two other Squadrons of Spitfires were also parked near the hangar, and just beyond them, men were transferring caissons, boxes and barrels from the holds of four large cargo planes into the back of lorry trucks.

Dobbers had gone inside the hangar but Eddy joined his Squadron mates who stood clustered around James "Tank" Roberts.

"I'll bet that lot's come from the boys in Calais," Tank said. "The Jerries must have really got 'em boxed-in over there."

"I suppose that's why we're here," said James "Hondo" Hundley. "Uxbridge won't have sent us down here to sit on the beach."

Eddy lit a cigarette and listened to their conversation with equal parts excitement and trepidation. He had just completed months of aerial combat training in Scotland and now that he had been posted to an active squadron he was ready to put his new skills into action.

In recent weeks, Eddy had met pilots who had been flying missions in France. They all knew the Germans were advancing through Western Europe. French Curtiss and Morane fighter planes had been no match for German Messerschmitts; nor had the British Defiants.

Germany now dominated the skies over France, and Eddy thought it was very likely that Nazi tanks were now rolling down the peaceful streets of Hazebrouck, the small town not far from the *Nord* coast where he had lived his first sixteen years. If the German forces weren't held back, they would keep going and subjugate him and his adoptive British family. He had been face to face with SS and Gestapo men before war was declared, and even then the cold eyes and hard lines on their faces had convinced him that they could only be stopped with brute force.

His fellow pilots might be as impatient as he was to fly and fight, but for them it was part of the defence of Britain, while for him, it was also Nazis on French soil that made the battle personal. He was burning to avenge Nazi aggression and defend the country of his birth.

But Eddy and his Squadron mates hadn't yet been called on. Dobbers had kept reminding them: "The brass hats are keeping our Spitfires in reserve for home defence. Our time will come." Surely it was his time to fight now!

Dobbers came out of the hangar and gestured to the Squadron to join him. They tossed away their cigarettes and walked over, passing the single Hurricane fighter parked at the open hangar doors. Inside they joined the pilots of the other two squadrons in a loose semi-circle around a tall, broad-shouldered man in a one-piece flying suit, who waited with an air of easy authority for Squadron Leader Dobson to collect his audience and introduce him.

Eddy already knew him: Air Vice Marshal Keith Park. He barely listened to Dobbers's introduction. He thought of his first flying lesson in the tandem seat of Park's Hawk, experiencing for the first time the wonder of looking down at the roads, rivers, woods, and buildings of Middlesex. He was well aware of how lucky he had been. Under Air Chief Marshal Dowding, Park had the great responsibility of commanding Number 11 Group, which must defend the southern coast of England. When Park began to speak, Eddy put away the memories and gave him his full attention.

"Men," Park said, "I'm sure you will have already heard that four hundred thousand soldiers of the British Expeditionary Force are trapped by the enemy in northern France. You, and many others of the RAF are going to work in close coordination with the Royal Navy to bring our men home. Our rescue effort is codenamed Operation DYNAMO."

He paused and scanned the faces of the three dozen pilots gathered around him.

"At this moment, hundreds of ships are converging on Dunkirk to pick up our soldiers."

Dunkerque! Eddy remembered riding the train there with *Maman* when he was eight or nine years old; they had walked along the beach, sand between his toes and the icy water lapping at his ankles. *Maman* had bought a *sandwich au fromage* for each of them and they had eaten in the sunshine while sitting on a bench overlooking the sea. She had pointed across the Channel to the opposite coast and told him, "That is where your father came from. It is called *Grande Bretagne*. Some day we will go there."

Park continued. "Navy gunships, ferries, fishing trawlers, barges, and even pleasure boats are assembling for the rescue. We know that the Luftwaffe will attack them and the soldiers who will be lining up on the beach to board them. Our job is to give both our ships and our soldiers air cover."

All the men took deep breaths and stood a little taller, as if they felt the weight of the responsibility they were required to take on.

"Your mission," Park went on, "is vitally important to the defence of your country. Every one of you is here because you're fully trained in aerial combat. You are the best men we have to tackle the Germans and defeat them. I'll be up there with you myself. My Hurricane will be a flying observation post—I shall be spotting enemy positions and surveying the beaches." He paused, and Eddy felt that the Air Vice Marshal was looking directly at him. "Men, I'm going to remind you of an important tactic you all learned in your training: When you're in the midst of combat, never fly straight. Fly with just a little rudder trim—it will give your Spit a slight skidding action and you'll see tracer go right past you." The Air Vice Marshal saluted his pilots. "God speed. I'll see you back here to debrief. Now, Squadron Leaders, review the operational details with your men."

Dobbers gathered his Squadron around him and gave orders in his nasal Australian twang. "We take off in ten minutes. They're refueling our planes as we speak. Maida and Red sections will be A Flight with me. A Flight will provide cover for the ships.

"Blue and White are B Flight. Tank will lead you; B Flight will cover the men on the beach." Dobbers continued in his usual clear and concise style, describing the flight route, landmarks, the German

Stuka bombers and Messerschmitt fighters they would be facing, and other mission details. "A final word. Stay in formation until the Messerschmitts engage us. Then use all the skills you've learned in training. Rolls, dives, tight climbs. Whatever it takes to get the upper hand on them." He paused. "Now, mates, take a pee, then strap in and wait for my signal. Good luck."

Outside, striding towards the waiting aircraft, Eddy found Air Vice Marshal Park alongside him.

"Edouard! Take care of yourself up there. Keep calm and remember what you've been taught."

"Yes sir." There was so much Eddy wanted to say, but there was no time. He stammered. "Take care yourself, sir."

"I intend to," Park said. "Remember—a little rudder trim. Now run!"

Eddy and the others climbed into their cockpits. Within sixty seconds, they had fastened harnesses, put on headphones and microphones, and completed their pre-flight checks.

Dobbers's voice came alive. "Line up for takeoff!"

The twelve Spitfires took off in turn and rapidly began to climb. Eddy took his place in Maida's Vic formation and his section became a flying triangle with Squadron Leader Dobbers on point, Eddy to starboard, and Hondo to larboard. Over his right shoulder, he could see Skinner leading Red section's Vic formation.

The wind whistled over the cockpit on a steady keening note, like an all-clear siren. Eddy checked his dials. The engine was up to working temperature, three-quarters: perfect.

They were heading south-east, the coastal town of Folkestone below and the sun in his right eye as they flew out over the Channel. Five minutes later, they were close to the French headland of *Cap Gris Nez*, a landmark that Dobbers had translated as the "gray nose."

"Echelon, turn to larboard," Dobbers commanded, and they wheeled north. "Dunkirk dead ahead."

Today, instead of the coastal *Dunkerque* scene from Eddy's memories, there were billowing black towers of smoke and the sea below was filled with ships—a scratch flotilla of vessels of all shapes and sizes. A dozen Navy gunships had moved in close to shore, a large destroyer among them, and dozens more ships, boats and trawlers stood out beyond them in a half-moon, the length of the *Dunkerque* beach.

The black smoke was coming from an oil storage depot a little way inland, and it partly obscured what was happening to the troops on the ground. Offshore, a Navy vessel was sinking, already three-fourths submerged, and it too was putting up a death pall of smoke.

Eddy could see a large three-deck ferry squeezing between two other Navy ships to dock at a long pier crowded with soldiers. On the beach, lines of men hundreds of yards long crossed and intersected around abandoned automobiles and light trucks that had bogged to the axles in the sand. Where the lines of soldiers met the tide, men were wading chest-deep into the water to reach the small boats, the only vessels able to come close into the beach to pick them up and tender them to the merchant ships. Every boat was being packed with men, nearly to the point of sinking.

Dobbers's voice in his headphones said, tersely, "Bandits, ten o'clock high. Attacking our destroyer! A Flight, they're ours. B Flight, hold formation."

Thousands of feet above them a cluster of gray planes had appeared above the row of British Navy ships. Dive-bombers were banking in a long line and Eddy recognized them as Stukas by their inverted gull-wings. They turned one after another and stooped into vertical dives towards the Navy destroyer. He had been taught about Stukas and their attack technique, but this was his first sight of their lethally fast dive. He could hear the rising howl of their engines as the Stukas gathered speed, even over the roar of his own. Another one followed, and another. Banshees from hell with their bombs all targeting the Navy ships. The first bomb hit next to the destroyer's rail and sea water rose in a fifty-foot plume.

"A Flight, attack as they bottom out," Dobbers ordered.

A Flight spread out and closed on the Stukas, each Spitfire picking out a target.

Eddy concentrated on the second dive-bomber. He got the Stuka's tail swastika in his range-finder, his thumb hovering over the trigger. He was nearly on his target's tail when he fired, but he'd come in too fast and overshot, and when he looked back, he saw the Stuka flying away. Damn. A waste of good ammo.

"A Flight," Dobbers said. "Stukas, two o'clock. Form up. Attack."

On the beach, the middle of a long line of soldiers vanished into a fountain of sand. The men to each side of the gap scattered, like fraying ends of a rope. Above the howl of the engines and the rat-a-tat of gunfire, Eddy could hear Hondo shouting. "Bastards!"

Hondo dived after a Messerschmitt 109. Dobbers shouted an order. "Maida three! Get back in formation!"

Hondo didn't answer. Three 109s dived across Eddy's sight, dropped behind Hondo and flew on his tail.

"Maida Two! Cover him!" ordered Dobbers, and himself dived after the 109s. Eddy followed, trying to keep sight on Hondo. Two of the 109s were rolling away. Dobbers locked on the third, two hundred yards behind it and closing. He fired a burst and smoke began to trail from its fuselage before it nosedived and rolled drunkenly from side to side as if it were rudderless. It crashed in a giant fireball on the beach.

There was another plane falling from the sky, twisting as it fell, but this one had the RAF's red-white-and-blue roundels and Hondo's tail number. Horrified, Eddy watched it plunge between a barge and a trawler and disappear into the sea.

"Maida two!" snapped Dobbers in his headset. "Bandit on your tail! Break right for God's sake!"

Eddy pumped the rudder bar to put slip into the Spit's flight path. Tracer fire streamed past his cockpit and a single bullet shot in through the canopy behind him and out through his windscreen. Shards of perspex peppered the left side of his face. Reacting before he was able to think, he turned and pulled back his throttle for a tight, climbing turn. A Messerschmitt 109 hurtled past, its nose like a yellow arrow. He saw the number 34 painted in white on its fuselage, and then it was gone—and it had missed its kill shot.

He went on climbing for thirty more seconds until he reached cloud patches, then he leveled off and looked down. Dozens of ships still dotted the wrinkled surface of the sea but it looked as though the mismatched flotilla was beginning to stream raggedly back towards the English coast.

Dobbers's voice came through his headphones. "A Flight. Head for home."

Eddy looked about to locate the others and spotted their contrails above the clouds and to his larboard. He banked left and climbed to join them.

"Maida two. Come in," said Dobbers.

"Maida two here."

"You okay Frenchy?"

"I caught one through the canopy." His face had begun to sting. He put his hand to his cheek and found the fingers of his glove smeared with red. Judging by the exit hole in his windscreen, the bullet had missed his temple by only six inches. "I may need an aspirin and a plaster. But my plane is fine."

"Can you make it to Hawkinge?"

"Yes."

"Good. Form up with the rest of A Flight if you can. See you on the ground. Out."

Flying back over the Channel, Eddy had time to replay the air battle in his head. That Messerschmitt that had nearly got him, Number 34. He'd seen it before, but where—Wunstorf? Over the Dornier factory? Was it the same plane? He couldn't be sure, but it had come close enough today for Eddy to see a thick white scarf around the pilot's neck. You got the jump on me this time, Jerry bastard!

Eddy had reached the white cliffs and relative safety. Once he was in sight of Hawkinge airfield he pushed his stick forward to drop the Spit's nose, eased back on the power, and let her glide to the runway.

When he rolled to a stop one of the ground men climbed up to unfasten his harness. Dobbers was on the ground already, waiting for him, so Eddy scrambled down the wing root and hopped off.

Dobbers grimaced over the blood on his face. "You look like you caught the wrong end of a shotgun."

"It's not bad," Eddy said.

"See the Medical Officer." Dobbers slapped his shoulder and climbed up into the Spitfire. Seeing the bullet hole in the canopy, he exclaimed, "Good Lord, Frenchy! That was close."

"Yes. Hondo went down in the drink."

"I'm afraid so," Dobbers said.

A Spitfire flew over, not landing but swooping low over the hangar. Eddy saw the number 72 on its fuselage. It rose again into a joyful loop, did a half turn as it came past vertical and leveled out, only to loop again in the opposite direction, as if drawing an immense figure eight in the air. A loud cheer rose from the groundmen. Some waved their hats at it.

"He got one! We gave it to the bloody Huns today!"

"For God's sake," Dobbers said, his Aussie accent even more marked than usual. "The rest of us are just glad to get home, but Tuner has to do a Cuban 8. Bloody show-off."

"The men seem to enjoy it," Eddy said.

A Hurricane followed the Spitfire, more soberly, and landed without fuss.

"Who is number 72?" Eddy asked.

"Dudley Thane. He flies with Duncan's 274 Squadron. His call sign is Tuner."

Eddy looked at Dobbers. "Did you say Thane?"

"Yes," Dobbers said. "Do you know him?"

Eddy didn't have time to reply. Dobbers drew his attention to Air Vice Marshal Park who was walking over from his Hurricane towards them.

"Dobson. Beane." He had pushed his goggles up to rest on top of his flying helmet, and he looked tired, but his first words were for his men. "Are you all right?"

"Yes sir," they replied together.

"What hit you, Beane?" Park put his hand under Eddy's chin and examined the left side of his face.

"Perspex, I think, sir. Just a scratch or two."

"Someone almost got you. A Stuka?"

"A 109, sir."

"Did you get him?"

"No, sir."

"I hope you've learned from it."

"I need to have eyes in the back of my head, sir. And it was your reminder that saved my life."

The Air Vice Marshal smiled. "Now you are one of my veterans."

Park turned to Dobbers. "How did it go?"

"We downed four Stukas, sir. But A Flight lost a man—James Hundley."

The Air Marshall grimaced.

"What about B Flight?"

"Roberts was leading B Flight, sir. They should be on the ground shortly."

"Okay." Thane's Spitfire came roaring overhead again to do a victory roll.

Park watched him with wry amusement. "I hope he had enough success to excuse that." The ground men were cheering again. "The men need a champion now and then, but he'd better live up to it."

Chapter 27

Eddy and James "Wall" Wallingford were flying with Squadron Leader Dobson in a three-plane 'Vic' formation. 57 Squadron had been making daily routine patrols of the South Coast since Dunkerque and the first part of their flight plan was familiar, with Eastbourne to larboard. Today, however, Dobbers was leading them west, out to sea to provide air cover for a ship convoy code-named "Silverload."

The July sky was bright and the Spitfire's Rolls-Royce Merlin engine was as reliable and as deafening as always. They skimmed through the top of a cumulus cloud, climbing easily at two hundred miles per hour, but by the time the Vic leveled out at Angels Twenty even Eddy's wool pullover, Irvin flying jacket and overalls were not enough to deal with the bone-chilling cold of high altitude. He tried to rub warmth into his legs. Tank had a story about a Spitfire pilot who had pinched his girlfriend's silk stockings to wear under his trousers, but Eddy was determined his legs would turn to icicles before he'd ask June for hers. He was glad of the white scarf she'd given him, all the same, and it was wrapped around his neck now, like it was on every flight.

The Silverload convoy was below, chugging east in the Channel towards Dover and trailing a long series of white-tailed wakes. It was a loose formation of sloops and steamers, with a naval warship positioned between the merchant ships and the coast of France. Maybe fifteen vessels in all.

An ominous-looking dark streak in the sky came from the direction of Cherbourg. Its slow north-eastward roll reminded Eddy of the moving stairway he and June had used at Piccadilly Circus. It might have been a layer of storm cloud, but he knew it wasn't. It was enemy planes, in huge numbers, flying up the Channel to bomb the convoy. Within seconds he was able to make out the angled wings of Junkers 87 dive-bombers, escorted by Messerschmitt 110s. Much higher,

Messerschmitt 109 fighters were flying apart from the main German force in an oval sweep, on the watch for RAF aircraft.

A squadron of wide-winged Hawker Hurricanes was diving towards the Junkers. Dobbers's voice crackled through Eddy's headphones: "There go the Bulldogs." The Hurricanes flew head-on at the German formation, the front of which burst in all directions like a gray dust cloud. In a matter of seconds vapour trails were lacing the sky as the fighter planes carved through it. Two Junkers fell into dives, trailing smoke, and disappeared into the sea, but the sheer number of German bombers meant that many got past the protection of the Spitfires and Hurricanes and released their bombs. Plumes of spouting water began to dot the sea around the ships.

Aerial patrols had taught Eddy not to waste time looking at details at sea level. He had to be aware of the whole airspace around him because the enemy might be anywhere and he had to spot them before they spotted him. And there they were, the Messerschmitt 109s, turning high above him.

"Bandits!" Eddy shouted. "Two o'clock."

Dobbers replied at once. "Climb!"

Eddy and Wall climbed behind Dobbers at full throttle. These were the first 109s he had faced since Dunkirk where they had attacked with unforgettable diving speed and shot down Hondo with ruthless efficiency. His stomach churned. He took deep calming breaths and forced himself to exhale.

Dobbers led them high above a four-plane schwarm of 109s.

"Tally ho!" he said, casually, and dived at them. Eddy went with him, keeping on his wing while Wall leveled out to provide high cover. Three of the 109s made steep evasive dives but Dobbers closed on the hindmost one and fired. Bits of metal flew off its fuselage before it, too, dived away. Eddy chased it, but the 109 had dived first and was far out of range before he could fire.

No more targets were in range so Eddy looked round to find Dobbers and leveled off beside him. With the skies strangely empty around him it was a moment of astonishing peace, but Eddy knew better than to relax. The enemy might be unseen but he was still there. Stay on the *qui vive!*

High overhead he could see Wall's Spitfire. Higher still there were tiny specks that flickered like diamonds in the summer sky—109s about to bounce Wall from high in the sun.

"Maida Three!" Eddy shouted through his radio. "Bandits. Twelve o'clock high! Break!"

With the 109s diving at over four hundred miles per hour, unless Wall moved there would be no escape. They fired before Wall gained momentum and dived under him, leaving his Spit trailing a ribbon of thick black smoke. Eddy followed it as it descended, now streaming black oil. Forty seconds later it was gliding over the wave-crests. When the Spitfire finally hit them, its wings threw up two wide fountain-sprays of water but it kept going, skimming the surface like a speedboat.

"Wall's pancaked!" Eddy reported to Dobbers.

"I see him," Dobbers replied. Eddy spotted him also, banking starboard to come back over the crash site. Below them, Wall had pulled back the canopy and was climbing out, while the plane slowly settled down into the sea. "Very pretty landing. The convoy's gone past him, so I'll have to call Coastal Command. They'll fish him out."

Only one ship remained behind them, a tanker engulfed by orange flames and a thick black pall of smoke. The crew had launched lifeboats and were rowing towards the Kent coast. The rest of the Silverload convoy had steamed on and was already miles to the east and approaching Dover. The Germans planes, having finished their strike, had turned back to France. The Hurricanes had disappeared homeward and the skies were clear again, except for the slowly dissipating vapour trails.

"Return to base," Dobbers said.

The entire engagement had lasted five minutes.

~ ~ ~

Kettlebury airfield's mess was a boxy, bricked building. The main room was spacious and open, carpeted and furnished with square tables to seat four men, plus a dozen arm chairs and a stand-up bar next to the door to the kitchen. A photograph of King George and RAF posters were displayed on the wall, one with a silhouette of a Lancaster bomber with crew positions in white lettering and a slogan that implored its reader to "Join An Air Crew."

57 Squadron had been posted to Kettlebury in June. Eddy found it comfortable, and its location in the Kent countryside was a little closer to London, and to June Stephenson.

When Eddy and Dobbers strolled through the entry arch to the mess, they found Tank, Robby and Burns seated at one of the tables, digging into plates of meat and mashed potatoes. Tank was accompanied by a yellow retriever puppy who lay under the table and waited with soulful eyes for a share of the meal. Skinner and Ox were smoking in armchairs either side of the wireless, listening to the Home Service.

"Any news on Wall?" Dobbers asked.

"Not yet," Tank said. "He radioed in that he's a bit bloodied-up and his leg's bothering him, but otherwise managing nicely, thank you. Hopefully, he'll be drying out in Eastbourne soon, having a pint, and The Home Guard will drive him over here when he's finished."

"That would be nice." Dobbers sat at the next table and motioned for Eddy to join him. "What are they serving up?"

"The usual shoe leather and lard," Tank said, drawing a chuckle from Robby.

Station Commander "Bull" Connell came through the mess door followed by two young men in RAF dress uniforms. Eddy recognized one of them as Dudley Thane. He sat back in his chair, keeping himself out of Thane's view. He was still high on adrenalin from Maida's encounter with the 109s and he needed to compose himself a lot more before he faced June's ex-fiancé.

"Meet Squadron 57's two new pilots," Bull said. "They're formerly of 274 Squadron."

Connell didn't need to explain that they were replacements. Two Squadron members had perished during the past week: one had limped home with a badly damaged plane but had crashed on landing; another had been ambushed by a Messerschmitt on a routine patrol.

Bull introduced the man on his left. "Archibald Griffin."

A tall, handsome young man stepped forward. His black hair was parted neatly in the middle and he wore a thin black mustache. "Griff will do," he said.

Bull turned towards Thane, who stepped forward. "And Dudley Thane."

Thane grinned and addressed Squadron Leader Dobson, as if it were only the two of them. "Afternoon, Dobbers."

Dobson nodded to him. "Tuner."

169

"Tuner?" Robby repeated, as a question.

Thane scanned the room. "Give me a piano? I'll play you whatever you like. If there's a local pub with a Joanna I'll lead you all in a sing-song."

"Well, Dobbers," Bull said, "this lot's all yours." He left the mess.

One of the pilots chuckled. "Afternoon, Tuner. I'm Tank. Remember me?"

"Should I?"

"Officer training in the north of Scotland," Tank said.

"You were there?" Thane asked Tank. "I'm afraid I can't bring you to mind."

"I might be forgettable, but you certainly aren't. At least for the CO's daughter."

The men chuckled, but Thane showed no sign of embarrassment. "It seems my past has come back to haunt me—"

"Dirty deeds will out," Dobbers said. "You'll have to tell us now, man."

Thane reached inside his jacket pocket for his cigarettes and lit up. He took a long drag and looked around to draw the attention of his audience before he exhaled. "All right. In my defence, the incident in question occurred over a year ago. It was just my second solo in a Spit. You'll all remember how take-off had to clear the trees at the end of the runway?"

Tank and several other pilots nodded.

"Now, admittedly, I hadn't yet mastered keeping my left hand absolutely still on the stick while I was pumping up the undercarriage with my right. So the nose dipped and my engine cut-out, and I clipped the treetops."

"Did you crash?" Dobbers asked.

Tank began to laugh.

"That might have been preferable," Thane said. "I was only knocked a bit off-course. When I looked down, I was dropping towards a small lake. My plane restarted, God bless her, but it was all I could do to keep her above the water. I was at the massive altitude of six feet when I flew over a little rowing boat in the middle of the lake. In which there was a courting couple. Doing what courting couples do."

170

"The CO's daughter!" Tank said.

Their laughter filled the room.

Thane kept a straight face, like a seasoned comic. "I don't know what shocked them more—the noise or my slipstream. Probably the slipstream because it upset the little boat and jettisoned them both into the drink. And the CO was in the worst of all possible humor when he tackled me about it."

Tank said, "I seem to remember that the lass's clothes had been on the seat beside her when the boat sank, so she had to swim to shore in her birthday suit!"

The pilots' laughter was even louder this time. Over by the wireless, Skinner reached forward and turned up the volume.

Tank rose and shook Thane's hand, then Griff's. "Welcome to 57."

One by one the pilots introduced themselves to Griff and Thane. Eddy was the last to step forward.

Thane paused and looked Eddy up and down. When recognition struck, his face creased in a knowing grin.

Eddy held his ground eye to eye with Thane, stone-faced. Neither of them said anything.

Dobbers looked at them both and asked, "What is going on here?"

Thane blew out a long breath. "This French bastard," he said, pointing his finger at Eddy's chest, "ran off with my fiancée!"

"Your ex-fiancée," Eddy said. "June and I are engaged."

Tank laughed loudly but quieted immediately when it was clear that neither Thane nor Eddy had softened towards the other or backed down.

Thane's face reddened and he turned on Dobson. "What the bloody hell is a Sergeant pilot doing in the Officers' Mess?"

Dobson replied, "Frenchy is welcome, same as any other man in my Squadron. He's a damn fine pilot."

Ox shouted from across the room. "Quiet over there! We can't hear the bloody radio!"

Dobson looked coldly at Thane, then at Eddy. "Keep your mating squabbles to yourselves."

The radio filled the silence with the voice of BBC War Correspondent Charles Gardner:

"Well now, the Germans are dive-bombing a convoy out to sea in the Channel. There are one, two, three, four, five, six, seven German dive-bombers—Ju 87s. There's one going down on its target now! Bomb! No! It hasn't hit a single ship. There are about ten ships in the convoy, but he hasn't hit a single one!" Gardner paused for a moment and Bull, Dobbers, Thane and Eddy and the rest of the men came closer to the wireless. They heard the sound of guns firing. "There! You can hear anti-aircraft going at them now! Now the British fighters are coming up! Here they come in an absolute steep dive, and you can see their bombs actually leave the machines and come into the water. You can hear our own guns going like anything now! Oh, here's a Spitfire coming down now! There's one coming down in flames! Someone's hit a German, and he's coming down completely out of control! There's a long streak of smoke! The pilot's baled out by parachute! He's a Ju 87 and he's going to slap into the sea! There he goes! Smash! Terrific funnel of water! Only one man has come out by parachute ... "

The mood in the room had turned solemn. Each of them knew that the downed Spitfire pilot could have been a man he trained with, or a friend. Tank turned to Dobson. "Where were the Spits from? Tangmere? Biggin Hill?"

"Probably Biggin Hill," Dobson said. "Or it could have been a squadron out of Kenley." He shot a steely look at Thane and Eddy. "We won't stand for your grudges here. Are you going to work together, or do I transfer you out of my unit? Which will it be?"

Thane spoke first. "Do I have to call him Frenchy?"

"Watch it, Thane," Dobson said. "This must be unconditional. You either stay and behave, or you go."

"Okay," said Thane. "I'll work with him."

Eddy looked at Dobson and unclenched his jaw. "As will I."

172

Chapter 28

Since Germany's Eagle Day attack had begun on August 12th, German raids had been fierce and unrelenting. 57 Squadron had been up patrolling multiple times each day and once again Eddy's earphones crackled to life.

"Maida Leader to Maida Two," Dobbers said. "Bandits, twelve o'clock."

The enemy was no more than a black speck, barely visible through the Spitfire's windscreen. Could have been a smashed bug. But in seconds, the speck grew to a bird shape, with gun pods under its wings. A Messerschmitt 109, barreling straight towards him.

"Maida Two to Maida Leader. I see them."

"Deal with him. I'll cover you. Tally ho!"

Eddy lined his Spitfire's nose up with the enemy and pushed her to top speed. The Merlin engine's voice rose from a whine to a scream and its vibrations shuddered through his body as the enemy plane filled his sight, bigger and bigger, like an expanding balloon. He switched on the firing toggle. His machine guns would spit out thirteen hundred rounds a minute. How could he miss? But as he fired, the 109's yellow nose dived under him, apparently unscathed.

Eddy pulled back on the spade stick and throttle, forcing the Spitfire into a climbing turn. G forces slammed his helmet against the back of the seat. In the middle of the turn he felt the tail section bounce. The plane whipped into a spin to port and jerked him sideways so he couldn't see the controls, only the horizon which spun in a kaleidoscope. The earth was corkscrewing towards him.

By pure instinct he floored the starboard rudder pedal, and the plane began to level. The sunlight dimmed and the temperature in the cockpit felt like it had dropped ten degrees. He had flown straight into a giant cirrocumulus cloud. The altimeter showed angels fifteen. There was no Messerschmitt, nothing to be seen but gray vapour.

He flew out of the cloud and Dobbers's voice drawled in his earphones.

"Maida Leader to Maida Two. You missed the bastard. You okay there, Frenchy?"

"Yes. Okay. Over."

"Your bandit dived away. But there's more of them above. I'm going up to angels twenty-five. Get on my starboard wing, over."

"Understood. Out."

Eddy pulled his throttle back and his Spitfire climbed at more than two thousand feet per minute. Dobbers's plane seemed to be suspended in the sky beside him, looking as though it was hardly moving. They shot through a layer of wispy clouds and out the other side. Three Spitfires of the White flight team came into view to starboard. Below them the gray and white puff ball clouds looked better suited for the walls of a nursery than a place of aerial combat. A strange sense of serenity came over him despite the adrenalin of the previous minute.

Dobbers said tersely, "Bandits to port!"

Through a break in the clouds, he saw six Messerschmitts in formation five thousand feet below. Beyond the fighters was a mass of bombers in a rolling rectangle of gothic dark gray with ominous black crosses on their wings.

"Maida Leader to Maida Two. Let's keep the 109s busy while White Flight goes for the bombers. Out."

"Understood. Out."

Three hundred yards to starboard, White Leader, White Two and White Three rolled into dives to attack the bombers: four ranks of six Dorniers.

"Tally-ho," said Dobbers.

Dobbers rolled to port and dove towards the Messerschmitts. Eddy followed, inverting, and tilting the Spitfire past vertical for maximum speed. Negative gravity pushed his helmet onto the hood of the cockpit and his head pounded with blood rush but his Sutton harness bit firmly into his shoulders and held him in place until he leveled the plane.

The Messerschmitts were chasing two Spitfires, and they hadn't yet seen Dobbers and Eddy. Dobbers opened fire on them, spirals of cordite trailing from guns mounted on the underside of his wings.

Chunks of metal flew off the enemy plane's fuselage. Flames shot from its port engine, and it began to lose height. Four Messerschmitts broke away from the group into tight spinning dives but the enemy leader greedily continued to hunt one of the Spitfires and his tracer bullets surrounded it like white wrapping ribbon. Eddy dropped towards him and waited for the two-toned gray wings to fill the rangefinder before he pressed off two long bursts. Pieces of metal sprayed over the top of his hood as he overflew the Messerschmitt.

When Eddy banked and came around he looked right and left through the glass canopy for his prey, but only saw puffy, scattered clouds. He changed his flight angle, to look upward. There were clusters of black specks flying two angels higher that must be German bombers, but they were miles away. Neither the 109 nor the hunted Spitfire were anywhere to be seen. He rolled for a look below, and saw another black speck, significantly closer, but dropping towards the sea with trailing smoke. Could that have been his target?

While he lingered, feeling cheated of his death blow, three tracer streams across his nose snapped him back to high alert. A Messerschmitt had closed to starboard and flames spat at him from under its wings. He instinctively covered his face. A tinging sound told him his Spit had been hit, but when he looked up again, the perspex of windscreen and canopy was unmarked. The bullets must have sprayed the underside of the fuselage.

The enemy plane had vanished, but he'd be back to finish the job. Eddy pulled the Spitfire into a tight, climbing turn, remembering Dobbers's advice: "We can out manoeuvre a 109 every time, but we'll never catch 'em when they dive." If his engine was still in one piece, then he'd have a fighting chance.

The plane was climbing all right but now little puffs of smoke were coming off the engine and he could smell something like baking bread. Damn. A glycol leak—a hot spot that could grow and explode the engine. He opened the radiator slightly to try and cool it but a trail of white vapour began to appear, which confirmed the damage.

Dobbers's voice sounded in his ears. "Frenchy! You're hit!"

"I know. Is the Bandit still on my tail?"

"No. Can you make it to Kettlebury?"

"She's steady. I think so."

"Land at Tangmere or Ford if you can't."

"I'll make it. Vector 060. Heading to base. Out."

Eddy leveled and set his course. Within minutes he was over Brighton, "Bandstand" according to today's code card: it was fifteen miles to the northwest of the afternoon's aerial combat that had been playing out over the Channel. There were no smoke plumes, so Bandstand hadn't suffered bombing strikes today. Its citizens would be carrying on as normal, women making meals, children playing, and men working.

But normal was gone. Hitler's bombers were raining death on England to soften it for invasion, and Brighton was a gateway. The sight of planes now ought to spread an infectious distemper through the good people below.

White smoke was streaming from the engine now. The glycol leak was growing. Northeast of Brighton, he scanned the horizon, first looking starboard for Tangmere, and then for Leith Hill Tower to the north. He checked his altitude and speed and was reassured his Spit would make it back to Kettlebury.

The relief came with a burst of self-loathing. His own inattention—his thirst for a kill—had put everyone at risk, not just himself but Dobbers and the others. Station Commander Bull Connell's final instructions at the morning's briefing had been: "Never follow a Jerry that you've hit. Come home with a probable rather than be shot down chasing a confirmation." He ought to have been covering Dobbers's attack instead of pursuing vainglory. 57 Squadron might have lost its leader due to his lapse.

With Kettlebury in sight, Eddy lined up the Spitfire into the wind. The runway was dead ahead. As he began to crank the wheels down he wondered whether the Jerry bullets had hit a tire. A flat would undoubtedly flip the plane as it touched down. But the alternative—to land the Spit on its belly—was worse. There were gallons of juice left in its tank and one spark would blow the lot, and him with it. A Hobson's choice.

He went on cranking down the landing gear. He tested the brakes. Air pressure was still good. He set the flaps and glided down.

One small bounce on the packed turf. No collapse. His Spitfire slowed, smoothly, and with huge relief he taxied to his position near the dispersal hut.

He was met by Mike, his ground man, whose greasy polo sweater and scuffed elbow pads belied his supreme competence. Eddy valued his comfortable comradeship and crucially, his conviction that backed every mission. As pilot, Eddy maintained some distance and the upper hand, but he still welcomed the attention as Mike climbed up and helped Eddy free himself from the harness.

Eddy balanced his helmet and earphones against the reflector gunsight and stuffed his flying gloves between the pitch control lever and throttle. Mike helped him out of his seat, and while he climbed down, Mike stowed the parachute on the wing nearest the hut, with its shoulder straps dangling for quick entry upon the next call from dispatch.

"Trouble? Glycol leak?" Mike asked.

Eddy grunted. "I caught a packet. Hope she won't need too many bandages." He tousled his hair into place and walked into the dispersal hut, where he pulled his tunic over his head and sat down on a squeaking iron-framed cot. He lit a Chesterfield while he waited for Intelligence Officer Carter. He was halfway down the cigarette when Carter arrived.

"Welcome back, Frenchy," Carter said. "What did you find up there today? Your crate's got some ugly holes in it. Lucky you made it back."

Eddy gave his briefing, often having to stop to answer Carter's questions. He could hear other planes coming in to land. He found himself counting them home. Would they all get back safely? Was Dobbers all right?

He exhaled with relief when Dobbers entered the hut and sat on the opposite bunk.

"Hallo, Lieutenant Dobson," Carter said. "Let me finish with Frenchy, and you're next."

"That'll be fine," Dobbers said. There were lines of tiredness on his face.

Eddy said a silent prayer of thanks and offered Dobbers a cigarette, which was accepted with a nod. Then he finished his report.

"Good show," Carter said. "One probable today, so far. We'll see what the camera shows." Carter's mention of the camera that was mounted to follow the discharge of Browning machine guns made Eddy realize how foolish he'd been to chase a confirmation. The film would vouch for his kill if he'd in fact made one.

Carter turned to Dobbers. "Well, Dobbers, tell me about your day."

Dobbers reported, taking more time than Eddy had because he detailed the orders he had given during the mission and the responses of his Squadron members. Eddy smoked in silence, not paying much attention, until he heard Dobbers say "number 34."

He looked up. "You saw Messerschmitt 34?"

"I did, mate," Dobbers said. "Passed by my nose so close I could even see the pilot's white scarf. It was his 109 that put the hole in your radiator."

"Bastard! He's the one who punctured my canopy at *Dunkerque*. Next time, he's mine!"

"That's the spirit," Dobbers said. He finished up his report and Carter saluted and left.

Dobbers pulled out a pack of cigarettes and offered one to Eddy, took one himself, and they lit up.

"You don't seem so happy about your probable," Dobbers said.

"I went after him, trying to get a confirm. That 34 bastard nearly killed me while I was looking. I was stupid. It put me out of the fight."

"Don't be so hard on yourself. It's a dog's breakfast up there, mate. 109s above and below, tracers, spinning debris."

"But I was your wing and put you at risk."

"Then learn from it. That's it." Dobbers stood up. "Come on. Let's eat."

Eddy went willingly, following behind Dobbers's long-legged gait and soothed by his easy-going reaction to the lapse. A tongue-lashing would have been justified, but that wasn't Dobbers's way. Eddy gave a silent thanks that he flew under him.

They entered the officers' mess where Tank, Robby, Griff, and Thane were sitting together having their dinners. Another three pilots were lounging in armchairs. There were nine including him and Dobbers. Eddy's heart sank. Three were missing.

"Where are Burns, Skinner and Ox?" Dobbers asked.

"They got back before you," Griff said. "They finished their dinners and they're gone to the Leeward Inn."

Eddy exhaled with relief.

"Twelve up. Twelve back," Dobbers said. "Good show."

Thane turned towards Dobbers and Eddy. He crossed his legs and took his time packing his pipe. He eyed Eddy, but he spoke to Dobbers, "We were wondering about you."

Dobbers grinned. "A Jerry did his best to keep me from my tucker. But, sadly, he missed his own."

All the pilots chuckled.

"Good of you to distract the 109s, Dobbers," Griff said. "That made it easy for us to drop in on the bombers—like shooting fish in a barrel. Tuner here got three."

"Or so he says!" Robby said.

"I did. My flight camera won't lie," Thane said.

"You and your counts," Robby said. "You've got a couple of lackeys polishing your DFC, haven't you?"

Eddy had not seen a Distinguished Flying Cross until two days before, when one of Dobbers's Aussie pilot friends brought his into the officers' mess. An elegantly-shaped silver cross, hung on a purple ribbon diagonally striped with white. Dobbers had explained to his Squadron's pilots that DFCs were rarely given, and only for exceptional valour in aerial combat.

Tank laughed. "He'll be lucky if he stays alive long enough for the pinning ceremony." He tapped the ashes off his cigar and rose from the table. "When you fellows have got changed, come and join us at the Leeward."

"Will do," Dobbers said.

Chapter 29

Eddy and Dobbers strolled into the Leeward Inn, where two gray-bearded seadogs wearing heavy pullovers, scarves, and working caps stood at the bar. A wooden model of a cutter was mounted behind it and pictures of navy ships rested on high shelves against the wall. A battered upright piano, with chips and scrapes marring its rosewood finish, stood in the center of the far wall. Three young women were sitting at the table next to it.

Raucous laughter rang out from an open door beyond the bar. Eddy and Dobbers went through into a dark room fugged with tobacco smoke. Two small wooden tables and a larger one were arranged in the small space and Tank sat at the center of the larger table, flanked by Griff and Robby. Next to Griff was Thane, at the end, with his elbow on the table and swirling a nearly-empty glass of whisky. The wall behind them was decorated with a shredded tire tread, a broken set of headphones, a fuel can and a pair of flying boots nailed to the woodwork. Dobbers sat down opposite of Tank and Eddy reluctantly took the only remaining chair, on Thane's right.

Tank had two whisky glasses in front of him, and smiled at Dobbers around a long, fat cigar.

"Naow, James Roberts! You look like you're nose deep already," Dobbers said.

"I am!" He slid one of the whiskies in front of Dobbers. "Jump in with me!"

"How did they get 'Tank' from James Roberts?" Eddy asked, curious since he rarely heard a Squadron mate's given name.

Griff answered. "We already have a Robby, so that was out. But during training, our friend here glided home not once, but twice, on fumes. He doesn't quite have a full tank!"

Dobbers and Thane chuckled heartily.

The barman brought another whisky to Thane, who was also smoking a cigar. He breathed in and then expelled its smoke with a contented expression. Eddy recalled Mr. Stephenson's observation on his worldly ways.

Griff said to the barman, "One for the Frenchman, here, Jack."

Eddy sensed Thane's stare boring into him, and he turned and stared back. He knew Thane was out to intimidate him. He regularly made patronizing observations such as, "Frenchy wouldn't know a Tripos score from an RPM," but close contact with him as a Squadron member was peeling away layer after layer of Thane's pretensions. Although June had told Eddy that Thane had studied at Cambridge, nobody seemed to know whether he had actually graduated nor what class he had achieved. Whatever Thane's education had been, it would be of no help if a 109 marked him over the Channel. Eddy suspected too that Thane's allegiance to King and Country was no stronger than his Church attendance, which seemed to be a social ritual without any serious faith. The hollowness Eddy saw made him question whether Thane had enough grit to do the job at hand.

Thane was by no means the only pilot in the Squadron with an Oxbridge mindset, but Eddy was civil with the others, having found that they were much less inclined to rub his nose in the fact that he'd joined the RAF through the Volunteer Reserve. Even Griff was pleasant enough, despite having been at university with Thane. Taking the same mortal risks flying Spitfires gave them all common ground, but Eddy would never expect to find common ground with June Stephenson's former fiancé. He looked away.

Thane turned his back on Tank and Griff and tapped his shoe against Eddy's chair. "Didn't see much action today, did you Frenchy?"

"I was there all right," Eddy said.

"Perhaps you were," Thane said. "But I saw you. Safe and sound. Five angels below, flying home on your own." He was keeping his voice low apparently to keep his criticisms private.

"You don't know anything about it."

"I know you're a liability to this Squadron." Thane leaned closer, still keeping his voice low. "But it's not your fault, old chap, not completely. The RAF put us all at risk when they opened the doors to your sort in '36. But to let in a Frenchman! Bloody hell!"

Eddy shoved Thane away, and whisky sloshed over Thane's sleeve.

"Easy lads," Griff said. He put his hand lightly on Eddy's wrist.

Thane jerked his arm away. "You'll be qualified to clean that, I suppose. Dobbers did tell me your trade is—laundry, was it, or tailoring? No matter, I understand your work in that line is quite acceptable. Nobody expects a tailor to be brave."

"That's enough, Thane," Dobbers said, the use of Tuner's actual surname making it a command. "Frenchy here got a Jerry today. A fighter, not one of yer lumbering great Junkers." Dobbers sniffed with an implication that Thane couldn't have missed. "Besides, he may have a bit of an accent, but so what? So've I. Are you gonna make something of it? Eddy's father was as English as George. Fought in Flanders, and he's buried there."

Thane wiped off his jacket. "Is that so? Well then, if he's so bloody English, why does he talk like he's Charles bloody Boyer?" he asked, letting the actor's name roll off his tongue with a sarcastic flourish. "Well, to hell with it; I'm going to liven-up this drab gathering with song!" He pushed away from the table and walked off into the front room.

Griff rolled his eyes.

"Here we go again—" Robby said, but he got up to go after Thane. So did Griff, Tank, and the others. Dobbers made a silent motion for Eddy to follow the rest of the pilots and he reluctantly complied.

Thane had made his way to the piano and was bowing to the three girls. Hearing his Squadron mates crowding in, he turned to face them. "Ah, Frenchy," he said. "Have a ringside seat. No hard feelings. After all, I have a song to sing-O. What is my song-O? I shall sing it for you and you alone. Consider it an olive branch."

Eddy and the others sat down at the tables around the piano, and Griff and Robby sat with the girls. The piano bench squeaked loudly when Thane sat down. He lifted his arms and made a show of clenching and unclenching his fists and wiggling his fingers. He turned to the girls who were sitting behind him and blew a kiss to the bosomy brunette closest to the piano. She giggled and the pilots laughed. Then he lifted the lid and warmed up with a series of pyrotechnic scales that ran the full length of the stained ivory keys. He pounded out a few big, fat romantic chords, then broke into a heavy waltz pattern.

"VTR," he announced, looking round his audience while his fingers maintained their oom-pah-pah rhythm. "That's Vamp Till Ready,

Frenchy." He cleared his throat and began to sing in a chesty tenor to the tune of novelty song 'The Spaniard That Blighted My Life':

List to me while I tell you

Of the French-man that bligh-ted my life; tralala.

List to me while I tell you

Of the man who pinched my fu-ture wife. Tralala.

Tank howled with laughter.

Eddy felt his throat tighten. He was furious that Thane had brought June into it—an inexcusable escalation of the usual insults to his French ancestry and working-class education. He took a drink of whisky, hoping it might help him to keep his temper.

'Twas in The Air Force where we met him,

We'd been watch-ing his work-man's display,

And when I went for some nuts and a cup-pa

The dir-ty dog stole her a-way

One of the girls, a strawberry blonde with round, freckled cheeks, pierced the interlude with a shrill giggle and buried her head into Griff's shoulder. Thane turned his head slightly towards Eddy, as if he sensed his ire, and he flashed a sardonic grin and continued:

Oh yes! Oh, yes!

But I've sworn that I'll have my re-venge!

If I catch the French A-Vee-Ator, the A-vee-a-Tor, tralala (OOM-PA-PA) tralala

With one might-y swipe I will dis-lo-cate his bal-ly jaw!

Eddy stood and took a step towards the piano. "That's enough!"

Thane stopped playing and faced him. "How's my girl, Monsieur *Crapaud Gigolo*?"

"She's not yours," said Eddy. "Another word about her and I'll break your jaw."

"Sit down, old man, and enjoy the song," Thane said. "There's a lot more, about dirty work with my stiletto. You'll enjoy it as much as I will; I'm quite sure." He stood up, picked up his whisky glass with a flourish and took a drink. "Here's to *Joie de vivre*! And to the lovely June!"

Eddy lunged and grabbed Thane by the collar. Their faces were inches apart. Thane tipped his whisky over Eddy's head.

183

"Now, hold on! Both of you!" Dobbers said, getting between them.

"Get back to the barracks, Froggie," Thane said, "Go home and darn my socks!"

Eddy pushed Thane away, aware that if he retaliated things would get out of hand. No matter how satisfying it would be to "paste one on" Thane, he would probably end up in the brig, and possibly his flying career would be over. He thought of June, and of his loved ones who had helped him rise from his humble beginnings in France. He thought of Air Vice Marshal Park and everything he had done to put him in a cockpit of a Spitfire. He must never risk all that for some toffee-nosed Cambridge fool. He clenched his fists and kept his temper. He wiped his face, strode out of the Leeward and set off on the long walk back to Kettlebury.

~ ~ ~

The following day the Squadron was grounded by heavy rain and low clouds. While the pilots were at breakfast, Eddy stole a few minutes alone to call his fiancée, which he hadn't had a chance to do in several days.

The male voice at the other end of the phone said, "Just one moment, sir. Please hold the line while I locate Miss Stephenson."

"Thank you, Rankin," Eddy said. As one minute turned into the next, he listened to raindrops pitter-pattering on the tin roof of the dispersal hut. He was hungry for the sound of June's sweet voice, but the previous evening's confrontation with Thane still rankled, and he had to take deep breaths to release the tension.

"Eddy darling?" June's use of his Christian name sounded odd since at Kettlebury he was known only by his 'Frenchy' call sign.

"Yes, darling. It's me."

"I'm so sorry if you had a long wait. Rankin had to come and fetch me. I was down in the gulley—you know, below the balustrade." She paused. "Our special place."

Eddy smiled. Six months before he had proposed to her on the stone bridge. How June's face had lit up when he opened the box and offered her the engagement ring. "Indeed it is," he said. "But I'd rather not have Rankin finding my sweet girl down the gulley."

"Don't worry," she said, "I was just helping Foster to find suitable spots for some more hydrangeas. We must keep our special place beautiful, now mustn't we?"

184

"I suppose so. Is it raining there?"

"Not at the moment, but Daddy thinks its going to—his knee is aching." She chuckled. "But I don't mind if it does rain. I'll enjoy the afternoon very much more for knowing you won't be in the skies fighting the Germans."

"I wish I was with you."

"So do I. Listen, Eddy, I'm going to Peckham this evening to see Lotte. Your Aunt Maddy and Uncle Al have taken the children to Lassingwood for a few days, and I told Lotte I'd visit her while she's on her own. I'll raid our kitchen and take dinner for both of us."

"That's wonderful. Give her a kiss and a hug from me. How is she?"

"She seemed very busy when I spoke to her on the telephone. She is working in Uxbridge now. She might tell me more this evening."

"I see." He wondered if Lotte's duties were now at 11 Group headquarters. If they were, she must be working under Air Vice Marshal Park's direction. "You girls get into the shelter at the very first sign of German bombers. The moment the air raid warning sounds."

"We will, don't you worry." She hesitated. "Eddy? I'm thinking of joining the WAAF."

"What?"

"The Women's Auxiliary Air Force. After all, I can fly! I'm hoping they'll let me deliver Spitfires to the air bases. There's a factory at Castle Bromwich and one at Southampton. Maybe I'll get to see you occasionally. Or, if I can't do that, maybe I can fly an air ambulance."

"No June! Absolutely not!"

June paused. "Why on earth shouldn't I?"

"Look! You can see German fighter planes almost anywhere in the skies above England. They'd shoot you down as quick as they would me, and you wouldn't have any guns to defend yourself! I couldn't bear the worry."

"But, Eddy, I have to do my bit," June said.

Eddy sighed. "I suppose you do, *mon amour*. But please, please, for me, find some other way that won't put you in such danger. Please, June, don't join up!"

"I'll think about it. Eddy—my dear—you sound edgy. What's the matter? Have you been injured?"

185

"No. I'm fine," Eddy said. "I suppose I am a bit tired."

"Ah," she said, knowingly. "Were you off base last night?"

"I went with Dobbers to the Leeward."

"Did you have a good time? Please tell Patrick I said hello. I so very much enjoyed the evening in July he joined us for dinner. He's my very favorite Aussie!"

"I will. He's fine."

"I wish I could have joined you."

"I'm glad you didn't. It wasn't much of a night."

"But you always enjoy an evening out with your Squadron mates."

"Not last night. Too much drinking. Too much bad temper."

"I see," she said. "Does that mean Dudley was there?"

"Yes."

June waited, and when he didn't say more she prompted, "What happened?"

"Oh, June. It's not worth the time—"

"Please, Eddy. Tell me."

He regretted opening the door for her to ask about her ex-fiancé. "Tuner—that's what the men call him—was drunk. He sat at the piano and sang a song about how I stole you away."

"He didn't!"

"Yes, he did."

"He's an awful liar! I had broken off our engagement months before I met you."

"That detail didn't register. We nearly came to blows."

June sighed. "It's an intolerable situation. Can't you transfer to another Squadron?"

"I could never do that to Dobbers. He's a great Squadron leader—the best. He taught me everything and he needs me on his wing. I'll never let him down."

"I thought you would say that. Then Dudley should ask to be posted, and leave you be."

"That won't happen either," Eddy said. "Tuner enjoys having someone around to needle. And I think he feels the same respect for Dobbers. I'll give him the benefit of the doubt, anyway."

The door to the hut groaned open.

"The men are coming back from breakfast," Eddy said. "I'll have to go, my dear." He said his good-byes and hung up the telephone receiver just as Dobbers stepped into the hut and closed the door behind him. He was alone.

"Weren't you hungry, mate?"

"I had more important things to do," Eddy said.

"Like talking with the Missus?" Dobbers asked, with a twinkle in his eye.

Eddy nodded.

"How is she?"

"She's well. She asked me to say hello to you."

"That's nice," said Dobbers. "Listen, Frenchy, about last night." He paused. "I've come looking for you because I need to tell you now what I told Tuner last night, after you flounced out. You're two of my best pilots, but this business between you has to stop. This is your last warning. If you can't put aside your differences, I'll have you both posted out of my Squadron."

As if to soften his words, Dobbers offered Eddy a cigarette, and they smoked in silence for a few moments.

"It's not easy getting on with Tuner and his pals, with their impressive educations and their family wealth, is it?" When Eddy didn't respond, Dobbers added, "For me either, mate; I didn't go to any fancy university, and I'm from a 'Colony,' remember?"

"But they know you are the best pilot in the Squadron, and you are our leader."

"Listen, Frenchy, you're no slouch yourself. Air Vice Marshal Park himself told me you'd make a fine pilot in this Squadron."

The mention of Park's name hit home. Park would expect Eddy to accept Thane as a squadron-mate, because it was wartime, and duty and service to the country were more important than personal feelings.

"The Air Vice Marshal was right. You're a good pilot, one of my best. Tuner's the same, but you've got a blind spot about him and he's the same about you."

"I get on fine with every pilot in the Squadron except Tuner," Eddy said. "June is a gap between us that he and I can never bridge."

"I can't have it going on here, mate. Tuner's one of those knife-edge fellas, and I need to make sure he doesn't fall off because he's fighting you instead of the Jerries. It's a waste of energy."

"All right. I understand. I can respect what he brings to the Squadron as a pilot. I swear I'll hold my tongue with him from now on."

Dobbers blew out smoke. "That's the spirit. You don't have to kiss and make up. But every man in this Squadron has to work together with every other like moving parts in a time piece. It's the only way we'll stay alive to beat the Germans."

Chapter 30

The following morning, the pilots of Squadron 57 were gathered in the dispersal hut before dawn, as they had been each day for weeks while the Battle of Britain raged. By eight o'clock, Thane and Griffin were passing the time by playing chess.

"Check," said Thane, moving his Queen to King's Rook five. "And mate in two."

Griffin studied the chess board and ruefully tipped-over his King.

Thane lifted his chin contentedly and reached for his tobacco pouch. As he began to pack his pipe, Dobson entered the hut.

"It's gin-clear up top. The bastards will be on their way."

"Probably," Robinson said. "Relax, Dobbers. The Groupie will come and tell us soon enough. Here, have a cuppa and look at the paper."

"What have you got?" Dobson asked. He sat down on the creaking cot and loosened the collar of his heavy pullover.

"The Times," Robinson said, tossing it towards him and following it with the Manchester Guardian and the Financial Times.

"Have you got a Daily Mirror for Frenchy?" Thane asked. The jibe drew a frown from Dobson, but Thane affected not to see it and added coolly, "Chuck me The Times, will you." He scanned the pages, puffing luxuriously on his pipe. "Dammit Griff, we've missed another Promenade concert. Chappie here describes it as 'rousing.'"

Griff murmured sympathy, without appearing at all troubled. "At least the Queen's Hall is still standing."

Thane continued. "And Sir Henry Wood says, 'The Show Must Go On.' Dear me, we've already missed Henley Regatta, and Ascot. How much more can we take?"

Thane was talking to the air, with his eye on Frenchy. It would be preposterous to think that he had ever listened to a symphony orchestra or watched a boat race, and Thane was mischievously determined to create a conversation that excluded him. Of course, he would have to be careful, because Dobbers had ordered him to be civil, but there was no doubt Frenchy was working class, through and through. Dirt under his fingernails. His sympathies would always be with the workers. Having grown up in France, too, he refused to see that England had become a great nation through the talents of its heads of commerce and its landowners. On top of that, Frenchy had probably only half as many years of education as the Oxbridge men. In the face of Thane's provocation, he was doggedly silent. Thane doubted he could forge even the slightest intellectual connection with such a man. Mutual tolerance was going to be as much as Dobbers could reasonably expect from either of them.

The door rattled as Roberts entered the hut. "The Groupie's coming."

Bull Connell was right behind him. "Attention! We're expecting a massive enemy force flying through Sector C. We think they'll hit the East End docks, Brooklands factories, and our airfields. You can expect to see two hundred or more bombers wing to wing. There will be 109s protecting them above and below."

Thane put down his pipe, dismayed by the poor odds.

"Then we'll be the Spartans before the Persian hordes, won't we?" Griffin asked. "Dying a noble death in a hopeless defence."

Bull favoured him with a pitying look. "Where did they teach you that fable? Pembroke? Peterhouse?"

"Trinity, actually," Griff said, with a glance at Thane.

Bull scowled at Griff. "You and your friends with your ancient universities and pseudo-intellectual leanings can't simply think your way out of this war. Think of our people in the East End, dammit— you're all they've got! You've gotta boot the bastards out of the sky, as many and as fast as you can, and I don't want you dying a noble death until you've absolutely bloody got to!"

Griffin looked down at his fleece-lined flying boots and an uncomfortable hush settled over the pilots.

Dobson said to Connell, "Now wait half a minute. You haven't flown with Griff. I have. He can fly on my wing anytime." He looked at the other pilots around the room. "Any one of 'em can. They'll knock the stuffing out of the Jerry bastards, all right." He fixed Bull Connell with a steely glare. "I won't put up with that kind of talk in here."

Thane was skeptical about the exchange. Connell had tried to bash the gilded brotherhood out of their smug sense of security, and Dobson had responded by taking up his Squadron's honor. Thane suspected the whole thing was a setup between Bull and Dobbers. He guessed that Bull had been lying in wait and would have preferred to pounce on one of Thane's own supercilious comments. But Griff had stepped into it, and the ploy was working: Robinson and Oxholt and Thane's Trinity classmate Griffin had all roused and were sitting taller in their chairs. Drama worthy of Shaftesbury Avenue—and Thane's guess seemed to be supported by the fact that Bull didn't take Dobbers to task over it.

"All right," Bull said. "Let's get to business. We expect the Jerries to be flying at Angels twenty. If they come in the usual tight, boxy formation we can bust 'em up. You're all experienced men now. You know how to do it. All twelve of you will fly under Dobbers's command. Maida and Red sections will be A flight and will attack the 109s from above. When we hit the Jerries they will form up in a defensive circle. It'll be synchronized and impressive as hell, but it's just what we want them to do. White and Blue sections—you're B flight—you will peel off and hit the Heinkel bombers. It is imperative that Maida and Red sections keep the fighters busy. Buzz their circle from above and below; turn it into chaos; a cluster of dogfights. While Maida and Red are scrapping with the 109s, White and Blue must bring down as many bombers as you can."

Thane knew that each of the six Spitfires of A flight would have to deal with at least three Messerschmitt 109 fighter planes, and if the Spitfires from Kenley and Westhampnett didn't join up in time it might well be more. He and the rest of B flight would be chased by any 109s that A flight couldn't keep busy and sprayed with bullets by the machine gunners in the rear turrets of the Heinkel bombers. The odds against the Squadron were going to be overwhelming. All of them knew that. Essential tactics ticked through his head: Never fly straight more than two seconds; close in to less than two hundred yards before firing; make tight, cork-screw climbing turns if a 109 gets behind you.

"We'll scramble as soon as they hit the Channel—so be ready. Good luck men," Bull Connell saluted and left the hut.

"Well," Griffin said, deadpan, "his defence of the working areas of London is admirable, but I'll have to remove him from my guest list at Brooks."

191

Thane said to Dobson, "Thank you for standing up for us, old chap."

Dobson nodded, but the room stayed quiet. The usual irreverent chatter had been silenced. Thane and his Squadron mates were thinking uncomfortably about the impending air battle.

Bull's words: "I don't want you dying a noble death" made Thane think of his father. He was far from on good terms with Pater, though that was no one's fault but his own. Thane was sure he'd die in aerial combat. No sane person could go up day after day and expect to survive, even with the greatest confidence in his ability to climb, dive, and fire accurately, or to turn tightly and barrel roll out of trouble. In every combat the skies became a death lottery where enemy fighters appeared out of the sun with guns blazing and vanished in seconds. To Thane, death was an inevitability, so nothing was more important than fighting bravely and removing as many enemy machines from the skies as possible. His own ferocity might earn him a posthumous measure of redemption in Pater's eyes.

Beyond the possibility of impressing the old man, Thane thought his death wouldn't leave much of a mark. His parents and their friends would attend a memorial service at the church in Norfolk and maybe put up a bronze plaque in his memory. But how much would they truly miss him? He rarely visited home. He hadn't helped out on the Thane family lands since his last summer break from boarding school, which had been during his early teenage years. As far as the Squadron was concerned, a replacement pilot would be posted in tomorrow or the next day, and within a week his Christian name would be a trivia question to everyone but Griff.

Like most of the Squadron's pilots, he had no wife or lover to mourn him. That was just as well because a steamy romance might cloud his judgement in aerial combat. There was no point, either, in regretting his breakup with June Stephenson. To dwell on it would only muddle his thoughts and distract him when there was life-or-death work to be done. Thane thought the others were probably thinking along similar lines.

The dispersal hut telephone rang, and Thane sat up, ready to jump to his feet. But when Dobson picked it up, he shook his head at the pilots and said, "They're only calling to let us know the tea van is on its way."

Roberts blew out a long breath. "Did you say there's a Daily Mirror?" he asked Robinson.

"I didn't, but there is."

"Give me the funnies page. I want to see what Jane is doing today!"

"She'll be having her clothes torn off—what else?" said Robinson, slinging the paper at him.

The pilots began to relax.

It was hard to keep your brain straight when you knew you were waiting for the call to action. Even afterwards, it was a struggle to master your wits. Wine, women and song were the age-old panaceas. Luckily, when Thane needed the occasional romp, it seemed to come easily enough. He and Griff and Robby piled into the back of his Vauxhall most evenings and he drove to the Leeward or the Sun. At the Sun, for instance, there was Maude, one of the auxiliary girls, whom he'd met the last time the weather had been too bad to fly. Over a couple of whiskies, she had smiled at him, then held his hand and asked what it was like to fly, and listened; and later she had sneaked him to her room for a few pleasurable hours.

The phone rang again.

This time Dobbers signaled them to action. "Scramble! Rendezvous over base, Angels ten!"

Thane grabbed his helmet and sprinted for his plane. His fitter, Percy, was standing by the wing waiting for him, holding open the straps of the parachute. Thane pulled it on, climbed the wing and hopped into the cockpit. His earphones and helmet hung on the reflector gun sight. He put them on and looked out of the cockpit, waiting for Dobbers's take-off signal.

Ten other pilots were also looking to Dobson for the signal. He was waiting for his mechanic who had climbed the wing to hand him a map he'd forgotten, and he grinned to his Squadron as if his lapse had been part of the plan. Then he gestured forward to indicate he was rolling. All the pilots acknowledged with a thumbs up.

Thane pulled the throttle back to check the engine's revolutions. Satisfied, he waved to Percy to pull the chocks, and then rolled to his taxi post.

Given the green light for take-off, he set the flaps at fifteen degrees, opened the radiator and throttle, and released the brakes. The aeroplane began to move and he closed the canopy. He tapped the rudder bar with his left foot like striking a bass drum. The Spitfire picked up speed, the wings lifted, and he felt the body frame shudder as the wheels left the ground. At six hundred feet he cranked the undercarriage into place and set the pitch lever.

A Flight was ahead of him, climbing south-east through thin cirrus clouds. He saw Frenchy's number 103 take up its position behind Dobson. Thane, in White Section, was formed up three hundred yards behind, to starboard. Soon, they were over the south coast, with the billowing dark-striped curtain of England's iconic White Cliffs below them, and the sight somehow magnified the task at hand.

Dobson's voice crackled through Thane's earphones. "Echelon starboard."

Ahead of Thane, Maida section formed a triangle: Dobson on point, Robby behind him to port, and Frenchy to his starboard. Thane's and the other two sections also formed triangles and took successive positions forty-five degrees to Maida's starboard. Together they created parallel diagonal lines of Spitfires a half mile long.

"Climb to Angels twenty-five."

They climbed through cirrus clouds that wisped round them and chilled the sunlight. When Thane flew back into sunshine, ahead of him was a thick, gothic gray mass of planes that reminded him of the sooty iron walls of Sheffield steel mills he had passed over on training flights. Layers of Heinkel bombers, maybe two hundred of them, and above and below them twice that number of Messerschmitt fighters.

The odds were appalling. The Spitfires were twelve against hundreds. The best they might do was to take down as many of the German bombers as they could to prevent some, at least, of the thousands of tons of ordnance from raining on London. With luck, other squadrons would join the fight and thin out the bombers a little more, but survival seemed out of the question.

"Keep climbing," Dobson ordered. When the Squadron had four thousand feet of height on the Germans, he ordered, "B Flight drop back five hundred yards. A Flight: Tally ho and good luck."

Thane had a perfect view of A Flight's attack on the Messerschmitt 109s. Dobson and Frenchy dove for the fighters with Robby and Red section following to starboard. Dobson closed to two hundred yards on the hindmost 109 and trails of black smoke pouring off his wings showed he had fired several bursts. Pieces of gray metal sprayed everywhere and Dobson broke to port.

The lead enemy fighter turned to port in response, and those behind it followed so in seconds the Messerschmitt 109s were spiraling in a giant circle three hundred yards above the bombers. Thane's White Section passed close by the circle as they positioned their planes to dive at the Heinkel bombers. He expected some of the Messerschmitts to abandon their defensive tactic and attack him and White Section, but Frenchy's Spitfire fired two short bursts at the forward 109's tail section and then dived between two of the enemy fighters, forcing them to tighten their circle.

"Maida and Red, attack the 109s!" Dobson ordered. "White and Blue sections break!"

Thane shoved the stick and rudder down to dive past A Flight and the circling 109s. Screaming downward at four hundred fifty miles per hour brought on pounding pressure that made his eyes feel as if they'd dropped into his throat.

Three hundred yards below A Flight, Thane locked onto a German Heinkel bomber and let loose both cannons at it. Glass from its cockpit shattered up around his Spitfire, and the Heinkel seemed to fall off a cliff, exploding as it went. Thane avoided the dying plane by banking tightly to port, then leveled and began to climb to re-enter the fray. Rectangular German fuselages filled the sky ahead of him. When their light gray filled his crosshairs he took dead aim and let off a burst, breaking only when he was within fifty yards of his target.

His Spitfire passed through the slipstream of a stricken Heinkel and the plane shook so violently it tore the stick from his hand. Tracer was streaming past his canopy and a quick glance told him that a 109 had broken formation and was on his tail. He regained control and pulled up into a vertical climb, searching for cloud cover. Ting. Ting. Bullets hit his port wing, but when he looked over his left shoulder the 109 was turning away because Frenchy's Spitfire number 103 was following his pursuer with tracer streaming from his guns. Given breathing space, Thane made a tight climbing turn that took him into gray cloud, and when he emerged five seconds later the 109 and Frenchy were both gone.

The sky was bedlam, full of whirling black-crossed wings and yellow noses of Messerschmitts. One with a swastika-marked tailfin passed to starboard, cutting white contrails with its wing tips. Thane saw that its prey was Ox's number 49 whose cockpit glass was running with blood, like scarlet rain.

Red rage lit Thane. He dived for the 109's tail, reckless of the damage to his own Spitfire. The stick was shaking violently, but he fought it to target the space on the German's mottled fuselage between a large black cross and a white circle. The 109 tried to dive away but Thane had dived quicker and faster. He was nearly upon the 109 when he fired and its engine exploded. Hot oil sprayed all over Thane's canopy and the windscreen turned black.

He toggled the stick to and fro, trying to use slipstream to throw off the oil, but that only cleared a few shilling-sized spaces. He hurtled on, knowing the airspace was thick with twisting and turning 109s and Spitfires, but completely unable to see or avoid them. He banged impotently on the windscreen, expecting impact any second. Then his head cleared, and he saw a solution. He throttled back to near stalling speed. Then he slid back the cockpit hood, released his harness and rose from his seat to wipe at the oil with his handkerchief, fighting through the freezing air that stung his cheeks like needles.

Tracers came zig-zagging in front of his propeller and he closed the hood fast and sat down again. Ting. Ting. Bullets were hitting his tail section. He closed the throttle and eased the stick back for a tight climbing turn, but the Spit had lost too much speed and it stalled and started to spiral downward, throwing off engine oil. As Thane struggled for control, it occurred to him that the 109 pilot might consider him finished. Maybe he could be fooled into leaving him for dead. He let his Spitfire go on falling towards earth, holding his nerve against the negative G for fifteen terrifying seconds before he opened the throttle and pushed his stick forward. The engine coughed and sputtered to life. He refastened his harness with shaking hands, considered the Spitfire's trailing plume of petrol, then turned away from the battle and headed west.

A thick cloud of black smoke to starboard blew aside and revealed a glowing red ball at its heart, falling earthward. He evaded it, instinctively, but not before he recognized a Spitfire's pointed nose cone. There was no parachute. He swallowed hard and flew on towards Kettlebury. Approaching the landing strip he had to waggle the Spitfire from side to side to see over his Spitfire's long nose in order to line up with the runway. He raised his flaps, eased the stick back more on instinct than vision, and was relieved when the wheels hit evenly.

Thane taxied towards the hut with black smoke pouring from his fuselage. He was met by Percy waving his arms frantically for the firefighters. As Thane climbed out of the cockpit Percy took his hand and helped him down. He looked to see which of the other planes had already come home. At least three were in. Jack Berry strolled over and waved to him.

"Bloody hell, man. Your windscreen! How the hell did you find the airfield?"

"Money for old rope," Thane said. "I can land here with my eyes closed."

"You damn near had to, old man," Berry said. They shook hands.

"Glad you made it, Straw. Who else is back? I know Ox has gone down."

Jack "Straw" Berry looked away. "I saw Split was in flames."

Lanky Morris Spiller had been another of the Oxbridge privileged, a quiet man with a soft smile and frequent words of encouragement. "I saw a Spitfire explode," Thane said. "Don't know if it was Split or someone else."

Two more Spitfires were descending towards Kettlebury. Frenchy's number 103 had just landed and was rolling to a stop. He climbed down and pulled off his parachute with the help of his mechanic and joined Thane and Berry.

"Greetings, Straw," Frenchy said. "Well, Tuner, you made it—with all that smoke pouring from your crate I expected you to land in a ball of flames."

Thane wondered if Frenchy was disappointed, but for once he was too shaken to make a joke of it. "No, I got here in one piece because you covered me. Thanks."

Frenchy nodded.

Dobson came over. "Any losses?

"We lost Ox—I saw him go down," Thane said. "And Straw saw Split go down."

"Ahh—Christ." Dobson looked for incoming planes. "I see Tank's come home okay. Griff should be landing soon. There's you three. Is that it?"

197

"So far," Thane answered. "You say Griff's coming in?" he asked and scanned the empty sky.

"He must be. He was covering me just minutes ago," Dobson said. "A Jerry had me taped. If Griff hadn't come along, I was finished."

The four pilots were looking up, watching for the return of Griff and the others. Air warriors who had given all they could and now were left to worry for their missing squadron brothers. Frenchy was one of them, whether Thane liked it or not. He had faced up to mortal risks, fighting with considerable aerial combat skills and he had probably saved Thane's life. Thane had to grudgingly admit Frenchy had every right to stand among them.

They heard the whine of Griffin's Spitfire before they saw it. The plane was coming in unusually low, its wing tips wobbling erratically like a drunk's knees. Yellow tails of flame flashed above the canopy.

"My God, there's a fire in the cockpit!"

Thane heard a 'woosh' as Griff opened the hood and air flow fed the flames.

"God!" Dobson said. "He's going to jump!"

They began to run, parallel to the stricken plane.

Griffin's right wheel hit the runway and the Spitfire bounced and lurched sideways. When the left wheel hit, in turn, its tail flicked upward and drove the prop into the ground and the plane vaulted over it, in a somersault. It landed on its open canopy two hundred yards further on.

Thane was first to reach the burning plane. He could see Griff's body under the cockpit. He pulled him from the smoldering wreckage and fell to his knees. He cradled Griff's head in his arms, checking in vain for a sign of life. Dobson put his hand on Thane's shoulder. "You can't stay here." He bent to lift Griff's legs. "Come on, Tuner. She could blow up any minute. Pull yourself together, man."

Thane got up, raising his friend by the shoulders, but Griff was shockingly limp and when they lifted him, his head fell back. They carried him away from the dying Spitfire at a shambling trot and when the fuel tank finally blew, they fell in a heap with him at the edge of the runway.

Dobson sat up first. "He must have unstrapped ready to jump out. But when the plane flipped, the drop broke his neck."

Thane lay face down on the grass beside his friend, not knowing whether the wetness on his face was tears or blood.

~ ~ ~

Only eight pilots had returned, of the twelve who had taken off. That evening, a dark pall loomed over the Officer's Mess. Thane sat opposite Jack Berry, with Frenchy next to him. He stared at his whisky glass feeling a deeper sense of melancholy than he ever had before. Alcohol was what they used to come to terms with the knowledge that four of their mates would never come home.

Thane was the first to raise his glass. "To Griff. My bunkmate at Neville's Court. A dear friend. A dear good friend. A man with talents. Top of the class, was Griff. A good shot and a cricketer who always presented a straight bat. And a wonderful, irreverent, bastard. Here's to you, Griff." He drank. "He never uttered a cruel word, you know, even though he never knew his mother—she died in childbirth. His father ran a Lloyd's syndicate in London. Raised by governesses and boarding schools. We've been together since Harrow."

Straw, Robby and Tank all nodded, knowingly.

"You're with your mother now Griff," Thane said. "*Benedic, Domine, nos et dona tua.*"

He raised his glass. "To Griff."

"To Griff," the men said in unison, and drank the toast.

Thane lowered his glass and added, "The Lord giveth and the Lord taketh away. The bastard."

The pilots went on sipping at their whisky. Straw stared blankly at the table. Roberts rested his head on his crooked arms and began to snore. These were the same young men who had sprinted so keenly to their planes that morning, who had made three sorties over the south coast in cramped cockpits, with all their senses engaged in life or death encounters with German planes. Now, the pendulum had swung completely the other way. Thane's squadron mates were spent.

Even at Trinity Thane and Griff had been like brothers. Fairbairn rowing on the River Cam, spending long hours in the casino, and arguing the relative merits of TS Eliot, Ezra Pound and WB Yeats— switching between points of view without ever intending to reach a sensible conclusion. The two of them had roared down Bridge Street in Griff's sporty two-seater towards the pubs along the river, out for fun with drink and girls. It wouldn't have occurred to either of them that life could end this way. Thane had a clear memory of Griff from the last time: An RAF brevet displayed proudly on his jacket, and his cap cocked just so. And then in his mind's eye he saw Griff under the burning plane, his body limp and his face blackened with soot. Thane shoved away the memory and pulled out his tobacco pouch to pack his pipe.

Berry looked up and said, "I'm sorry about Griff. He was a helluva pilot. He was hard done by Bull this morning. I've a mind to take it up with him."

"Ah, don't worry about that," Thane said. "Bull was bracing us for a fight. But you are entirely correct: Griff was a helluva pilot."

Thane lit his pipe and watched Frenchy sip his whisky. He did it almost reluctantly, as if it was medicine. He did everything differently from everybody else. How in the heavens could such a working-class foreigner have captured June Stephenson's heart? Surely June's parents were appalled by Frenchy's station in life. Thane couldn't work out why her Pater had allowed the match. But Thane had to acknowledge that old man Stephenson was no fool. There must be something in Frenchy he trusted.

Thane went on smoking and as the whisky worked its consoling magic he wondered whether there might in fact be more to Frenchy than he had given him credit for. Achieving an engagement to an heiress was remarkable. It wasn't Frenchy's fault, Thane realized, that the heiress in question had chosen Frenchy rather than himself. Perhaps it had been spite on her part, or a rebound after she had rejected him—but there was no denying that Frenchy had risen from a foreign, uneducated upbringing to earn his place in the cockpit of a Spitfire. That took grit. And Frenchy's flying skills were undeniably top notch, perhaps even better than Thane's.

"Thanks again, old man, for peeling that 109 off me."

"You're welcome. You'd do the same for me," Frenchy said, with a slight smile.

Thane said, "I must concede, old chap—I saw some fancy flying from you today. I saw you dive between the wings of two 109s and I thought you were lucky. When you blasted one to pieces from underneath and came up behind him—I knew you were good. With you keeping the 109s on the hop the bastards couldn't protect their bombers."

Frenchy's shoulders relaxed. "I saw you get a Heinkel. I thought you were going to come down right on top of him."

"I let him drop through my sights at right angles and took him beam on." Thane leaned towards Frenchy as if he were telling him a secret. "They have sting in their tail, old man. A Heinkel's rear gunner can put up a sheet of metal. If you come in from behind you can only collect bullet holes and hope for the best. But my way, you see, he never gets a shot."

Frenchy said appreciatively, "It was a textbook kill. We must pass that on."

"Thanks." Thane patted Frenchy's shoulder. "Let's both try to make a go of things, eh?" Frenchy seemed genuinely moved, but Thane couldn't think of anything else to say.

Dobbers had watched the exchange. "How about that, Frenchy? I thought it would be a cold day in hell before Tuner here took note of how you zigged and zagged through the 109s."

Thane looked Frenchy over and toasted him with his whisky glass. "One of these days, you must tell me where you learned to fly. You're bloody good."

That must be why he earned such respect from Dobbers, and Dobbers, blast his bloody Aussie hide, was a man of integrity. He had helped to carry Griff away from the fire of that fatal crash. Griff, who would never fly again.

Thane realized that Frenchy was staring at him. So were Dobbers and Tank and Robby and Straw. He stood up, swaying slightly. "Yes, I want to know how you got to be so bloody clever. But not tonight. Tonight, I'm Garbo. Want to be alone." He drained the glass and walked out.

Chapter 31

Later in the week, Bull Connell came into the dispersal hut and closed the door against the wind and rain. He took off his hat and slapped the water from it, but his overcoat was sodden and below its hem his trouser legs were wet. Eddy and his squadron mates, equally wet, were standing round the pot-belly coal stove to get warm.

"Bloody weather, eh?" said Bull. "You men had your breakfasts?"

There were subdued murmurs or careful nods in reply to his question. "Good. Now, you may be waiting here for some time. Nimbostratus is eight-eighths damn near all the way to France. The cloud layer's too cold to fly through this morning."

"Hopefully the dumb Jerry bastards try it," Tank said, "and ice particles jam their air intakes!"

"Don't relax too much though because Bentley Priory is not standing us down just yet. We may see some clear sky later and if we do, you'll be needed." Bull turned to leave, and said over his shoulder, "Take it easy for now." The door banged shut behind him.

"Bless the pagan gods for that," Thane said. He sat down gingerly and shut his eyes. "I'm at death's door."

Eddy smiled to himself. His own head was aching, but Thane surely felt worse since he had consumed enough whisky with his uncountable number of toasts to Griff to float a flying boat. How he had even got out of bed this morning was a mystery.

Thane said, with his eyes still shut, "Tank: When did the pub start lacing their whisky with arsenic? Remind me not to drink any more of it, there's a good chap."

Roberts laughed. "You needn't worry about that. You drank the lot, so tonight's stock is guaranteed to be fresh. We just need to get there at opening time and guard it properly."

Eddy chuckled.

Dobson had put on his flying helmet and his yellow Mae West life jacket. He moved in front of the stove and gathered the men's attention. "You all know we have four new men. Quinn, Stevens, Lofting, and Wingfield: We're glad to have you with us."

"Lofting did you say?" Thane said, interrupting. "What's your call sign, old man?"

"Loft."

"That won't do," Thane said. "You'll have to be Doctor Doolittle."

Lofting grimaced.

"Enough Tuner," Dobson said. "You new men have been through training but now it's time for the real thing. Remember the basics. Don't leave your flight leader's wing until we engage. Close in to less than two hundred yards before you fire. Your best evasive move is a tight turn with a steep climb. Most of all, remember that when we work as a team, we survive. So stay in formation until the fighting starts. Sergeant Beane: tell them what to expect."

"On most of our sorties," Eddy said, "we fly southeast to Hellfire Corner. Once we get there, it's usually Spits and 109s going round and round in circles."

"Yeah," Tank said. "The fur will be flying."

"Hellfire Corner?" Quinn asked.

"Over the white cliffs," Eddy said. "You won't need to be told you've arrived. Enemy action will tell you. And when it does, for God's sake don't ever fly straight. I was bloody lucky I wasn't killed on my first sortie because I almost forgot that. Every aerobatic you learned in training, put it into play—aileron rolls, tight turns, loops, or half Cubans—everything you know and anything else you can invent. Throw your crate about all the time, or else you won't come back from your first trip. Survival is your main goal for today. Anything else is a bonus."

Quinn looked at the floor and Lofting nervously shifted from one leg to the other.

Dobson said, "When we're called, we scramble." He smiled tightly. "For now—at ease."

The hours passed slowly by. The weather outside remained grey and wet. All the men smoked constantly.

"This waiting is worse than the training classroom," said Wingfield.

203

Thane dragged himself upright, got out the chessboard, and invited Jack Berry to join him at the table. Dobson, Quinn and Lofting sprawled in chairs, reading newspapers or novels. Straw and Skinner played mah-jong. Roberts put a record of "The Lambeth Walk" on the turntable of the Victrola, wound the handle, and let it play. But when the telephone rang, they all sat up immediately.

Dobson answered the call. "Understood. Angels Twenty. Yes sir."

He clattered the phone onto its cradle. "Scramble!"

Eddy was first out of the hut, sprinting to his Spitfire where Mike helped him into his parachute and Sutton harness. He plugged the cords of his headphones and microphone into his flying helmet. The rain had eased to a light drizzle that shimmered down the wet windshield.

Dobson's voice came through. "Squadron. There's partial clearing overhead. Radar picked up bombers coming over the Channel from Wissant at Angels twenty. There will be fighter escorts. We'll attack from above. Take off, form up, and climb to Angels twenty-five."

Eddy hit the ignition and his engine began to crank. When he checked the oil temperature gauge it was rising towards the usual three fourths level. He taxied into place behind Lofting who, in turn, had taken his place behind Dobson. Dobson stretched his right arm outside the cockpit and signaled with his hand fore and aft, then he closed his canopy and sped down the runway.

Eddy's engine roared like a hungry beast. He raced in Dobson's wake and at eighty knots his wheels were up and he was airborne along with the rest of the Squadron.

Less than ninety seconds had elapsed from leaving the dispersal hut.

The twelve Spitfires joined in formation at one hundred seventy five knots. In four minutes they had reached Angels ten. Eddy kept an eye on the performance of the new pilots. So far, they were doing all right; but the flight had barely begun. The nimbostratus was a swirling, angry gray layer where enemy pilots would be unlikely to spot them, but a momentary break in the clouds gave Eddy visibility to starboard.

"Maida leader. This is Maida two."

"Go ahead Maida two," Dobson said.

"Bandits to starboard," Eddy said. "Three 109s. Two o'clock. Estimated range three thousand yards at Angels twenty."

"Are you certain?"

"Yes sir."

"They might not have seen us. Bring them in, Frenchy."

They had flown together long enough for Eddy to know that Dobson meant him to be the bait. "Understood."

"Good luck," Dobson said.

Eddy turned his Spitfire into the cloud bank. Ice crystals popped against his fuselage. Freezing cold rain dripped into the cockpit through cracks in the perspex onto his knees. He flexed his calves repeatedly to keep warm. When the Spitfire broke into the clear above the clouds, he immediately saw one of the 109s; it was within fifteen hundred yards, part of a flat triangle formation with a leader and a third plane. Judging by their undeviating progress, stooging along towards Kent, they were completely unaware of him or the Squadron.

It was his job to change that. He dived towards them. He had closed to eight hundred yards before the leading 109 reacted, banking towards him. Eddy adjusted his dive to larboard and the 109s followed, closing rapidly. He pointed the Spitfire's nose cone at the cloud bank, aware that he had just thirty seconds to reach it before the leader was within firing range. Tracer crossed his propeller and he made a slight evasive adjustment to port which resulted in a gray flash passing him safely to starboard. Then he was wrapped in the safety of swirling white vapour.

He dived out of the clouds past Angels fifteen at four hundred miles per hour. The lead 109 was still dangerously close behind him. Crack. A bullet struck in front of his windscreen. He needed to bring these hounds within reach of the Squadron, or they would catch their fox in seconds. He heard a blast of cannonfire from his left and prayed it came from a Spitfire.

Yes!

Dobson, Thane, Roberts and the rest set on to the German fighters like a pack of wolves. A square of dark grey metal flew off a 109's fuselage and turned in the air above him like a pinwheel. Roberts's Spitfire dived to larboard and below him a 109 spiraled wildly in a swirl of smoke until it dropped nose first to the sea.

"Double Top! Good shot, Tank," Dobson shouted. "All flights. Climb to Angels twenty-five. Maida two, Maida two! You have a white trail."

"Roger," Eddy said, rapidly scanning what he could see of his fuselage. If a bullet had pierced his radiator, the white smoke might only mean he had a glycol leak. When he checked his gauges, the altimeter was unwinding at a dizzy rate and the temperature gauge was stuck at the far right, in the red. He pulled back on the throttle, but his plane didn't give him the usual jump. Then he saw flames shooting from the engine cowlings. Damn the luck!

"My engine's on fire."

"Maida two. Head for land."

"Roger. Willco."

"You'll be hitting the silk, Frenchy. I'll radio your course to Bull. God speed."

Dobson was right about him needing to bale out, but by now the Spit had fallen thousands of feet, and he had lost too much height to parachute safely. He had to regain some altitude.

He pulled back the stick and hoped.

The Spitfire began sluggishly to climb, but the engine fire was growing, and even in the cockpit he could feel the heat. The engine coughed, missed, coughed, missed again, and stopped. There was a terrible absence of noise.

The Spitfire still had the airspeed to glide for miles, but flames were licking at his windscreen now and he had lost too much height to parachute safely. He turned off the ignition and the fuel. The stick, flaps and rudder bar were still responsive, so he stabilized the Spit into a gliding descent.

He was already over the stony headlands of Dungeness. At least he wouldn't go down in the drink, but he must keep well to the west of Romney Marsh because if he landed there, the wetlands would suck his Spitfire under in seconds.

At five hundred feet, he cranked the landing gear into place and tried to choose a landing path that didn't have too many trees or hedges. He took aim at a wheat field and came in flat, keeping his wing tips level, skimming the pale stalks that were ready for harvest.

Lower.

The underside of his fuselage began to cut through the wheat with rapid slapping sounds then his left wing caught in the crop and the plane jerked ninety degrees to larboard. In spite of his harness he was thrown against the inside of his cockpit and everything went black.

~ ~ ~

Thump. Thump. A hissing noise and a whiff of burning oil. His left shoulder was shrieking with pain. But the Spitfire was about to explode—he must get out.

A cheerful voice said, "You've been through the wringer, mate, and no mistake."

Eddy opened his eyes to the sight of a fat-cheeked middle-aged man peering into the cockpit. He had a wispy brown mustache, glasses with thick, circular lenses, and a mud-colored cloth cap. Eddy tried to lift his hand to his face. His arm didn't obey him. There was a strap cutting into his throat, half strangling him. Nothing made sense.

Another voice said, "Take his helmet off, Brown. The strap's caught up in his collar." Brown's hands fumbled under his chin, and the strangling abruptly ceased. Brown drew off Eddy's helmet and threw it down onto the ground.

"*Merci...*" Eddy mumbled.

Brown said, "Eh, that's foreign talk."

The other man said, "Well, this is a Spit, so he must be one of ours. We'd better get him out of here before his engine decides to blow up."

The two men hauled Eddy out of the cockpit, roughly but quickly, dragging him away from the wreckage.

His shoulder felt as though it was being torn from its socket. "Ah! *Mon épaule*," he groaned.

"Yes, yes, all in good time, son," Brown said. "You don't want to be blown to Kingdom Come, now do you?"

They dragged him backwards along the path where the Spitfire had flattened the wheat. He wanted to get his legs up under him and walk, but the stalks caught his heels every time he tried and he felt extraordinarily helpless. His shoulder stabbed with every step but the two men didn't put him down until they were a safe distance away from the burning plane.

"Now then," the second man said, "Who are you?"

207

"Sergeant Edouard Beane. Where am I?"

"You're in my field. You've made a grand mess of my crop." His breeches and jacket were newer and a better cut than Brown's, but to Eddy both men seemed elderly.

"S—sorry, sir."

"Ah well, it doesn't matter. We saw three German planes go down into the sea, so I'd say it's worth it. We'll take care of you, lad. I'm Ted Tofer, by the way, and this here is Walter Brown. We both serve in the Home Guard."

Eddy tried to pull himself together and thank them properly, but he could see they were anxious to get him away in case the plane blew up—despite his assurances that if it were going to blow, it would have done so by now. When they saw that he was able to walk, they helped him to the gate where Tofer's cart was waiting, the horse tied to the gatepost. In the middle of the field, number 103 lay abandoned under its rising column of smoke.

"Meet us at my house," Tofer said to Brown as he helped Eddy into the cart. Eddy took a last look at the wreck with a melancholy feeling that he was leaving an old friend behind.

Brown mounted a bicycle and pedaled away. Tofer took up the reins and called to the horse, and the cart bounced over the grass and into the rutted road.

Eddy cradled his injured arm with his good one and stifled a groan.

~ ~ ~

He woke to the smell of lavender and linen. His eyes felt gritty and he wasn't sure he could open them, but when he thought about moving his hand to his face, the shoulder flared back to life and he abandoned the idea. He unstuck his eyelids and found he was in bed in a small room wallpapered with a pattern of green leaves and orange buds on a sky-blue background. It was someone's spare room: from his supine position he could see a wicker-seated chair by the bed, a small table on the other side with a water pitcher and a glass, and the top of a chest of drawers against the opposite wall. The window curtains stood open but outside it was dusk. He had no idea whether he'd been unconscious for ten minutes or ten hours—or merely asleep. Rummaging his memory, he recalled diving with 109s on his tail, and his elation as his squadron destroyed the pursuers. Then the flight home, and the crash.

The door opened.

"Hello!"

Tofer came to the foot of his bed, a heavy-set figure in the gloom. Behind him, a middle-aged woman wearing a kitchen apron went to the window and meticulously closed the blackout and the curtains before lighting a lamp and placing it on the chest of drawers. When she came over to the bed he saw that she had a kind smile.

"Nice to have you back with us, lad," Tofer said.

Eddy tried to sit up, but his shoulder seared with pain, and he decided not to.

"Stay quiet, lad. Martha will bring you some tea."

"I have to get back to base," Eddy said.

"Just rest lad. You're in no hurry. I told Brown to telephone the Home Guard HQ, and now the people at your base know you're here. They want us to tend you overnight. Someone will take you over there in the morning."

Eddy relaxed. "Thank you, sir."

"Don't mention it, lad," said Martha. "While you've been sleeping it off, I've made a pot of pheasant soup." Her tone conveyed that she was used to dealing with half-conscious young men, whether from accident or alcohol. "Will I bring you some? The broth'll do you good."

Eddy tried to sit up and winced again. "My shoulder is troubling me."

"I put Brown on that, too," said Tofer. "I told him to phone the doctor at New Romney." He glanced at Martha and added, apologetically, "The soup may have to wait. It will be better if you don't have anything to eat before Dr. Eberly comes."

It was fully dark by the time the doctor arrived.

"Now, then, young man. Let's have a look at you."

Eddy lay as quiet as he could, and the Tofers stood in the doorway while Dr. Eberly examined him.

"You're in better shape than I expected. Mr. Tofer tells me your aeroplane is a smoldering wreck."

"I need to get back to base," Eddy said. "My squadron needs me."

"Hold on now, son. Your shoulder has popped out. I'm going to give you some morphine for the pain and pop it back in again. Most people wouldn't do much of anything for two weeks after that."

"I must get back and fly—as soon as they get me a new plane," Eddy said.

Dr. Eberly chuckled, and said to the Tofers, "The unbridled hubris of youth." He turned to Eddy. "I admire your fighting spirit, son."

He helped Eddy to sit on the edge of the bed then he opened his medical bag and pulled out a vial of morphine. "Relax. This will help." He stuck the needle into Eddy's upper arm. "It'll take a few minutes to work." He closed his medical bag and sat on the side chair. "You speak with a French accent. You are a long way from home, aren't you?"

"No sir," Eddy said. "I was raised in France; that is true. But I moved to London in 1932. I live with my Aunt and Uncle and little cousins."

"Jolly good. Whereabouts in London?"

"Peckham."

Martha put her hand over her mouth.

"I'm sorry to tell you this, lad," Tofer said. "Brown reported to me that London has copped it pretty badly this afternoon—especially south of the river. He mentioned Balham, Camberwell, and Peckham."

"*Mon Dieu*—my family," Eddy said, aghast.

Mrs. Tofer patted his good hand. "It will be all right."

"Perhaps your commander will give you a few days to check on your family while you heal," Dr. Eberly said. "Now, let's get your shoulder into place."

Dr. Eberly took a firm grip on Eddy's damaged left arm and extended it straight in front of him. Eddy bit his lip, wishing that the medicine's relief would come on faster. The doctor pulled Eddy's arm and guided the ball of his arm bone back into the shoulder socket with a jolt like the blow of a sledgehammer.

"*Merci*," said Eddy, and fainted.

Chapter 32

The next morning, Mr. Tofer's man Brown helped Eddy into the farm's ancient Austin Swallow. The weather had closed in again and rain was falling steadily across the Kent countryside. Eddy kept his arm sling tight against his body as Brown swung the starting handle and drove out into the lane. The automobile bounced and splashed through the puddles like a drunken old dodger and Eddy winced at every pothole. He had taken another vial of morphine after breakfast, but the dull ache in his left shoulder confirmed Dr. Eberly's assessment that flying today would have been impossible.

The windshield wipers were slapping through streams of water. The left front tire dropped into a particularly deep rut and Eddy grunted with pain. Brown said, "Sorry. Visibility's not very good, is it?"

Eddy tried to smile. "I am thankful for the rain. It means my squadron will not be flying, so my absence is not so important."

Peckham, and the previous day's bombing, loomed very large in his thoughts, and he wished Brown was driving them on to the Weldys' house. Even so, it was a relief when, at the end of their drive west, Brown managed to find RAF Kettlebury and turned into the access road to the base. Eddy directed him towards the Officers' Mess. As he got out, he said, "Thank you for the ride. And for saving my life."

Brown nodded as though it were an everyday occurrence. "It was no trouble lad." Then he drove off, leaving Eddy beside a shining black Autovia limousine parked at the mess entrance, its driver waiting patiently at the wheel. Eddy hurried in out of the rain, only vaguely wondering which bigwig must be visiting.

Inside the mess, the squadron's pilots were standing about, talking with several well-dressed officers whom he did not recognize. Dobson, in his grease-stained flying suit, was conversing with an officer wearing impeccable striped trousers and a shiny blue jacket.

Both men turned to see who had entered, and Eddy at once recognized Air Vice Marshal Keith Park. There was a lot more gray in Park's hair than last time he had seen him.

"Edouard!" Air Vice Marshal Park shook Eddy's hand. "I'm glad to see you're in one piece. The first reports about you at Uxbridge last evening were not encouraging. Lieutenant Dobson has just been giving me the details."

"It was a lucky shot, sir," Eddy said. "I believe only one bullet hit me, but it was square in the radiator."

"Yes. Sometimes it's all down to providence. Your arm took the brunt of it?"

"It was the landing that did that, sir. I'm a bit banged up, but I'll be fine. Two men from the Home Guard found me and then called a doctor."

"Good for them," Park said. "I'm always heartened by the kindnesses people show to our chaps."

Eddy agreed, remembering how philosophical Tofer had been about the damage the Spitfire had done to his wheat field.

He felt everybody's eyes on him while the Air Vice Marshal showed him such distinguishing attention. He asked, quietly, "Why are you here, sir? Not just to check on me, I'm sure."

"Inspection, my lad. You just missed it. And I have a Citation to make." Park lowered his voice. "But I came myself because I did want to check on you. I don't know whether you have heard, but Peckham was badly hit yesterday."

"I heard from one of the Home Guard men, sir. I'm worried sick about my family."

"I haven't heard any news about them, which may mean there is no bad news, or may mean very bad news indeed. I can't tell you whether your family is all right, but I spoke with Commander Connell and you'll have a few days' compassionate leave—go home and see what's happened. Spend some time with your Aunt and Uncle and little cousins and that girl from the Mosel—what's her name—Lotte?"

"Yes, sir."

"Very well. Good luck." Air Vice Marshal Park nodded to him and stepped away to address the room.

"This Squadron has made us proud. The Royal Air Force, Air Chief Marshal Dowding, and myself. The King and the Prime Minister. And all of England." He turned towards the men standing at his left. "Commander Connell. Squadron Leader Dobson. You lead the best we have." He led a round of applause.

"One of your number, Flight Lieutenant Dudley Thane, has made ten confirmed kills of enemy aircraft. He has exemplified valour, courage, and devotion to duty whilst flying in active operations against the enemy. Today, I am here to present Flight Lieutenant Thane with the Distinguished Flying Cross."

Air Vice Marshal Park shook Thane's hand. Thane kept his expression solemn, but Eddy had no doubt that inwardly he was smiling from ear to ear.

"We will be releasing this statement to the London Gazette," Park said, and read out the citation:

"Flight Lieutenant Thane has led his flight both on operations in France and throughout the aerial fighting in defence of his country. He has destroyed at least ten enemy aircraft. His fearlessness and courage under fire have been an example to other pilots and have contributed to his Squadron's impressive successes against greatly superior numbers of the enemy."

As he concluded, there was another round of applause.

"You'll have to forgive him, Air Marshal, if Lieutenant Thane is a little preoccupied," Dobson said. "The Germans tried to keep him from coming to his award ceremony. He landed very late yesterday because he had seventeen bullet holes across the bottom of his fuselage."

"I caught a full packet, sir," Thane said. "My plane's in the hangar for a few days."

Park nodded. "Good show, Lieutenant Thane." He addressed the other members of the Squadron. "All of you men have fought valiantly and have had great success. I have no doubts that RAF command will be returning to this air base soon to present this honor to some of the rest of you.

"Now, Pilots; gather round," Park said. Dobson, Eddy, Thane and the others formed a semi-circle around the Air Vice Marshal. "We've been at this long enough to learn a fair bit about our enemy. We know that when their bombers come in force, they layer 109s above and below them, and the fighters keep tight formation with the bombers."

His listeners nodded.

Dobson said, "Like a protective shield."

"Indeed. When they do that, they sacrifice their fighters' speed and manoeuvrability. And that plays into our hands." The Air Vice Marshal scanned the pilots' faces. "I want you to fly at their formation and dive straight through it. Ignore the 109s and fire at the bombers. Roll away, climb, and do it again."

"That's a serious change in tactics, sir," Dobson said.

"Exactly. We must make the most of the element of surprise. Eventually the 109s will break, of course, and you will not avoid aerial combat. But until they do, ignore them and hit the bombers like bats out of hell. It's the bombers that are killing our people, not the 109s. Deal with them."

The Air Vice Marshal saluted his pilots and they saluted in return.

Park said his parting phrases, shook hands around the room, and departed. All the pilots took a turn congratulating Thane. Eddy held back, not wanting to push his sore shoulder in among them, so he was among the last to reach Thane. "Well done. You deserve this honor."

Thane shook Eddy's hand. "Thank you, Frenchy." He looked down at the cross on his jacket breast, with its airplane propeller engravings, and embossed RAF monogram. "Funny isn't it? The cloth and bits of metal probably aren't worth two shillings. But no price would be high enough for me to part with it."

"It means everything," Eddy said. "Honor and courage."

"I don't know about honor," said Thane. "But I say, after that prang yesterday you must be all-in. Come and sit down. As they say, any friend of an Air Marshal is a friend of mine." He grinned.

Eddy took a seat next to Thane as plates of beef and potatoes were brought from the kitchen for an impromptu luncheon in Thane's honor. "My friends are nothing compared to yours. Aren't you an Earl or a Viscount or something equally wealthy?"

Thane laughed. "Touché Frenchy! My family doesn't have a title and let me tell you there isn't much wealth either: Pa's estate is a wasteland. An outdated, eighteenth century monstrosity of a manor house, with stables that depend on the horses to keep them upright.

Old grassland with decrepit fences, declining rents and steadily increasing taxes...." He shook his head. "The cost of it all! The only saving grace is that the War Ag is paying my Pater to plough up pasture, even though he knows nothing about growing cereals."

"Well, that helps, I suppose," Eddy said.

"A temporary fix. I'm afraid keeping the estate in the Thane family will prove more difficult than fighting off any number of 109s."

Eddy wondered whether a thaw was beginning in their frosty relations. Perhaps the common threat to their mortality, day after day, had become a bridge between their very different backgrounds.

Thane asked, "How do you come to be on such good terms with the top brass?"

Eddy considered whether he should answer, but there didn't seem to be any malice in the question. "I know the Air Vice Marshal from my days at Hanworth."

"He seemed more familiar than a casual flying buddy," Thane said, moving food around on his plate. "He certainly knows more about your family than I do. Come to think of it, I remember him chatting you up at Hawkinge, way back in May. There appears to be layer upon layer of you, Frenchy—like peeling back the skins of an onion."

"Isn't that true of everyone? What about you, Tuner? You have shot down a dozen Nazis. You are the most aggressive pilot in the Squadron. Tank said you flew through a shower of tail gunner fire yesterday. We all think you have a death wish."

Thane smiled. "We have that in common, don't we now? But let's get back to my point. Who is this girl that the Air Marshal mentioned —the girl from the Mosel. She lives with your family?"

"You were eavesdropping?" Eddy asked, but Thane raised his brow as if to admonish him, and he changed it to, "Sorry—I meant, you overheard."

"Well. What about her?"

"There is nothing to tell."

"Really? The Mosel, I am quite certain, is squarely in Germany. Come on, Frenchy," Thane said. "A German girl? Just when I was starting to like you, the tiniest bit." He lifted his cup of tea and cocked it towards Eddy's chest with a quizzical expression, and Eddy reddened.

"Lotte is like my sister."

215

"Excellent answer," Thane said. "I was beginning to wonder what June might think." He paused. "Actually, that's pretty remarkable!"

"What is?"

"We've been talking for ten minutes and it's the first time June's name has come up."

"Let's keep it that way," Eddy said.

"Okay. Back to your *fraulein*. I'm partial to people's sisters." Thane chuckled. "Tell me about her. Is she pretty?"

Eddy put down his cup. "Look, Tuner. At the moment, I don't even know if she is alive. Or my family. Peckham was bombed yesterday. That's where my family lives. I heard about it last night—I would have taken it with a pinch of salt, but Air Vice Marshal Park was worried, too. I can't get a telephone call through. I must go and see if everybody's all right."

Thane dropped his teasing and put his hand on Eddy's good shoulder with what seemed like genuine concern. "Sorry about that, old chap. How are you going to get there?"

"I'll catch the train this afternoon when Bull releases me."

"That won't do! I'll drive you. Pater lent me his Vauxhall to drive down here." Thane pushed his plate aside. "One of the last vestiges of his wealth."

"But aren't you on duty?"

"My crate is unserviceable for at least two days. Bull says he's got nothing for me to fly tomorrow and I can celebrate the DFC with a clear conscience. But what's another drink, more or less? I'll drive you to Peckham instead. I've got a feeling your *fraulein*'s still alive, and I need to find out if she's pretty!"

Chapter 33

Thane's car was a two-toned beige and black Vauxhall, a soft-topped sedan with spoked wheels painted beige to match the body. The front grille was crowned by an enameled griffin badge and flanked by four big headlamps.

"Get in, old man," he said, "I'll pretend I'm your chauffeur."

"You're a regular comedian," said Eddy, grimacing as he slid across the leather of the seat. "But your car's a beauty."

"Like I said, she's my Pater's, old man. A one-off." Thane shut the door for him and got behind the wheel. "She's a Tickford Saloon. A bit dusty, but not bad, eh?"

The car smelled manly: brown leather, tobacco, shaving cologne, gasoline and damp-dog tweed—the folded blanket on the back seat that Pater's hound usually sat on. Its dashboard was walnut, the dials shiny chrome.

Eddy said, "This isn't the one you brought to Hanworth the day you came to see June."

"No. I'd borrowed Griff's two-seater that day." Thane was discomforted at being reminded of his fallen best friend and instead of saying more about him, he declaimed, "Home, James, and don't spare the horses." Gravel flew from the wheels as he set off.

They each lit a cigarette and smoked, while the Vauxhall purred through the countryside that lay golden in the September sunshine.

"I see the barley's ripe," Thane said. "Like a buxom blonde, eh? Ready for harvest."

Eddy said, carefully, "I don't know much about farming."

"No?" Thane glanced at him and was amused to see that Eddy's cheeks had reddened. He chuckled but decided not to press the point. "I suppose you wouldn't, being cooped up in Peckham with needles and pins and all that. My father's men will be wrestling with acres of it."

217

"On your estate, I take it. Where is that?"

"Norfolk."

"So, when you've dropped me off in Peckham, you'll rush off to help with the harvest?"

Thane laughed loudly. "Now you're the funny one! Not likely, old chap. My life's sole purpose is to avoid work."

Eddy took a drag on his cigarette. "Life on a country estate sounds good to me. Live in a manor house, give your orders to the tenants, and feast with fine wines in the great hall."

Thane burst out laughing. "If only! My Pater works as hard as any man I know. Drives a tractor. He can fork cow-muck into the spreader as well as any of our men. And the fruit of his labor is to hold on to the estate by his fingernails."

"I don't understand."

"I didn't think you would. The taxes and the upkeep costs go up and up. But not the crop revenues. Either the weather is poor and decimates the harvest, or the cattle and cereal prices go down. Or both. My parents rarely leave the estate any more."

Thane tossed his spent cigarette out the window. "I'd die of boredom, which is why I don't live there. Estate lands mean solitude —drudgery. There aren't many educated people round our way. No professional theatre or music. No clubs. No dining. And just try and find an interesting woman!"

"I can see why you enlisted in the RAF."

"*Touché* again Frenchy!" Thane winked at him. "There's wit hidden inside your Gallic skull, after all. Mind you, Pater graduated from Trinity and I think he was quite pleased when I followed in his footsteps." He paused and the car slowed a little. "Frenchy. About Griff. He was the best friend I ever had."

"I knew you were close."

"I can't believe he's gone." After a moment, he had gathered himself and continued. "We were up at Trinity together. We learned to fly at an airfield outside Cambridge."

"Fen Ditton, wasn't it?"

"Yes. After we graduated, we told our Paters that we were going to delay looking for suitable employment—no banks or diplomatic for me, thank you very much! We said we would get more experience, and then start a flying business."

218

Eddy nodded. "Were you teaching? How did that go? I've had a few hairy moments with novice pupils."

"Not too good, old man. If I'm honest, we never got as far as pupils. We spent most of our time absorbing the subtle nuances of single malt whiskies."

"Oh."

"My Pater and Griff's decided in the end that we had to talk about our futures. We were summoned to discuss it in a gentlemanly fashion over dinner. Unluckily, Griff and I outdid ourselves that afternoon with a bottle of Bowmore and we made complete fools of ourselves. After that, my choice was either to enlist in the RAF, or stay home and take over the tractor. Here I am."

"Are you sorry you joined up?"

"Far from it." Thane remembered sitting at a table in the RAF recruiting office, pen in hand. Not only had Pater given him an ultimatum, but Tom Howard, his instructor at Fen Ditton, had banished him from the airfield altogether. Signing the RAF papers was the only way to keep flying and he had done it gladly. "They call educated lads like Griff and me 'The Lost Generation.' We had to find our Holy Grail. I suppose that's flying for me. I'm right where I belong."

Thane down shifted for a sharp bend and nodded towards a plume of smoke that came into view above the fields. "That must be Biggin Hill tidying up. Yesterday's raid must have hit them, too." Earlier that morning the groundcrew at Kettlebury had been dealing with a hangar that had been destroyed, bull-dozing the wood into a big pile to be burned before Air Vice Marshal Park had arrived.

"I suppose so," Eddy said.

They were passing a farm now where a dozen men and women were working, bending between rows of dark, leafy plants.

"Cabbages," Thane said. "Not my favourite plants."

"I can see why you don't want to be a farmer," Eddy said.

Thane chuckled. "I believe, old man, you're starting to understand me." He drove for several minutes without speaking. "Well, Frenchy, haven't you got any news to entertain me? What about your German sweetheart?"

Eddy blinked. "If you mean Lotte, she's a nice girl, but she's not my sweetheart."

"Too much of a strapping blonde Viking, eh? Are you not up to it?"

"Do you have to reduce everything to the farmyard level?" Eddy snapped. "I'm sure you remember that I'm engaged to be married. I'm worrying about my family. I don't know if they are even alive and you're sitting there making off-color jokes."

Thane realized for once that he had crossed the line. "Sorry, old chap. No offence meant." Eddy didn't reply. "Listen, Frenchy, I do hope your family will be all right. I do honestly. I'll keep the jokes to myself. But if I'm about to meet Lotte, why don't you tell me how she came to be in England. It'll pass the time."

Eddy seemed to consider his request and said, "All right. Lotte's story really begins in Flanders. My father and my Uncle Al—who you're about to meet—served together in the Great War."

"Good lord, as far back as that? I sense this story may take a while. Right. I'm all ears."

Eddy told the story of Jens's capture and The Christmas Truce while Thane drove on between the late summer hedgerows, the wheat and barley fields and copses of trees. He choked up just a bit recounting that Uncle Al had been badly wounded and his own father had died saving him. After he'd gathered himself, he described Jens's letter to Uncle Al. "Before the war I flew to Trier for Uncle Al to meet Jens and Lotte and find out what was going on. And just like the letter said, Lotte was having trouble with her brother because he was a Nazi thug. An SS man. He would have killed Lotte if she continued to stand up to him." He paused. "So I brought her back to England with me, and now she lives with Uncle Al and Aunt Maddy."

"Well, now, Frenchy, you really are a *preux chevalier sans reproche*, aren't you?"

"Hardly."

"But you saved the damsel in distress. If you hadn't been otherwise attached—with June—who knows, love might have blossomed." Thane flicked his cigarette out the window. "But, then again, one can't fall in love with a German fraulein."

Eddy said, irritably, "If you mean to imply that she's a Nazi because she's German, you're wrong."

"Her countrymen are dropping bombs on our people. They killed Griff. I'd just as soon we killed the lot of them—although we can leave your Lotte out."

"Listen," Eddy said, "I don't care for Germans either. They killed my father. But Lotte's lived with my Aunt and Uncle for two years now. I've grown to like her."

"Like brother and sister? Isn't that what you said?"

"I really can't say—I don't have one of either—but I'll do anything for her, and I'm sure she feels the same about me." Eddy paused. "And I can tell you she is no Nazi. Her heart is broken by what they have done to her country. She's doing everything she can to defeat them."

"How?"

"I can't tell you. It's classified. I can only say she's fluent in English, French and German, and Air Vice Marshal Park gave her a job where she can use them."

Thane put a palm on his forehead, flummoxed. After a few moments of thought, he asked, "Where does Park come into all this?"

Eddy didn't respond.

"Don't you trust me?" Thane asked. Eddy stared out the passenger side window and didn't answer. Thane tried again. "Look, Frenchy. Okay, I'm a wastrel, and a bit of a scoundrel. But I keep my confidences. For instance—Griff's worst debaucheries will go with me to the grave!"

That worked. Eddy gave him a reluctant grin. "I met Air Vice Marshal Park when he came into the family shop. Weldy & Beane. Tailors. Go ahead and laugh."

"Would I do such a thing? A man's tailoring secrets are a confidence of the utmost sensitivity," Thane said, tongue in cheek. "I'll bet there's more to it than meets the eye."

"Not really. I got to know the Air Marshal when I was training at Hanworth. After I got my license he hired me occasionally to fly on RAF business. Drop off and pick up papers, that sort of thing. When he realized that Lotte could be useful, he made it possible for her to stay in England, despite being a German refugee. Because of him she's officially a Class C alien. Papers and everything."

"Well now."

They had left the quiet villages of Surrey behind, and Thane had to drive more slowly as the Vauxhall encountered more traffic. He didn't speak for several minutes, then lit a cigarette and said, "That's some tale. A flight to the Continent to save a girl running away from

221

the Nazis. And hobnobbing with an Air Marshal, too! Unexpected depths, Frenchy! You punch with more weight than I would have expected from a man of your background."

"You're surprised? Have you forgotten I fly a Spitfire and risk death from German guns every day?"

"*Touché* once more, Frenchy."

They were running into the outskirts of London now. The Vauxhall nosed its way down a street lined with bombed-out shops where masonry and bricks had been shoveled into heaps at the edge of the pavement. One shop was shut off with barricades, and chunks of concrete lay scattered on the road. Men wearing tin hats were shoveling and brushing up the debris and throwing it onto the bed of a truck. A bombed-out shell that had been an automobile sat by the kerb, its interior a maze of twisted metal and bent panels.

A little further on, everything appeared normal. A greengrocer in his work apron stood at the entrance to his shop and watched the Vauxhall go by. A young woman came out of a doctor's surgery, pushing a baby in a pram. Two blocks further on, several buildings in a row had been hit. Windows had been blown out, and chunks of bricks were gone from exterior walls, like missing puzzle pieces. "The bastards that did this can't have been targeting the airfields," he said. "If they were, they are rotten shots. Croydon and Biggin Hill are miles from here. And the docks are not close, either."

Two skinny lads were climbing through a gap in a brick wall into a building. "I don't like this," Thane said. He pulled over at once and got out.

The lads came back through the gap, one carrying an armful of cardboard-cased records and the other a gramophone player in a wooden box. Thane ran at them. The one with the records dropped them with a crash among the broken bricks and sprinted away. His partner, encumbered by the gramophone box, was slower. Thane grabbed him. "You little bastard! This is looting!"

"Tisn't. Let go'a me!"

The lad's partner, now a safe distance away, shouted back, "It's not your stuff, is it? Bugger off!"

Thane took a grip on the lad's collar and turned to Eddy. "We need a policeman, Frenchy—is that a bobby at the end of the street? Bring him here, quick as you can, there's a good fellow."

Eddy walked slowly, favoring his injured shoulder, but he attracted the constable's attention and returned with him.

"Well, now, look what we have here," said the policeman. "Jonny Marlowe. Shame on you!"

"I ain't done nuffing!"

"No? What's that in yer hands then, Scotch mist? I'm putting your name in the notebook—see? You put that gramophone back where you found it and get on home. I'll be along later, and I'm going to talk to your mother about you. You can let him go now, sir."

Thane released his grip and the lad turned sulkily away to replace the box inside the building.

"And I'll be on duty on this street for the rest of the day, so don't you and your mates think you can sneak in when my back's turned, neither."

"Bloody looters, they want locking up," Thane said as the lad ran off. "A lad his age ought to be in school."

"And you ought to be flying," said the constable, angrily, "then those German bastards wouldn't get 'ere to bomb us, and we wouldn't be reduced to this, now would we?" He looked at Eddy's sling. "At least your friend has an excuse."

Thane took an impulsive step towards him and Eddy quickly got between them. "We haven't got time for this, Tuner." He turned to the bobby. "We're grounded because our planes are shot up."

"Well then." The policeman eased his shoulders inside his tunic, like a cockerel settling his feathers. He said to Thane. "If that's the case, then I apologize, sir."

Thane nodded curtly, and the policeman added, "I appreciate what you lads are doing. We all do. We're just a bit on edge."

Eddy said to Thane, "Come on, Tuner. Let's be on our way. I've got to get to my family."

They returned to the Vauxhall and drove on.

"Sorry about that, old man," Thane said. "I didn't mean to hold us up, but I had to stop. Those looters are a bloody outrage." He offered Eddy a cigarette and they both lit up.

"Don't worry about it."

"This bomb damage must give you the shivers, when you don't know how your family is doing."

223

When Eddy didn't reply, Thane regretted the remark. He wished he hadn't put Eddy's mind on the unknowns. He drove for several minutes before Eddy spoke again to direct him through Elmers End.

"Well, Tuner, a day ago if someone told me you would be driving me to see my family, I would have said *c'est une plaisanterie.*"

"A joke indeed," Thane said. "June Stephenson's fiancé and ex-fiancé sitting in the same car without coming to blows."

"*D'accord,*" said Eddy.

"Remember the Dennison wedding?" Thane asked. He steered round a pile of rubble that had tumbled onto the road.

Eddy coughed, as though he had breathed in the dust that was hanging in the air. "I was there."

Thane sighed. "I was a real shit to you, old man. And I've carried it way too far since then. That bit on the piano—"

"It's water under the bridge," Eddy said.

"The wedding was the day I realized June was never coming back to me." Thane looked at him. "Whether you believe it or not, I was gutted. I'd made rather a mess of it, I'm afraid. But you know all about that."

"Actually, I know very little about it and you don't owe me an explanation," Eddy said.

"It's all rather obvious," Thane said. He took another long drag on his cigarette. "I told you about my summer of Scotch with Griff."

"Yes."

"Rather bad timing for Griff and me to spend the summer in a drunken stupor, but you see I didn't much care for all the parties and socials June's mother arranged. I missed date after date. Her Pater threw a party when she graduated; I missed that, too." But Thane would never forget June driving the little red sportster her father had given her—roaring down the street, with a silk scarf over that flowing brown hair, and smiling with pure pleasure.

"Her Pater said he'd had enough of my shenanigans," Thane said. "So, June cut me loose. I suspect at his insistence. Dashed ironic to lose June in June, eh?"

Eddy said, slowly, "I haven't had much sympathy for you, Tuner, before this week. But losing her must have been a blow. I hope you'll find another girl."

"Thank you, Frenchy, but I may never have the chance. Flying a Spitfire these days, the odds aren't in my favour, now are they?"

Eddy did not reply and stared out the window again. They were driving through a residential neighbourhood and the houses were all intact.

"You don't have to agree with me. Open the glove box, please, and give me my flask."

Eddy complied, silently. Thane unscrewed the cap of the flask and held it up. "Here's to the two of us--linked together by the best girl in the entire world." He took a long gulp. "God, I needed that. Well, Frenchy, she's all yours now."

"*Mon Dieu*, Tuner, why can you not be silent? *Tais-toi!* You have said far too much!"

It dawned on Thane that an hour or two of cordial dealings didn't make them friends. He took another drink; something about Frenchy was genuine and a part of Thane wanted to know more and maybe even develop their relationship. He hadn't helped his case by reminding Frenchy they were likely to die in aerial combat and— even worse—why had he spilled his guts on his failings with June?

"Sorry, old chap. I hoped we were having a *détente*. Like you said— its water under the bridge."

"*C'est ca, exactement,*" Eddy said coldly.

Thane considered asking him to put the flask away and thought better of it. He slipped it into his jacket pocket and drove on.

They had reached Peckham High Street before Eddy spoke again. "We're nearly at my Aunt Maddy's house. Take the next left turning." He was observing the shops and the road ahead more attentively than was necessary but, Thane guessed, in a moment of empathy, that he was looking for bomb damage in the area.

Thane blew smoke out the window. "Looks like they got off lightly, thank God!"

"I hope so. Turn here." Eddy glanced at him. "Where are you going on to? Did you say you were celebrating the DFC tonight?"

Thane laughed. "I'll have to find the party first, old chap, and from the look of some of the places we've passed, that may be impossible. I'd only thought as far as delivering you here. Which house?"

Eddy pointed. "Just beyond that cream-and-blue bus. It has green wooden gates."

Thane pulled up close to the kerb and set the brake. Eddy said suddenly, "Look, Tuner, why don't you come in for a few minutes and meet everyone?"

Thane recognized that Frenchy had forgiven him so he agreed.

"I admit I'm looking forward to seeing your fraulein." Seeing Eddy's expression change he said quickly, "Sorry, my farmyard mind again, eh? Can't seem to settle down, with all this death and daring-do. Yes, I'd like to meet your people." He remembered his medal and unhooked it and put it in his pocket. "Bit pretentious, wouldn't you say?"

Eddy nodded, understanding. "If you stay off the blue jokes, Aunt Maddy will probably feed you."

"Thanks. Oh—er—June won't be here, will she?" Thane asked.

"Oh no," Eddy said. "I spoke to her this morning by phone. She's at home at Longmarsh."

"Did you tell her about the crash?"

"No. She'd only worry. My arm will be all healed up before she sees me."

Chapter 34

Edwardian style houses were the norm on Aunt Maddy's street. They were set back from the pavement, fronted by waist-high brick walls, privet hedges and small, neat gardens of summer bedding and late roses. The houses themselves were red-brick, with parlour turrets and decorative porches, and to Eddy's relief, they were undamaged. His Morris Eight was still parked on the driveway that had replaced the garden, while on the other side neatly pruned laurels gleamed in the late afternoon sun. Everything was exactly as it had been when Eddy last visited, apart from two things: a pungent, smoky smell that seemed at odds with the normalcy of the street, and the twenty-seater bus which was parked at the kerb. It had eighteen-inch headlamps that looked like bug eyes and above its windscreen the destination sign read: Heather & Crane: Country Tours.

"Joining your family on holiday, old man?" Thane asked Eddy, with a straight face. "It looks as though nobody here has even heard there's a war going on."

Uncle Al poked his head out of the driver's window. "Eddy!" He climbed down rather stiffly and shook Eddy's hand. "Well, now, what's the sling in aid of?"

"He limped home from a dogfight with a glycol leak," Thane told Al, "and he put the plane down in some wheat. Careless of him not to find a proper airfield, but that's Frenchy all over."

Al cocked an eye at Eddy, who grinned, but added nothing to Thane's account.

"Then I hope the other fellow came off worse?"

"I hope so, but I didn't stay to ask. This is my Squadron mate, Dudley Thane. We heard Peckham had been hit last night, so he offered me a lift to come and see if you were all right."

"Kind of you, Mr. Thane." Uncle Al shook Thane's hand. "Alan Weldy. I'm pleased to meet you."

"Call me Dudley, please, sir. I'm glad to see your house is all right."

"We've been very lucky," Al told him. "Two streets away, a family with four children were all killed."

"I'm sorry to hear that," Eddy said.

"But come in, won't you? Maddy will be so pleased to see you. She'll get you some tea."

"Uncle Al—what's the bus here for?"

"Oh! I've borrowed it from one of my customers at the shop. Albert Crane. He had a touring business, before the war put a stop to things like that. With all the bombing—there are a fair number of children who live near the docks who need to be evacuated to safety. We're going to use the bus to take some of them to Lassingwood."

Eddy opened the door and looked inside. "You'll have room for a dozen at least. Are you taking Aunt Maddy with you, and little Georgie and Anna Thérèse?"

"Of course. Crane managed to gather enough petrol coupons for one trip there and back—but after that, I daresay any other children will have to go by train. So this may be our only chance to go touring for the foreseeable future. Dudley, have a look round, if you want to, but don't be long, will you? We're on alert for an air raid warning, and I don't know how much time we've got before the bombers start coming over again."

Al limped away towards the house, jingling the bus keys. Seeing Thane's enquiring expression, Eddy murmured, "War wound." Thane nodded.

As soon as Al was out of earshot Thane said, "You wouldn't catch me travelling in one of these, old man. Let's walk round it for the sake of appearances, and then go and claim our cups of tea."

Aunt Maddy met them at the door, kitchen apron over her dress. "Eddy! Al told me you were here. What a lovely surprise!" On seeing his sling, she exclaimed, "Isn't that just like Al—he never even mentioned you'd been wounded. Is your arm broken?"

"No. I'm not even wounded. I only dislocated my shoulder. I'll be fine, Aunt Maddy. It's already feeling better. Give me a hug." Eddy embraced her with his good arm. "Meet my Squadron mate, Dudley Thane. He drove me here from the airfield."

"Well, come on in, both of you," she said. "You must be famished." She took Thane's hand. "Please stay for dinner of course," and led them into the dining room before he could respond. "If you want to wash your hands," she said to Thane, "the lavatory is upstairs and to the right."

Lotte entered the dining room. "Eddy!" She took his hand and drew him to her. "*Tu est blessé?* Does your arm hurt you very much?"

Eddy kissed her on the cheek. "Nothing serious. I'm feeling much better, now that I know you are all safe. Tuner, this is Lotte," he said to Thane.

"*Enchanté,*" he said, and took her hand. "I am Dudley Thane. *A votre service, Mademoiselle.*"

"Thank you for driving Eddy," she said. "I suppose you don't have a break from your duties very often, these days."

"You're right," Thane said, still holding her hand. "But my Spitfire needs some repairs and our commander gave me tomorrow off."

Georgie, a seven year old blond-headed dynamo, pushed between Aunt Maddy and Uncle Al and flung himself at Eddy. Eddy caught him and winced a little. "*Bonjour, petit coquin!*"

"Be careful of Eddy's arm now, Georgie," Aunt Maddy said.

"Did you shoot down some Germans, Eddy?" Georgie asked, still with a grip around Eddy's hips.

"I shot a few," Eddy said. "Whether they went down, I'm not sure."

"I bet they did. Wheeee—crash!"

Aunt Maddy was setting out the tea service beside a plate of home-made biscuits. Thane was still taken up with Lotte and had not yet released her hand. Lotte was smiling back at him, but when Eddy glanced at her she freed herself and said, "I will go and bring Anna Thérèse. She will want to see you."

"Everybody sit down," Uncle Al said. "There's tea on the table now, and enough chairs, surely!"

"Don't expect much, Mr. Thane," Aunt Maddy said, "I'm afraid rationing limits our fresh meat. I didn't know Eddy was coming until the Air Marshal telephoned, and the market didn't have much left."

Thane seated himself at the oak table with an air of being at home. "We're grateful for whatever we get, Mrs. Weldy." he said.

"I'm sorry that I forgot to call you. Things have been rather a muddle," Eddy said.

"A young Captain called on Air Marshal Park's behalf —was it Captain Kilgore?" Aunt Maddy asked Uncle Al, and without waiting for his answer continued, "He told us you were likely to come tonight or tomorrow to look in on us," Uncle Al said. "He didn't mention that you'd been hurt, but it was very good of him to take the time to call."

Thane glanced at Eddy with a slightly bemused expression, as though he had not really believed the connection with Park, and now he was impressed in spite of himself.

Eddy pretended not to have noticed and put a spoonful of mashed potato on Georgie's plate, then took some for himself. "It was. We saw the Air Vice Marshal this morning at Kettlebury. He asked if I knew Peckham had been bombed."

"Doesn't he work at Uxbridge?" Aunt Maddy asked.

"Yes, but he came to the airfield to present an award to Tuner, here. Show them," Eddy said to Thane.

Thane pulled his DFC from his pocket. Georgie reached for it, but his mother stopped him.

"Manners, Georgie," Aunt Maddy said. "Mr. Thane's medal is very precious." Thane handed the DFC to Aunt Maddy and she showed it to Georgie, then passed it around the table.

Eddy caught Thane watching Lotte as she examined the cross. He doubted that Thane was seriously interested, and suspected that he just fancied a fling with Lotte, the way he and other pilots fancied the girls at the Leeward and the Sun. He would have to keep an eye on him. Then Lotte looked up at Thane and handed the medal back to him with an expression of amusement. Eddy realized with relief that she was more than capable of dealing with Thane.

"We are very honored to have you with us," Uncle Al said to Thane. "And your DFC, too."

"It was well-earned," Eddy said.

Uncle Al suggested, "Perhaps a brandy after dinner to celebrate?"

Thane nodded. "Thank you." He turned to Aunt Maddy. "This meal is delicious, Mrs. Weldy." He put his medal back in his pocket.

Bravo, thought Eddy.

"You're very welcome. Have another hard-boiled egg," Maddy said. "I'm just sorry there isn't much bacon."

"But it goes well with the potatoes and the cabbage," Thane said, adding, "and I'm very fond of cabbage."

Eddy opened his mouth in astonishment, but before he could say anything Thane kicked him in the ankle. Lotte glanced from Eddy to Thane and back and smothered a smile. Eddy cautiously moved his foot away from Thane and said to Maddy, "I feel guilty about us over-stretching your rations. Where have all these eggs come from?"

Young Georgie piped up, "We've got hens now, Eddy!"

Uncle Al explained: "The Mitchell family got some hens last month, but they couldn't keep them out of their vegetable garden. Well, you know your aunt and I have never been very good at gardening, so we suggested to the Mitchells that we put the hens in our garden instead. They get the scraps from both houses, and we share the eggs and vegetables between us."

"That won't go on much longer, though," Thane said, "once the dark nights come along."

Aunt Maddy said, sadly, "I know. And we can't get any more corn to keep them going so I'm afraid when this bag is finished the hens will become—" she dropped her voice to a whisper and mouthed over Georgie's head, "—Sunday dinners."

"Indeed," Uncle Al said.

There was a short pause. Georgie built a mashed potato castle with his knife and fork, and Aunt Maddy told him to stop messing about and eat it.

Eddy said to her, "Uncle Al tells me you are taking some children to Lassingwood."

She said with sudden energy, "Yes. My friend, Tess Walden, is with the Women's Voluntary Service. She needs volunteers to take children to the country. You see, the bombing has flattened whole neighborhoods near the docks. Lots of children have lost their homes. Some have lost their parents. Al and I went to the East End to meet with Tess and others at the WVS a few days ago and it's all set. We are going to care for a dozen at Lassingwood. I will put them up at The Four Bells."

"Really? Does Bill Jenkins know?" Eddy teased.

"Of course he does! He is putting sleeping pallets in the ladies parlour. His wife Gladys and my cousin Rose are going to help me to feed and clothe them. The children will go to school in Lassingwood, but we'll do everything else for the duration."

"I'm going to drive the bus down to Surrey Docks and pick them up," Uncle Al said. "Otherwise they'd have to go by train like all the other poor mites."

"Tess told us she'll call in a few days when the WVS has the children ready. Being sent away from their homes with just a suitcase. A luggage label tied to their coat!" Aunt Maddy said, indignantly. "I can't abide the idea."

"Are you going to live in Lassingwood with them?" Eddy asked, looking from his aunt to his uncle.

"Your Aunt and Georgie and Anna Thérèse are going," Uncle Al said, "and I'm going to travel down there as much as I can. Business has been slow in the shop since the bombing started, but I'm going to fulfil any orders we receive."

"I admire your charitable spirit," said Thane.

"Thank you," Aunt Maddy said.

"What about you?" Thane asked Lotte.

"I have my duties," she said, "so I will stay here in London." But she smiled as she said it.

Aunt Maddy had made a summer pudding, a juicy, dark purple construction of brambles and sliced bread. "Georgie picked the brambles, didn't you, my love. I'm sorry it isn't holding together as well as I'd like," she said. "I normally let it sit overnight, and there isn't as much sugar as there ought to be."

"Don't worry Mrs. Weldy," Thane said. "We're going to enjoy it just the same, aren't we Georgie?"

Georgie, with his mouth full of brambles, caught his mother's warning glance. He didn't attempt to speak, and instead nodded vigorously. Anna Thérèse finished her portion and snuggled sleepily against her mother.

"She's tired, poor lamb," said Aunt Maddy. "The bombing is disrupting everybody's sleep. I know we're better off than the poor souls who have to go and shelter in the Tube stations, and we should be thankful we've got room for the Anderson shelter, but it isn't cosy like your own bedroom, is it, my pet?" She completed the meal with Anna Thérèse cuddled under her arm. "Will you boys help Lotte to clear the table?"

"Of course," said Thane, getting to this feet at once.

Eddy began to move but Lotte told him, "You go and sit in the parlour, and rest your arm. Mr. Thane and I can wash up."

"Good man," Uncle Al said to Thane. "Then you can come and listen to the wireless with me while we take a brandy."

"I'd like a glass of water," Eddy said. "My shoulder's aching. I'll take a couple of aspirins."

Aunt Maddy poured him a glass and said, "I'm going to put the children to bed in the shelter. When you've taken your tablets, come and have a look." With Anna Thérèse on her hip, she led Georgie out the kitchen door.

Following them into the garden, Eddy looked up into early evening darkness. He could hear a railway engine puffing and rattling in the distance, but at the moment everything else was quiet. Despite the rumour of another air raid, there were no searchlights and no sirens warning of incoming bombers.

His Uncle Al had also come out, possibly having found himself alone in the parlour after all. They walked down the path to the Anderson shelter, which had been set into the ground at the end of the garden, its arched top covered with sod and patchy grass.

"I dug down four feet for the floor," Uncle Al said, "just like the Government advice tells you. And then I piled the earth up round the outside of the walls, and over the roof. It's made of corrugated iron. It's small, but it's supposed to sleep six people, and Maddy's made it comfortable enough. Go in and have a look, while I shut the hens in."

Eddy went down the steps and opened the door. Inside the windowless hut there were bunk beds on either side with little room between them, blankets folded on top of them, water jugs lined up against the far wall, and a lantern, which Aunt Maddy proceeded to light so the children could see their way in. "This is a fine *auberge*, indeed," he said.

"There's no fireplace," Maddy said. "It will be cold and damp if we have to go on using it during the winter. That won't matter so much for me or the children, because we'll be in Lassingwood, but Al and Lotte will be here a lot of the time. We should put in a little stove, or at least a paraffin heater, and keep the blankets in the house during the day. Georgie, take off your shoes and get into your bunk, and if you are very good and quiet, I expect Eddy will tell you a story."

Georgie hurried to obey his mother's instructions. "Will the story be about Babar the elephant?"

"*Bien sur,*" said Eddy.

"I like Babar," said Anna Thérèse shyly.

"Nobody at school knows anything about Babar," Georgie said. "Eddy says he's *le p'tit éléphant de notre famille.*" Aunt Maddy smiled and helped Anna Thérèse get into her night clothes.

Chapter 35

Thane couldn't believe his luck. Frenchy, his Aunt and Uncle and their children had all gone outside to the shelter, leaving him alone with this beautiful blonde, her long hair tucked neatly behind her ears, accenting the cheekbones of a face that seemed both strong and feminine, like a Nordic queen. She carried herself with a classy grace that was out of the league of any girl he'd met at the pilots' pubs.

He dunked a plate into the soapy water, rinsed it, and handed it to her for drying. She smiled at him. Her lips were perfectly full, and rose-red, and his heart raced a little.

"What a difference a day makes," he said.

"How do you mean?"

"Yesterday evening I was mucking-in at our air base with a dozen sweaty young men, breathing in aviation fuel and dust. Tonight, I've eaten my dinner in a comfortable family home and now I'm making the acquaintance of a beautiful woman who is indubitably more fragrant."

Lotte laughed. "So, I am a nice-smelling kitchen-maid, am I? I have heard a lot about pilots." Her accent was barely noticeable, perhaps even fainter than Frenchy's. "Is it true that when you're not flying you're always surrounded by girls? Is that where you practice your flirting?"

"Don't believe everything you hear," Thane said. "Sometimes a man must chase quite a few women before he catches the right one." She laughed again, and he added, "Frenchy speaks very highly of you"

"Who is Frenchy?"

"Oh, Eddy. That's what we call him at base."

"He has been very good to me. So have Maddy and Al. They are my family now." She took a handful of cutlery from him and toweled

235

them off. "It was nice of you to drive Eddy here. Of course, we are all delighted to meet one of his friends."

It dawned on Thane that neither Lotte nor the Weldys had any idea about the love triangle between himself, Frenchy, and June, but he decided to deal with it straight away. "As a matter of fact, Lotte, I can't exactly say Frenchy and I are friends. We serve in the same squadron, but we've had some differences ... "

The kitchen door opened, and there was June Stephenson standing in its threshold. When her gaze met Thane's, he drew back, feeling the menace in her glare. Uncharacteristically, he was speechless.

"June!" Lotte exclaimed. She set down her towel and embraced her warmly.

"Hello, Lotte," June said. She hugged Lotte back but stared coldly at Thane. "Dudley. What are you doing here? Where's Eddy?"

"You know each other?" Lotte asked, with a puzzled look.

"We were once engaged to be married," June told her, "but I broke it off—for several very good reasons."

Thane said to June, "I'm not here to make any trouble if that's what you're thinking. I drove Frenchy up from Kettlebury and Mrs. Weldy invited me to stay for dinner. I wouldn't have accepted if I had known you would be here."

"Humbug," she said. She had never shot him an icier glare, not even on the many occasions during their engagement when he'd given her good cause to do so. "Where's Eddy?"

Thane hesitated at June's aggressive tone of voice, and Lotte stepped in front of him and took June's hand. "Dearest, Eddy has been wounded."

"My God!" June exclaimed. "Where is he? In the hospital?"

"No, he is here, but you should be gentle to him. His arm is in a sling. He's in the shelter with Maddy, reading to the children."

"Oh thank goodness!" June's relief let Thane breathe. She hurried to the garden door, opened it, and looked back at Lotte. "I must make sure he's all right. But then I've got to talk to you."

She went out, almost bumping into Al who was on his way in. "She's in a hurry! What it is to be in love, eh."

"I had no idea June was coming here tonight," Lotte said.

"I suppose she's come because Maddy phoned to say Eddy might be here. June wanted to surprise him." Al looked at Thane and rubbed his chin. "Full of surprises yourselves, you and Eddy, aren't you now?"

Thane, not sure exactly how much of the conversation Al had overheard, said, ruefully, "I take it you didn't know I had been engaged to June, sir."

"No we didn't."

"It ended two years ago."

"I see. Well, these are strange times we live in." Al sighed. "It was still very kind of you to drive Eddy here. Judging by your DFC you must be a fine pilot too. So I'd still like to offer you that brandy—as soon as you've finished the washing up."

"Thank you very much, sir," Thane said with relief.

Al went off towards the parlour and Thane and Lotte turned back to the dishes.

"Lotte—" Thane said.

"Let's just finish what we're doing," she said firmly.

When they joined Al in the parlour, he was sitting peacefully listening to the wireless. Thane made himself comfortable on the settee but Lotte sat in a separate armchair. Clearly he was no longer in her good books.

The radio crackled and whined. Al adjusted the tuning and a man's voice began to speak.

"Good evening. This is the BBC Home Service. Here is the six o'clock news... and this is Alvar Lidell reading it. Up to midnight yesterday, 175 German aircraft had been destroyed in yesterday's raids over this country. Yesterday was the most costly for the German air force for nearly a month. In daylight raids, between 350 and 400 aircraft were launched in two attacks against London and south east England. About half of them were shot down."

"That must be what you boys were doing!" Al said.

"Yes," Thane said, "But we can't tell you any details, of course." He glanced at Lotte who nodded coolly.

"Fair enough. Shall we have those brandies now?"

While Al was busy with the bottle and the glasses, the radio announcer said: *"Here they come. We have just received a report that hundreds of enemy war planes are approaching the Kent coast. The expected target is the docks in East London. All residents in that area are urged to seek shelter."*

Thane stood up to accept his glass of brandy but he carried it to the window and looked out over the rooftops.

"Shouldn't you be with your Squadron?" Lotte asked him.

"We don't go up at night," Thane said over his shoulder. "My Squadron will be ready to fly at dawn, but my Spitfire was shot full of holes yesterday, so I won't be with them. There is no plane for me to fly in the morning. We have almost no replacements. And I didn't tell you that."

"Of course not," Al said, soberly.

The chilling wail of the air raid siren sounded in the distance and Al sighed and turned off the radio. "Here we go again. Close the curtains, please, Dudley, while I check upstairs and turn off the lights and the gas."

Thane closed the curtains and went out with Lotte into the back garden where the wail of sirens was much louder. Maddy was sitting on the steps down to the shelter. "I'd better go in," she said, standing up. "Where's Al?"

"He's turning things off in the house, Mrs. Weldy. I'm sure he won't be long."

"Of course. Don't stay out here too long—come into the shelter immediately if anything sounds close. The children are settled and June's sitting with Eddy. He's taken some Veronal, so he'll be out cold for the night. It will be a tight squeeze in here, but we'll manage." She went down the steps into the shelter and quietly shut the door.

Thane stood in the garden beside Lotte, watching the searchlights crisscrossing the sky to the north as they hunted the German bombers. His suave demeanor at the dinner table had vanished and he wasn't even thinking about his uncomfortable encounter with June. He was a fighter pilot, burning to do something about the bastards who were about to open their bomb bays on London. Fleetingly, he wondered what Lotte felt about it all.

He didn't want to join the Weldy family in the shelter, not now that June had arrived. He had to decide what to do instead. Going into Town was hardly an option during an air raid. Even if he risked gate-crashing a social engagement, he didn't feel any desire for drinks and laughter. What he really wanted was to jump in the Vauxhall and drive back to Kettlebury.

"Everything all right here?" Al asked, appearing out of the dusk. He pulled his pack of cigarettes from his jacket pocket and let Lotte pick one out. "We shouldn't show lights outdoors, I know, but what the warden doesn't see, he won't grieve over." He offered the pack to Thane, who waved it off. "What's up? Are you leaving?"

"I ought to go back to base. My station commander might be able to find me a crate to fly tomorrow." He looked at Lotte, and hoped he saw a hint of disappointment. "But I'll smoke that cigarette before I go and thank you, sir."

They smoked, watching the sky above the row of houses. More searchlights had come on, creating a lattice of white over the river.

"How close are you to the docks?" Thane asked Al.

"Two miles, three at the most."

"If one of those pilots misjudges his run by a degree or so, you're for it."

Al sighed. "I know. That's why I built the shelter. And that's why I am taking Maddy and the children away to Lassingwood. It's not an entirely selfless action, taking on these East London children. I want Georgie and Anna Thérèse far away from here."

They listened to the oncoming low drone of massed aircraft engines. "Heinkels," said Thane. "If my family was living here and the bastard Germans were dropping bombs, I'd feel the same as you." Lotte sighed, and he added, "My apologies. You're in a difficult position, aren't you."

Lotte said, sadly, "Everyone here confuses Germans with Nazis. The soul of Germany is in the good people who work hard and raise their families. They don't want war with Britain or France or any country. But the Nazis are in control there and they are evil—so our people must do what they are told—or else. Some day that will change."

"It will," said Al, comfortingly. "We'll never give up fighting for that to happen."

Thane realized that this quintessentially English family had accepted Lotte. So had June. They were able to keep their anger at the Nazis from tainting their love for her. The thought calmed him. He reached for Lotte's hand and squeezed it reassuringly. She squeezed back and smiled before she released his hand.

Anti-aircraft fire began to crackle as the searchlights caught and illuminated the incoming bombers. Then there were louder, heavier explosions, and the ground shuddered under their feet.

Thane said, "A lot of people are going to get hurt."

The telephone rang inside the house. Thane, closest, said, "Shall I answer it?" Al nodded, and Thane ran inside.

"Hello."

"Hello. This is Tess Walden from the Women's Voluntary Service. Is Mr. Weldy there?"

"He is out in the garden," Thane said.

"I see. Well perhaps you can give him a message?"

"Of course."

"He and Mrs. Weldy are to pick up some children that they will be evacuating to the country. The children need to be collected tomorrow morning. Mr. Weldy mentioned he would be borrowing a bus. Does he have it?"

"He does."

"Please ask Mr. Weldy to drive the bus down to the WVS station— it's where he and Mrs. Weldy met me last week. He and Mrs. Weldy need to be there by ten o'clock to do the paperwork."

"Yes, mam, I'll tell him."

After concluding the call, Thane rejoined Al and Lotte and recounted Tess's request.

Al threw down his cigarette. "Dear me. Who will look after Georgie and Anna Thérèse? The docks are no place for them. All the smoke and debris. And who knows what macabre sights they might see? I'd like to spare them those kind of memories." He sighed. "But you'll be going to work," he said to Lotte. "So will June. And you and Eddy must return to your base in the morning?" he asked Thane.

"Yes sir."

"I'd worry about taking any of you anyway. It's dangerous near the docks."

Thane laughed. "Dangerous? I'm sorry, sir. You are talking to a man who took seventeen bullets in his fuselage yesterday."

Thane stole a glance a Lotte and her incredulous expression seemed to search him for answers. Was she wondering how he had survived? How Eddy had survived. Whether strafing by German machine guns was an everyday occurrence for Spitfire pilots.

"Fair enough, then," Al said. "At first light Maddy'll have to ask Mrs. Robson or Mrs. Ferguson to sit with the children while we're gone—or they'll just have to come along."

Part of Thane wanted to stay and join Al and Maddy on their bus ride to the East End. RAF fighter pilots saw the devastation from German bombing runs only from the cockpit, at Angels twenty or higher. Al and Maddy were going to see it from the ground. But his duty was to get back in the cockpit of a Spit as soon as possible and stop as many bombers as he could.

A bomb hit close enough for the blast to shake the ground under their feet.

"Christ!" Al said. He looked at Thane and Lotte. "We all need to get inside." He went into the Anderson shelter.

Chapter 36

"MY GOD! That's bloody close," Al said, looking out from the shelter door.

"Too close," Dudley said. He looked to the sky with his hands on his hips, and Lotte saw an angry scowl replace the cheery expression he made when he looked at her.

"We must all get in the shelter," Al said, and he disappeared inside.

Lotte was following but she waited on the top step for Dudley. He was still looking into the sky. "Aren't you coming?"

"I ought to get back to base," Dudley said.

"Are you mad? You heard how close those last bombs were. You can't drive during a raid! You can't have your lights on, and how will you see if the road's damaged or not?"

"But, Lotte—"

"And what about Eddy? Are you just going to leave him here?"

"If he's taken Veronal he's probably asleep. I expect when he's awake he's in more pain than he will admit," Thane said. "Let June look after him. It'll be the best medicine. When he wakes, I'm sure she will gladly drive him to Kettlebury."

Another blast hit, too loud to talk over, and Dudley hesitated. At last he said, "Being caught in this raid—and unable to do anything about it—well, it makes my blood boil. If I can get to back to base, maybe there'll be a plane and I can go after some of these murderous bastards."

To Lotte, his fury at the German bombers had outrun his good sense. "A few minutes ago there had been no plane for you and it had been all arranged that tomorrow was your day off. There won't be a new plane magically ready for you in the middle of the night! Come on." She held out her hand. "We must go into the shelter."

He took her hand and she tightened her grip. He followed her into the narrow space between the bunks, and they sat on the floor of the dark shelter, wedged together with their thighs touching. Lotte could make out the shape of Eddy asleep on a lower bunk, and June cuddled up with Anna Thérèse on the bunk above him.

Maddy was on the opposite top bunk, comforting Georgie, who was sobbing. "There, there," Maddy soothed him. Then she whispered to Lotte and the others: "The explosions upset him. But he'll be all right."

Georgie's sobs became fainter and fainter. Lotte heard him sigh as he snuggled into the security of his mother's embrace. The bombs and the sense of helplessness in their cramped shelter might still disturb him throughout the night, and she doubted that Maddy would get much sleep.

Another whisper, just a little louder, came from Al. "I'm sorry for the tight quarters, Dudley. Perhaps the All Clear will sound before long and we can go back into the house."

Lotte felt Dudley's arm press against her shoulder as he settled into position. He whispered back to Al, "It's fine. Thank you for offering me space in your shelter, sir."

There was a pause, during which another stick of bombs rumbled across the neighborhood, and dust wafted down from the roof of the shelter.

"For God's sake, Lotte," came a whisper from June that was more like a hiss. "Did you have to bring Dudley in here—with the family!"

"Now, June," Maddy said, loud enough that Georgie stirred and moaned.

They all fell silent, listening while Georgie sniffled several times and finally settled again. Then Al whispered, as softly as he possibly could and still make himself heard, "Everybody. Mind your manners in here. Please."

In the uncomfortable quiet that followed, Lotte realized that her personal space was absurdly confined. Her knees were tucked into her chest. Her right hip was jammed against a water jug and the storage box that Maddy had packed with dry goods, towels and bandages. Yet being in such close quarters with her English family gave her a sense of contentment.

Her left hip was pressed against Dudley's. He was certainly an outsider to the Weldy family, but the warmth of his arm against her was comforting. She turned towards him and made her softest whisper into his ear, "Aren't you uncomfortable, sitting like this?"

His blond hair brushed against hers as he bent to murmur back. "I think I have more room here than I have in the cockpit. It's quite cozy."

She wasn't quite sure how to respond, and just accepted it as British pilot's humor. "I'm glad you decided to stay."

"I am eager to get back to base. But the morning will have to do."

It seemed as if everyone in the shelter had settled in for the night. Al had fallen into a raspy, slumbering breathing pattern. Little Georgie was sleeping, making a quiet moan now and then that sounded more contented than troubled. Lotte hoped that even if June or Maddy were still awake, they might not hear her and Dudley whispering.

She felt his breath on her ear as he said, "Al and Maddy are very generous, agreeing to take those children to safety, along with their own. I can't imagine my parents doing such a thing."

"Why wouldn't they?"

"Well, perhaps they would. I don't really know them very well."

"I don't understand."

Whispering required an intimate rhythm where Lotte spoke softly into Dudley's ear, then straightened to let him whisper in return.

"I went off to boarding school at a young age. I wasn't home much after that. Even when I did come home, Pater was working and didn't have time for me. Mother seemed content to let the nanny look after me."

"That is sad," Lotte said.

She felt him shrug. "It's just how it was. Was yours the perfect, happy family?"

Lotte hesitated. "No. My father died in the last war. And my mother also died, years ago."

"Then we're united in our miseries." Dudley moved abruptly, fishing for something in his jacket. Then she heard metal on metal and realized he was unscrewing a bottle top and offering it directly in front of her. She caught a whiff of spirits. "Want some?"

"No! Not in here with the children. And Eddy's in your care. You need to have your wits about you to drive him back to your airbase."

A soft, mocking whisper came from above. "Just like old times, Dudley."

So June had been listening, after all. Perhaps she couldn't sleep, cramped as she was between her current and ex fiancés! Worried about Eddy's injury, worried about the bombing raid, and worried about what mischief Dudley would make, she was making it quite clear to Lotte that she should keep away from him and his drinking at all costs.

Dudley chuckled quietly. "Same old June." Lotte heard him screw the cap back on. "Of course, she's right," he whispered in her ear. "She always is." He adjusted himself to set the flask on the floor between their legs, then settled back against Eddy's bunk.

"I'm sorry," Dudley whispered in her ear, fainter this time so she could barely hear, apparently taking it down a level in the hope that June wouldn't be able to listen in.

Lotte didn't reply and the only sounds in the shelter were Al's occasional snores and Georgie's fitful breathing.

After a lengthy pause, Thane whispered, "I'm sure you would concede there are two sides to every story. But I fear you think the worst of me."

Lotte hesitated. Trying not to disturb the others had forced her to wedge her arm tightly into his, but there was no comment from anyone, not even June, so she replied. "How can I judge? I don't know you. But please, don't drink tonight. Not here."

"Rest assured; I'll mind my manners."

"Good." Lotte understood that she must keep her distance. But her heart beat faster when she felt the warmth of his body next to hers and pleasant softness of his breath when he whispered into her ear. "What do you think June would tell me about you?"

"That I'm irresponsible and a louse. But that was two years ago. I've grown up a bit since then."

"I expect you have. In fact I know you have. I believe there must be some goodness in you. You brought Eddy here to see his family, even though—you didn't have to."

"I am a lucky man, not a good man. The only thing I am good at is killing our enemy," Dudley said.

She had no idea what to say to him next. Part of her wanted to find out if he had changed and grown into a decent man since his falling out with June. He seemed content to sit quietly side by side with their bodies pressed together.

He said, "Frenchy told me a little about your life in Germany. My parents were perfectly delightful compared to your brother, the Nazi."

"Thank you, and you're right," Lotte said, "but now's not the time to talk about that. It makes me sad to think of him."

"Don't be sad, dear girl," Dudley said. "You're safe in here. I'm starting to think this is the safest place on earth."

She laid her head on his shoulder and he put his arm around her, and she found herself hoping that the All Clear siren wouldn't sound for hours.

Chapter 37

The next morning, Thane's eyes were heavy from lack of sleep. The All Clear had sounded barely three hours earlier. He and Lotte and Al had gone into the house where he'd dozed for maybe thirty minutes. Even in that snatched sleep, he'd been thinking of Lotte, remembering how she'd been pressed against him in the shelter, and the scent of her floral perfume.

After splashing water on his face, he went down the stairs to the dining room. Maddy and June were placing two pitchers of water and a dozen cups on the table.

"I'm sorry for the inconvenience, Dudley," said Maddy. "We're arranging things for the children that Al and I will pick up with the bus."

"Aren't you taking them on to Lassingwood?"

"Yes. But once we collect them in Rotherhithe we must bring them here. I've arranged for Mrs. Ferguson to sit with Georgie and Anna Thérèse until we return. I thought we'd give the children a drink and a toilet break before we leave for the country. We'll feed them some sandwiches on the bus."

Lotte came into the dining room with Georgie.

"Mummy, are the children here?"

Maddy chuckled. "No, dear. The children I told you about— They'll be arriving here later."

"I can't wait to play jacks with them!"

"I'm sure there will be time for that later, dear." Maddy shuffled him up the stairs.

Thane took Lotte's hand. "Good morning."

"Good morning, Dudley. Let me get you some tea."

Thane saw June roll her eyes.

Lotte turned to Maddy. "After I get Dudley's tea, I'll wake Anna Thérèse and get her dressed."

247

"Thank you, dear," Maddy said.

Lotte went into the kitchen.

Thane wanted a moment with Lotte to tell her how much their night in the shelter meant to him, and to make plans to meet her again. He hoped he wasn't too late. It was apparent that the three ladies had risen before he had to prepare for the East End children, and if June had cornered Lotte and warned her away from him, his hopes would be as good as dashed.

"Do you know anything about these children you will be collecting?" Thane asked Maddy, who was scurrying between the parlour and the kitchen, carrying a handful of towels.

"They are a sad lot, Dudley. They are from the East End, but most of them have no place to live. Their family home was bombed. Others are being sent with us because their parents want them in a safer place. One I know is an orphan. Lost her parents in a bombing." She paused. "All of them will be better off in the country—until the German bombings stop."

Thane flinched. It was his job to stop the Heinkels and Dorniers from getting through but this morning he was sitting idly at the Weldys' table instead of strapping into his Spitfire. Part of him wanted to leave immediately to return to Kettlebury and do his bit. But his heart was tugging at him to stay until he could talk to Lotte.

Maddy sighed. "The little orphan girl—Esther—I met her. She had streaks running down her cheeks, so she'd been crying. She was sitting beside a pram. I asked her what was wrong. She told me her family's flat is gone. And her parents are gone."

"The poor girl," June said, taking notice.

"Esther has been staying with a WVF lady. The poor lamb is fiercely attached to her pram and Judy—that's her doll. Because they are all she has."

Thane handed Maddy a five pound note. "Would you buy some things for Esther after you get to the country, Mrs. Weldy? Whatever she needs: some clothes, or toys, perhaps."

"I will, Dudley. God bless you."

June didn't say anything, but nodded slightly, acknowledging his action even though her expression betrayed she wasn't convinced of his sincerity. "I'm going to the shelter to check on Eddy," she said. Maddy followed June out of the dining room.

248

Lotte returned and poured Thane a cup of tea.

With Maddy and June out of the room, he took Lotte's hand and drew her in close enough to whisper. "I can't stop thinking of you. I want to see you again."

Lotte smiled, politely, and said, "I'll have to think about it, Dudley. Please excuse me; I must tend to Anna Thérèse." She hesitated. "I'll be leaving for work soon. Be safe, Dudley."

"I will. While you're thinking on it, please have good thoughts, my dear." He kissed the back of her hand and released it.

Lotte turned away and he watched her climb the stairs. As the warmth of her touch faded, he yearned for more. Please, please, he mused, let there be a next time.

Reluctantly, Thane turned his thoughts to the day's business. He knew he should be leaving for Kettlebury, but he hadn't seen Eddy yet this morning. He joined Al, who was smoking in the garden near the Anderson shelter, but there was still no sign of Eddy. He pulled out his own cigarettes.

"Are the women finished making their arrangements for the children?" Al asked.

"I think so," Thane said.

"Maddy and I will be leaving in the bus soon," Al said. "Listen, Dudley, everyone here in Peckham and all over England appreciates what you boys are doing."

"Thank you, sir."

"Please look out for Eddy."

"I will."

"He's very dear to all of us, you know."

"I've learned that, sir."

Al shook Thane's hand. "Good luck and may God protect you." He went into the house.

Thane stayed by the back door, smoking.

After a few minutes, Eddy came out of the shelter, stretched, and drew a deep breath. Seeing Thane, he exclaimed, "My God, Tuner, what have you done to the world while I've been asleep? It smells like fire and brimstone."

"Twilight of the Gods, old man. Quite Wagnerian. It's probably treason to say it in German."

"Let me have a ciggy, would you?"

Thane gave Eddy one and lit him up, and they smoked without speaking, each leaning on a doorpost, looking idly down the length of Al's garden. Silence hung in the air.

At last, Thane asked, "Something bothering you, old man?"

"June said you were in the shelter with us last night. And you were whispering back and forth with Lotte. She didn't like that one bit."

Thane threw down his cigarette and stomped on it. "Then why don't you say your good-byes. I'll drive us back to Kettlebury. We have a war to fight."

Chapter 38

When Thane drove the Vauxhall away from Peckham, there was still a reddish-yellow haze hanging over the Thames.

"I hope Aunt Maddy's and Uncle Al's route to the East End isn't closed," Eddy said to him. "It must be still burning there."

"That's not Northern lights. That's Manderley."

"What?"

Thane chuckled. "Sorry. Never mind."

Commercial Way was dotted with craters and littered with chunks of concrete and blown-out car frames. Thane was certain buildings were badly damaged along the route, but smoke and dust were thick as fog. When the air cleared, slightly, he could see a man and a woman were walking along the sidewalk, toting suitcases and cloth sacks, and hurrying along three young children. Then a father was carrying his toddler, an old man trudged past with the aid of his cane, and a middle-aged woman with her hair in curlers was carrying a puppy. All wore grim, almost blank expressions as if they never expected bombs to fall on their homes, three miles south of The Thames.

They could hear the wail of a lone siren, even though the German bombers had turned back for France hours ago.

"I don't remember any of this damage on the way in," Thane said. "They've copped it pretty bad overnight."

"I don't know how to help these people," Eddy said.

"Our job is to get back to Kettlebury and fly our Spits to protect them."

Eddy sighed. "We need to get off Commercial Way. Take the next left turning."

"Will do."

Two blocks more and things seemed normal. There was a grey pall over the street, but through it they could see brightly-colored awnings were out and adverts on an easel that beckoned customers into the newsagent's shop. A quarter mile further, Thane was forced to stop behind a line of automobiles. He tapped the Vauxhall's steering wheel impatiently, but the line wasn't moving.

"What's happening here?" he asked, rhetorically.

"Let's see," Eddy said, getting out.

Thane followed him to the front of a dozen waiting cars. On the street just beyond the cars, debris had been pushed into several piles. A man wearing a tin helmet strapped tightly under his chin was watching a bull-dozer push one of the piles to the kerb.

"When can we get through?" Thane asked him.

"Ten minutes, probably. No more than fifteen."

Thane nodded his thanks. He said to Eddy, "We'll have to wait our turn, old man."

Air had a pungent taste: was it smoke or dust or both? Dark billows rose over a row of buildings; smoke from fires that hadn't yet been put out. A black rat darted by Thane's shoe. Its eight inch tail brushed his heel. He jumped and swore.

"Let's have a look over there," Eddy said. Round the corner a crowd had gathered, standing before a clean hole in a row of residential buildings. Like a missing tooth. All that was left was a sunken rubble field strewn with bricks, stones, mortar and roof tiles, and odd bits like a desk chair, file folders and a gabardine work cap. A section of a brick wall was standing, but it had been reduced to a jagged, sooty triangle of bricks.

Brick walls and window frames of buildings adjacent to the hole were intact, except that the glass was gone. Three firemen were manning a firehose that shot water into the window of a flat. Even with water streaming in, black smoke was billowing out.

A boy covered in soot like a chimney sweep descended the front of a building, swinging from window frames to wires to gutters and back like a monkey.

"Good lord, lad, stay out of there!" Thane said to the boy. "That building could collapse at any moment."

"I 'ad to check on Mr. Holland. He's an old man, you know."

Thane looked at the building. "Is he following you out?"

"No. He's still there."

252

"Where?"

"The second floor hall. Where the flats stop 'cause a bomb blew off the back of the building. He's in the last one."

"Is he okay?" Thane asked.

The boy shook his head. "Ceiling fell in on 'im. So he's dead."

"You're sure?"

"'Is hand was cold and he had lots of blood on his face." He pointed to a canvas that was covering ten body-sized lumps. "They need to put him under that." The boy approached the firefighters.

Thane saw that the canvas did not completely conceal a dead woman's day dress and scuffed black shoe. Eddy was staring at the tarp.

"Come on. Let's get back to the car," Thane said.

"These poor people live no more than a mile from Aunt Maddy and Uncle Al and they've been in for it. I—I just want to do something," Eddy said.

"At least, now I know what the Germans are doing to our people," Thane said. "I know why I'm fighting. The bastards will pay if it's the last thing I do."

Chapter 39

Eddy found himself outside the dispersal hut the following morning an hour before dawn, even though the Squadron's pilots weren't due until first light. Unable to find a position that was comfortable for sleeping, he had wandered outside the sleeping barracks towards the hut, watching the stars without making any sense of their endless patterns in the still blackness of the sky. Before long pilots began filing into the hut, Dobbers, a new man called Stack, and two more new men he had only met at dinner last night and couldn't recall their names. These men and the others would be dressing in their flying suits and Mae Wests, ready to scramble, and he wanted to be among them. He took his elbow out of his sling and raised his shoulder, testing it, but the movement caused him to wince in pain.

When the rest of the Squadron's pilots had appeared, Eddy followed them into the hut and after a moment's hesitation he took off his sling and left it on the seat of a folding chair. Minutes later, Bull Connell arrived. "You all here? Good. The rain has gone and the sun is shining."

"Bloody lovely," Thane said, stretched out on the couch, without opening his eyes. Eddy wondered how he could still be tired since he had napped on and off for almost all of the previous day to recover from his night in the Anderson shelter.

Bull began to fill out duty listings on the blackboard on the center of the wall. "We have thirteen pilots and twelve Spitfires." Bull looked at Eddy. "You're going to be on base radio with me."

"No! I want to fly," Eddy said.

Bull stared at him. "Have you chucked away your sling? Lift your arm to shoulder height."

Eddy tried and winced.

"See? What the bloody hell are you going to do when you're dodging a 109? You'll lose control and dump a perfectly good fighter into the Channel. Six thousand pounds-worth of plane that somebody else could be flying!"

Bull turned to Thane. "Tuner, we've got you a Spitfire from Aston Down. They were using it as a trainer, but Mike and I have checked it top to bottom and sighted its guns and it's ready to go. You can fly that until your own has been repaired."

"Bull, I can fly it!" Eddy said, desperately.

"Quiet, Frenchy. It'll be yours to fly in a day or two when your arm is better. Put your sling back on."

Bull finished writing the duty listing in chalk and turned to Dobson. "Right! It's all yours."

When Bull left the hut Dobson gathered his Squadron around him. "We've got four new pilots. Most of you met them yesterday, but Tuner you missed them since you slept through dinner. Meet Dunk, Tobin, Stack and Harwell."

"Hello, chaps," Thane said in the direction of the new men, "we had rather a time of it in London—and I'm afraid I couldn't muster the energy to introduce myself."

Stack gave him a knowing smile, and they all shook hands.

"You new men, gather round," Dobson said, from the blackboard. "My veterans are welcome to stay, it might do you some good."

Tank and Straw got up and left the hut. Eddy looked at Thane, who seemed oblivious, and stayed in his own seat.

Dobson chalked on the blackboard in all capital letters:

NOTHING IS NEW.

NOTHING IS TRUE.

KEEP SIGHT.

"If you want to stay alive, remember these words. Tobin: what advantages do you think our Spitfires have over the 109s?"

Tobin spoke confidently. "The Spitfire has a tighter turn radius and better overall manoeuvrability. Its maximum range is four hundred miles further and its service ceiling is seven thousand feet higher."

"Very good," Dobson said. Tobin smiled. "But ninety-nine percent of the time none of that matters a tinker's damn. The Germans know everything you just said and have tactics to deal with it. Nothing is new. If a 109 dives on you with more speed than you are carrying, your turning radius and range will not save you from getting shot down."

Dobson picked up models of a Spitfire and a Messerschmitt 109 that were mounted on sticks. He held the Spitfire with its nose pointed at the 109's tail. "Stack, which of these planes would you rather be flying?"

"The Spitfire, sir," Stack said.

"But if the Spitfire's cannons are empty, and the 109's are loaded—nothing is true."

Dobson put the models down. "More than anything, men, always keep looking. Starboard, larboard. In front, over your shoulders. Watch for the position of the sun. The 109s want to drop down on you with the sun at their backs, just as you are trying to do to them. Keep sight.

"All right. Have a brew. Think about what I've said. Be prepared to scramble at any time." Dobbers picked up his chair and carried it outside and sat down in the sunshine with Tank and Straw.

"Come on, old man," Thane said to Eddy. "Let's have a look at my new crate."

"Our new crate," Eddy said.

They walked across the grass infield towards the row of parked Spitfires. The air was heavy with the smell of fuel, reminding Eddy of the paraffin lantern in the Anderson shelter. They had no difficulty identifying the new plane—a white band with the number 1700 in black was painted in front of its tail.

"Lucky number?" Thane asked Eddy.

"We'd better hope so," Eddy said, shaking his head when he noticed that the duralumin skin of the Spit's fuselage was dented in several places.

Thane walked around the plane, examining it. "At least it has guns."

There was a parachute packed and hanging over the edge of one wing. "Mike's set the brolly," Eddy observed. "Let's have a look at the office. Help me up, would you?"

Thane cupped his hands for Eddy to step into and boosted him onto the wing root, and then climbed up behind him. They leaned into the cockpit.

"Look at this," Thane said. "Chipped paint. The oil dial has a crack in it... this crate's been hammered. What do Aston Down do with their students, for God's sake?"

"At least they cleaned up the vomit," Eddy said. "Still—it has a stick, a toggle switch, a throttle, and a trigger. What more do you need? Just bring it back in one piece, would you?"

"I plan to," Thane said. "Thank heavens you're in better spirits than you were during our drive from Peckham yesterday. For God's sake, I thought you were going to throw me out of my own car!"

"So I made my point?"

"How could I have missed you want me to stay away from Lotte? You even called me *scélérat*, remember? But I've been thinking it over and I can't lie to you, old man. I spent enough time with her to know she's an angel, honestly she is." He looked at Eddy. "I'll never do anything improper. But, I'd like to see her again."

Eddy tried to speak, and Thane spoke over him. "We both know the odds are that I won't get the chance."

"Look, Tuner, Lotte is a darling, and a very clever one. She's doing great work for England, and when the War's over she will have a great future. But it's a hard time for a German girl to live in London right now. If you're honestly smitten, that's one thing. But if your attentions are going to make her life more difficult, I'll have something to say about it."

"Point taken."

Eddy exhaled sharply. "Ahh, hell. It's my fault."

"What are you talking about, old man?"

"You dealing with Lotte. June being mad as a hatter at me for bringing you to the Weldys' home—I should have realized Aunt Maddy might call her over. I should have never invited you in."

"I see. Well, I'm sorry I put you in a bind with our—your—girl. But I must say: The night with your family meant a great deal to me."

When they returned to the hut, Dobson greeted them. "Satisfied?"

"Not much of a looker," Thane said, "but she'll fly."

"Then get into the cotton wool and stay hidden," Eddy said to Thane. "I want my crate back in one piece."

"I'll do that," Thane said. "But not before I've given three or four Jerry bastards a full squirt."

257

Dobson and Tank laughed. "You lads must have kissed and made up," Dobson said. "Your trip to London did some good."

The telephone rang and Dobson rushed to answer it.

"Scramble! Angels ten."

The twelve pilots sprinted to their planes, put on their parachutes, and climbed into their cockpits. Envy tore through Eddy as he watched propellers twirl into motion, smoke puffs drift along the fuselages, and the ground men pull away chocks in a pattern of economical actions that brought to mind a dance troupe. While the planes taxied into position, Eddy reluctantly took himself to the command post, which was a small building on the other side of the officers' mess. Its wooden front wall was splintered where shrapnel had struck it. He and Bull stood at the front door, watching the Squadron take off to the south-west, into the wind. As the airplanes circled to take up positions, one of them began to plunge up and down like a swimming porpoise. Eddy recognized the plane's reaction to a novice's heavy-handed pumping of the undercarriage lever.

"Christ!"

Bull looked despairingly at Eddy. "I thought Uxbridge said our new men are well-trained."

Another Spitfire went over with its engine bellowing like a bull elephant. "What the hell does Harwell think he's doing, still in fine pitch?"

Bull hurried into the command post and radioed Dobson. "Tell Harwell to switch to coarse pitch or he'll spit out all his engine oil."

Information was coming in from Uxbridge and in a moment Bull spoke again to Dobson. "Set course for vector forty. Two bandits at Angels twenty."

"Okay," Dobson said.

"Only two?" Eddy asked Bull.

"Two reconnaissance planes. Should be easy pickings."

"You scrambled the entire Squadron for two spotters?"

"Dobbers suggested it. He wanted to have a look at these new men before we call on them for serious action," Bull said.

"I can see why."

It took ten minutes for the Squadron to make the climb. Bull had turned back to the radio transmissions and Eddy listened as he passed on orders to Dobson which positioned the Squadron five angels above the German reconnaissance planes. Dobson ordered Stack to break and attack the trailing plane, and when Stack shouted, "I got him!" Eddy thumped the desk in triumph.

Bull asked Dobson, "What about the second spotter?"

"He's dodged into the cotton," Dobson said.

Eddy imagined the Squadron flying round the cloud like terriers hunting a rat in a haystack.

Tank's harsh baritone came on the radio. "I see him to starboard. I'm going after him."

There was silence for almost a minute.

"The bastard's run between my legs!" Tank said.

After another minute Eddy began to wonder if Tank had lost him, but the radio came in again. "Got 'im," Tank said jubilantly. "I'm circling two brollies. They're going to splash down off Dungeness. About a mile out. I'll return to base once the boat spots them."

"Okay."

Tank's voice came through the speaker again, this time singing, "Bang, bang, bang, bang goes the farmer's gun, so run rabbit, run rabbit, run, run, run."

"It's the bloody funny farm," Bull said.

~ ~ ~

Eddy was sitting in the sunshine, on the grass infield. Several other pilots were lounging a short distance away. Beside him, Thane was sleeping flat out, and had been for a good two hours. A persistent fly was doing circuits and bumps around his face, and eventually it woke him, and he stretched and groaned and sat up.

"You've sure caught up with your kip," Eddy said.

"It's helped. I'll be ready when they scramble us for the real thing."

"What's the new machine like?" Eddy asked.

"Oh, yes. Well, she's a bit sluggish on take-off." Thane lit a cigarette. "It takes the full left rudder to hold her straight. But the old girl cruises all right. I tried some rolls and a steep turn, and she's lively enough."

259

"A good report, overall?" Eddy said. He was still not quite sure what to think, because a pilot would never speak ill of any plane he flew, respecting the superstition that a scorned machine, like a scorned lover, would cause him problems.

"Good enough for me to tape a few of the bastards next time they come over."

Dobson came striding across the infield. "Gather in the hut!"

The pilots dragged themselves to their feet, yawning and stretching, and went indoors. Someone had made tea, and they all helped themselves.

"Well done this morning, men," Dobson said. "I was pleased with the sortie. We kept formation reasonably well. The main thing is, we got the job done."

The new men nodded.

Dobson asked, "How did it look from the ground, Frenchy?"

"The Squadron scrambled as one. You took off neatly. I noticed a couple of minor errors of technique, but I am quite certain they will not be repeated."

Harwell looked down at his flying boots. Eddy hoped the new men appreciated Dobson's wisdom in giving them an easy, low-risk sortie. They had taken off together, formed up and hunted quarry successfully. That exercise would give them confidence when they scrambled to face a major raid, and they just might have learned something that could save their lives.

Eddy concluded, "And Tank is a terrible singer!"

"We shan't have time for singing this afternoon," Dobson said. "We are expecting two hundred or more bombers coming over the south coast and heading for London. They will be covered above and below by 109s. Remember the instructions the Air Vice Marshal gave us: climb above them and dive straight through the 109s to hit the bombers. We will be attacking at very high speed. Four hundred miles per hour or more. You must keep your plane stable to shoot—no skidding as you fire. Deflection shooting is imperative—send your packet into the bomber's flight path. You practiced deflection shooting at training school, didn't you Dunk?"

Dunk nodded.

"Good lad. Remember, don't shoot from right angles because it's damn near impossible to hit them. You have to attack from above or

260

below. You only have fifteen seconds of firing—four or five short bursts. Make them count. Now, all of you, be ready. Keep sight. Anything to add, Tank?"

"If you see a 109 behind you, roll over and make her sing," he said.

Chapter 40

While the Squadron's pilots waited for the order to scramble, Eddy checked the blackboard out of habit, reading the list of pilots, duty, and section. His name still wasn't there. He wanted to be flying, facing the same risks as the other men, and feeling the surge of adrenalin that flowed through his veins when he climbed into the cockpit.

Left of the blackboard was a three foot long poster of aerial tactics.

To its right was a chart with overhead views of enemy aeroplanes. Next to the chart were two pin-up girls, a redhead and a blonde. Harwell was looking at them with a silly smile on his face. Eddy decided not to ask him which one he preferred.

The room was quiet, like the stillness before thunder. Tension was palpable and it could only be relieved by the scramble order.

Tank was reclining on a cot, reading a Graham Greene novel. His yellow-haired retriever lay curled beside him. Stack sat in a leather chair with his feet up on the windowsill. A writing pad rested on his right thigh but his fountain pen was idle, as if he were contemplating his next sentence. Tuner puffed on his pipe behind a copy of The Times and cursed under his breath at something he was reading.

Dobbers had an unfolded letter on the desk in front of him. Eddy thought his expression was strangely serene, almost sad. Was it bad news from home? A break-up message?

The telephone rang, Dobson answered and gave the order to scramble, and the twelve pilots sprinted to their Spitfires. Eddy watched them harness up. It was as if he were in Tuner's place, facing a florid panel of dials, buttons, and levers. His mind ticked through procedures during those highly-charged seconds: Throttle slightly open, stroke the priming pump, set to fine pitch, brakes on, stick back, and press the starter. The pilots slid their canopies closed. Propellers began to turn, and purplish-white smoke rose from the cowlings of the supercharged Merlin engines.

Twelve Spitfires roared into action. Eddy watched Tuner take off. He accelerated smoothly—not so fast that he would risk catching the long prop blade in the turf. A couple of bounds on the grassy infield and the plane rose as if it were kicking the ground clear. Now Tuner would switch hands on the stick to put his right on the undercarriage lever. Pull. One Hail Mary and rotate.

The twelve Spitfires were circling round to the east as one. The Squadron was perfectly spaced. Time for Tuner to reduce the engine pitch and start climbing. Minutes later Eddy could see nothing but contrails leading into the altostratus clouds.

~ ~ ~

Thane kept a light touch on the controls as he scanned the flaps position and the buffet warning and the rest of the dials. He tried to free his mind of anything but the task at hand, seeking an instinctive harmony with his machine that almost gave the plane life to fly itself.

His stomach had its usual peculiar feeling of slight nausea induced by high altitude. But today it was something more. He glanced over his right shoulder at Stack. Would Stack cover him if a 109 was on his tail? He thought of Frenchy standing on the infield with his hands on his hips, watching the Squadron take off without him. Frenchy had been glum all right, and Thane understood completely. The truth was that he and Dobbers and Tank all needed Frenchy. They were flying into aerial combat against dozens of Messerschmitt 109s alongside four new men who'd come straight from training. He didn't know yet whether they were reliable or a liability.

At Angels seventeen he saw three distinct, long gray layers of enemy planes, too many bandits to count, all spaced with meticulous German efficiency; a grim flying set-piece delivering ordnance to London. It brought Lord Tennyson's lines to mind: "All in the Valley of Death Rode the six hundred." The twelve Spitfires of his squadron, only eight with aerial combat experience, were even more out-numbered than the Light Brigade. Thane's memory of the Bible was hazy, but he decided that the passage from Samuel—David against Goliath—would be more apt.

He turned on his oxygen mask as the Squadron continued to climb. Around thirty thousand feet, Dobson positioned the Squadron above and to the west of the German formation. The sun was behind them. Perfect.

He looked down on the German formation, preparing to dive, and was struck by the insanity of his task. He had to fly through a gap in the 109s, which were traveling more than two hundred miles per hour and keep his wits while they shot at him. Would this wreck of a Spit Aston Down had sent over even hang together at diving speed? When he cleared the 109s he had to line up a shot on a Dornier bomber below and somehow avoid crashing into a German plane on the way through. Take the dare, he told himself, for the Weldys and Lotte and their neighbors in Peckham, and for the people who lived in the East End.

"Tally-ho!" said Dobbers, through his headset.

Thane fixed on a 109's yellow nose, kept pace three hundred feet above it for five seconds, then timed his dive through the gap behind its angular wing. White tracer streamed wildly above his cockpit, but as he was diving through the 109s at more than twice their speed, he knew only a miraculously lucky shot would hit him.

As soon as he was below the protective layer of 109s, Thane waited for a Dornier's glass canopy to come squarely into his sights, then toggled off a long burst and broke right. He was confident his packet had found the target but bringing down a bomber twice as long and three times as heavy as his plane was like elephant hunting. He couldn't be certain he had scored unless he saw it go down.

The back of his neck tingled and glancing over his left shoulder he saw that two 109s were breaking formation to chase him. He rolled to starboard into a tight climbing turn, aiming for the cloud base. Orange flashed to his left and he saw a Spitfire with flames shooting from its cowlings and over its windscreen. He recognized Harwell's tail number before it fell away behind him.

He leveled off when he'd climbed above the German formation. There seemed to be mist rising from the Spitfire's hood. Damnit! It was a spot of ice forming on the lower half of his windscreen, shrinking the plane's small field of vision just when he needed it most.

Dobson's Spitfire was two hundred yards in front of him, starting to dive through the tight layer of enemy fighters. Thane rose in his seat to look over the icy patch and as he did so, he saw Dobbers's starboard wing clip a 109 and his plane began to spin. Thane dived to cover him. Somehow, Dobbers regained control before he reached the bombers below, but a 109 was diving after him with cannons flashing. Pieces of the fuselage broke away. Flames erupted in the cockpit. The fuel tank exploded and the plane, a fireball, fell end over end out of the sky.

Thane growled and opened the throttle to roar after the 109 that had shot down his Squadron Leader. He was closing on it and lining up on the number 34 painted on its fuselage for a shot when another 109 zipped between them. He pressed off a long burst, pretty sure he would miss both his enemies but too furious to stop himself. A single shard of metal bounced off Thane's windscreen. The 109 he was chasing flickrolled to larboard before it vanished as completely as a ghost.

You bastard!

A third 109 hurtled past him, so close that he ducked, but when he looked again through the windscreen the enemy planes had disappeared. He had no idea which way they had gone, so diving after them would be a fool's errand.

Thane judged that he had one good burst of ammunition left, six hundred rounds or so. He gave his Spit full throttle, then made a half Cuban turn to line up head on with the Dornier formation. Looking through the wisps of cloud below, he could see the serpent of the Thames, the docks and the ravaged boroughs of London—Rotherhithe where Al and Maddy Weldy had gone to evacuate the dockland children and Peckham, where Lotte was alone in the Weldys' house with only that stuffy, tin-framed Anderson shelter for protection.

It was time for these bastards to pay!

He flew directly at the leading Dornier, hoping to break the nerve of its pilot. He held steady until the last moment and fired all of his final burst into the glass cockpit before he pulled the spade stick back to climb clear of it. He went on climbing into the clouds, till he was well above the German formation. He was sure that this time he couldn't have missed.

"Tuner," Bull's voice crackled over the radio. "RTB fuel?"

Thane looked at his fuel gauge. Nearly empty. "Yes. And my packet is spent."

"Return to base."

"Okay. They got Dobbers. And the new man." He heard anguish in Frenchy's voice in the background but couldn't make out his words.

Bull exclaimed, "Dobson!—and Harwell?"

"Yes. Both of them."

"Damn."

Thane flew on, southwest, to get clear of the German formation before he throttled back. The exhaust was making an ominous crumpling sound which told him that his fuel tank was nearly empty. As he lined up for Kettlebury, he didn't have to think through the landing procedure: his mind was in automatic, and he let the Spitfire glide towards the airfield, with the conscious part of his mind replaying the mission over and over.

After Dobbers had clipped wings with the 109, the loss of speed had left him a clay pigeon. At that point, everything had depended on his wingman, on him, Dudley Thane. He should have been covering Dobbers. Had he been too bloody slow? In aerial combat, fractions of a second could mean life and death. Had he watched Dobbers's plane spin for one instant too long when he should have begun to dive?

For a moment a strange sense of envy washed over Thane. Patrick Dobson had returned to earth like a flaming rocket, spent but glorious, having given everything for his cause. His was a heroic death, and that seemed immeasurably better than growing old slowly and waiting for one's organs to fail. If Thane went out the same way, he would have no regrets: neither of them had ever stood down in the face of the enemy.

An engine roared, behind and to his right, and as he recognized the sound of an enemy plane his body jerked him back into survival mode. A lone 109 was diving at him. From its angle of attack, Thane knew he was taped. He instinctively pulled back the throttle. Nothing. Of course, he was out of fuel. Out of ammo. Out of luck. So this is it, old man. He leaned his head back and waited for the cannon shells that would send him to join Dobbers.

Thane wasn't expecting the crackle of Browning machine guns that broke out above him. He looked to starboard and there were bullet holes starting at the 109's engine and running all along its fuselage. Its nose dropped and its propeller stopped turning and it fell out of his field of vision towards the Kent countryside. Then Stack was alongside him, flashing a thumb's up, waggling his wings, and sprinting ahead of him towards Kettlebury.

Thane was more astonished than relieved. Surely the war could be won if they sent 11 Group some more new men like Stack.

~ ~ ~

Eddy was standing in the doorway of the dispersal hut, leaning against the jamb, while Thane sat on the edge of a cot and gave his flight report to Intelligence Officer Carter. Five other pilots had gathered round them. The hut was unnaturally quiet. They were all listening.

"You saw Dobson clip his wing against the 109. Do you consider he overshot his dive?" Carter asked.

"For God's sake man, no," Thane said. "Dobbers was the best flyer here. Maybe in the whole bloody RAF. I told you: we were at thirty thousand feet. My windscreen was starting to ice up. My bet is Dobbers couldn't see."

Carter wrote something on his clipboard. "I have noted this condition in previous reports."

"Then note it again you bloody idiot! This time, tell them to put Gnomist in every Spit's office, before the next man dies. And have them give us a reserve cannister of oxygen while you're at it! Dobbers would have been dead anyway, if he had hit the silk at that height without oxygen. You and your damned pencil-pushers need to get your heads out of your arses!"

Eddy sat down next to Thane and put a hand on his shoulder. Carter was low in the SIS's hierarchy, but Thane might be testing his capacity to make trouble.

"Have a cigarette," he suggested, offering his case.

Thane accepted, abruptly, and lit up. He exhaled a stream of smoke and turned to Carter. "Sorry old chap. Today was a rough one."

Carter nodded as though he saw outbursts like Thane's every day. "Anything to add? Anything to make the next sortie easier, quicker, safer?"

"No. But I'll have nightmares about the number 34," Thane said. "After the bastard got Dobbers I thought I had him lined up. I was that close; I could see the bugger's scarf. White wool. Clear as day. And then somehow, he spun his crate and got away."

"Did you say 34?" Eddy asked.

"Yes," Thane said. "Why, have you seen him too?"

"I've seen that bastard, all right." Vivid memories came back to Eddy of Wunstorf, where a Messerschmitt number 34 had followed his Aeronca into the clouds, and of Dunkirk when number 34 had put a shell through the Spitfire's canopy. He had been too green then to know what to do. Not any more. "That's the bloody Jerry who put the hole in my radiator. If I see him again, I'll kill him."

"Not if I see him first," Thane said.

Just then, Stack walked through the door. Thane exclaimed, "See the conquering hero!" He popped up from the cot and bear-hugged Stack.

"You two are rather friendly all of a sudden," Eddy said.

"I owe him my miserable life. I was bone-dry coming home and felt a ring twitch and there was a bloody 109. It had me lined up and I thought I was a dead man. But Stack took care of business for me."

"Bravo! *Vive le héros!*" said Eddy.

"I thought you could use some help," Stack said to Thane.

"A moment longer and I'd have been eating cannon shells," Thane said. "But the Nazi was a bit too slow. He was probably having a laugh at me, floating my crate home." He turned to Eddy. "The bastard must have thought he was about to bag a sitting duck. But Stack bagged him instead."

Bull Connell entered the hut and shook hands somberly with Thane, Eddy and Stack. "We lost three pilots today. The new men, Harwell and Duncan. And Squadron Leader Dobson."

The pilots took the news in silence. They were all thoughtful; it was unsaid but hanging in the air that the next mission might be their last, too.

Bull said to Thane, "I plan to appoint you Squadron Leader. It will become official when I receive approval from Uxbridge."

"No," Thane said. "Don't do that."

"Whyever not?"

Thane looked across at Carter. "I lack the temperament. Frenchy here would be a better choice."

Eddy was taken aback. Squadron Leader? And proposed by Thane, of all people?

Bull nodded, looking a little perplexed. "You don't really have the option to refuse, but I'll consider what you've said." Bull turned to Carter and said, "They need you over at the brig. A 109 has been shot down and landed in a barley field just east of here. The Home Guard have brought the pilot to us." Eddy saw Thane and Stack exchange a look of fierce satisfaction. "Uxbridge wants you to interrogate him. Get his unit's location and strength, that sort of thing. The Air Vice Marshal expects a report immediately, so get over there."

"I don't speak any German, sir," Carter said. "At least, not enough to interrogate a prisoner."

"Uxbridge is sending us an SIS translator," Bull said.

"Ahh, that will be Park's girl," Carter said.

"What's that?" Bull asked.

"Park keeps a girl at Uxbridge," Carter said. "She's a looker! He sends her round to the air bases when they've captured German pilots, and she acts as translator for interrogations. I saw her at Biggin Hill last week driving a very smart Morris Eight."

Thane and Eddy looked at each other, wide-eyed.

Chapter 41

Lotte and Intelligence Officer Carter were interviewing the captured German pilot in the "brig," a small barracks buildings. It had two cots for the use of visitors, a toilet, and a wash basin. A coal stove and a small cupboard were its only other amenities. The prisoner sat in a chair on the opposite side of the desk from Lotte, guarded by two military policemen who stood at either side of the door.

"What is your name?" she asked, in German.

"Lothar Hintz," he answered.

"Where are you from?"

Hintz drummed his fingers on the desk and did not answer.

"Please stop that," Lotte said.

Hintz ignored her, until Carter sat forward and frowned. Then he folded his hands in his lap and stared insolently at both of them.

"Where are you from?" she repeated.

"Hamburg. You are a German girl," he hissed at Lotte. "Why are you helping the British?"

She had become used to prisoners using her as a target for their anger. "What I am is not your concern," she said. "Answer the questions, no more."

"All right," said Carter. "Let's get on with it. Ask him...."

The door burst open and Dudley Thane charged in. The two MPs intercepted him, but he still struggled to get at the captured German. "You're the bastard who shot down Dobbers!"

"Take it easy now, sir," one of the MPs said to Thane. "You're not wanted here."

Lotte said, "Please, Lieutenant Thane—we are conducting an interrogation."

Thane shouted at her. "He shot down Patrick Dobson." He struggled to throw off the MPs' grip.

Hintz, seeing that the MPs had control of Thane, turned back to Lotte and Carter and said disdainfully, in German, "Tomorrow we will blacken the skies with our bombers. They will keep bombing until they demoralize your degenerate little country. When you are finished, my comrades will release me." He nodded at Thane. "Then I'll take care of this one."

Lotte waited as calmly as she could for him to stop. Such threats were not unusual. She dismissed them with a single glance and then she said to Thane, "Dudley. Please go away. You are not helping me to do my job."

"What have you asked him? Has he admitted that he shot down Dobbers?"

She didn't reply, hoping that her silence would encourage him to leave.

"Whose side are you on, Lotte?"

Thane's face twisted. Was it hatred for the prisoner? For her? For both of them? He pulled free of the MPs' hold and stormed out, almost colliding with Eddy Beane, who was on his way in. Thane hesitated, then ran out without closing the door.

Eddy came into the room and shut the door, and the two MPs faced him as a precaution, but they could see he didn't pose the threat that Thane had.

"I must apologize for Lieutenant Thane," he said. "I'll go after him and try to calm him down."

Carter firmed his lips and nodded. "Thank you, Frenchy. Now, if you don't mind—?"

Lotte asked Carter, "May I have a word with my cousin, for a minute, sir?"

He sighed, irritably. "As the interview is already disrupted, you can have a minute, but no more."

Lotte went outside with Eddy, and he hugged her.

"I thought I might find you here."

"It is so good to see you," she said.

"Yes, it is. And you calling me Cousin! That was clever."

271

"I do my best," Lotte said. "I was hoping to find you once this interview is completed, of course. Lieutenant Tinker has sent me here from Uxbridge, to translate."

"Lieutenant Tinker is it now?" Eddy asked, then added, "Good for him."

"I mustn't be long. But Eddy—will you go after Dudley? He stormed in here and tried to attack the prisoner. He shouted something about the man shooting down Dobbers. Then he was very angry with me— he questioned my loyalty." She paused. "I didn't see this side of him at the Weldys' house."

"I'm sorry, dear," Eddy said. "He's shaken up. We all are. Our leader —our friend, Patrick Dobson—was shot down by the Germans in front of him, no more than an hour ago. I think Tuner's mistaken—your prisoner is probably not the man who killed our friend—but he isn't thinking straight right now and when we heard there was a German pilot here I was afraid he might do something rash. I was talking to our Station Commander and I warned him. He told me to get over here as quick as I could."

"I see. That explains it. I am so sorry."

Eddy embraced her and they stood silently for a moment, looking across the airfield in the direction of the line of Squadron 57's parked Spitfires. Fitters and riggers were tending to engines and ammunition boxes.

"You see the Spitfire with the hose from the fuel wagon connected to it?"

"The plane with the number 1700 in front of its tail?" she asked.

"Right. That is my plane," Eddy told her. "Tuner flew it today, but I'll fly it tomorrow."

"But your shoulder?"

"It's better," Eddy said. "Besides, we've lost three pilots, so I'm needed. Listen, Lotte, it has been a rough day here. Come and find me at the officers' mess when you finish your job here. If you have time, we can go to the Leeward Inn and talk to Tuner. He should have calmed down by then."

~ ~ ~

An hour and a half later, Lotte had completed her interrogation of prisoner Hintz and then freshened up, and she and Eddy walked down to the Leeward Inn together, companionably arm-in-arm. The

272

Leeward and its customers had a harbour-side atmosphere: there were bearded older men at the bar, dressed in dungarees and caps, who looked as if they'd just come off the boat. There were no young men in the main bar. Four young women sitting at the other end of the room all stopping talking and stared at Lotte. Two had pursued their lips and were glowering with an intensity that made Lotte uncomfortable.

She looked at Eddy, and he grinned and whispered into her ear, "They think you are competition. Come on."

He led her to a door beyond the bar and they entered a small room that was much quieter than it should have been, given that it held nine young men in RAF uniform. One of them was Dudley Thane, who was sitting at the large table in the middle of the room. A cigarette dangled from his mouth and there was a glass of whisky in front of him. He was watching another pilot who was standing on a small table and using his lighter to scorch his name into the plaster ceiling.

"That's it, Stack," Roberts said. "Record your score for posterity."

"And a very important score it was," Thane said. "Jack!" he shouted at the landlord. "Another whisky for my hero. And another for me."

Dudley seemed surprised to see Eddy and Lotte.

"Please join me," he said. He pulled out a chair for Lotte, and she and Eddy sat down. Stack jumped down from the table having rendered 'Stack - 1' on the ceiling, sloppily, but legible. Other names with tallies next to them had been written on the plaster, some in ink, some in paint, a few burned in by lit cigarettes, and the name 'Tinky' had been marked in lipstick.

Eddy introduced Lotte to his Squadron members, and they nodded politely to her.

"I owe you an apology for my behavior this afternoon," Thane said to her.

She nodded. "It's all right, Dudley. I understand you lost a friend."

"Yes," Dudley said. "I got it into my head that your prisoner was the man who shot him down. The odds are he didn't, I suppose, but I was seeing red. Still, that is no excuse. I shouldn't have said what I did. I'm terribly sorry."

"I forgive you, Dudley."

"Let me order you both a drink."

"Thank you."

He called Jack over again. "Whatever they fancy, to drink to the memory of Patrick Dobson. Chalk it up to my account, old man."

"Dobbers was the best of us," Eddy said to her. "We'll say a few words to remember him tonight."

"Am I intruding?" she asked, looking from Eddy to Dudley and back.

"No," Dudley said. "Not at all. I take it you and Carter finished your interrogation?"

"Well, I translated everything the prisoner would say. I don't know how satisfied IO Carter will be with what he told us, but that is not my concern. The MPs took him away—for his long trip to Canada. As soon as we finished, Carter left to deliver his report to Uxbridge."

"I see," Dudley said. "Are you going back to Peckham tonight?"

"No. The Station Commander offered me a bed in the brig. I accepted so I could spend the evening with Eddy, and you."

"I'm glad you did," Dudley said. "Are you allowed to tell us about the Nazi? I'm curious. What do you ask in interrogation?" There was a barely noticeable slurring of his words.

"I'm required to keep my work in confidence," Lotte said. "I'm sure you can understand that."

"Of course," Dudley said. "We were told that you work for Air Vice Marshal Park. I was surprised—what you do must be quite important."

"Thank you."

"It can't be easy for you."

"You mean, dealing with German men? That's true," Lotte said. "These prisoners mostly consider me a traitor. They look at me with hateful eyes. They'd like nothing more than to snap my neck. I have learned to ignore that and do my job."

"You're a tough lady, then," Dudley said. "Any military secrets that you and Carter pried out of him are meant for much higher ranks than us. But do you learn anything about the man himself when you're translating?"

"No, not very often." She thought for a moment. "This man, Hintz, he claimed he was not a Nazi."

"Then why does he fly with them?"

"I asked him that. He quoted a motto: 'there must be order.' In other words, he had to follow the rules when he was called to serve."

Jack arrived with brandy for Lotte and whiskies for Eddy and Dudley. She took a sip, remembering her questioning of Hintz.

"I can also tell you this man's politics were rather interesting."

"Why?" Eddy asked.

"He considered himself a patriot. He said he fought for Germany, not the party."

"What's the difference?"

"He believed that Germany suffered a great injustice following the last war. The Treaty of Versailles drove us into poverty. One and a half million Germans were handed over to Poland and suppressed culturally and racially. And Danzig and German East Prussia were cut off. He sees the war as justified to right those wrongs."

"Is that what you think?" Dudley asked over his glass.

Eddy said, "That's hardly a fair question, Tuner."

"It's all right," Lotte said calmly. "No. I don't agree with him. Those are political issues that should be dealt with by diplomacy, not war."

"Amen to that," Dudley said. He sipped his whisky, then looked at Eddy. "Well, Frenchy, I think we need to say a few words about Dobbers."

He stood up and tapped the table with his glass, calling them to order. "Gather round, please." The other seven pilots and Bull Connell came to the table where Lotte was sitting with Dudley and Eddy.

"Today we lost our leader, Patrick Dobson. It happened right in front of me, and I can swear to you that Dobbers was attacking our enemy with all his usual vigor. I've flown in the RAF for more than two years and Dobbers was the finest fighter pilot I have ever seen. It was a freak occurrence that gave the Jerries a shot at him: he clipped wings with a 109. Losing a man like Dobbers only proves the hazardous nature of our duty, because on skill alone, nobody could ever best him." Dudley raised his glass and said, "To Dobbers."

The men repeated, 'To Dobbers' in unison. Dudley drained his whisky and shut his eyes for a second. Lotte yearned to comfort him but this moment was for the men alone.

Thane sat down and nodded to Eddy to take his turn.

"Like me, Dobbers was born in another country. He learned to fly in Victoria and joined the Royal Australian Air Force four years ago. He took a commission with the RAF in '37 and was our Squadron's longest-serving member." Eddy paused. "Dobbers led us by making us see the bigger picture—it was up to us to protect our good citizens and fight until we are victorious!"

The men gave a cheer.

"He believed in the Commonwealth and the merits of our cause. He wouldn't let anything get in the way—he made sure we all put aside our grievances with one another and worked to the good of our Squadron." He looked at Thane, who nodded in agreement. "As Tuner said, Dobbers was the best of the best." Eddy raised his glass. "My brother Dobbers—Tally Ho!"

The men raised their glasses and answered his cheer.

Tank Roberts stood up and spoke in an uncharacteristically serious voice. "Dobbers was our leader and none of us can fill his shoes, but Tuner, Bull, and I all agree that Frenchy is the man who should lead our Squadron." He raised his glass to Eddy. "May God grant you wisdom and a steady hand, Frenchy, my friend."

"Hear, hear," said the men, in unison.

Tank and Stack came over to shake Eddy's hand and the pilots began to drift away from the table. Bull Connell and Straw went out into the main bar, Lotte guessed to flirt with the table of girls.

She said to Eddy, "Congratulations. You have a lot to live up to."

He nodded and cleared his throat, as if embarrassed by the weight of authority he had never expected to be given.

"Frenchy," Tank shouted, from the dartboard. "I need a partner, and the dog's aim is rubbish." He pointed to Stack and Tobin. "Let's show these upstarts how it's done."

Eddy stood up. "Do you mind Lotte?"

"Not at all," she said, smiling. "I'll keep Dudley company while you play."

Dudley shouted to Jack, "Another whisky. A double this time!" He gave Lotte a half-crooked grin. "Will you risk another brandy with me?"

She hesitated. She was not used to spirits and it was a fair distance back to the airfield. She didn't want to make the return journey hanging drunkenly from Eddy's arm.

"What?" he asked, apparently reading her thoughts. "Are you counting?"

"Dudley, don't you think you have had enough?"

"You can't feel like I feel. I've lost a good friend. We all have. It is a frequent occurrence here. We drink to remember him, and to forget."

"I'm terribly sorry. I really am." She took his hand. "When I was ordered to come to Kettlebury I was excited because I wanted to see you. But I didn't expect you to be—"

"To be—what? Drunk? My good girl, you don't know me. I am not drunk. Yet. Jack! Where's that whisky?"

"Dudley, please don't. Will you be flying tomorrow?"

"I will. With Frenchy, my pal, as the new Squadron Leader. Bull offered me the job, you know, and I turned it down. S'not the job for me."

"But if you are going to fly, you shouldn't drink any more, should you? It is not safe for you to fly tomorrow if you are still—"

"Still what? Drunk?" Thane said. "Right now I'm only half as drunk as I have ever been, and I intend to get much drunker. I'll thank you to leave me alone now. Jack! Where the hell are you, man?"

Lotte stood up, her cheeks hot with anger. "How dare you speak to me like that! I tell you I am worried about you and you answer as though I am a barmaid." She paused to suppress shaking in her voice. "I will leave you to your whisky since you care more for your drink than for me."

~ ~ ~

Eddy saw Lotte storm out, and Thane get up clumsily to follow her.

"Tuner! What the hell did you say to her?"

"I did it again," Thane said. He put his arm around Eddy's shoulder. "Frenchy, my friend. I like Lotte. Really, I do. She thinks I insulted her, again, and I didn't mean to. Tell her I'm sorry. Please. Tell her!"

Eddy shook his head. "You are drunk. Again."

He turned away from Thane, apologized to Tank, Stack and Tobin for leaving the game of darts and went after Lotte. He regretted his decision to bring her to the pilots' pub. Thane had never once left the Leeward sober so why should a visit from Lotte make any difference?

277

But Eddy still felt that there was a good man inside Thane, and he sensed that Lotte agreed.

She hadn't gone very far yet. He could hear the tapping of her shoes as she walked, a few hundred yards along the road towards the airfield. He jogged after her. When he caught up, he said, "I'm sorry, Lotte. I thought—well, no, I suppose I didn't think. Tuner is not himself tonight."

"Oh!" she said. "I think he is. Tell me, Eddy, is that the sort of behavior I can expect from him?"

Eddy considered his answer, but found he was at a loss for words.

"Your silence tells me all I need to know."

"Lotte, I've come to know Tuner. I can't believe I'm saying it—but I like him. He's witty. The men look up to him as a pilot. He has principles and courage."

"But alcohol changes him! It is not necessary for you, is it? But Dudley carries a flask with him, all the time, doesn't he?" She reached into her bag and showed Eddy the silver flask he had left in the Anderson shelter at the Weldys' house. "I meant to give it back to him tonight."

"Shall I give it to him for you?" Eddy asked.

"No. It would be better if he can go through the day without it."

"I'm not sure he can. Maybe it is the war," Eddy said. "No one outside the cockpit can feel the pressure we live under."

"I do not doubt that is true," she said. "But the night in the shelter, I connected with Dudley. I felt that I could love him. I thought he felt the same about me. But now—I'm not so sure—"

Eddy sighed. "*Eh bien.* I don't think you will change him by worrying." He took her hand and drew it through his arm. "Come along and try not to fret. I'll walk you to the brig."

"Yes. I'll be leaving early tomorrow."

~ ~ ~

Dawn was just breaking as Lotte finished brushing her hair. She applied her lipstick, took a last look in the mirror, and put her bag strap over her shoulder. She opened the door to the chatter of birds and the sight of Dudley Thane standing outside, hands in his pockets, leaning against a lamp-post.

He looked pathetic in his rumpled uniform; his dress shirt bunched up over his belt with a tail hanging down. His sad expression suggested he wanted to make amends for his drunken exhibition the previous evening, but her senses urged her to acknowledge him cordially and leave immediately. And hopefully never see him again.

"What are you doing here? How long have you been there?"

He looked at her, solemnly. The morning light did not flatter the lines on his face or the bags under his eyes. "I'm so sorry for what I said."

"Go to bed and get some sleep."

He held a hand to her; but she dodged.

"Stay away from me, please."

"Let me make it up to you. Please!"

Lotte reached into her bag and tossed him his silver flask. He caught it, clumsily.

"You left this in the shelter. At the Weldys' house. I'm sure you'll be needing it."

Thane stared at the flask for a moment. "If you give me another chance; I'll never touch another drop. Look—I promise!" He heaved the flask as far as he could into the long grass between the barracks and the infield.

She stood irresolute for a moment, then pushed past him towards the Morris Eight. "I have to go," she said.

"Lotte," he said, following her.

She opened the door and turned to face him.

"What is it, Dudley? What have you got to say that I ought to hear?"

"Lotte. Will you see me again?"

She sensed a heart-felt sincerity in his plea and despite her deep misgivings over his drinking behaviors, she knew that deep down something about him had touched her. She said, "Honestly, I don't know." She got into the car and drove away.

Chapter 42

Eddy heard the familiar heavy rumble of his Morris Eight and came out of the dispersal hut to find Thane watching the rising trail of dust as Lotte drove away.

"Tuner! Where the hell have you been?" Eddy asked. "Have you talked to Lotte?"

"Yes. I owed her an apology."

"You did." The Morris rounded a bend and they lost sight of it. "Sun's up. You're due in the hut. Come on."

Thane asked, "Does Uxbridge pay enough for her to drive a Morris Eight?"

Eddy laughed. "No. It's my car. I let her use it."

"I'm quite certain the RAF doesn't pay enough for you to afford it."

"No. But my flying business paid well and I thought I deserved a treat. Lotte keeps it in good order for me, so I don't mind her using it."

"Frenchy, you continue to surprise me."

"I'll surprise you with a trip to the brig if you don't get your *derrière* into the hut."

"Oh I see. I'm already in trouble with the new boss."

Eddy slapped him on the shoulder. "Let's go."

~ ~ ~

Later in the morning Thane was asleep, flat on his back on a cot in the dispersal hut. He was dressed in his flying suit and wearing his Mae West, technically ready to scramble, but snoring, still sleeping it off. The other pilots around him variously read, wrote, and rested.

The telephone rang and Eddy answered. He recognized the voice at once. "Edouard, this is Air Vice Marshal Keith Park."

"Good morning, sir."

"I have been told we lost Lieutenant Dobson yesterday. I'm sorry. He was one of our best men and is a big loss to your Squadron and 11 Group. Please give your men my condolences."

"Thank you, sir. I will. Yes, we are all missing him a great deal."

"However, we must carry on. We honor him by defeating the Germans."

"Yes, sir."

"I understand the men have decided that you shall be the new Squadron Leader. Accordingly, I have promoted you to Flight Lieutenant. That's a rare honor for one of our Sergeant-pilots."

"Thank you, sir."

"Your Squadron will be getting three new pilots today. I need you to use all of your wit and knowledge to keep them alive."

"I'll do my best, sir."

"Let me tell you something, in confidence. Just half of our new fighter pilots survive their first sortie." He sighed. "You mustn't tell them that, of course, because we must keep sending them up—we owe that to our citizens. The Germans want to break our morale. But so long as we can send fighters up every time there are German bombers in the sky, British morale will remain steadfast. We are close to turning the tide, Edouard. Lord Beaverbrook has our factories running at full capacity and turning out more and more Spitfires. The only way we can lose is if we run out of pilots. We have asked so much from you and your comrades. But we need the men with experience to teach the new men what they need to know in aerial combat. If you do that, we can win!"

"Sir, I understand that. We will carry on."

"Now. Is there anything you need from Uxbridge?"

Eddy scanned the worn looks and tired eyes of the pilots around the room. What they needed more than anything was a day off. "How about a good rain storm this afternoon to keep the Germans on the ground?"

The Air Vice Marshal chuckled. "I'll see what I can do. That's all, Lieutenant Beane."

~ ~ ~

Later in the day, Eddy waited on the infield with Bull Connell watching three Spitfires approach from the north. The roar of their engines lowered to a gentle drone as they throttled down to land, their wide wings graceful as seabirds.

"These new fellows are Armstrong, Green and Jones," Bull said, looking at his clipboard.

"Okay."

"Armstrong is George. We could give him the call sign Custer."

"Why?"

Bull explained. "George Armstrong Custer was a Yankee general. He pitched his cavalry against thousands of Indian warriors."

"Did he win?" Eddy asked.

Bull shook his head. "He and his men were slaughtered."

"I would prefer not to call him Custer!"

"Your pal Tuner would find it funny," Bull said.

"Maybe he would. But if you call him Custer, the lads will change it to Custard. We'll call him Army. What about Green? Olive? Grass? And the other one?"

"Jones."

"They'll find a nickname that fits. That will do for the moment." The three Spitfires were on the ground now, taxiing towards the hangar. Eddy hesitated and said, "Bull? Can I ask you something?"

"What's up?"

"How do I lead our Squadron now that we've lost Dobbers? He knew more than any man here about aerial combat. He taught us so much. And we all loved him."

"We just keep buggering on, son." Bull put his hand on Eddy's shoulder and Eddy grimaced at the touch. "What's this? You're not healed enough to fly!"

"I'm tip top, Bull," Eddy said, stubbornly.

Bull gripped the injured shoulder and Eddy gritted his teeth through the pain but didn't move. "Hit me if you need to. I've got to fly if I'm going to lead this Squadron."

Bull let go. "Okay. Listen, Frenchy. Everything you said about Dobbers is true, so remember what he taught you and pass it on as you please. But you know plenty about aerial combat yourself now, so be your own man when you address them." He paused. "Most of all, you need to remember that Tuner and Tank want you for Squadron Leader. They are sure the men will respect you. Now get your men to the mess. They can meet the new pilots and have something to eat. Then you can get to it."

~ ~ ~

'KEEP SIGHT.' Eddy pointed to the words he had written on the blackboard. "The best fighter pilot this Squadron ever had liked to remind us about that. Always be aware, and always keep looking. It's not about focusing on something in the distance. It's being aware, with your eyes relaxed and your brain engaged. Spot that motion, that speck in the sky. Finding the enemy before they find you is everything. Keep sight.

"An engagement in aerial combat happens fast. Jones: How far away could you identify a single Messerschmitt 109?"

"From a few miles, I'd say," Jones said.

"Not that far. In clear skies," Eddy said, "you can see a lone 109 from two miles. If its flying head-on at you it will hit you within twenty seconds. Twenty seconds—that's how long you've got to make your tactical decisions, and it's less if you're late spotting the 109. On the other hand, you can see a bomber formation from four miles. Your Spitfire needs two and a half minutes to overtake it, so you must establish attacking position and be ready to fire inside that time. Army, what is the single most important factor when you attack?"

"Accuracy?" Army suggested.

"Ambush," Eddy said. "Four out of five victims never see their attacker. You can score most reliably when you ambush them. The other side of the coin is that if you don't see them coming, you'll be dead. Keep sight."

"Frenchy is right, men," Thane said. "We keep it simple. We find them. Climb above them. Keep the sun at our backs. Dive. And shoot them down. At all times with confidence."

Rain began to pitter patter on the roof and Thane went to the door and looked out. "It's coming down hard. And the sky's dark. We're not going anywhere until this lets up."

Eddy grinned, half-inclined to credit Air Vice Marshal Park with a direct line to the gods of weather. "Green, Army, and Jones—come and sit with me. I'm going to review the Squadron's procedures with you—take-off, landing, and the various rules we follow when we're flying." The new men gathered around Eddy. "We may not fly today,

283

but as soon as the rain lets up we're going out to have a look at my Spit's office. I'm going to make sure you know everything I know about the dials and the controls—over and above what you've picked up in training."

"No flying today, eh?" Tank said to the room in general. The yellow retriever thumped his tail gently. "Well, Tuner, shall it be the Leeward or the Sun tonight?"

"Neither for me, old man," Thane said. "I'm staying in. I say—if you're going out, can I borrow your novel? Is it a Graham Greene?"

"No, *Rebecca*."

"Ah, du Maurier. Remember her line about the blaze, Frenchy?"

Eddy looked from Tank to Tuner. "Who?"

Thane grinned. "Don't worry about it, old man. I'll tend to the literature."

Eddy smiled at the thought of Tuner immersed in Tank's book rather than downing glasses of scotch and went on preparing his new men for their tasks.

Chapter 43

Lotte was driving to RAF Uxbridge in the Morris Eight. The windshield wipers slapped in a monotonous rhythm and she was glad of the wet weather. It meant Eddy and Dudley would be held back from another fight against the Germans. She wished it would never let up.

Passing Osterley Park House she estimated she would arrive at No. 11 Group Fighter Command in fifteen minutes. Standing water here and there slowed her down, but she made steady progress. It was still raining when she pulled into the lot at Group headquarters and parked behind the only visible structure at 11 Group headquarters, a concrete block house ringed by a brick wall. A guard was on duty there and another was stationed by the path that led to a set of stairs that descended down into the earth. The stairs were hidden behind a row of bushes, just beyond two pipe stacks that rose from the ground, fifty yards away.

A shiny black Autovia drove into the lot and pulled into the parking space marked for the Air Vice Marshal. Lotte's immediate superior Lieutenant Tinker got out of the door nearest to her and Air Vice Marshal Park got out the far door. Both wore immaculate RAF uniforms.

"Good morning, Miss Schroder. I trust you are well."

"Good morning, sir. Yes, I am. Good morning, Lieutenant Tinker," she said. "Let's get in, out of the rain," Park said.

They went in through a vestibule that led to the stairs, where the Air Marshall paused and drew Tinker and Lotte aside, before they reached the busier parts of the underground structure.

"I have read Intelligence Officer Carter's report on your interrogation of the Messerschmitt pilot, Gerhardt Hintz." He smiled wryly. "I understand you had to deal with one of our pilots who wanted to take a piece out of the prisoner's hide. Lieutenant Thane, wasn't it?"

"Yes, sir. Emotions were running high," Lotte said, "but Officer Carter and I managed."

"Indeed you did. You obtained excellent information about Hintz's airfield, his aeroplane's flying characteristics, and his views on his superiors. I very much enjoyed his admission that Göring had told his unit that the British have only one hundred fighter planes left. This report is the best interrogation of a German pilot I have received and Carter tells me that much of the credit must go to you, Miss Schroder."

"Thank you, sir. Intelligence Officer Carter is giving me more praise than I deserve. We were a team, and he was the leader."

"What was the key, do you think, that unlocked this prisoner's tongue?"

She paused to gather her thoughts. "I must say that the interrogation started badly, sir. Hintz was very hateful towards me when he realized I was a German. He refused to speak at first."

"Is that common?" Park asked.

"Yes, sir. German prisoners consider me a traitor. But I talk to them about Saarburg, where I'm from, and I ask them about their homes and families. When we start to talk about Germany most of them relax. With Hintz, I asked him about his politics as I am sure you saw in the report. We found common ground there, and after that, I just let him talk. Intelligence Officer Carter suggested some questions. I asked them, and the results are in the report."

"I see," Park said. "The report states that in regard to his treatment by his captors the prisoner should receive due consideration for co-operating with us. Did you insert that?"

"I suggested it, sir. I told the prisoner that if he were forthcoming we would note his co-operation in our report and perhaps he would receive better treatment when he got to the prison camp in Canada. Did I go too far?"

"On the contrary, it was brilliant. Miss Schroder, we are capturing German pilots nearly every day and if I can extract detailed information from them quickly, we can save lives. From now on, Tinker here will send you on as many pilot interrogations as you can manage. Please use all your wits to gather me every scrap of information I can use to win this war."

"Yes, sir. I will do that willingly," Lotte said.

Park nodded to them both and hurried away down the stairs.

"Of course," Tinker said to Lotte, "after he's said all that, we haven't got any prisoners to interrogate right now. However, I have a job for you." She followed him as they descended two flights of stairs to a subterranean ring corridor where a balcony overlooked a massive map table. She knew it was the Operations Room, and Air Vice Marshal Park worked in there. She didn't have access, but wished she did, because it was the area of Fighter Command where the details of Eddy's and Dudley Thane's flying missions were known.

The desk Tinker offered her had only a typewriter and a telephone on it.

"Here," he said, opening his satchel and handing her a stack of papers. "These are SIS reports of recent interrogations of German pilots. You'll find that very few of the captured pilots have given any meaningful information to their questioners. I want you to read through this little lot and see if you can pick out anything we might have missed."

"Yes, sir."

"Be ready to shelve it if I call you," Tinker said. "Even though it's bloody weather up top, it's dry across the Channel, so it's likely the Germans will attack. When we capture a pilot, I shall need you PDQ."

After he left, Lotte began to work through the reports. As she read, questions occurred to her that she would have asked, about wives and girlfriends, hobbies and pastimes, sport, music and the arts, and politics. She made notes about anything that might facilitate an open conversation in which a prisoner would keep talking and inadvertently reveal details of military importance.

Several hours passed and she had two pages of observations to pass on to Tinker. She broke off to have lunch.

Soon after she returned to her desk he popped his head round the door. "We have a captured pilot for you to interview. He is at Biggin Hill. Please leave immediately."

~ ~ ~

Biggin Hill was a haphazard collection of buildings set in the midst of vast green grounds: barrack blocks, offices, huts, sheds, hangars, a mess building, and a chapel, surrounded by runways and the infield. Lotte steered the Morris Eight around a crater in the roadway and realized with some concern that the buildings themselves were pocked with bullet holes. There were artillery emplacements throughout the complex, big guns with their barrels pointed to the sky. With the center of London no more than fifteen miles away, the importance of Biggin Hill was obvious.

Lotte looked at the map of the base that Tinker had given her and with its help she found her way to the brig. A middle-aged, paunchy man wearing a well-cut but old-fashioned suit was waiting for her outside the entrance.

"Good afternoon," she said. "I am Lotte Schroder and I am a translator. I have been sent by Lieutenant Tinker to help interrogate a German pilot."

"Good afternoon, Miss Schroder. I am Intelligence Officer Scott. May I call you Lotte? I have been told that you are skilled at gaining the confidence of a prisoner."

"I am pleased to meet you, as well, sir. I try to do my best."

"Come, in, come in. Lieutenant Tinker wants you to take the lead here and try and establish a rapport with the prisoner. Generally, I direct the questioning. But we would like to see what you can do. Just remember to translate the conversation regularly for me in case I need to direct your questions."

"Yes, sir."

Scott seated her at a table inside the brig, with a single folding chair opposite them. A German prisoner was brought in by two MPs. He was about Lotte's age and had curly blond hair and tired eyes. He put his hands on his hips and stretched his back before he sat down, then he loosened his collar and straightened the gray wool scarf that was draped around his neck.

"Oh what a shame," the prisoner said, in German, looking her over with a scornful expression.

"Good afternoon. What is your name?" she asked.

"A beautiful woman who is also a traitor," he went on.

"Your name," she said, sharply.

"Karl Schmid. Who are you? May I call you Mati Hari?"

"We must get something straight," Lotte said. "You will answer my questions truthfully and without jest. If you do not, you will go directly to a stockade sealed with barbed wire and begin your long journey to prison camp."

"All right, all right. I understand." Schmid, looking directly at Scott, said, "You will send me to my squadron mates at Jagdgeschwader fifty-one, won't you?"

Scott nodded in reply, and then said to Lotte in English, "He flew in an elite Messerschmitt 109 unit. Take your time with this one. Let's see what he will tell us."

Lotte nodded.

"Ask him if I may have a cigarette," Schmid said. "I suspect it may be a very long time until I am with a beautiful German woman again and I want to enjoy the sight of you for as long as possible."

Scott agreed, and when Schmid was smoking the cigarette he said, "Now then, what shall we talk about?"

Lotte studied his expression. Though he was clearly exhausted, she sensed an unusual purposefulness in him that had to be approached carefully.

"You look tired," Lotte said.

"I am," Schmid said. "I flew six sorties yesterday over Kent and three more this morning. The only reason I'm sitting here with you is that my eyes were so heavy I didn't see my attacker."

"My colleague tells me you fly with an elite Nazi unit."

"My squadron mates are elite pilots, that is true. But I am no Nazi, and neither are you."

"Do you object to the Nazis?"

Schmid took a drag. "You first. If I am to give my views on the party, I must know where you stand."

Lotte translated Schmid's proposal to Scott. He nodded to Lotte to proceed. "But be careful," he added.

"I came to England over two years ago, to live with friends of our family," Lotte said to Schmid.

"Why" Schmid asked.

"My brother is SS. He tried to kill me."

"Again, I ask, why?"

"Our parents are dead," Lotte said. "I lived with my brother. I saw him and his friends do horrible things in Saarburg, where we lived. He wanted me to join the party and be like him. I refused."

"But joining the party is the easy thing to do in Germany."

"Yes," Lotte said. "But I saw what the Nazis did to my Jewish friend's family. And to communists. They are animals. They must be defeated if Germany is to find its way."

"So you left your country and your family because you hate the Nazis. Couldn't you have stayed and resisted—if only in subtle ways?"

"I told you my brother tried to kill me."

Schmid sat back with a thoughtful expression. "I suspect there is much more to your story," he said.

"There is always more. But you have no time for my story. If you don't say something soon that interests this man," Lotte nodded at Scott, "you will be taken to the stockade."

"Would it surprise you to know many German pilots feel like you do?" Schmid asked her.

Lotte translated for Scott, then turned back to Schmid. "Then why do you fly for the Nazis and kill English civilians?"

"These are difficult questions. I am German and have answered my country's call."

"*Ordnung muss sein?* There must be order?"

Schmid sighed. "That's right. I believe a time will come when we take back the soul of our country from the Nazis but right now, they are victorious. Germany has taken Austria, Czechoslovakia, the Low Countries, France... these victories have captured the hearts of our people. But I know we will be stopped, in the end. And then, those of us who believe like I do must be ready to deal with the Nazis as soon as the opportunity comes."

Lotte translated this for Scott, who raised his eyebrows in surprise. What Schmid was saying would have brought him before a Nazi firing squad if he were on the other side of the Channel. When Lotte looked back at Schmid she noticed that his scarf was monogrammed with the letters "EL." Were they his own initials? Perhaps he was concealing his real name. And if he was lying about that, perhaps he was exaggerating his views to bargain for better conditions in captivity; she had seen how Hintz had been motivated by the prospect of better treatment. She ought to suggest to Scott that Schmid's military ID be checked, but that would surely end the afternoon's interrogation and send him to the stockade with his information untapped. She decided to press on.

"Why do you think Germany will be stopped?" Lotte asked him.

"We will stop ourselves, because the Luftwaffe is run by Nazis who are idiots—Göring and his lapdog Kesselring. They are stuck in the last war. Their tactics cause good German men to be killed by the hundreds. Göring's senior officers have no backbone. They don't stand up to him. You are a woman and you have more courage than any of them."

Lotte translated for Scott. She thought he was startled by the things he was hearing, but he concealed it well and asked her to find out what tactics Schmid was referring to. "Ask him what Göring is doing wrong."

She relayed the question and Schmid replied. "Until last week, we were attacking England's airfields. We were damaging your radar surveillance, and your shipping. We were keeping your air force under constant pressure by bombing and strafing your bases. As a result, your Spitfires and Hurricanes could not attack our bomber formations in an organized manner. Many of us believed we were gaining the upper hand." He took a drag on his cigarette.

"Go on," Lotte said.

"Then, just days ago, Göring changed our target to London, exclusively. There is no more pressure on English airfields, so your RAF can now prepare and coordinate its attacks on our formations. Spitfires and Hurricanes slash at our slow-flying bombers like wolves preying on a herd of sheep. The balance has shifted now in favor of the English."

"Will the attacks on London continue?" Lotte asked, prompted by Scott.

"Oh yes. Göring—at Hitler's direction—has ordered the Luftwaffe to bomb London until Churchill accepts peace terms."

"Why should we believe you?"

"Why wouldn't you?" the prisoner asked.

"Because you lied," Lotte said. "Your name is not Karl Schmid. Your initials are EL. They are on your scarf."

The prisoner blew smoke to the ceiling. "I have a sweet girlfriend who embroidered her initials on my scarf to keep me warm."

"Then you will not mind telling me her name."

"Elise," he said with a weary grin. "Her second name is Leonora."

Lotte stared at him. "I too am familiar with the music of Ludwig van Beethoven," she said. "You are not Karl Schmid."

He shrugged tiredly, accepting defeat. "What I have told you would be considered treason in Germany. What will become of my family if I give you my real name and your report comes into Nazi hands? I can't dismiss the possibility that the Nazis will invade England and seize all the records. I will remain Karl Schmid."

Scott considered the exchange, and said, "We can conceal his identity with a code that is known only in classified records that will never fall into enemy hands. But we must have his name."

Lotte translated.

The prisoner stared at Scott. For a moment, Lotte thought that he might lunge at him, but then he took a deep breath and said, "Very well. My name is Ernst Lange. My brother is Horst Lange. At this moment, Horst is lying in a hospital bed in Berlin, blind in his right eye. He can barely speak. He is unable to form a sentence."

Hiding her triumph, Lotte said, "I'm sorry about your brother. What happened to him?"

"He trained to be a Nazi officer in the Kriegsakademie in Berlin. He took up with a girl, but another officer candidate wanted her. His rival was the son of a Nazi official—one who knew Hitler personally. Horst was beaten by this boy and his thug friends and left to die in an alley. Horst's assailants have not been punished. The Nazis treated Horst's beating as if it were his own fault after a night of drinking. Except that cannot be true because Horst never drank."

"I'm sorry," Lotte said.

"I am no traitor. I am a patriot," said Lange. "Tell your officer that. I know better than anyone that the Nazis are evil and must be removed from power."

Lotte translated for Scott, who made notes and said, "Ask him about the raids over London."

"Yes, I understand," Lange said, before Lotte could translate. "He wants to know about London. Göring forces our fighter planes to fly at the same speed as our bombers all the way to London. This strips us of our advantages of speed and manoeuvrability. Your RAF knows this."

Lotte translated again. "What else can you tell us?"

"My airfield is Saint-Inglevert, and it's not far from the Normandy coast. Still London is at the extreme range for my 109. If I have fought with your Spitfires or Hurricanes at all, my warning light comes on at the river. I have barely enough fuel to return to base. Two days ago, I ran out of fuel and had to land on the beach at Wissant. Over two dozen 109s have fallen into the sea or landed in France short of our airfield since Göring changed our target to London. May I have another cigarette?"

Scott lit one for him, and waited, tense with expectation, while Lange continued.

"If your Spitfires had attacked me as I returned from London, I could not have fought them because any rolls or dives or other manoeuvres would have spent my fuel reserves and I could not have got back over the Channel."

Lotte took a moment to consider Lange's admission. "So you are telling me that your Messerschmitt's fuel range is inadequate for you to defend the German bombers when they attack London?"

"You are a smart girl," Lange said. He blew out smoke. "I'm telling you this because we cannot defeat the RAF. We see more Spitfires attacking our formations every day even though Göring keeps telling us your Fighter Command is nearly finished. When he realizes the insanity of his attacks on London he will have to stop. The sooner that happens, the sooner we stop sending good German pilots to their deaths."

Lotte translated for Scott, who sat back, as if mulling Lange's information. "That will do for now," he said to Lotte, "We have a lot to write up."

Lotte told Lange they were through. Scott asked her to tell Lange that he would be interviewed again and that his identity would be concealed. He offered Lange a couple of cigarettes to take with him. Scott nodded at the military police, who escorted Lange away.

"Please type up my notes as quickly as you can," Scott said to Lotte. "If the Air Marshal doesn't know London is the limit of the effective range for a Messerschmitt 109, we need to make him aware of it at once. I will try to catch him by telephone but he will need our written report as soon as possible."

"Yes, sir."

Within an hour Lotte had typed their report of the interrogation. Scott read it, inserted a few pencil corrections and comments in the margin, and went off with it for Uxbridge.

Lotte took up her bag and left the brig. Dusk was drawing a dark cloak over the infield and the September breeze was brisk on her face as she walked back towards the yard where she had left the Morris Eight.

Biggin Hill was still a beehive of activity, with groundmen refueling planes, working in open cockpits, or rolling planes into hangars. A pilot and his groundman were examining a long, open gash in his plane's fuselage. The pilot said, "The air was whistling through there like a dashed football referee."

"I can fix that, all right, sir," the groundman said. "I could cut a strip from a Shell fuel can and rivet it on."

"By first light?"

"Yes, sir."

"You're a marvel, Thompson. But make sure you put it on inside out or paint over it." The pilot laughed. "Don't want to go about looking like an advertisement for a squalid little garage!"

Lotte recognized the laughter at once. It was Dudley Thane! As astonished as she was to see him, she had only an instant to decide if she should call out and greet him or let him walk away without knowing she was at Biggin Hill. And probably never see him again. He shook hands with the groundman and walked towards the hangar. Time stood still as June's cautionary tale and scenes of Dudley's troubles with alcohol rolled through her mind. But her heart wouldn't let him go.

"Dudley!" Lotte called. He looked over and waved, and then jogged across the infield to her.

"Lotte! What a surprise," he said. "Are you interviewing a prisoner?"

"I have just finished. Is your plane damaged? What happened?"

"They made a lucky shot," he said, smiling. "It tore a big hole in my fuselage and I couldn't fly back to Kettlebury. But the groundmen will repair her tonight and I'll fly out at first light."

"Thank God you're not injured. Did Eddy make it back to base?"

"I'm sure he did."

"Where are you going to stay tonight?"

"Oh, there must be a visitors' barracks around here somewhere." There was a smudge of dirt on his cheek in the shape of a paw print. His expression was tired. His eyes reminded her of Ernst Lange: he had been through too much and used his last reserve of energy.

"Dudley," she said severely, "you need someone to look after you."

He managed to smile. "Are you offering?"

"As long as I'm not hosting the man I met at the pilots' pub."

Dudley looked away for a moment, then said, "Once again, I'm very sorry to have behaved like a boorish drunk. Rest assured I'll be a perfect, sober, gentleman."

She smiled. "Well. You won't get much comfort in a drafty barracks. Come with me to the Weldys' house. It's not far. You can have a bath and I'll make you some dinner."

"Are you sure?" Dudley asked. "I don't want to disturb them."

"You won't," Lotte said, "they are with the children in Lassingwood. I'll bring you back here in the morning."

Chapter 44

Lotte drove carefully from Biggin Hill to Peckham. It was a dull night with no moonlight, and the Morris Eight's headlights were masked to emit only a dim, narrow beam which did very little to illuminate the apocalyptic dusk-gray of Bromley and Catford. The streets were eerily quiet, with the house windows blacked-out with heavy curtains, or unlit. She had not yet heard an anti-raid warning, but as Lange had told her, Göring had ordered German bombings of London to continue, so everyone expected to have to leave their homes and go to the public shelters, or Underground stations, or, as at the Weldys' house, their home-made shelters.

Dudley Thane sat in the passenger seat. He seemed subdued and she deduced he was very tired, so she concentrated on driving and didn't trouble him with questions.

After some time, he said, "I didn't expect I would have another chance to apologize to you."

"For what?"

"For my behavior at the Leeward. I'd like to say the man you saw then wasn't the real me."

She glanced at him but in the darkness she could barely make out his profile.

"Is that true?" she asked. "I mean no offense, but there are some men who take pleasure in drinking and tavern banter above all else. It wouldn't be strange if that were simply your nature."

Dudley stared out the side window at the buildings reeling by in the dimness. "Perhaps I'm trying to convince myself. I confess I have been that kind of man. My best mate was called Griff and we lived to drink Scotch and have a time of it with our friends. I was engaged once to a lovely girl and my drinking caused her to end it."

"June," Lotte said.

"Yes," Dudley said. "I won't let that happen again."

"When I saw you the other night with your fellow pilots, you were still taking one whisky after another. Honestly, it seemed like there was no place you would rather be than with them with a glass in your hand. Are you telling me you are suddenly changing your ways?"

"I don't know. I can't tell you. I love being with the men. When we blow off steam after aerial combat we drink a lot—far too much—and we laugh a lot. It gets worse when we lose a squadron mate. We go way too far, maybe it's our way of celebrating that it wasn't us. We are still alive and have to prove it. That is what you saw." He sighed. "That night, when you left the Inn, I walked back to the barracks and made a cup of tea. I carried a chair outside and I sat alone out there, looking into the darkness, and asking myself who I was. The answer was brutally simple. I am a pilot who fights for his country. If I have to give everything, included my life, that's what I'll do. But—Lotte—I am also a man who wants to earn your trust. And then your heart. I know a drunkard doesn't deserve you, so I will no longer be one."

Lotte could hardly speak for the lump in her throat. "Dudley, I ...."

"You don't have to say anything," he said. "I expect you find all that hard to believe, but I want you to know how I feel. I am asking for a chance to show you that I am a good man."

They had reached Peckham and, even with her concentration on making the last turnings in near darkness, Dudley's admission had pushed out all other thoughts. Never had such heartfelt words been spoken to her and she yearned to learn more about him.

As she drew up to the Weldys' house she was dismayed to see that a light delivery truck belonging to June Stephenson's family was parked outside. *Oh God—how could I have forgotten?* The previous evening, June had called and offered to come over so they both would have company if there was a raid.

Dudley noticed the truck at once. "Hullo! Who does the Austin Twelve belong to?" He got out and walked towards it but Lotte quickly switched off her lights and the engine, so he couldn't see clearly. Before she could explain, June opened the front door, and she saw him.

"Dudley! What are you doing here?"

Dudley asked Lotte, "Why didn't you tell me she was here?"

"I didn't know." Lotte looked from one to the other, upset by their stony expressions that seemed to accuse her of scheming to bring about this confrontation.

"Explain, please!" June said.

"It's just a series of coincidences," Lotte said to June. "I was leaving Biggin Hill after an interrogation and Dudley had landed there for emergency repairs to his plane."

"Oh—"

"It had slipped my mind that you might be coming tonight. He's tired and I said I'd let him have a bath and a hot meal."

"He has to go!" June said, while moving towards her truck. "Get in," she said to Dudley. "I'll drive you."

"Go? Where?" Lotte asked.

"Well—back to Biggin Hill, I suppose," Dudley said. "That's where my crate is."

"Now wait a minute, Dudley," Lotte said, and then turned to June. "Both of you! It's much too late for that, We're expecting an air raid and once the siren sounds, we all need to go into the Anderson shelter. We shan't be driving anywhere until we hear the All Clear. And what a waste of petrol! Come in! It's too cold to be standing out here in the dark."

Dudley hesitated until June let out an exasperated sigh and said, "Dudley—you must be on your best behavior here!"

He sighed. "Yes ma'am."

They went indoors, not looking at each other. Lotte went upstairs to put clean towels in the bathroom.

"I can't promise there will be much hot water," she said to Dudley, "unless June lit the fire as soon as she arrived. Even so, don't let it run too long or your bath will be a cold one." Once he'd closed the door behind him, she went down to talk to June in the kitchen. It was steamy in there and she could smell the carrots and potatoes in the two pans on the gas stove.

"I'm at a loss to understand why you brought him here," June said as she put a frying pan on the gas ring. "Surely you saw how I reacted to him a few nights ago—and surely you paid attention when I told you about our shambles of an engagement—wasn't that enough of a warning for you?"

Lotte said, "I just happened to meet him at Biggin Hill. He was so tired, June! A bath and a hot meal isn't too much to give him."

"And you 'just happened' to meet him? Purely by chance?"

"June. I told you—his Spitfire was damaged—I saw it. He couldn't have flown on to Kettlebury."

"I'm sorry to hear that." June took a little parcel of sausages out of the meat safe and used a knife to separate the links with quick angry movements. "But Al and Maddy are away at The Four Bells. You thought the house would be empty, and you were so keen to bring him that you forgot I would be here! You were going to be alone with him all night!"

"I hope you're not implying—"

"Hmmph."

June was cooking six sausages, far more than either of them would be allowed on their ration coupons. "Oh June, did you get those on the black market?"

June pushed the sausages about in the hot pan. "I wheedled them out of Mummy this morning. I have no idea where she got them from. I thought you and I could have a little treat. But instead I've got to feed them to Dudley Thane. How am I going to tell Eddy that we spent this evening entertaining my ex-fiancé?"

"June, dear, this puts you in a difficult position and I'm sorry. But maybe Dudley can give us some news about Eddy."

"Oh I do hope you're right," June said, crossly. "But not even that makes it worth having him here."

Lotte went into the dining room and set the table. June's cross words couldn't prevent her replaying in her head, over and over, what Dudley had said. A big part of her had been elated when he had confessed his feelings. She felt drawn to him. But she hadn't yet decided if it were genuine, or a fleeting attraction forged by wartime emotions. Maybe it was the same for him. Dudley flew over England every day under crushing life and death pressure that forced him to be daring in the sky, yet he had to be a responsible young man on the ground. How could he make any kind of sense of what he truly felt for her?

When he came down the stairs, the cleaned-up sight of Dudley stirred Lotte. His blond hair was slicked back, his green eyes were cheerful and he had a smile on his face. Even in the heavy trousers and wool sweater he had worn all day while flying he was just as handsome as she had remembered.

June brought plates of sausages, potatoes, and carrots and set them on the table with sharp thumps that told Lotte she was still cross.

"This looks delicious," Dudley said, taking his seat.

"I hope you don't want any tea, yet," June said to Lotte. "We can have it later when the kettle boils."

"Well," he said, savoring a bite, "it is delicious. A meal from home?"

"June provided the sausages," Lotte said. "The vegetables are from the garden next door."

"Oh yes, I remember. How are the hens? Still laying?"

"I am saving the eggs for breakfast," June said, stiffly.

"You haven't wrung their necks just yet, then." He glanced at the two girls and went on eating.

Lotte wondered how much of their conversation had carried up the stairs while he was having his bath. Then she blushed thinking of Dudley in the bathtub.

June asked, "Is Eddy at Kettlebury?"

"Yes. He was flying today."

"But his shoulder!"

"It might have been better for him if he had stayed on the ground, but he wouldn't hear of it," Dudley said. "He's a good leader. The entire Squadron will have come home safely today, except me, and I'm pretty much all right. I saw them bag three bandits."

"Thank God," June said.

"Did someone drive you here?" Dudley asked June. "You didn't drive yourself in that farm wagon, did you?"

"Of course I did. Why shouldn't I? It's normally at Longmarsh; Daddy bought it for Foster to haul his plants and tools about."

"Why didn't you drive your MG?"

"I was working close to here," June said. "And there isn't much petrol in the MG at the moment."

"Oh? What are you doing here? What work, I mean."

"I'm with the Women's Voluntary Services for Civil Defence. I help to run a day kitchen in the East End. Daddy said if I parked an open

300

sports car in the East End it wouldn't be there when I went back for it. And anyway, I would feel I was flaunting."

"Ah. Anyway, I'm glad you're doing your bit." He poked at his carrots and looked up. "I know the East End's been battered by the bombings. How are people doing?"

June's expression softened. "They're trying to carry on, but the bombings have gone on, day after day, night after night. Some of them are losing hope; I see it in their faces." She paused. "They're counting on you, Dudley, to stop the Germans. You and the RAF. You're all they've got."

Dudley's expression became serious. "Be assured, dear girl, every one of us is prepared to give all to defend them."

June nodded. "How's Griff? He's in the Squadron with you and Eddy, isn't he? But he wasn't with you the other night, and he isn't here tonight, and that seems strange. You two were always together."

Thane drew a deep breath, before he said quietly, "Griff—Griff's gone for a Burton."

"Does that mean what I think it does?"

He nodded.

Lotte wasn't familiar with the phrase either, but she couldn't misunderstand his meaning.

"Less than a week ago," Dudley said. "He is a big loss to the Squadron." He looked down and set down his fork and knife over uneaten food.

"I know he was your best friend," June said, softly. "I'm sorry."

Dudley gave her a thin smile and changed the subject. "I remember Mr. and Mrs. Weldy had made plans to set off from here with a dozen children in a bus and head for a pub in the country. How are they doing? Have you heard? I must say, right now I'd rather like to be in a pub in the country, too."

Lotte glanced at him. Sometimes RAF humor passed her by, and in light of Dudley's vow to change his drinking habits, she was unsure of his meaning, but decided to let it go. "Yes. Those children are living with Maddy in her pub in Lassingwood. She writes to me when she can."

"Of course. How are things there?" he asked.

"Uncle Al has been living here and working at the shop, but he went down to Lassingwood yesterday. He'll be there for a few days. Maddy wrote and told me the children have settled at The Four Bells. They go to school in the daytime, and Maddy and her cousin and their friends arrange activities in the evenings and on weekends, going for walks, playing football, fishing, things like that."

"Do they mind being away from their parents?" Thane asked. "But perhaps country life does them good. In terms of broadening their outlook. It must be a big change from Rotherhithe."

"Several of the children do not have parents any more," Lotte said. "Some of them were killed in the air raids."

"Yes. I remember Maddy telling us about little Esther. It's a pity."

"Maddy told me that if I should see you I should thank you again for the money you gave her," Lotte said. "She bought Esther some clothes."

"I hope she liked them."

"I'm sure she does. There was half a quid left, so she bought apples for all the children."

Dudley grinned at her.

June looked from Lotte to Dudley and back again. She cleared her throat and said, "Lotte, let's clear the table. I'll wash the dishes. Come with me and brew a pot of tea, then we can sit by the fire, together."

Lotte stood up and said, "Go on, Dudley. If you sit in the parlour you can listen to the wireless."

When the two girls went back into the parlour with the tea tray, Dudley was sprawled in Al's well-upholstered armchair, almost asleep. Lotte set the tray down on the side table, and the rattle of the cups roused him. "Would you like some tea?" she asked.

June said, "I expect Dudley would prefer the bottle of brandy that Al keeps in the cabinet."

Lotte hesitated. "I'm sure Al wouldn't mind, Dudley, if you do want some."

Dudley looked at her with surprise.

"You can still have a drink with your squadron mates," she said, "even though you said you'd give it up. I wouldn't expect you never to drink anything ever again!"

"No," he said. "Tea is fine."

June listened to their exchange without commenting.

Lotte switched on the wireless and watched Dudley sink back into Al's chair.

A scratchy voice came through the speaker. *"Now it is eight o'clock. Jerry is a little late tonight."* Sirens wailed in the background. *"Search lights extend like long fingers into the blackness of the night."* The radio carried the boom of distant gunfire. *"The Air Ministry has issued a warning to expect an especially heavy bombing raid tonight and over the next several days, as Hitler's Nazi Germany seeks to bring England to her knees. London is again the target."*

The rising wail of air raid sirens outside began to drown out the radio. Lotte switched it off. "We will have to go to the shelter."

"You two go," June said. "I'll turn everything off, then I'll join you in just a few minutes."

Lotte led Dudley through the garden. They could hear the engines of approaching bombers, a low droning noise like a swarm of bees that underpinned the rise and fall of the air raid sirens.

"They must be right above us," he said. "They fly too high for us to see them at night."

They stood at the doorway of the shelter, looking up and listening for the first bombs to fall.

"For God's sake our guns are loud," he said. Lotte held his hand. "We put up flak fields and barrage balloons against the German bomber pilots and whenever they're in the air in daylight, we go up and harass them. They're flying from France to London and back, so the bastards must be more tired than we are. But they've come over in nonstop waves for two days. On that level, I respect them." He sighed. "Yet we will fly harder than they will and never stop. They won't admit it, but we will battle them to our very last man. Because they are attacking our homes. The sooner they learn we won't give in, the sooner they will stop coming."

Lotte remembered Ernst Lange saying much the same about the German Air Marshal Göring. *When Göring realizes the insanity of his attacks on London he will stop. The sooner that happens, the sooner we stop sending good German pilots to their death.*

"Before we met this afternoon," she said, "I was interrogating a German pilot." She hesitated for a moment, considering her obligation to keep her work in confidence. "He told me something that you and Eddy should know."

"What is it?"

"I'm sure Fighter Command will tell you pilots, if its important information, but it could take a day or two to reach you. I think I ought to tell you now, because if it might help, and if you or Eddy didn't come home tomorrow and I did not tell you, I could never live with myself."

"Okay," Dudley said.

"This prisoner was the pilot of a Messerschmitt 109. He said that London is his maximum range. When he crosses the river his fuel light comes on and he must fly straight and level back to his base in France. He said that if the RAF had attacked him on his flight back to base, he would have to concentrate on escaping rather than fighting. If he fought he would run out of fuel and fall into the Channel."

"That's very interesting. We had noticed some German bomber formations don't have 109 escorts when they turn for France. They're easy pickings. Now we know why. This is information we can use." Dudley hugged her. "Thank you, my angel. Keep digging for information to help put this bloody war behind us. And then it will be time for us," he said. "If you will have me."

She put her hands on his shoulders and leaned towards him, as if drawn by a magnet. Dudley kissed her. Passion for him surged through her, and she held on tight and kissed him back with a hunger that made everything else in the world disappear. They broke apart, breathing hard, and she put her hand on the back of his head, bringing his cheek to hers. She felt the strength in his embrace and wished the moment would never end. She kissed him again. Never had she felt this way and she craved more.

"Come," she said, leading him into the shelter. "Oh no! I took the blankets indoors to keep them dry. I'll be just a moment." She kissed him again, then reluctantly drew away and headed for the house.

June met her at the back-door.

"Are you expecting me to stay in the house so you two can have the shelter?"

"Of course not!"

"Then I don't know what you're doing," June said. "I could see you, you know, from the kitchen window. Are you out of your mind?

304

Dudley Thane will never give up his drinking, even though he put on a show of it tonight."

"I am falling in love with him," Lotte said, simply.

"Look dear," June said, "I more than anyone else won't deny Dudley is very handsome. He can be very charming, too. But he is irresponsible. He let me down, time after time. I don't trust him, and I think you shouldn't either."

"I will give him a chance," Lotte said. "I will find out for myself."

"Well," June said, turning away with resignation, "I admit it's been over two years since I spent any time with him. Perhaps I ought to hope he's changed. Once, my Daddy told Eddy he would judge him by what he sees, on his own merits. So I will say the same for Dudley. I will wait and hope he's changed and can be good to you."

"Thank you, dear," Lotte said. She gave June a kiss on the cheek and gathered up the blankets. The joy she'd felt from Dudley's kisses had swept over her like a tidal wave. She couldn't wait to join him in the shelter, though she'd have to maintain decorum when June came in. If June hadn't been here—what might she have done? She crossed the garden and hopped down into the shelter with her armful of bedding. The dark, cramped space was strangely quiet. It took a moment for her eyes to adjust. Dudley lay on his back on a cot, fast asleep, his chest rising and falling peacefully. She shivered in spite of her self-control. Even the sound of his breathing carried hints of his rich tenor voice. She removed his boots and straightened his legs, placed his hands across his abdomen, and covered him with a blanket. An air warrior at peace.

She went to the doorway and sat on the stoop that led down to the shelter and stared up at the black sky and the rolling search lights. Along the docks the ack-ack guns were rattling and the air raid sirens continued to wail. A plane dropped burning from the sky in an arc like a shooting star. The rumbling explosions of falling bombs made the ground beneath her shudder constantly.

She looked into the dim interior of the shelter towards Dudley but could barely see him. He was in there all right yet they were separated. Sleep did that to people. She remembered with a drop in her spirits that he was heir to an estate of northern lands. She could offer nothing in return but her heart. Surely, a common-born girl wouldn't be good enough to earn his parents' approval. Beyond that, could an English pilot, one of the 'few' lauded by the Prime Minister in a speech last month, really love a woman born in an enemy country? And if Dudley did choose to pursue her, she wondered whether the country of her birth would draw her home after the war ended. She truly didn't know.

Another explosion lit the sky, revealing barrage balloons tethered with cables, like fat, menacing spiders.

June would be coming out of the house any minute, with her swallowed criticisms giving her an air of disapproval. Lotte shivered again, recalling the feel of Dudley's cheek on hers. Would he be safe tomorrow when he flew again? Nobody could guarantee it. She knew that German pilots were shot down every day, and the ones she interrogated were the lucky ones who had been captured but hadn't died or been wounded and disfigured by air battles. British pilots were shot down, too, some taken and imprisoned by her compatriots, separated from their loved ones until the war ended. Dudley or Eddy could be next. Every time their Spitfires left the earth, they risked death. She dreaded having to take Dudley to Biggin Hill in the morning.

~ ~ ~

The air raid was over. The All Clear sounded in the early hours and Lotte and June had returned to the house and gone to bed, leaving Dudley deeply asleep in the Anderson shelter. Lotte's alarm clock roused her at 4:30 and although she felt dreadful she dressed and went downstairs to the kitchen where she toasted bread and brewed tea and put eggs into hot water. Then she made her way through the dark garden to the shelter.

"Come to the kitchen," she said to Dudley, lightly shaking his shoulder. "I have poached eggs, toast, and tea ready for you. Then I'll drive you back to Biggin Hill."

"What time is it?"

"Five o'clock."

She led him into the house and set out his breakfast while he washed and shaved.

"What time did you wake up?" he asked, joining her at the dining room table. She poured tea for them both.

"Oh, I don't know. Some time ago," Lotte said, concealing that she hadn't slept a wink.

When they had eaten she stacked the dishes on the draining board, and braced herself to say, "It's time to go."

He followed her out to Eddy's Morris Eight.

Upstairs, June opened a window and leaned out. "Take care of yourself," she said. "Look out for Eddy. If I lost him I couldn't live."

Dudley nodded to her.

Lotte drove away with Dudley in the stillness of the false dawn. Here and there, fires were still burning, with plumes of water being directed onto them by the fire brigade. Neither spoke for several miles.

"Thank you for giving me that intelligence about the 109s' limited range," he said. "I'll tell Eddy as soon as I get to Kettlebury."

"If anyone asks, I did not tell you," Lotte said, "but I'm glad I did."

He nodded and they drove on through the sleeping streets.

"I believe I kissed an angel last night," Dudley said. "I hope you didn't think I was forward."

"No. I kissed you back."

"May I see you again?"

Lotte burned to say yes, but her head was steadier than her heart. "I want you to concentrate on your duties," she said. "At the moment, nothing else matters. But when the war calms down, if you choose to call on me, I would like nothing more."

He put his right hand over her left hand as it gripped the steering wheel. "Until that day, my darling."

Chapter 45

By ten o'clock that morning, Eddy was leading the Squadron in a steady climb. To starboard, Bewl Water glinted in the distance. To larboard, there seemed to be mist rising over Croydon or maybe Crystal Palace. No, it was too late in the morning for mist; what he was seeing must be smoke from yesterday's bombings.

The air controller's voice crackled through his headphones. "Three hundred plus coming in over Folkestone. Vector one hundred, Angels twenty."

"Okay." Eddy switched to Squadron frequency. "Echelon starboard. Climb to Angels twenty five."

He glanced over his shoulder through the canopy to make sure Jones was on his wing. Beyond him Tuner was leading Red Flight. They were keeping formation well, even though they were climbing hard. Creamy white contrails streamed from the Spitfires' wing tips.

This was the moment Eddy lived for, when all the power of his machine was perfectly balanced in his hands and feet and body. And the Squadron flying under him strengthened him by a power of twelve. They were his to launch like arrows at the heart of the German Luftwaffe.

The raid approaching London was the biggest Eddy had ever seen. He could see vapour trails rolling and curling over the coast, evidence of deadly dogfights already taking place. He was still too far away to make out any details, but Bull Connell had briefed the Squadron that Fighter Command would scramble 32 and 64 Squadrons first, to peel off the German fighter escort who were flying in a protective layer above the bombers. That was probably the battle he could see. He and 57 Squadron had been ordered to attack the Heinkels and Dorniers in the second layer.

So far, everything was going to plan.

A minute later, he was in the thick of it. There were white pencil lines of enemy tracer crisscrossing everywhere. A plane fell into a flaming arc to Eddy's larboard, whether friend or foe he couldn't tell. Above him there were more Spitfires than 109s. In the distance, some of the 109s were turning away towards France. Eddy was grimly pleased. Evidently, what Lotte had told Tuner was true. The 109s didn't dare burn fuel in dogfights over London if they wanted to survive and return to their bases. It eased the Squadron's task a good deal, but they still had to deal with the relentless tide of bombers pouring towards London.

"Line astern," Eddy said into the microphone and in each of the Squadron's four flight ranks two planes lined up directly behind the flight leader.

Maida Flight was poised above the bombers, and ready to strike, three hundred yards to starboard and flanked by Tuner's Red Flight.

"Going down!"

The line of Spitfires swooped in a downward curl towards the middle of the mass of bombers, diving at nearly five hundred miles per hour. Eddy had to brace his neck and shoulders to avoid blacking out. His injured shoulder complained, but he had to ignore it. A gray wing filled his rangefinder and he toggled off a long burst of gunfire, then shoved his stick and rudder downwards to skid sideways and throw off the aim of his target's front gunners.

There was a sudden giant puff of black smoke to starboard. He saw Jones's Spitfire in mid-dive. He didn't think Jones was hit—the smoke was more typical of an engine cutting-out and stalling.

"Maida two! Break right!" Eddy shouted.

Jones's Spitfire regained power and turned away, but the Dornier gunners had got off a long burst at him and dark pieces of metal exploded from his wing.

"Jones, you're hit," Eddy said.

"Yes, but she seems stable."

"Good. Return to base. Okay?"

"Roger. Willco."

A falling Dornier crossed Eddy's path to larboard. Its canopy opened, and three crew members ejected into the sky. One of them somersaulted past Eddy's propeller and missed being gutted by only inches. A lucky bastard, Eddy thought. He didn't die an agonizing death in a fire either. Chances are he'll float in his silks to the ground and spend the war in prison camp, while the rest of us fight and die.

Eddy spotted several Spits from 57 Squadron above and below him, having scattered in all directions during the first attack. Tuner was to his larboard and gave a thumbs up.

"Squadron 57, form up around me and Tuner," Eddy ordered. "Climb to Angels twenty."

Eddy lined up the Squadron for another dive. Below him the Dornier formations had begun to look ragged, disorganized and vulnerable, no longer the precise grid pattern of a Luftwaffe bombing run. Perfect. He focused on a black swastika two angels below and shouted, "Going down!"

He pushed the stick forward and pulled back the throttle. As the Spitfire plunged into the dive, the familiar stress of negative gravity forced his body up against his harness, again with searing pain in his shoulder. But this time, without warning his straps gave way and his head bounced against the perspex, jamming his helmet into his body and disorienting him. When he regained his senses his rangefinder was filled with the gray of a Heinkel fuselage, so he let off a long burst. Blood was seeping from a cut on his forehead into his left eye, and he wiped at it with his gloved hand. Then he found that he had exhausted his ammo. He'd be a sitting duck for enemy gunners if he didn't move fast. He dived away, instinctively tweaking his rudder bar and throttle to confuse their aim.

He leveled the plane and pulled off his gloves to find his handkerchief and wipe the blood from his face. When his vision was clear again, he checked the skies. There were four, no five, Spitfires to starboard. Still flying. Part of 57 Squadron was still with him.

"Return to base," he ordered. The men with him would heed his order. He switched to base frequency. "Squadron 57 Leader to base."

"Base here," said Bull Connell.

"Probably half the Squadron is returning to base with me. Establish communications with the others, please."

"Will do. Out."

For the last fifteen minutes, his world had been all cannonfire, twisting aeroplanes, vapour trails, and tracers. Four miles above London it had seemed to be an honest match of the RAF against the Luftwaffe, almost sporting in nature, but a glance downward showed rising plumes of smoke that reminded him the fight had been

310

anything but fair play for the people below. Dozens of planes had crashed to earth, but the Luftwaffe had still been able to drop most of its deadly load. Bombs had fallen and exploded. For all the beings and buildings on the ground that he couldn't see but knew must be there—people, animals, homes—destruction or survival had been a matter of blind luck.

As he and the Squadron approached Kettlebury, Eddy saw with satisfaction that Jones's Spitfire was safely down and parked on the infield. The groundmen already had ladders up against its left wing and were making repairs. Ahead and behind him the rest of the Squadron was lining up to land. He recognized Greenie in front of him. Good, another new man returning.

Greenie came down steeply and fast and when the wheels hit his plane bounced back into the air. Eddy held his breath, dreading the moment when it returned to earth, because if the propeller blades caught the turf they would send the Spitfire spiraling end over end. He was relieved that Greenie managed to hold the plane level enough to come down correctly on three wheels and under control.

Following him in, Eddy reduced the engine power to idle. He pitched back, flared to a three point attitude, and as a reaction to Greenie's near-miss, delighted in setting his plane down on the grass lightly as a butterfly to taxi to the refueling position.

Eddy pushed the canopy back, released the treacherous straps of his harness and climbed out onto the wing. Thane was standing against the trailing edge with Eddy's groundman Mike, waiting for him. He pulled off his gloves and wiped his eyes again so he could see to climb down.

"Christ, Frenchy!" Thane said. "You're hit!"

Eddy looked at the blood on his hand. "Oh, this? Nah."

"That's a bad gash, old man," Thane said. "What happened?"

"It was the second dive. My head banged on the perspex like a bouncing ball. One of the harness straps was loose. I damn near left the crate through the ceiling."

Mike was mortified. "I'm sorry, sir. That was my fault. I didn't pull the one over your hurt shoulder quite as snug."

"Don't worry about it, old chap," Eddy said. "It was such fun when it stopped."

Thane laughed and offered Eddy his hand to jump down from the wing.

"I'll get a Medical Officer right away, sir," Mike said.

Chapter 46

Eddy and Thane reclined side by side on the infield grass with the Indian-summer sunshine warming their faces. Eddy had a strip of gauze taped to his forehead and was propped on his elbows, smoking, and Thane was asleep. The sky was strangely empty of aircraft noises.

Thane woke and stretched his arms over his head. "Ah, a nap is heavenly, old man. I doubt we've averaged four hours kip since the Germans started coming."

"That's about right," Eddy said, as he looked down the line of the Squadron's Spitfires. "We're damned good at parking, aren't we? Proper intervals, like hurdles on the track. Now we need to fly in formation just like that."

"You're the boss. Tell them." Thane sat up and studied the line of planes. "Truthfully, old man, I'd rather not see them empty like this. I can see the ghosts."

Thane's batman, Baxter, approached with cups of tea. "Thank you, Baxter. Bring me The Times, would you? And the Daily Mirror for Frenchy, here. I'm afraid he has fallen behind on Popeye."

Baxter chuckled. "Yes, sir."

"If you bring the Daily Mirror, I'll put my boot up your arse," Frenchy said to Baxter.

Baxter grinned and went back into the dispersal hut.

"Once a toff, always a toff," Eddy said to Thane.

"Perhaps so, my friend," Thane said. "By the way, how's the shoulder?"

"I'd be lying if I said it was right as rain, but I can do everything I need to."

"We'll never be right as rain again," Thane said.

Eddy spotted Greenie walking towards the dispersal hut. "Come and sit with us for a minute. Did you score?"

"I'm not sure," Green said, sitting down on the grass opposite them. "There was a lot of tracer all around me and I managed to get off a good burst in both of the attacks, but I didn't see a bomber go down. To be honest, it was all so fast I wasn't sure what I was doing. My heart was beating like a drum."

"It's a nervy business old man," Thane said, "but you came through all right. The thing is, Heinkels are hard to bring down. Like piercing a rhinoceros's skin."

"By the way," Eddy said, "I was behind you when you landed. Your Spit bounced down the runway like a football, old man. Damn fine work to keep it in one piece."

Green stammered, apparently unsure whether to apologize or thank Eddy.

Eddy said, "You were carrying too much power—that's why your front wheels bounced."

"Sorry, sir."

"You got her on the ground safely, so it doesn't matter now, but if you'd caught your prop in the grass that would have been the end. Here's the thing, Greenie: our crates need a three point landing. Idle down on approach, and she'll drop in for you very sweetly."

"If you're coming in too hot, raise your flaps just a bit," Thane said to Green. "Once you get the hang of it, old man, you'll touch the grass like a feather every time."

"Thanks." Green stood up. "I'll get the hang of it. I have to."

"That's the ticket," Eddy said. "Oh, if you're going back in, send Jones over here, would you?"

"Another lesson?" Thane asked, as Green walked away.

"If we don't give them, who will?"

Thane nodded.

"I say, Tuner?"

"Yes?"

"I was thinking about what you said to Greenie—about our fighting being nervy. Do you get frightened? I hate to admit it, but I do."

"When we're lining up to take off—Yes. I'm scared deep in my gut. But when the fur starts flying I'm calm as a stone."

Eddy nodded. Jones was walking over to them, so he said no more.

"Jones. Can the groundmen patch up your crate?"

314

"They've already done it," Jones said. "I'm ready to go back up."

"Good. Do you know what happened to you up there?" Eddy asked him.

"Only that the damned engine cut-out and left me a sitting duck," Jones said.

"Do you know why?"

"I'm not sure. I just know I don't want to be in that position ever again."

"Right," Eddy said. "The black smoke was a clue. It's what is called a rich cut. You were negative G for so long that your float no longer controlled the fuel going into your carburetor. The engine flooded and that's why you stalled. The trick is to bring her nose up just on the edge of that happening."

"I'll have a better feel for it next time I dive," Jones said.

"Of course you will," said Eddy. "I had an engine cut out last month when I was diving onto a 109's tail. It gave the bloody Jerry time to get away. It's one of those things you don't learn until you've dived too hard. The truth is it can happen to anyone."

"Thank you, Lieutenant," Jones said.

"Everything else all right? Not just with the plane—with you?"

"I think so. A bit ragged around the edges, but aren't we all?"

"Away you go then. I prescribe tea and toast and kip."

Jones grinned and went off towards the hut.

"You have a nice touch with the sprogs, Frenchy," Thane said. "Maybe as good as Dobbers."

"Nobody is as good as Dobbers. Sometimes when we're flying I wonder how he would handle things. The best I can say is that so far we haven't lost any of my chicks—and I want to keep it that way."

Thane laughed.

"What?"

"Chicks," Thane said. "That's what Air Chief Marshal Dowding calls us."

"Then I'm in good company." After a moment, Eddy added, "Jones was exceptionally lucky. He might have been shot to pieces when his engine cut out. I think the only reason he wasn't is because most of the 109s had already turned for France."

"What Lotte learned about 109s is crucial, isn't it? They don't have the range to fight over London."

"Right," Eddy said. "I think Dowding and Park used that information when they sent 32 and 64 Squadrons up first today, to dogfight with the 109s. We had a clear path to attack the bombers because the 109s were heading home."

"God bless you, sweet girl," Thane said to the air.

Eddy flicked his cigarette away. "How is Lotte?"

"She is well. Listen, Frenchy, I want you to hear it from me rather than from anybody else. Lotte invited me to your Aunt's house last night. She made dinner for me and I slept in the Anderson shelter."

"What? That was very gentlemanly of you Tuner. Was Uncle Al there, keeping a beady eye on you?"

"No. But June was."

Eddy sat up and stared at Thane. "If you took advantage of Lotte— or upset June—"

"I didn't," Thane said. "I told Lotte I'd be a good boy and try to deserve her affections. Then I slept in the shelter on my own like a dead man. It is rather like a family crypt, wouldn't you say?"

Eddy was speechless for a moment. "All right, I believe you. But dammit, you shouldn't have been at the Weldys' house with the girls."

"Okay. Point taken. Listen, Frenchy, I hope there's a spark between Lotte and me, but she's a sensible girl. She says she doesn't want to start anything between us and distract from my flying."

"That's a relief," Eddy said.

"Just as well," Thane said. "Apparently, I also need time to prove my worth to you."

Eddy looked off into the distance, over a copse of trees beyond the infield. He, of all people, knew about being given a chance. Air Vice Marshal Park, Tiger, and Mr. Stephenson had all trusted him without asking for proof, and now here he was, an expert pilot engaged to the greatest girl in the world. He had a wonderful life to look forward to if he could just survive this bloody war.

Thane broke into his thoughts. "You are a million miles away, old man. Women?"

"One woman."

"June?"

"I'm not going to talk to you about her," Eddy said.

"Remember, I'm her ex-fiancé," Thane said. "And if I'm honest, you didn't take her from me. I managed to lose her all on my own. I think she chose the better man."

Eddy grinned at him. "If that's true, Tuner, one day I might just come around—"

The moment was broken by a distant yell from Bull Connell. "Frenchy! Tuner! In the hut, please."

They got up, stretched, and joined the Squadron's semi-circle around Bull, who was standing in front of the blackboard, hands on his hips, waiting for them. On the board in white chalk were the words Frenchy, 57 Squadron Leader, and Maida 1. Eddy took a deep breath to cope with the mix of pride and serious responsibility that they implied.

"We have word from Uxbridge, gentlemen," Bull said. "We will shortly be facing the biggest German bombing raid we've seen yet. Fighter Command estimates that six hundred planes are going to attack London. September 15th. Mark it on your calendars. The Air Ministry believes that this is the day the Germans expect to break us and force England to her knees. Now, we can't allow that, can we? This afternoon, our job is solely to attack the 109s." He shook his fist. "The Hurricane Squadrons from Tangmere, Kenley and Croydon have got the job of attacking the bombers."

"Frenchy will be leading you up," he said. "Stay in formation and do your bit. Listen: the Hun planes have been coming over in waves all day long. They'll be everywhere in the skies between London and France. Once you're in the midst of it, stay alert! The Huns will be like rats up there—you'll never be more than a few seconds away from one. So spot him and take him before he gets you." Bull briskly yet thoroughly reviewed the Squadron's operational details, then left the hut.

Knowing how vital the Air Ministry thought this sortie was, the waiting was somehow different. Tank was reclining on a cot, as usual, but today his book lay closed on his chest. He was staring at the ceiling and his dog curled, ignored by its master, on the floor.

The telephone rang and Eddy picked it up. "Scramble! Rendezvous at Angels ten."

317

Eddy sprinted to his Spitfire and climbed into the cockpit. He adjusted the seat to its furthest ratchet and opened the foot screws for the rudder bar, plugged in the wireless lead and fastened his harness. Mike cinched down the straps until Eddy's shoulder burned under the pressure. Full petrol. Cocks on. Throttle tight, elevator and ailerons set. Oxygen, full.

He turned on the wireless and reception was good.

Last, as always, he checked the gun sights. They were clear. Eddy nodded at Mike and slid the canopy closed with a bang.

Eddy remembered how Dobbers used to call all this preparation 'pulling his machine on.' The easy-going Aussie in his one-piece flying suit, his wavy hair slicked back, with a smile on his face. The propeller began to turn and the memory was gone.

Even carrying her four tons of metal and ammo, the Spitfire lifted from the grass and climbed with a ballerina's elegance and speed. The Squadron had scrambled so fast that they were all airborne before the air controller said in his headset, "Vector ninety, Angels twenty-five."

Eddy repeated the coordinates to his pilots on squadron frequency and whirled his Spit around to the required vector.

Looking out of the bubble to starboard Eddy was well satisfied with the Squadron. Their positions in the air were as neatly spaced as they had been that morning on the ground when he'd commented on the parking. He led them into the cotton, ready for the hunt.

Chapter 47

The bright skies over Kent were at odds with Bull's prediction of poor visibility. In fact, through scattered clouds Eddy could see from the Isle of Sheppey to the Isle of Wight. Below him were golden rectangles of fields ready for harvest and patches of green forest interspersed with the red and brown ovals of villages.

At Angels fifteen, his eyes began to ache with the brilliant sunshine.

The air controller's voice broke the hum in his headphones. "Five hundred plus now past Warmwell on approach to London. Good luck, chaps."

Eddy addressed the 57 Squadron. "Stay together. Sight in one minute."

It was ninety seconds later when the enemy appeared as twelve horizontal, perfectly parallel dark lines against the whitish-gray sky. They seemed to stretch all the way back to France.

He alerted the Squadron, "Bandits, two o'clock."

Another thirty seconds passed, and he could see a further ominous cloud above the parallel gray lines. Closer still, they became an extensive flight of Messerschmitt fighters, like a swarm of wasps keeping company with a flock of fat pigeons—which were the German Heinkel bombers.

He said to the Squadron, "Keep form."

As they approached the massed formations, tracer from the bombers' gunners began to crisscross the sky in a haphazard white maze. In the distance, silver dots began to dive in—Hurricanes from squadrons closer to London. He could mark their successes by the smoke columns that arched up from damaged bombers and black trails of planes falling from the formation.

He kept 57 Squadron climbing, to thirty thousand feet, where he leveled off. As he scraped at the frost that was beginning to form on the windscreen he spotted a formation of 109s directly below and, with predatory glee, lined the Squadron up to attack.

"Tally Ho!" he shouted.

He pushed the stick forward to put the Spitfire into a dive. The new man Army should hold position five hundred yards behind him to back up his attack. The speed of his dive made his ear drums crack but he sighted a black cross on the rearmost 109 and pressed off a burst. The cross exploded. He broke left away from the flying debris and the 109 that had been immediately in front of his victim spun back towards his Spit with tracer streaming past its propeller. Eddy grinned, with amusement, and tucked into the tracer stream, confident that the machine guns of a moving 109 wouldn't hit the same spot twice.

He looked to starboard just in time to see Army blasting away at the second 109. It would have been a textbook kill, except Army didn't break away. Instead, he followed the smoking 109 and emptied his guns into it a second time.

"Army, break right!" Eddy ordered.

Army didn't respond.

"Break, Army. Now!"

Still, Army flew level. Perhaps he had been shaken by the continuous discharge of his guns, but now he was hanging by his straps for the enemy fighters. What the hell was wrong with him?

"Dammit Army, break!"

The 109 that had been ahead of the one Eddy destroyed peeled away, dived and put a cannon shell squarely through Army's canopy. The Spitfire exploded into pieces and Eddy had to roll away to avoid being taken with it. Now he could clearly see Army's killer. A white number 34 was painted on its fuselage.

"You!"

It was the same plane that had crossed his nose cone during his mission over Germany. The man who had shot down Army. The wolf who had destroyed Dobbers. Every bit of Eddy's being concentrated on the tail fin of the killer. *You'll pay, Jerry!*

Number 34 rolled through a cluster of 109s and Spitfires, all firing their guns and executing twists and dives, some as targets desperate to break free, others as pursuers intent on destruction. Eddy chased after 34 with the rage of Nemesis but the tracer streams, puffs of engine smoke, and metal pieces spinning off damaged aeroplanes all reminded him that he was on his own, without Army to back him up.

He called the rest of the Squadron. "Red One. Blue One. Maida Three, come in."

Nothing.

"Come in. Red One. Blue One. Maida Three, come in."

Still nothing.

"Tuner! Tank!"

Dead air. Not even white noise. His connection was broken. He would have no opportunity to fix it.

At twenty five thousand feet Number 34 disappeared into the cotton of a cumulonimbus cloud and Eddy followed. White cloud wisps spun round the Spit like curdled cream. He dived through them, anticipating number 34's evasive move, but when he broke through the sky was strangely devoid of the aerial bedlam he had just flown through. There was nothing in front of him except the Thames Estuary.

His altimeter read twenty thousand feet. Where in God's name were all the planes?

A sixth sense made him glance over his left shoulder and there was his foe, diving at him from two thousand feet above! He responded by turning the Spitfire onto her back, twisting through three hundred sixty degrees at the very limit of her capability. Tracer streamed over her left wing, barely missing as he dived away. But Number 34 was still there, so he put his wing over, hard, to the left and lined up the wingtip with a lighthouse on shore. He pulled a one hundred eight degree turn to reverse course and even then he wasn't sure he had thrown off his foe.

That bastard is skilled, Eddy thought. He had too many scores not to be.

When he leveled off and checked again over his shoulder his enemy was still there, but safely beyond firing range. He had no backup now, but neither had his enemy. They might have been alone in the sky.

Below them, the curling snake of the Thames had broadened to meet the sea.

By God, he thought, the Jerry is still on me. Why isn't he heading due south to France instead of following me east to the North Sea?

321

He won't have enough fuel to make it home—he must know that—but he would rather hunt me than give in!

Eddy had opened a gap between himself and Number 34. He hoped it gave him the advantage—the leeway that would let him change from prey to predator.

He loosened the white scarf June had given him and pulled back the stick for a tight turning climb. "All right," he said into dead air, "let's see who is the better man."

Chapter 48

A Messerschmitt 109 was coming at Thane head on. He went full throttle and charged at it in a mortal game of chicken. He pressed off a burst just as the 109 disappeared under his nose. Its slipstream shook the Spitfire and slowed him.

Not five minutes before he had seen a Spitfire go down, its nose section tumbling earthward, followed separately by its fuselage and tail. Its cockpit had disappeared entirely. Messerschmitt number 34 had been diving away from the kill and Frenchy had been hot on its tail. Thane had felt to his core Frenchy's lust for vengeance, and now he was seized with a desire to follow him into the hunt.

He was over Gravesend, heading for the convergence of the Thames with the North Sea.

Frenchy and number 34 had been flying eastward, their machines rolling and twisting through the scattered dogfights yet somehow avoiding collision. In seconds they had reached the eastern most fringes of combat, then they had disappeared into cloud. Frenchy had popped out of the cotton with number 34 above him diving in for the kill, until, with total mastery of his machine, Frenchy had spun into a violent flickroll and dived away, and then executed a wingover to reverse course to safety—quite the most remarkable evasive manoeuvre Thane had ever seen.

But it was a fool's errand to go on racing east when he had no idea which direction Frenchy had flown.

"Maida One," Thane said into his microphone. "Frenchy, are you there?"

Nothing.

"Maida One, come in."

Still nothing.

"Red Two, come in," Thane said.

"Red Two here," Jones said.

"I've lost sight of Maida One," Thane said. "He was hunting."

"Okay."

Thane noticed his red low fuel warning light was on. The full-throttle climb to six miles high coupled with rolls, dives and tight turns had cut his Spit's combat range to less than half of normal.

"Are you RTB fuel?" he asked Jones.

"Close."

"Return to base. I'll see you there."

"Roger. Willco," Jones said. "Look after yourself."

Thane took a last look. Seeing no sign of Frenchy, and with no radio contact, he banked to the west to return to base.

A scattering of 109s were making a grim parade south, retreating to their bases in France like Attila's defeated Huns leaving the Catalaunian Plains. There was even one directly below him, completely unaware of his presence. Bull had been right; the bastards were everywhere. Disregarding his low fuel warning light, he dropped in behind the 109 and followed it south, towards Maidstone, closing steadily but waiting, waiting, until the 109's tail filled his rangefinder. Then his fingers found the firing toggle and he pressed down for four seconds. The 109's rear section flew off in a sunlit shower of silver.

His killing high was cut short by a slight cough in the Merlin engine. Thane eased off his throttle. He couldn't ignore the warning light now. He was almost out of fuel.

"Red One to base," Thane said.

"Base here."

"I'm out of juice."

"What's your location?"

"I can see Leeds Castle."

"Okay. Land at Eastchurch. I'll alert them."

"Roger. Maida One is engaged with a 109. Eastbound at Canvey Island. No radio contact. I lost him."

"Okay."

Thane powered down and glided towards the runway at Eastchurch. The infield around the flattened landing strip was pocked with massive craters. Some of the buildings surrounding it were only blackened shells.

The Spit's three tires set down gently on the grass and he taxied to the fueling station. He slid back the canopy straight away and leaned out, shouting at the ground men, "Fuel and new boxes and be quick about it!"

"Yes, sir."

A tractor pulling the fuel wagon parked in front of the Spitfire's propeller and the ground man climbed onto the wing and was handed the hose.

Thane climbed out of the cockpit. "Where's the weapons team?"

The ground man pointed to a brawny man wearing a sleeveless cotton shirt who was straining under the weight of two metal cartridge boxes. Another was following him.

Thane hopped down from the Spit's wing and walked away to a safe distance before he pulled his cigarettes from his jacket. He turned to the west to face the sunshine. Even now, there were tiny gray specks silhouetted in the late afternoon sky. Most were flying straight and south, but a few were swooping to attack or twisting to evade.

He thought over what Frenchy might be doing. He must have seen number 34 get Army—the first loss of any of his 'chicks.' Frenchy knew that number 34 had killed Dobbers, and apparently he had an axe to grind with the German ace that dated at least as far back as Dunkirk. Thane took a deep drag on his cigarette and hoped that Frenchy's lust for vengeance hadn't clouded his judgment.

The weapons team had removed the panels on the undersides of the Spitfire's wings. One inspector was examining its propeller, and another leaned over the cockpit to check its radio and oxygen supply.

Frenchy and number 34 had been flying east when they had disappeared, but the bends and rolls of aerial combat could take them any direction. To Foulness Island or the mouth of River Crouch to the north? Or south to Margate? If number 34 was determined to finish their fight once and for all, they could be miles out over the North Sea. Thane was convinced of Frenchy's aerial combat skills and believed he would prevail, but he would probably run out of fuel over the ocean, much too far out to make it to dry land.

Dammit, he wasn't going to let that happen! Frenchy had captured his heart. Like Lotte had, and like Griff had. He wouldn't lose someone else he loved. He was going after his friend. But where?

Frenchy was off the grid and it was up to him to find him. Tension rolled in the pit of his stomach.

The weapons technician was cleaning the last of the Spit's gun barrels with a ramrod. The fuel tractor was pulling away. Thane threw his half spent cigarette into the grass, readying himself to climb back into the cockpit.

Chapter 49

Lotte typed up her report of her latest interrogation. The words on the paper, stripped of emotion and conveying only facts, didn't impart the depth of hostility she'd felt interviewing the most recently captured German pilot, Friedrich Becker. Becker had been unflappable, and to her consternation Lotte had not been able to extract any meaningful information from him. His eyes had been black and cold, and his jawline set like stone. She had taken him for a determined Nazi and wished there had been a place on the report form where she could condemn him to an igloo prison in Canada's frozen Yukon.

"Don't you wish we could stop and have a gasper?" asked the girl at the next desk. "I don't know about you, but I've been here for hours and I can hardly see straight."

Lotte looked up from her papers. "No. I must get this to Lieutenant Tinker."

"I've never seen things so hectic," the girl said. "They're saying every fighter Squadron is up there."

Lotte thought of Spitfires twisting and turning through the skies. She imagined the enemy fighters and bombers, as dense as flurries in a snow globe, all of them shooting at Eddy and Dudley. Please, lord, she prayed, bring them home safely.

She reached into her bag for her handkerchief and found a neatly-folded paper that on closer examination she identified as a page torn from her notebook. It was addressed, "Lotte," in bold, sprawling handwriting.

My Darling Lotte,

Thank you for taking me in and feeding me. And thank June, too, though it's you I'll be thinking of, sweet girl: Your beauty, your goodness, and your kiss. I will cherish the memory of that kiss whatever confronts me. Now I've found you and I never want to let you go. Give me a chance to show you I can be as good for you as you are for me. You are my light. May our feelings for each other grow deep and strong. Until the moment we are together again,

All my love,

Dudley

She had to force herself to breathe. Never had she received such a note, or even such an expression of a man's thoughts in conversation. But Dudley's words were genuine; she felt them in her heart. She saw him in her mind's eye, smiling at her, with a flash in his green eyes and confidence in his strong profile. They were of a single mind; he was the man she wanted in her life.

Lieutenant Tinker appeared at the doorway and broke into her thoughts.

"Lotte! Have you finished the report? Come with me."

She stood up from her chair. "Another interrogation, sir?"

"No. I need you in the Operations Room. Today is the biggest German raid so far and information is coming in from everywhere faster than we can make sense of it. I need you on a phone line."

"I will try—but I haven't been trained..."

"Think on your feet," Tinker said, giving her no further chance to argue. He led Lotte into the Operations Room.

Young women wearing headsets and gray-blue Women's Auxiliary dresses were using rakes like a croupier's to push wooden blocks across the surface of a giant wooden table marked with grid lines. She realized it was a map of the aerial combat operations taking place over southern Britain. One block was marked 'HO5' and '50+'. An arrow behind the block pointed towards London.

Tinker explained in a low voice, "That block represents the fifth hostile raid we've identified today. It means more than fifty enemy aircraft are flying towards London."

A chill ran through Lotte as she thought of the many people she had met since she moved in with the Weldys in Peckham. Many of them were at their homes or in shelters this very moment, defenseless. The room she stood in controlled all the orders being sent to the pilots who were trying to save their lives.

Air Vice Marshal Park was standing at the center of a balcony overlooking the table, with six officers flanking him. Park leaned towards one, said something, and the officer immediately relayed it to a young officer on the telephone at the wing of the balcony.

"Radar data comes in from Chain Home stations and we filter it here," Tinker said. "The girls plot it on the table to track the progress of raids. In addition to the radar, we have thirty thousand observers in a thousand posts throughout England. They use binoculars to spot German planes and our own falling aeroplanes. Information is called into here on those telephone lines." He pointed to the women wearing headsets who sat at a line of switchboard desks against the wall. "The girls pass it on to an officer who matches it up against our radar plots or acts on it as he deems necessary. That's all you really need to know. Do you understand?"

"Yes, sir. What do you want me to do?"

"I'm putting you on a phone line with our group from the east coast, near Manston airfield and Margate. The enemy bombers passed over Kent for London some time ago, and they're going back now, but they seem to be taking a route well to the west of Manston, over Maidstone. So your line should be fairly quiet, but even a single call may be vital."

He indicated a desk against the wall. "Sit here, please."

Lotte noticed a hairbrush next to the telephone. "But isn't someone sitting here?" Lotte asked.

"Yes. She has—had enough." Tinker handed Lotte a headset. "Put this on."

He raised his arm to catch the attention of an officer at the control board at the end of the row of desks. "Test her line, if you please."

Lotte heard the man's voice through the earphones. "Test. One, two. Do you copy?"

"Yes, sir."

Lotte gave Tinker a thumbs-up.

"You're on duty now, Miss Schroder. Good luck."

Chapter 50

Eddy had a quick look over his shoulder to confirm that number 34 was still behind him. They had cut through the scrum of dogfights over East London like a couple of booze-fueled brawlers outside the pub; intent on each other and consequences be damned. The pilot chasing Eddy had skills every bit his equal, and they both knew it. Either of them could have dived away, but neither had. They would finish it. Eddy knew his own reasons for not turning back: Dunkerque, Dobbers, Army. But number 34? He must be equally driven. Maybe he had been pushed through too many missions and too many perils and had decided it was time to make his stand. Or was it just bloodlust?

"Come on, bogey," Eddy said out loud. "I have a few tricks of my own."

He tried his radio. Still nothing. He jostled the plug-in. Still nothing. His low-fuel warning light was an unrelenting red.

North Thanet was below to starboard. The seaside towns and sandy beaches of Herne Bay were remarkably unaltered by the bombing attacks not far to the northwest.

He began a gentle descent, knowing the 109 behind him would be tempted to close the gap.

Steady now, he told himself. He pushed the spade stick forward and steepened his dive. His compass shook violently, fouling its bearings, but he didn't need it, because he knew his plane's nose was pointed due east. In less than a minute he was low enough to see the lightening rod on Margate's Clock Tower, and in twenty more seconds he was two miles offshore, flying towards the Netherlands. He started to climb in a tight, twisting spiral, bracing the stick against his leg and pressing his back into the seat. His head jammed into his neck, making the pain in his left shoulder nearly unbearable. The muscles in his forearms were taut as ropes as he applied constant pressure to his spade stick and throttle positions to avoid stalling out.

He knew number 34 was still following him but his enemy would be unable to draw a bead on his endless movement. He aimed the Spitfire at a layer of grayish clouds, ten angels up. After three minutes at maximum intensity of mind and body he judged that number 34 would enter the layer just behind him, and he rolled his plane right to pretend to his enemy that he had leveled off. He looked over his right shoulder, but nothing was there. He pulled back and climbed again, shot up and out of the cloud and gave his engine full power for thirty seconds.

He was flying past vertical. He gave the rudder a gentle nudge, his wing came over and he was looking straight down at the sea. The late afternoon sun was behind him, and there was number 34, two thousand feet below, and climbing.

Eddy's heart beat faster. He was going to win this duel. He began to dive, pointing the Spit's nose directly at his victim, and his fingers moved to the firing toggle as he lined up his shot.

White tracer crossed his windscreen from over his right shoulder. Another Messerschmitt 109 had him taped!

Its cannon shell hit in front of his canopy. A second burst his reserve tank, spewing fuel over his legs. Black smoke began to curl around the sides of his cockpit like demons from hell. Time to bale out.

He pulled off his oxygen mask and microphone, dumped his flying helmet and headset and unfastened his harness. He kicked the left rudder hard and pushed the stick forward to stall out his engine.

Flames were already shooting up the left side of his windscreen, so he crabbed the plane to its right to clear his way out of the starboard side. It took three hard jerks to slide the canopy back. A blast of cold air hit him in the face. He unstrapped himself and kicked the control column to point the Spit's nose upwards. He jumped up and negative gravity popped him through the open roof like a cork from a toy gun. He pulled his legs into a tuck to somersault away from the flaming Spit. Then he straightened his legs and threw his arms wide, like a cross, for maximum drag while he located the ripcord and pulled. The parachute unfolded rapidly and as it filled with air his weight hit the straps and his body jerked like a rag doll.

Then he was hanging under the silk, nursing his injured shoulder while in the distance his plane fell flaming towards the sea, like a comet. Then it was gone.

But the sky was not silent. Ahead of him was the Messerschmitt 109, its yellow nose cone pointed directly at him. The bastard was coming to finish him! Eddy wasn't going to wait there, slowly falling into the sea, and doing nothing to retaliate. He reached into his right boot, pulled out his Colt 45 pistol and released the safety and pointed it at the plane.

"Come on then, you bastard!"

The 109 didn't fire. Instead it banked around Eddy in a wide circle, then made a tighter pass that seemed to flaunt the painted number 34 at him. Floating under his chute, he had enough time to study the Messerschmitt 109. The lines of its angular profile were straight and businesslike, a total contrast to a Spitfire's elliptical, artistic wing design.

"Dammit!" he shouted at his foe and the open sea, "I had you taped!"

The German pilot wore a white scarf, like his own. He had raised his goggles, revealing his eyes. He gave Eddy a grim smile and put his fingers above his brow, saluting, as if acknowledging theirs had been a fair match.

Eddy lowered his pistol and saluted back.

It's all very well you playing the merciful victor, he thought, but you only won because you had a working radio. If it weren't for the mate you called in, I'd be landing at Manston now, and it would be your crate sinking down there.

Number 34 flew away to the south.

He could hear the rumble of his foe's engine growing fainter until its tail fin disappeared from view. Then the engine sound stopped altogether. It was bitter satisfaction for him to realize that his foe was out of fuel, and falling, like him, somewhere off the French coast.

The water was turning from green to blue as he dropped towards its surface. Squalls frothed in white roils and the evening sunshine sparkled coldly on the waves. It might make an idyllic portrait, and it might be the closing scene of his life, but he refused to let the sea take him without a fight.

He reached for the metal disk of the parachute harness release that rested on his stomach like a belt buckle. As soon as he hit the water he would have to turn it ninety degrees and give it a hard whack, because if he didn't free himself the silks would quickly drag him under and drown him.

Three... two... one... He hit the buckle and plunged through the brilliant yellow streak painted on the water by the setting sun.

Chapter 51

Waiting in the Operations Room for her telephone to ring, Lotte observed the uniformed young women with determined expressions who were scurrying between officers and the giant grid map on the center table. One of them was the girl who had wanted to take a cigarette break, though her friendly smile had now been replaced by a look of intense concentration. Lotte watched her hand a note to one of the girls at the map table.

"Take detailed notes of any call," Tinker had said. "I will be nearby if you have questions."

Each five minute segment of the clock on the wall was colored in red, blue, or yellow. The arrow on the table, behind the block Tinker had pointed out, was colored blue, which she assumed meant that the plot showed current data. A board with Squadron numbers was fixed on the wall in full view. The light bulb next to Eddy's and Dudley's 57 Squadron was lit. Every bulb was lit.

A man's gravelly voice said through her headset, "Manston, here."

"Go ahead, Manston," Lotte said.

"Nineteen Do-17s flying south. Estimated at Angels fifteen, just east of Canterbury," the man said.

"Okay. Anything else?"

"Negative."

Lotte wrote it rapidly on her pad, tore off the sheet and held it up, and a young officer with round glasses came up and took the message.

"Okay," he said, reading it quickly. "Is this a seven?" he asked.

"Yes. Sorry, sir," she said, realizing that she had fallen back on her German handwriting, putting a dash through the digit.

"And is that a nine?"

"Yes. I'll be more careful."

The officer hurried off.

Lotte felt a sense of satisfaction that she had successfully accomplished her first task, despite the bedlam of the Operations Room. Air Vice Marshal Park was still standing at the center of the balcony, a position from which he could observe the whole of the massive three-dimensional grid. It dawned on her that Park and the RAF had devised a system that could distill the chaos of a conflict between more than a thousand English and German planes into information he could assess and act on to influence the battle that was still underway. The blocks, arrows, airfields, cities, and geographical features all had to be considered in his calculations and turned into orders to men like Eddy and Dudley who were face to face with the enemy.

Park turned to an aide and gave instructions, pointing at a location on the grid. The aide hurried away.

Another man's voice came through Lotte's headset. "Uxbridge. Manston, here."

"Go ahead," she said.

"We have a sighting at Margate."

"Go ahead," she said again, writing.

"An observer has spotted a Spitfire being chased northeast by a ME 109 off Margate," the man said. "We have a further report that one of our brollys fell into the North Sea. Estimated four miles due east of Viking Bay."

Lotte recorded the message, and asked, "Okay. Anything else?"

"Yes. The Spitfire was low enough for our observer to see its number. 1700."

"No!" Lotte screamed.

The young officer was first to her desk. "Miss Schroeder, you must calm down! Otherwise, I'll have to remove you—like the last girl who sat here."

Lieutenant Tinker came over and nudged the young officer aside. "What's wrong?" he asked Lotte and examined her message pad.

"It's Eddy!"

"Frenchy?"

"He's been shot down! He is in the North Sea, off Margate."

335

Lotte's outburst had attracted the attention of Air Vice Marshal Park. He signaled Tinker to come to him. Lotte watched as he took in Tinker's message, and heard him say, "Ask Coastal Command to send a boat for Lieutenant Beane."

"I'll call, sir, but I believe all the boats are out."

"I see." Park signaled to the officer who was manning a telephone at the end of the balcony. "Get Bull Connell on the line."

Chapter 52

Thane climbed up his Spitfire's wing, but as he grabbed onto the frame of its cockpit to step in, a ground man came running up.

"Lieutenant Thane! There's a phone call for you."

"A call?" He was inclined to dismiss it. Every second counted if he was going to spot Frenchy, and anything important could be radioed to him. "Tell them you just missed me," Thane said.

"You better come, sir. It's Air Vice Marshal Park."

"How on earth does he know I'm here?" Reluctantly, Thane climbed down and followed the ground man to the telephone in Eastchurch's dispersal hut which had a corner of its roof blown off but was still standing.

He picked the receiver off the desk and said, "Sir?"

"Lieutenant Thane?" said Park.

"Yes, sir."

"I have just spoken to Bull Connell at Kettlebury. He tells me that you sighted 57 Squadron Leader Beane's Spitfire eastbound off Canvey Island—is that correct? And you are at Eastchurch for refueling?"

"I am, sir."

"Lieutenant Beane has been reported parachuting into the North Sea, approximately four miles off Margate. Due east of Viking Bay to be exact. Since you are nearby, I need you to go up to spot him for the rescue boat. You don't have much time because it's going to be dark very soon."

"I'll take off immediately, sir."

"And Lieutenant Thane," the Air Marshal said.

"Yes, sir?"

337

"Beane is one of my more special chicks—a particular protégé of mine. Do your best to find him."

"Frenchy is special to me, too, sir. If he's there, I'll find him."

Thane dropped the phone and sprinted to his Spitfire. The groundman shouted to him: "Lieutenant!"

"What, man?"

The ground man handed Thane a map. A circle was drawn around an inlet half way up the eastern-most coastline of southern England. "They launched a fishing trawler from Viking Bay to pick up your flyer. When you find him, circle above him until the boat sees him."

"Okay!" Thane strapped in quickly. Throttle half an inch open, brakes on, fine pitch, and stick back. He pressed the starter button and the propeller turned over.

Waiting while the engine warmed, he reflected that Park wasn't the only person who thought Frenchy was a man worth saving. His ascent from humble beginnings, his skill as a pilot, his character, his leadership—all of it made for one of the finest men Thane had ever known. Park's last words had been telling: The secrets that connected Frenchy to the Air Marshal must be the best of him. Secrets that perhaps Frenchy would share with him one day.

He had to find Frenchy for Lotte, too. The love between her and Frenchy was platonic, but it was obviously deep, and somehow rooted in her move to England. She would never be the same if Frenchy didn't come back, and because Thane loved her, he wouldn't let that happen.

The ground man pulled out the chocks and Thane released the brake and eased open the throttle. He turned his plane into the wind and began his run-up. Then the vibrations of wheels on grass were replaced by whistling sounds and he was soaring towards Margate at three hundred miles per hour. Soon, the grey waters of Viking Bay were beneath him. He ought to be above Frenchy's position in less than a minute.

Thane saw a fishing trawler below him, men at the rail scanning the sea with binoculars. He circled to lose height, dropping under a thousand feet as he searched the sea, using the tawny swath made by the setting sun. Either side of it the water was dark, like gleaming gun metal, in an endless three-foot swell and the rolling troughs of water, crested by occasional white roils of foam, all looked the same.

He couldn't see Frenchy so he flew lower, sacrificing scope of vision for detail. Down at this level the sun was a hazy ball close to touching the horizon and the shadows in the wave troughs were deeper. He didn't have much time.

Then he spotted a roil that didn't melt back into the pewter surface like the others. He pushed the stick forward to drop lower and get closer and he recognized that the roil was Frenchy's white scarf. He banked around to keep the scarf in sight. Frenchy was there—he was floating—but he didn't make any signal to acknowledge Thane's plane.

Thane approached at tree top height, dropped a wing close to a wave top, and a plume of sea water showered Frenchy. "Wake up, old man!"

This time Frenchy raised his good arm and Thane waggled his wings in acknowledgement and banked to make tight circles over Frenchy in a protective cocoon. He could see the rescue boat turning towards his position. Then he pressed the button on his microphone. "Red One to base."

"Base here," Bull Connell's voice came through Thane's headset.

"Jolly good news, Bull! I've spotted Frenchy. And the search boat is approaching."

"Thank God!" A loud roar drowned out Bull's voice.

"What's that!"

Bull said, "Tank and the rest are dancing around here celebrating like naughty schoolchildren."

Thane laughed. "You might want to take up your ruler and rap some knuckles. I'll keep circling Frenchy until I'm sure the boat sees him."

"Make for home the minute you're sure he's safe."

"Too dark to make it to Kettlebury," Thane said. "Call Manston, would you, that's a good man. I'll land there and find a ride back to Viking Bay and meet Frenchy."

"Okay," Bull said. "Tuner—"

"Yes?"

"You did well."

"All in a day's work, sir!"

"And what a day's work its been!" Bull said. "Uxbridge told me we stopped more than half of the German bombers from reaching the docks. We've shot down dozens—maybe hundreds—of 'em. Hun planes are crashing all over southern England and into the Channel. It's our best day yet!"

"Thank God for that! I'll see you tomorrow morning."

"Very well. Out," said Bull.

Having confirmed that the rescue boat was preparing to pick up Frenchy, Thane turned west into the dusk. The steady thrum of his Spitfire's Rolls Royce engine was his only companion. Flying through grayish-murk was strangely relaxing after surviving a day of bright skies filled with hundreds of metallic glints that had been Messerschmitt 109s and Heinkel bombers.

Three, maybe four minutes more and his wheels would be on the ground. Thane throttled down, beginning his approach to RAF Manston, and finally easing his mind of the taut intensity demanded of him each moment since 57 Squadron's morning take-off. Imagining Frenchy on a rescue boat, swaddled in a wool blanket, swelled him with pride. Thane hadn't known Frenchy long—because he'd wasted time with jealousies over June's affections and petty social class and nationality badgering—yet his new friend was already a driving force in his life. Their bond would grow, Thane was sure of it, and the possibilities for them in the RAF and beyond were endless.

He and Frenchy wouldn't be the types to discuss it, but he had certainly earned a measure of respect in Frenchy's eyes, and he delighted in knowing that perhaps even more than in earning his DFC. And respect would come from the Squadron's pilots and his Pater, and maybe even redemption from June and Mr. Stephenson. Could he dare to think June would accept him back into her life, this time as a friend to her fiancé, and maybe even as her own friend? But most of all, he couldn't wait to see the joyous look on Lotte's face. Recounting the day, slowly, with her at his side, would be the prize, indeed.

Chapter 53

At Uxbridge, just over a hundred miles to the west of RAF Manston, thoughts of Eddy cold and alone in the sea were tumbling through Lotte's mind. She looked at the clock: nearly seven. He couldn't have much time...

Lieutenant Tinker returned to Lotte and said confidently, "We will find him, Lotte." He added, "Air Vice Marshal Park has sent Lieutenant Thane to search for Lieutenant Beane. It will just take a little time."

"He sent Dudley?" Lotte said. "Oh, God. I can't bear to think of them both out there."

Tinker looked at Lotte. "You know Lieutenant Thane?"

Lotte looked away, but she nodded. Her heart was thumping. *No!* Eddy struggling in the sea, trying to keep his head above the cold waves, and Dudley flying somewhere above him, searching the endless water as daylight faded.

The minute hand on the wall clock moved on and on, and the uncertainties made her head ache. If Eddy survived his parachute jump, how long could he stay alive in the freezing water? If Dudley lost visibility in the darkening skies, would he run out of fuel and have to ditch in the sea himself? Her wait for answers was unbearable.

Her gaze went constantly from Tinker to Air Vice Marshal Park at his usual perch at the center of the balcony, searching for even a hint of an answer. An aide approached the balcony and handed Park a note. He read it and took a few steps down the rail towards Lotte. He was smiling.

"Lotte—Lieutenant Thane has spotted Edouard," Park said. "A boat was sent off from Viking Bay. Thane's circling him, so they can't miss him. He'll be fine." The Air Marshal returned to the center of the balcony and turned his attention back to the aerial battle being shown on the grid.

"Thank God," Tinker said.

Lotte hugged him, feeling at last she could exhale, with that crushing weight of worry lifted from her shoulders.

"Steady on," Tinker said, smiling as she let him go. "Now that it's dark I think you won't be getting any more calls, so go on home. You've had quite a day."

"Yes, sir. Thank you." She paused, gathering her wits. "Sir—may I use the telephone? I would like to let his fiancée and his family know he's safe."

"Certainly," Tinker said.

Lotte sat at her desk and dialed Longmarsh. Rankin answered. When Lotte asked to speak to June, he responded in his usual unruffled manner and she could hear his feet padding away across the hall. It seemed a century before she heard the clatter of shoe heels on the tiled floor, and June picked up the receiver and answered.

"Lotte! What is it? Is everything all right?"

"Yes—it's all right now. But listen, dear, Eddy has been shot down."

June gasped. "You say everything's all right!"

"Yes! He had to parachute. He went down into the sea, but Dudley went looking for him. Air Marshal Park says Dudley's spotted him, so a boat's going out to pick him up and bring him to shore."

June gave a little moan of relief.

"There, there," Lotte said. "He will be safe by now, I'm sure."

"Oh, God. Where is he?"

"Viking Bay."

"I could drive up there," June said, half to herself.

"Why don't you wait, dear. We should get more news once the boat lands. Eddy was in the sea for some time, so they may take him to a hospital. I'll phone you if I hear any more, but it's good news, remember. Dudley has found him, and he's going to be all right."

There was a pause on June's side.

"Then thank God for Dudley. He has his uses, after all."

Lotte said, "Listen dear, I'm going to call The Four Bells and tell Uncle Al and Aunt Maddy that Eddy is safe. I'll call you again if I hear anything more."

"Thank you," June said, and hung up.

Lotte sat for a moment, thinking of Dudley who was flying back from the sea, and looking forward to hearing about the rescue. How she would hug him and kiss him—so many kisses for the life he had saved! There would be no end to them.

She picked up the receiver again and began to dial the number of Maddy Weldy's pub in Lassingwood.

Chapter 54

Eddy was exhausted. He was wet through, chilled to the bone and he couldn't feel his hands or his feet. His teeth were chattering uncontrollably. He resorted to humming *Rule, Britannia* to try and still them. The restless North Sea had battered him and forced him to gulp down mouthfuls of seawater, until he had realized the futility of swimming at all and simply lay in the embrace of his Mae West, floating up and down with the waves. He knew he couldn't survive this cold very much longer.

He could see Thane's Spitfire flying away west towards Thanet. What had Tuner been doing flying over the sea—fifty miles northeast of 57 Squadron's aerial battle? When he first saw it he wondered if he were hallucinating. But he wasn't. Tuner had flown low enough that he could see the number 72 on the fuselage, and the Spit had circled and circled above him, the familiar roar reassuring him he was being looked for, until at last another note joined it, the sound of a heavy boat engine, distant but closing. He had a firm enough grasp on his senses to realize that rescuers were coming, and he lifted his good arm to wave his thanks to Tuner, but the effort cost him a heavy slap from the sea and he gave up. Tuner must have understood, though, because he had waggled his wings before he had turned away for the coast.

Eddy went on floating listlessly, waiting for the rescue boat to arrive. There was nothing else he could do.

He saw the enemy plane before Tuner did. A dark streak diving out of cloud cover straight at the Spit. A 109.

"Break, Tuner, Break!" Eddy croaked, a helpless observer with no one to listen, not even a seabird. "Roll and climb, man!"

He watched as Tuner's Spitfire spun to starboard and her nose lifted. The 109 was coming round to try and gain Tuner's tail. Then the Spit climbed into the cloud bank with the 109 trailing it, and both vanished.

There was no gunfire, no explosion. Both planes were gone, swallowed by the cloud, and any sound was covered by the oncoming throb of the boat engine.

The water was cold, so cold. Eddy felt he couldn't live much longer. Night was falling and the boat still hadn't reached him. It would only pick up a dead body. Tuner, his friend, had risked his neck to spot him in the sea, but his efforts might have been for nothing.

Eddy couldn't tell whether Tuner had evaded the 109. If he hadn't he might be dead now, and if they both died they would learn what came next—mankind's great question, now wasn't it? Perhaps Tuner would be waiting at the Pearly Gates and they would arrive at the Judgment Seat together. Part of him feared punishment—both of them had killed enemy pilots and maybe neither the British nor the Germans deserved God's absolution. But if God condemned air warriors along with those on the earth—at least he would find his father, the Eddie after whom he had been named, and who had died in the Great War without ever meeting his son.

The cold seemed somehow less now. His body no longer shuddered and tried to warm itself. He drifted, muddled but still conscious. He closed his eyes and forced himself to remember June's smiling face, her white teeth gleaming and her hazel green eyes dancing. *Ma Belle, mon amour.* Dear one, he thought, I've got to hold on. I have to survive to come back to you.

The throbbing engine sounded very close. He opened his eyes to darkness, split by the beam of a headlamp. A fishing boat, black-painted and salt-stained, was coming towards him. How fast it moved over the relentless surging waves. He was suddenly terrified that it would run him down. He croaked, "Here! Here!" but he couldn't raise his arms to signal it. Then the lamp shone in his eyes and half-blinded him, and a voice shouted, "He's there, look! Reverse engines!"

Men were at the rail, waving to him. The throb of the engine dropped back to idling speed so they could reach down to pull him from the sea.

A boat-hook snagged his harness and steadied him. Friendly hands caught hold of his flight suit to haul him over the rail, and he tumbled into the boat headlong, pouring seawater across the deck. There were men leaning over him, turning him onto his side, onto his stomach. Someone grasped his arms and pulled them forward, forcing air into his chest, and he gasped and retched up the seawater that had almost drowned him.

He heard one of the men say, "He's still kicking, Captain."

He began to regain his senses. There was a strong, cold smell of fish. A portly bearded man stood looking down at him, with his hands on his hips.

He vomited more water and coughed and rolled onto his side, seeing lifelines, fishing pole stanchions, legs wearing seaboots and knitted stockings, and then a rough grey blanket being flung around him. He struggled to sit up.

A gruff male voice from the Captain said, ironically, "This is a daft time to go swimming, son."

"Thank you for picking me up," Eddy said.

"The credit goes to your mate. We would've had a helluva time spotting ya before dark if he hadn't been circling over you."

"His name is Tuner. He's my friend," Eddy said.

"Hope he got away, then. A Nazi plane was on his tail when we last saw him," the Captain said.

"I know," Eddy said. "But he probably did a wing-over, outflew the bastard and shot him down. I hope he did. He's the best damned pilot in the RAF."

Another man handed him a cup of tea. "This will warm you up."

Eddy needed both hands to manage the cup. His hands felt like frozen paws and his fingers wouldn't work. But the tea had rum in it. It was strong and very sweet.

"We'll have you in front of a warm fire within an hour, son," the Captain said. "You've had a rough time. War or no war, they ought to give you a few days leave to get over it."

"Thank you," said Eddy, "but I think not. The Germans will be coming back tomorrow, and the next day, and the next. They will not wait politely because I am *un peu malade*. I need to get to my Squadron, and fly."

The Captain chuckled. "Still have some fight in ya, don't ya, son. You French, by the way?"

"No," Eddy said. "I'm an Englishman." He was certain that Tuner would agree.

Chapter 55

It was Christmas Eve and Eddy and June had driven down to Lassingwood, to Aunt Maddy's Four Bells pub. Maddy had closed the pub early and the family had settled into the main room which was still as Eddy remembered it: parquet floors and hardwood tables, the elegant beveled wood and glass back bar, and a cozy coal-fired hearth. A small Christmas tree stood in the corner and Aunt Maddy's home-made tin-can carolers were arranged on the mantle on the chimneypiece, as they had been every holiday season since her childhood.

Eddy and June were seated at a table in the middle of the room with drinks in front of them, his a pint and hers a port and lemon. Aunt Maddy and the pub's landlord, Bill Jenkins, were washing glasses and wiping down the woodwork behind the bar. Uncle Al and Bill's wife Gladys were seated at the bar, engaged in happy reminiscing with Maddy and Bill while they worked.

To Eddy, it was astonishing that he was here at all. 1940 had been an exhausting and terrifying year. It was only through the dogged endurance of soldiers, seamen and pilots like himself that the British people, June and Uncle Al and Aunt Maddy and millions like them, remained safe from Nazi aggression. Despite victory in the Battle of Britain, which Eddy had managed to survive, they were still enduring the Luftwaffe's nightly bombings of cities and factories, and no-one was really sure that the Nazis could be pushed back inside Germany's borders.

Eddy's little cousin Georgie was desperate to start up the Father Christmas automaton that Maddy had set on a tall plant-stand—the aspidistra having been banished to the parlour for the Christmas period.

Georgie tugged at Eddy's sleeve. "Eddy! Gimmie a penny. A penny, please!"

"Okay, monster. Here," Eddy said, handing him the coin.

"Look, Miss Stephenson!" Georgie said to June, "Watch this." He dropped the coin into the slot and the little Father Christmas began ringing his bell to the tune of "Good King Wenceslas." His red velvet belly jiggled ridiculously and Georgie laughed joyfully until the act was over.

"My turn!" Anna Thérèse said.

"But of course it is," Eddy said. He scooped her up and put a penny in her little fingers. She fed it into the automaton and Father Christmas began to jiggle again. Anna Thérèse squealed with delight.

Aunt Maddy glanced over from the bar.

"Now, don't get them too excited, Lieutenant Beane," she warned, but smiled as she said it. "Maybe I should send you upstairs with them, to get them to sleep?"

"I can always read them a Babar story—"

Eddy was interrupted by the creak of the heavy front door. He turned to see Lotte Schroder enter, followed by Dudley Thane.

"*Mon Dieu!*" Eddy said, jumping to his feet to greet them. He hugged Lotte and shook Thane's hand.

"There now, isn't that a wonderful surprise!" Aunt Maddy said, with a wink at Lotte.

June hurried over to hug Lotte. "Happy Christmas, dear! I'm so happy you're here!" She gave Thane a polite peck on the cheek.

After greetings all around, Eddy punched Thane's shoulder. "Trust you to turn up in uniform, Tuner. Another surprise appearance. Like when you cut short my bath in the North Sea."

Thane laughed. "Happy Christmas, old man! My beautiful dear girl, here," he paused to hug Lotte, "suggested a visit to a pub in the country, which I had to agree is a fitting respite given the year we've had!" He helped Lotte take off her coat and hung it on the stand.

Lotte said, "June dear, did you receive my letter? I can't believe I haven't seen you since you set the date of the wedding. Let's hope the war will be over by then."

June pulled a face, half laughing, half sad. "I must send a telegram to Herr Hitler. 'Stop ze varr, I vish to get married.'"

Bill Jenkins came over to shake Thane's hand. "I gather you're the pilot who spotted Eddy in the sea? I'll look forward to hearing more about it. You and Lotte make yourselves comfortable. What can I serve up?"

"Oh," Thane said, "a cup of tea will do."

"I would like tea, as well," Lotte said, calmly, and before Eddy or June could make any comment she bent down to hug Georgie and Anna Thérèse.

"Happy Christmas, Auntie Lotte!" Georgie said.

"Happy Christmas," Anna Thérèse echoed with her tiny voice.

Georgie looked eagerly at the two wrapped packages in Lotte's bag. "Are those for us?"

"Yes, they are," Lotte said, "Happy Christmas to you, my little loves! But—" She took Georgie's hand off a package— "You can't open them till the morning."

"Oh," Georgie said, longingly. "All right then."

Maddy said, "And now it's bed time for you and Anna Thérèse. I've cut up some carrots so you can fill your shoes and leave them under your beds for *Gui*."

Thane made a baffled expression. "*Gui?*"

"Oh," Maddy said, with a little laugh. "*Gui* is a French donkey, a special tradition of the children's Aunt Thérèse—Eddy's mother. He's Father Christmas's donkey."

"*Père Noël*," Georgie corrected her.

"*Bien* little one. *Gui* makes a special journey to visit us every year," Eddy said with a smile.

"Ah," Thane said, "he must like flying with the reindeer."

Maddy said, "Well, he can't come before the children are washed and into their nightclothes and fast asleep. Al, come upstairs and give me a hand, would you, dear?"

Gladys got up at that and embraced Maddy. "It's time we went, isn't it, Bill? We have our four to get home to."

"Aye, we have, the rascals." Bill finished his pint and stood up beside Gladys.

"Happy Christmas, dear." Maddy hugged Gladys and Bill, and Al said his good-byes.

Maddy turned to Eddy, June, Lotte and Dudley. "As soon as the children are in bed, we'll have another tradition—Al and I will serve up our Christmas toddies. We'll try not to be long."

Maddy and Al escorted Georgie and Anna Thérèse through the door at the rear of the bar.

349

"Before we go," Bill said to Dudley, "I've got to hear about the day you rescued Eddy."

Dudley grinned. "The girls have heard it all before." He glanced at Lotte and June for permission. "Would you mind if I repeat it for Bill?"

"Of course not," Lotte said.

"Go on, Dudley," June said. Eddy felt her hand squeeze his.

"Well, on September 15th our Station Commander warned us the Nazis were going to try to finish us. German planes were coming over from France like a cloud of locusts. So Dowding and Park sent every available Spitfire and Hurricane to attack them. Between the white cliffs and London I'm proud to say we destroyed hundreds of the bastards. Frenchy and I had been in the thick of it. Then they shot him down. But he ought to tell you about that himself."

Eddy explained briefly that his aerial combat with Messerschmitt number 34 was unfinished business from previous encounters and had turned into a deadly chase to the North Sea. But another Messerschmitt had appeared from nowhere and shot him down and he had parachuted into the sea.

"*Mon Dieu!* Was it cold! I was nearly out of hope when Tuner flew over me," Eddy said, nodding at Dudley, "but I still had enough of my wits to see that it was him. There was a Messerschmitt on his tail. I lost sight of him and was afraid he was done for."

"What happened?" Bill asked Dudley.

"I looked over my shoulder and saw the 109 diving towards me. So I rolled away and climbed full throttle into the clouds. I expected him to follow me so I put a wing over and dived straight down to attack him. But he was gone."

"Just gone?" Bill asked. "You'd think he'd stay to try to see you off. Bloody funny!"

"Well, no—it was nearly dark, you see. I'll wager he was running out of fuel so he had to make a run for his airbase in France. Anyway, I'd done what I set out to do—I found Frenchy and got the boat out of Viking Bay to pick him up. So then I radioed Manston. The groundmen lit the runway with paraffin lamps. I landed safely—warm and dry—which is more than I can say for Frenchy."

"I did very well, all the same, thank you," Eddy said, putting his arm around June.

Upon arriving at Viking Bay, she had crept under the blankets with him to warm him. Sheer relief had poured out of both of them, and the closeness they had shared during those hours would be in his heart as long as he lived.

"Well, thank God you spotted him," Bill said.

"Yes, thank God," June said, kissing the top of Eddy's head.

"What's next for you?" Bill asked Dudley. "Are you still on active combat duty?"

"As a matter of fact, my orders just came in," Dudley said.

Lotte sighed just a little.

"I'm off to the Western Desert the beginning of January."

"Hold on!" Eddy interrupted. "I thought you and I were going to Debden to train pilots on Spitfires? It was settled more than a month ago."

"Not any more, old man. Sholto Douglas called me in. Lotte and I have come straight from Uxbridge." Eddy nodded at Thane's mention of Air Chief Marshal Dowding's recently-appointed successor.

Thane continued. "Sholto has asked me to lead a Squadron in Libya. He needs experienced hands down there. We've beaten the Italians but the Nazis will be coming and the Air Ministry wants to beef up our air support in the region." Dudley put his hand on Eddy's shoulder. "I think I should go, and Lotte agrees. I ought to lead the men."

"Of course you should," Eddy said, his voice tight with emotion. "Does Keith Park know?"

"Ah, Park," Thane said.

Eddy and Thane had met with Keith Park at the administrative offices at the CFS Cranwell Instructors Course just a week after the King had received Park at Buckingham Palace and made him a Companion of the Most Honorable Order of the Bath for his leadership of 11 Group during the Battle of Britain. It had been strange to see Park at a training base and even stranger to hear him say that his new assignment was to raise the standard of pilot instruction. Learning that Park had recently been relieved of his command of 11 Group had been a complete shock.

Later, Eddy had pieced together that Dowding's and Park's removals had been due to wily Air Ministry politics—though Park's audience with the King proved that their achievements in leading

Fighter Command to victory over the Nazis would never be undermined in the eyes of history. So Park had undoubtedly been at a low ebb on the day at Cranwell, but he had swallowed his hurt and enthusiastically welcomed Eddy and Thane as new training instructors, even telling them that he was counting on them to be two of his best.

"I'll write him," Thane said. "And he probably won't be surprised. Do you remember the last thing he said to us?"

Eddy smiled. "He told us the war won't end soon and that they'll need us again. He told us to stay ready."

"Right-O."

There was a little pause. Before it could grow too long, Gladys said briskly, "Well, we ought to get off home, I suppose." She hugged June, then Eddy. "I'm thrilled you're here with your family."

As Bill followed her out, he said to Dudley, "I wish you the very best of luck in Libya," and shook his hand.

Eddy and June and Dudley and Lotte sat down again but no one spoke. Finally, Lotte looked at Dudley and said, "I still wish you had decided to train pilots with Eddy. But I know you must do your duty."

"For God's sake, Lotte," June said, "I don't see how you can be sanguine about Dudley being sent off to fight again. He's done his bit. So has Eddy. It should be someone else's turn."

"Oh, dear girls," Dudley said, looking first at Lotte and then at June. "Don't fret. I'll do my bit and after that I can come back and train new pilots."

"Tuner has to go where our superiors need him," Eddy said to June. "We all must until the war is won. After all, Fighter Command could order me back to an operational squadron at any time." June looked away, but he said as cheerfully as he could, "It is quite a surprise to see you here tonight, Tuner. I thought you would spend your Christmas leave at your family's estate."

"We shall," Dudley said as he smiled at Lotte, "we're driving to Norfolk bright and early."

"We're leaving early, too," June said. "We're going to have Christmas dinner with my parents at Longmarsh."

The thought of Christmas at Longmarsh appealed to and even excited Eddy. June and her mother would talk endlessly about the wedding plans while he and Mr. Stephenson talked business. In previous conversations, Mr. Stephenson had seen beyond the war years, predicting that when commerce resumed aviation would boom. Eddy took that with a grain of salt because he saw firsthand that the British military continued to be stretched by nightly bombings and fighting in North Africa and in Asia, so to him the end of the war seemed a long way off. Still, Mr. Stephenson's optimism encouraged Eddy to dream of the day when he and June could start a flying business.

"We came tonight," Lotte said, "because Maddy called and invited us to come for Christmas Eve so we could all be together. And I'm so happy we are here!"

"All together—hear, hear!" Dudley said. He raised his tea cup and clinked it with Eddy's pint glass.

The door at the bar opened and Aunt Maddy and Uncle Al returned. Al was carrying a steaming kettle. He set it on the draining board while Maddy lined up six glass mugs on the counter. She had served up her Toddies this way each Christmas Eve since Eddy had been in England and his mouth began to water as he anticipated sipping the tart and sweet flavors.

"Now then." Maddy poured boiling water into each mug and then squeezed in some lemon and dropped in a clove and teaspoon of sugar. She measured a tot of whisky and a half tot of brandy into each mug and gave the mix a brisk stir with a cinnamon stick. Al brought the tray of drinks to the table.

"Here we are," Al said. "Everyone, take one, please."

"May I offer a toast, dear?" Al asked Maddy.

"Of course."

He raised his mug. "To Christmas Eve. It was this very night nine years ago when my darling Maddy and I fell in love again. And many years before that it was on Christmas Eve when the war in Flanders stopped and we soldiers on both sides put down our weapons. For a Christmas Truce. The German army sang to us, *Stille Nacht, Heilige Nacht.* Simply beautiful. Then we sang it back to them in English. The next day, Eddy's father and I had a Christmas meal with Lotte's father, Axel." He waved his mug, flashing a huge smile. "A toast to all of us, being together on this special night."

Everyone clinked mugs.

"I've read a bit about the truce back in the War," Thane said to Al. "It must be quite a story."

353

Uncle Al's eyes brightened which was a sure sign he was about to spin up a long-winded recollection. "Indeed. You see—"

"Before you start—" Aunt Maddy said, with a small wink at Eddy. "I would also like to make a toast."

Al's mouth was still open in mid-sentence but he nodded in agreement.

Maddy raised her mug. "To all the people in all the countries who live with war. To all good, hard-working people who only wish to raise their families and live in peace. May wars end forever and their wishes be granted."

Thane said, "Amen to that." He raised his mug. "And here's to you and Al. Lotte and I were remembering on the way up here that you had taken in children from the bombed-out East End areas to keep them safe."

"Thank you."

"Where are the children? We haven't seen them tonight. Have they gone back home?"

"Most went to be with their families at Christmas for a few days," Maddy said. "My cousin Rose took in three tonight who had nowhere to go—so we could have family time. I hope all the children are enjoying Christmas."

Uncle Al said to Maddy, "I'm sure they are, dear."

Everyone sat back, contentedly, with the only noise in the pub room the crackling of the coal fire at the hearth.

As they settled, bells rang briefly.

"Church bells?" Dudley asked Uncle Al.

"Indeed. They must be calling for the Christmas service at one or the other of the four churches round here."

"Ah. The Four Bells?"

Al nodded.

"Let's go outside," Aunt Maddy suggested. "Just for a few minutes."

The six of them stood under the eaves. It was brisk, but clear. Each man held his lady love tightly to him.

"Al and I stood out here and listened to the carols nine years ago," Maddy said. "Snow was falling and it seemed like a Dickens set."

"Tonight is no less wonderful," June said.

Choir voices began to sing the first strains of "Silent Night." The six of them joined in for the last two stanzas and savored the final notes, until the night fell silent.

Uncle Al had closed his eyes. A tear was falling down his cheek.

"What is it, Uncle Al?" Eddy asked.

"It's all coming back to me. The Christmas Truce. A most unlikely fellowship, it was."

Lotte was smiling.

"And now, Al," Dudley said. "Why don't you tell us about it? Let's go back inside."

Eddy raised his eyebrows, but Dudley just smiled.

"And take your time, good fellow," Dudley said. He kissed Lotte on the cheek. "We have all night."

THE END

Notes and Acknowledgements

ANGELS AND BANDITS has been a true joy to research, due to the rich historical record of the Battle of Britain. Diving into the vast chronicle of when England stood alone and incredible accounts of aerial combat during the battle was a history-lover's joy.

My story ultimately focuses on Britain's elegant warplane, the Spitfire, and the courageous RAF pilots who flew it. Fortunately, there is a wealth of video productions and on-line video of the Spitfire in flight and in aerial combat action during the Battle of Britain. Philip Kaplan's *The Spitfire: An Icon of the Skies* has an amazing collection of photographs and explanations of the Spit's capabilities and operation. My understanding of the battle itself was most informed by Stephen Bungay's thorough and well-paced *The Most Dangerous Enemy: A History of the Battle of Britain*.

My aerial combat scenes are largely inspired by auto-biographies of combatant pilots. Pilot recollections present some of the most compelling action scenes I've ever read, non-fiction or fiction. In particular, Richard Hillary's *The Last Enemy*, Gordon Olive's *Spitfire Ace*, and Pierre Clostermann's *The Big Show*.

Air Chief Marshal Keith Park hasn't universally been lauded as one of the greatest military commanders of the Second World War, but his operational control of Fighter Command 11 Group's defense of southern England was masterful and undoubtedly influenced the outcome of the Battle of Britain. I have tried to be true to Park's career, relying in part on Vincent Orange's biography, *Park*.

A big thank you to my editor, Sue Millard, for shaping up ANGELS AND BANDITS in a fashion I couldn't possibly by myself. Thank you to my advance readers, Mark Bloom, Annie Chaloupka, Sjoerd Hoogwater, and Rhonda Jackson for your invaluable feedback and encouragement. A special thank you to my son Zack, who took breaks from his studies at Boston College to read and critique the book, chapter by chapter. Another special shout-out to my friend since boyhood Mike Helwig who flew F-14 Navy jets. Wigs, his call sign as a naval aviator, schooled me on the realities of flying a fighter plane. *Keep sight!* Thanks so much to wife Sue and son Dane for being part of my writing journey.

About the Author

Brodie Curtis is the author of THE FOUR BELLS, a novel of The Great War. Curtis is a big fan of World War fiction and has posted more than 100 brief reviews on his website brodiecurtis.com. He also reviews historical fiction for the *Historical Novels Review* and his published reviews can be found on his website.

Westy Vistas Books

https://www.brodiecurtis.com